ALSO BY PETER SWANSON
FROM CLIPPER LARGE PRINT

The Girl With a Clock for a Heart

The Kind Worth Killing

....

....

DE			
HG			

This item is to be returned on or before the latest date above.
It may be borrowed for a further period if not in demand .

The Kind Worth Killing

Peter Swanson

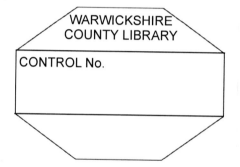

W F HOWES LTD

This large print edition published in 2015 by
W F Howes Ltd
Unit 4, Rearsby Business Park, Gaddesby Lane,
Rearsby, Leicester LE7 4YH

1 3 5 7 9 10 8 6 4 2

First published in the United Kingdom in 2015
by Faber & Faber Limited

A CIP catalogue record for this book is available
from the British Library

ISBN 978 1 51001 221 9

Typeset by Palimpsest Book Production Limited,
Falkirk, Stirlingshire

Printed and bound in Great Britain
by TJ International Ltd, Padstow, Cornwall

MIX
Paper from
responsible sources
FSC
www.fsc.org FSC® C013056

For my mother, Elizabeth Ellis Swanson

PART I

THE RULES OF AIRPORT BARS

CHAPTER 1

TED

'Hello, there,' she said.

I looked at the pale, freckled hand on the back of the empty bar seat next to me in the business class lounge at Heathrow Airport, then up into the stranger's face.

'Do I know you?' I asked. She didn't look particularly familiar, but her American accent, her crisp white shirt, her sculpted jeans tucked into knee-high boots, all made her look like one of my wife's awful friends.

'No, sorry. I was just admiring your drink. Do you mind?' She folded her long, slender frame onto the leather-padded swivel stool, and set her purse on the bar. 'Is that gin?' she asked about the martini in front of me.

'Hendrick's,' I said.

She gestured toward the bartender, a teenager with spiky hair and a shiny chin, and asked for a Hendrick's martini with two olives. When her drink came she raised it in my direction. I had one sip left, and said, 'Here's to inoculation against international travel.'

'I'll drink to that.'

I finished my drink, and ordered another. She introduced herself, a name I instantly forgot. And I gave her mine – just Ted, and not Ted Severson, at least not right then. We sat, in the overly padded and overly lit Heathrow lounge, drinking our drinks, exchanging a few remarks, and confirming that we were both waiting to board the same direct flight to Logan Airport in Boston. She removed a slim paperback novel from her purse and began to read it. It gave me an opportunity to really look at her. She was beautiful – long red hair, eyes a lucid greenish blue like tropical waters, and skin so pale it was the almost bluish white of skim milk. If a woman like that sits down next to you at your neighborhood bar and compliments your drink order, you think your life is about to change. But the rules are different in airport bars, where your fellow drinkers are about to hurtle away from you in opposite directions. And even though this woman was on her way toward Boston, I was still filled with sick rage at the situation with my wife back home. It was all I had been able to think about during my week in England. I'd barely eaten, barely slept.

An announcement came over the loudspeaker in which the two discernible words were *Boston* and *delayed*. I glanced at the board above the rows of backlit top-shelf liquor and watched as our departure time was moved back an hour.

'Time for another,' I said. 'My treat.'

'Why not,' she said, and closed her book, placing

it faceup on the bar by her purse. *The Two Faces of January*. By Patricia Highsmith.

'How's your book?'

'Not one of her best.'

'Nothing worse than a bad book and a long flight delay.'

'What are you reading?' she asked.

'The newspaper. I don't really like books.'

'So what do you do on flights?'

'Drink gin. Plot murders.'

'Interesting.' She smiled at me, the first I'd seen. It was a wide smile that caused a crease between her upper lip and nose, and that showed perfect teeth, and a sliver of pink gums. I wondered how old she was. When she first sat down I'd thought she was in her midthirties, closer to my age, but her smile, and the spray of faded freckles across the bridge of her nose made her look younger. Twenty-eight maybe. My wife's age.

'And I work, of course, when I fly,' I added.

'What do you do?'

I gave her the short story version, how I funded and advised Internet start-up companies. I didn't tell her how I'd made most of my money – by selling those companies off as soon as they looked promising. And I didn't tell her that I never really needed to work again in this lifetime, that I was one of the few dot-commers from the late 1990s that managed to pull up my stakes (and cash out my stocks) right before the bubble burst. I only hid these facts because I didn't feel like talking about them, not because I thought my new companion might find them offensive, or lose interest in talking with me. I had never felt the need to apologize for the money I had made.

'What about you? What do you do?' I asked.

'I work at Winslow College. I'm an archivist.'

Winslow was a women's college in a leafy suburb about twenty miles west of Boston. I asked her what an archivist does, and she gave me what I suspect was her own short story version of her work, how she collected and preserved college documents. 'And you live in Winslow?' I asked.

'I do.'

'Married?'

'I'm not. You?'

Even as she said it, I caught the subtle flick of her eyes as she looked for a ring on my left hand. 'Yes, unfortunately,' I said. Then I held up my hand for her to see my empty ring finger. 'And, no, I don't remove my wedding ring in airport bars in case a woman like you sits down next to me. I've never had a ring. I can't stand the feel of them.'

'Why unfortunate?' she asked.

'It's a long story.'

'It's a flight delay.'

'You really want to hear about my sordid life?'

'How can I say no to that?'

'If I'm going to tell you I'm going to need another one of these.' I held up my empty glass. 'You?'

'No, thank you. Two is my limit.' She slid one of the olives off the toothpick with her teeth and bit down on it. I caught a brief glimpse of the pink tip of her tongue.

'I always say that two martinis are too many, and three is not enough.'

'That's funny. Didn't James Thurber also say that?'

'Never heard of him,' I said and smirked, although I felt a little sheepish trying to pass off a famous quote as my own. The bartender was suddenly in front of me and I ordered another drink. The skin around my mouth had taken on that pleasurable numb feeling one gets from gin, and I knew that I was in danger of being too drunk and saying too much, but it was airport rules, after all, and even though my fellow traveler lived only twenty miles from me, I had already forgotten her name, and knew there was very little chance of ever seeing her again in my lifetime. And it felt good to be talking and drinking with a stranger. Just speaking words out loud was causing some of my rage to dissipate.

So I told her the story. I told her how my wife and I had been married for three years, and that we lived in Boston. I told her about the week in September at the Kennewick Inn along the south coast of Maine, and how we'd fallen in love with the area, and bought some ridiculously overpriced shorefront property. I told her how my wife, because she had a master's degree in something called Arts and Social Action, decided she was qualified to codesign the house with an architecture firm, and had been spending the majority of her recent time in Kennewick, working with a contractor named Brad Daggett.

'And she and Brad . . .?' she asked after sliding the second olive into her mouth.

'Uh-huh.'

'Are you positive?'

So I gave her more details. I told her how Miranda had been growing bored with our life in Boston. For the first year of our marriage she had thrown herself into decorating our brownstone in the South End. After that, she had gotten a part-time job at a friend's gallery in the SoWa district, but even then, I knew that things were getting stale. We had begun to run out of conversation midway through dinner, had started going to bed at different times. More importantly, we had lost the identities that had originally defined us in our relationship. In the beginning, I was the rich busi-nessman who introduced her to expensive wine and charity galas, and she was the bohemian artist who booked trips to Thai beaches, and liked to hang out in dive bars. I knew that we were our own kind of strained cliché, but it worked for us. We clicked on every level. I even enjoyed the fact that even though I consider myself handsome, in a generic sort of way, no one was ever going to look at me while I was in her presence. She had long legs and large breasts, a heart-shaped face and full lips. Her hair was a dark brown that she always kept dyed black. It was deliberately styled to look tousled, as though she'd come straight from bed. Her skin was flawless and she didn't need makeup, although she never left the house without applying black eyeliner. I had watched men fixate on her in bars and restaurants. Maybe I was projecting, but the looks they cast her way were hungry and primal. They made me glad I didn't live in a time or place where men habitually carried weapons.

Our trip to Kennewick, Maine, had been spontaneous, a reaction to a complaint from Miranda that we hadn't spent time alone in over a year. We went the third week of September. The first few days were cloudless and warm, but on Wednesday of that week a rainstorm swept down from Canada, trapping us in our suite. We only left to drink Allagash White and eat lobster in the inn's basement tavern. After the storm passed the days turned cool and dry, the light grayer, the dusk longer. We bought sweaters and explored the mile-long cliff walk that began just north of the inn and wound its way between the swelling Atlantic and its rocky edge. The air, that had until recently been heavy with humidity and the smell of suntan lotion, was now crisp and briny. We both fell in love with Kennewick, so much so that when we found a piece of rosehip-choked land for sale on a high bluff at the end of the path, I called the number on the for sale sign and made an immediate offer.

One year later, the rosehip bushes had been cleared, a foundation dug, and the exterior of the eight-bedroom house was nearly complete. We'd hired Brad Daggett, a rugged divorcé with thick black hair, a goatee, and a bent-looking nose, as our general contractor. While I spent my weeks in Boston – advising a group of recent MIT grads that had created a new algorithm for a blog-based search engine – Miranda was spending more and more time in Kennewick, taking a room at the inn and surveying the work being done on the house, obsessing over every tile and every fixture.

In early September, I decided to surprise her by driving up. I left a message on her cell phone as I got onto I-95 north of Boston. I arrived in Kennewick a little before noon and looked for her at the inn. They told me she'd been out since morning.

I drove to the house site and parked behind Brad's F-150 on the gravel driveway. Miranda's robin's egg blue Mini Cooper was there as well. I hadn't visited the property for a few weeks and was happy to see that progress had been made. All the windows appeared to be in place, and the bluestone pavers that I had picked for the sunken garden had arrived. I walked around to the back of the house, where every second-floor bedroom had its own balcony, and where a screened-in veranda along the first floor led down to an enormous stone patio. In front of the patio a rectangular hole had been dug for the pool. Walking up the stone steps of the patio I spotted Brad and Miranda through the tall ocean-facing kitchen windows. I was about to rap on the window to let them know I was there, when something caused me to stop. They were each leaning against the newly installed quartz countertops, both looking out through the window with its view toward Kennewick Cove. Brad was smoking a cigarette and I watched him flick an ash into the coffee cup he held in his other hand.

But it was Miranda that had caused me to stop. There was something about her posture, the way she was leaning against the countertop, angled toward Brad's broad shoulders. She looked completely at ease. I watched her casually lift a hand as Brad slid the lit cigarette between her fingers. She took a long drag, then returned the cigarette to him. Neither had looked at the other during the exchange, and I knew then that not only were they sleeping together, but that they were also probably in love.

Instead of feeling anger, or dismay, my immediate feeling was panic that they would spot me out on the patio, spying on their moment of intimacy. I backtracked toward the main entrance, crossed the veranda, then swung open the glass door and shouted 'Hello' into the echoey house.

'In here,' Miranda yelled back, and I walked into the kitchen.

They had moved a little bit apart but not by much. Brad was grinding out his cigarette in the coffee cup. 'Teddy, what a surprise,' Miranda said. She was the only one who called me that, a pet

11

name that had started as a joke, since it did not fit me at all.

'Hey, Ted,' Brad said. 'What do you think so far?'

Miranda came around the counter and gave me a kiss that landed on the corner of my mouth. She smelled of her expensive shampoo and Marlboros.

'It's looking good. My pavers arrived.'

Miranda laughed. 'We let him pick one thing and that's all he cares about.'

Brad came around the counter as well, and shook my hand. His hand was large and knuckly, his palm warm and dry. 'Want the full tour?'

As Brad and Miranda took me around the house, Brad talking about building materials, and Miranda telling me what furniture would go where, I began to have second thoughts about what I had seen. Neither seemed particularly nervous around me. Maybe they had just become close friends, the type that stand shoulder to shoulder and share cigarettes. Miranda could be touchy-feely, linking arms with her girlfriends, and kissing our male friends on the lips hello and good-bye. It occurred to me that there was a chance I was being paranoid.

After the house tour, Miranda and I drove to the Kennewick Inn and had lunch in the Livery Tavern. We each got the blackened haddock sandwiches and I drank two scotch and sodas.

'Has Brad got you smoking again?' I asked, wanting to catch her out in a lie, see how she would react.

'What?' she said, her brow furrowing.

'You smelled a little like smoke. Back at the house.'

'I might have snuck a drag or two. I'm not smoking again, Teddy.'

'I don't really care. I was just wondering.'

'Can you believe the house is nearly done?' she said as she dipped one of her French fries into my pool of ketchup.

We talked about the house for a while and I began to doubt what I had seen even more. She wasn't acting guilty.

'You staying for the weekend?' she asked.

'No, I just wanted to come up and say hi. I've got dinner tonight with Mark LaFrance.'

'Cancel it and stay here. Weather's supposed to be beautiful tomorrow.'

'Mark flew in just for this meeting. And I need to prepare some numbers.'

I had originally planned on staying in Maine through the afternoon, hoping that Miranda would agree to a lengthy nap in her hotel room. But after seeing Brad and her canoodling in the very expensive kitchen that I was paying for, I had changed my mind. I had a new plan. After lunch, I drove Miranda back to the house site so she could get her car. Then, instead of driving directly to I-95, I got onto Route 1 and drove south to Kittery and its quarter-mile stretch of outlet stores. I pulled up to the Kittery Trading Post, an outdoor outfitters that I'd driven past on numerous occasions but had never visited. In the space of about fifteen minutes I spent nearly five hundred dollars on a pair of rainproof camouflage-print pants, a gray raincoat with a hood, some oversize aviator glasses, and a pair of high-end binoculars. I took the gear to a public restroom across from the Crate and Barrel outlet and changed into my new getup. With the hood up and the aviator glasses on I felt unrecognizable. At least from a distance. I drove north again, parking in the public lot near Kennewick Cove, squeezing my Quattro in between two pickup trucks. I knew there was no reason for Miranda or Brad to come down to this particular lot, but there was also no reason for me to make my car easy to spot.

The wind had died down but the sky was a low, monochromatic gray, and a warm misty rain had begun to pepper the air. I walked across the damp sand of the beach, then clambered over the loose rocks and shale that led to the start of the cliff walk. I moved carefully, keeping my eyes on the paved path – slick with rain, and buckled in places by roots – instead of on the dramatic sweep of the Atlantic to my right. Some of the paved portions of the cliff walk had eroded away completely, and a faded sign warned walkers of its danger. Because of this, the path was not particularly well traveled, and I only saw one other person that afternoon – a teenage girl in a Bruins jersey that smelled as though she had just smoked a joint. We passed without saying anything or looking at one another.

Toward the end of the path, I walked along the top of a crumbling cement wall that marked the back property line of a stone cottage, the last house before a quarter mile of undeveloped land that culminated in our lot. The path then dipped down to sea level, crossed a short, rocky beach strewn with chewed-up buoys and seaweed, then continued along a steep rise through some twisted spruce trees. The rain had picked up, and I took off my wet sunglasses. The chance that either Miranda or Brad would be outside of the house was very slim, and my plan was to stop just short of the open sweep of cleared land, and position myself in a copse of hardy shrubs along the low part of the bluff. If either looked out and saw me with my binoculars they would assume I was a bird-watcher. If I was approached, I could retreat quickly to the path.

When I could see the house looming above the scarred land, it struck me, not for the first time, how the rear side – the side that faced the ocean – was stylistically opposite from the side that faced the road. The front of the house had a stone veneer with a smattering of small windows and a towering set of dark wood doors with exaggerated arches. The rear of the house was beige-painted wood, and all the identical windows with their identical balconies made it look like a medium-size hotel. 'I have a lot of friends,' Miranda had said when I asked her why the house needed seven guest bedrooms. Then she'd shot me a look as though I'd asked her why she thought indoor plumbing was necessary.

I found a good spot under a stunted spruce that was bent and twisted like a bonsai tree. I lay down on the damp ground on my front, and fiddled with the binoculars till I started to get the house in focus. I was about fifty yards away and could easily see through windows. I swept along the first floor, not spotting any movement, then worked my way across the second floor. Nothing. I took a break, surveying the house with my naked eye, wishing I had a view of the front driveway. For all I knew, there was nobody at the house at all, even though Daggett's truck had still been there when I dropped Miranda off.

A few years earlier I'd gone out fishing with a colleague, a fellow dot-com speculator who was the best open water fisherman I'd ever known. He could stare out at the surface of the ocean and know exactly where the fish were. He told me that his trick was to unfocus his eyes, to take in everything in his visual range all at once, and by doing that he could catch flickers of movement, disturbances in the water. I tried it at the time, and only succeeded in giving myself a dull headache. So after completing another sweep with my binoculars, and seeing nothing, I decided to use this same trick on my own house. I let everything sort of blur in front of my eyes, waiting for any motion to draw attention to itself, and after I'd been staring at the house for less than a minute I caught some movement through the high window of what was to be the living room on the north edge of the house. I lifted my binoculars and focused on the window; Brad and Miranda had just entered. I could see them pretty clearly; the lowering after-noon sun was hitting the window at a good angle, lighting up the interior without causing a glare. I watched Brad walk over to a makeshift table that had been set up by the carpentry crew. He picked up a piece of wood that looked like a section of ceiling molding and held it out for my wife to see. He ran a finger down one of its grooves and she did the same thing. His lips were moving and Miranda was nodding at whatever he was saying.

For one brief moment I felt ridiculous, a paranoid husband dressed up in camouflage and spying on his wife and his contractor, but after Brad put the molding down I watched as Miranda slid into his arms, tilted her head back, and kissed him on the mouth. With one big hand he reached down and pressed her hips against him, and with his other he grabbed a handful of her unkempt hair. I told myself to stop watching but somehow I couldn't. I watched for at least ten minutes, watched as Brad bent my wife over the table, lifted her dark purple skirt, removed a pair of tiny white underpants, and entered her from behind. I watched Miranda posi-tion herself strategically along the table, one hand braced on its edge, the other between her own legs, guiding him inside of her. They had clearly done this before.

I slid backward and into a sitting position. When I regained the path I pulled my hood back and threw up my lunch into a dark, wind-ruffled puddle.

'How long ago was this?' asked my fellow traveler after I'd told her the story.

'Just over a week.'

She blinked her eyes, and bit at her lower lip. Her eyelids were pale as tissue paper.

'So what are you going to do about it?' she asked.

It was the question I'd been asking myself all week. 'What I really want to do is to kill her.' I smiled with my gin-numbed mouth and attempted a little wink just to give her an opportunity to not believe me, but her face stayed serious. She lifted her reddish eyebrows.

'I think you should,' she said, and I waited for some indication that she was joking, but nothing came. Her stare was unwavering. Staring back, I realized she was so much more beautiful than I had originally thought. It was an ethereal beauty, timeless, as though she were the subject of a Renaissance painting. So different from my wife, who looked like she belonged on the cover of a pulp novel from the 1950s. I was about to finally speak when she cocked her head to listen to the muffled loudspeaker. They'd just announced that they were boarding our flight.

CHAPTER 2

LILY

T he summer I turned fourteen my mother invited a painter named Chet to come and stay with us. I don't remember his last name; don't know, in fact, if I ever knew it. He came and stayed in the small apartment above my mother's studio. He had thick glasses in dark frames, a bushy beard that was always flecked with paint, and he smelled like overripe fruit. I remember the way his eyes darted down toward my chest when we were introduced. The summer was already hot and I was wearing cutoff jeans and a tank top. My breasts were no bigger than mosquito bites but he looked anyway.

'Hi Lily,' he said. 'Call me Uncle Chet.'

'Why? Are you my uncle?'

He released my hand and laughed, a sputtering noise like an engine dying. 'Hey, I already feel like family here, the way your parents are treating me. A whole summer to paint, man. Unbelievable.'

I walked away without saying anything.

He wasn't the only houseguest that summer. In fact, there was never only one guest at Monk's House, especially in summertime, when my

19

parents' teaching duties died down and they could focus on what they truly loved – drinking and adultery. I don't say that in order to make some sort of tragedy of my childhood. I say it because it's the truth. And that summer, the summer of Chet, there was a rotating cast of hangers-on, graduate students, ex-lovers, and current lovers, all coming and going like moths to a flickering porch light. And these were just the houseguests. My parents, as always, had endless parties – I would listen to these parties hum and roar through the walls of my bedroom as I lay in bed. They were familiar symphonies, beginning with bursts of laughter, discordant jazz, and the slap of screen doors, and ending, in the early morning hours, with the sound of yelling, sometimes sobbing, and always the slam of bedroom doors.

Chet was a slightly different breed of animal from the usual houseguest. My mother referred to him as an outsider artist, meaning, I suppose, that he was not affiliated with her college, neither a student nor a visiting artist. I remember my father calling him 'the homeless degenerate your mother has housed for the summer. Avoid him, Lily, I think he has leprosy. And God knows what's in the beard.' I don't think it was genuine advice from my father – my mother was in earshot, and he was speaking for her benefit – but it turned out to be prophetic.

I'd spent my entire life at Monk's House, my father's name for the sprawling, rotting hundred-year-old

Victorian mansion an hour from New York City in the deep woods of Connecticut. David Kintner – my father – was an English novelist who'd made most of his money off the film adaptation of his first and most successful book, a boarding-school sex farce that caused a brief sensation in the late 1960s. He'd come to America as a visiting writer at Shepaug University, and stayed on as an adjunct when he met Sharon Henderson, my mother, an abstract expressionist with a tenured teaching position in the school's art department. Together, they bought Monk's. It didn't have a name when they purchased it, the year I was conceived, but my father, who rationalized the six bedrooms by plans to fill it with creative and intelligent (and young and female) houseguests, thought he'd like to name it after the house that Virginia and Leonard Woolf shared. It was also a reference to Thelonious Monk, my father's favorite musician.

There were many peculiarities to Monk's, including some unused solar panels that were smothered in ivy, a screening room with an old film projector, a wine cellar with a dirt floor, and a small kidney-shaped swimming pool in the backyard that was rarely cleaned. Over the years it had devolved back into a murky pond, its bottom and sides covered in algae, its surface constantly filmed in rotting leaves, its unused filter clogged with the bloated corpses of mice and squirrels. At the beginning of that particular summer, I had made an attempt to clean the half-filled pool myself, pulling off the mold-blackened tarp, finding a butterfly net that worked for skimming the leaves, then filling the pool from the hose over the course of one tepid June day. I asked my parents separately if they would pick up pool chemicals the next time they went shopping. My mother's response: 'I don't want my darling daughter swimming around in a bunch of chemicals all summer.' My father promised to make a special trip to the store, but I watched the memory of the promise fade out of his eyes before we even finished the conversation.

I swam in the pool, anyway, for the first half of the summer, telling myself that at least I had it to myself. The water turned green, and the bottom and sides became slippery with dark algae. I pretended the pool really was a pond, deep in the woods, in a special place that only I knew about, and my friends were the turtles and the fish and the dragonflies. I swam at dusk, when the cricket whine was at its highest, nearly blocking out the sounds of parties starting up on the screened porch at the front of the house. It was on one of those dusk swims that I first noticed Chet, a beer bottle in his hand, watching me from the edge of the woods. 'How's the water?' he asked, when he realized he'd been spotted.

'It's all right,' I said.

'I didn't even know this pool was back here.' He stepped out of the woods and into the remaining light of the day. He wore a pair of white overalls that were spattered in paint. He sipped at his beer, foam clinging to his beard.

'No one uses it but me. My parents don't like to swim.' I paddled in the deep end, glad that the water was green and cloudy, so that he couldn't see me in my bathing suit.

'Maybe I'll go swimming sometime. Would that be all right with you?'

'I don't care. You can do what you want.'

He finished his beer in one long pull, making a popping sound when he pulled it away from his lips. 'Man, what I really want is to paint this pool. And maybe you'd let me paint you in it. Would you let me do that?'

'I don't know,' I said. 'What do you mean?'

He laughed. 'Just like this, you in the pool, in this light. I would like to create a painting. I mostly do abstracts, but for this . . .' He trailed off, scratched at the inside of his thigh. After a pause, he asked, 'Do you know how goddamn beautiful you are?'

'No.'

'You are. You're a beautiful girl. I'm not supposed to say that to you because you're young, but I'm a painter so it's okay. I understand beauty, or at least I pretend to.' He laughed. 'You'll think about it?'

'I don't know how much more swimming I'll do. The water is kind of dirty.'

'Okay.' He looked into the woods behind me, slowly bobbing his head. 'I need another beer. Can I get you something?' He was now holding the empty bottle upside down by his side, drips of beer falling onto the unmown grass. 'I'll get you a beer if you want one.'

'I don't drink beer. I'm only thirteen.'

'Okay,' he said, and stood watching me for a while, waiting to see if I would get out of the water. His mouth hung open slightly, and he scratched again at the inside of his thigh. I stayed put, treading water, and spun so that I wasn't facing him.

'Ophelia,' he said, almost to himself. Then, 'Okay. Another beer.'

When he left I got out of the pool, knowing that I was done swimming for the summer, and hating Chet for wrecking my secret pond. I wrapped myself in the large beach towel I'd brought to the pool and ran through the house toward the bathroom nearest my room on the second floor. My chest hurt, as though the anger inside of me was a balloon, slowly inflating but never going to pop. In the bathroom with the rattling vent turned on and the shower going, I screamed repeatedly, using the nastiest words I knew. I was screaming because I was mad, but I was also screaming to keep myself from crying. It didn't work. I sat on the tiled floor, and cried until my throat hurt. I was thinking of Chet – the scary way he looked at me – but I was also thinking of my parents. Why did they fill our home with strangers? Why did they only know sex maniacs? After showering, I went into my bedroom and looked at myself naked in the full-length mirror on the inside of my closet door. I'd known about sex for almost my entire life. One of my earliest memories was of my parents doing it on a large towel in the dunes on some beach vacation. I was three feet away, digging in the sand with a plastic trowel. I remember that my baby bottle was filled with warm apple juice.

I turned and looked at my body from all sides, disgusted by the patch of red hair sprouting between my legs. At least my breasts were barely noticeable, unlike my friend Gina who lived down the road. I pulled my shoulders back and my breasts completely flattened out. If I held a hand between my legs I looked the same as I had when I was ten years old. Skinny, with red hair, and freckles that darkened my arms and the base of my neck.

I dressed in jeans and a sweatshirt, even though the night was still sweltering hot, and went downstairs to make myself a peanut butter sandwich.

I stopped swimming in the pool. I don't know if Chet continued to look for me there. I would see him sometimes on the top step that led to the apartment above my mother's studio, smoking a cigarette and gazing toward the house. And he was occasionally in our kitchen, speaking with my mother, usually about art. His eyes would find me, then slide away, then find me again.

My father took off that summer for about three weeks. It happened immediately after a visit from several of his English friends, including a young poet named Rose. He introduced us by saying, 'Rose, meet Lily. Lily, meet Rose. Do not compete. You are both beautiful flowers.' Rose, skinny and with large breasts, smelled of clove cigarettes, and when she shook my hand she stared at the top of my head. I was worried that after my father disappeared Chet would show up in the house more often. Instead, another man showed up, with a Russian name. I liked him, but only because he had a beautiful shorthaired mutt named Gorky. We hadn't had any animals at the house since Bess, my cat, had died three months earlier. With the Russian around, Chet disappeared from view for a while, and I was beginning to feel safe. Then Chet came to my bedroom late on a Saturday night.

I knew it was a Saturday because it was the night of the *important* party, one that my mother had been talking about for over a week. 'Lily, darling, take a bath on Saturday because of the party.' 'Lily, you'll help your mother make the spanakopita for our party, won't you? I'll let you hand them out the way you like.' It was strange that she cared about this particular night. She had parties all the time, but usually with teachers and students from the college. For this party, people were coming from New York to meet the Russian. My father was still gone, and my mother was nervous, her short hair sticking out at the back because of how often she ran her fingers through it. I stayed away from the house for most of that Saturday, walking through the stretch of pine trees to my favorite place, a meadow edged with stone walls that abutted a long-abandoned farmhouse. I threw rocks at trees until my arm began to ache, then lay back for a while on the soft hummock of grass near the willow. I daydreamed of my other family, the imaginary one with boring parents, and seven siblings, four boys and three girls. The day was hot. I could taste salty sweat on my upper lip, and as I lay there, I watched dark, swollen clouds build in the sky. When I heard the first low rumble of thunder, I stood, brushed grass from the back of my legs, and returned to the house.

The thunderstorm pelted Monk's for a dark hour. My mother drank gin and pulled things from the oven, telling the Russian how perfect the storm was – how she couldn't ask for a better sound track to her party – although I could tell she was upset. When guests began to arrive the skies were blue again, the only evidence of the storm the cleanness of the air, and the steady dripping from the swollen gutters. I passed appetizers to people I'd never seen before, then snuck away to my room, bringing two cold Pop-Tarts with me for my dinner.

I ate in my room, and tried to read. I had taken a paperback from my mother's stack of books by her side of the bed. It was called *Damage*, by Josephine Hart, and I'd heard her talking about how she didn't like it, how it was just trash dressed up as something literary. It made me want to read it, but I didn't really like it either. It was about an Englishman, like my father, who was having sex with his son's girlfriend. I hated everyone in it. I gave up and pulled a Nancy Drew from my shelf. Number ten: *The Password to Larkspur Lane.* I knew I was too old to be reading Nancy Drew but it was by far my favorite. I fell asleep while reading it.

I woke to the sound of my bedroom door being opened. Light fell in from the hallway and I could hear loud rock music coming from downstairs. I was curled on my side, a single sheet pulled up to my waist, facing the door. I cracked open my eyes and could see Chet standing in the doorframe. The light was coming from behind him, but he was easy to identify because of the beard, and the dark-framed glasses, an edge of which had caught the yellow light from the hall. He swayed a little, like a tree in a strong wind. I didn't move, in the hopes that he would go away. Maybe I wasn't who he was looking for, even though I knew I was. I considered screaming, or trying to run from the room, but there was a steady thump of bass and drum throughout the house and I didn't think anyone would hear me. And then Chet would kill me for sure. So I closed my eyes, hoping he would go away, and with my eyes closed, I heard him step into the room, quietly shut the door behind him.

I decided to keep my eyes shut, pretend I was

asleep. My heart beat in my chest like a jumping bean, but I kept my breathing regular. In through my nose and out through my mouth.

I listened as Chet took a few steps forward. I knew he was standing right over me. I could hear his own breath, ragged and wet, and I could smell him. The fruity, musty smell, mixed with the smell of cigarettes and alcohol.

'Lily,' he said, in a loud whisper.

I didn't move.

He leaned in closer. Said my name again, a little quieter this time.

I pretended I was in a deep sleep, and couldn't hear a thing. I pulled my knees up a little tighter to my body, moving the way I thought a sleeping person would move. I knew what he was doing in my room, and I knew what he wanted. He was going to have sex with me. But as far as I knew that was only something he could do if I was awake, so I planned on staying asleep, no matter what he did.

I heard the creak of his knees and the rustle of his jeans, then smelled the sour, beery smell of his breath. He had crouched down beside me. The song from downstairs – its thumping bass – stopped, and another song, that sounded the same, started up again. I heard the sound of a zipper being slowly unzipped, one tiny, metallic pluck at a time, then a rhythmic sound, like a hand being rubbed rapidly back and forth across a sweater. He was doing it to himself and not to me. My plan was working. The sound got faster and louder, and he said my name a few more times, in low hoarse whispers. I thought he wasn't going to touch me but I felt the air shift a little in front of my chest, then felt a finger graze along the pajama fabric that stretched across my breasts. It was warm in the room but cold prickles coursed over all my skin. I willed myself to keep my eyes closed. Chet pressed his fingers against my chest, his sharp nails pinching, then made a sound that was halfway between a grunt and an intake of breath, and he pulled his hand away from my nipple. I listened as he zipped his pants back up and quickly backed out of the room. He thudded into the doorframe on the way out, then pulled the door closed behind him, not even trying to keep quiet.

I stayed in my curled-up position for another minute, then got off the bed, took my desk chair and tried to jam it up under the doorknob of my door. It was something Nancy Drew would do. The chair didn't quite fit – it was a little too short – but it was better than nothing. If Chet came back it would be hard for him to open the door, at least, and the chair would fall over and make a noise.

I didn't think I would sleep that night, but I did, and when morning came, I lay in bed, thinking about what I should do.

My worst fear was that if I told my mother about what had happened, she would tell me that I should have sex with Chet. Or else she would be mad that I let him come into my room, or that I let him watch me in the pool. I knew that this was something I needed to take care of on my own.

And I knew how I would do it.

CHAPTER 3

TED

At nearly midnight, I stood on the front steps of the bay-fronted brownstone I owned with Miranda, the taxi's red lights receding down the street, and tried to remember where I'd stowed the house keys when I'd left for London a week earlier.

Just as I was unzipping the outside pocket of my carry-on, the front door swung open. Miranda was in midyawn. She wore a short nightshirt and a pair of wool socks. 'How was London?' she asked, after kissing me on the mouth. Her breath was slightly sour and I imagined she'd been asleep in front of the television.

'Damp.'

'Profitable?'

'Yes, damp and profitable.' I shut the door behind me, and dropped my luggage on the hardwood floor. The house smelled of takeout Thai. 'I'm surprised to see you here,' I said. 'I thought you'd be in Maine.'

'I wanted to see *you*, Teddy. It's been a whole week. Are you drunk?'

'The flight was delayed and I drank a few martinis. Do I reek?'

'Yes. Brush your teeth and come to bed. I'm exhausted.'

I watched Miranda climb the steep stairs to our second-floor bedroom, watched the muscles in her slim calves tense and untense, watched the nightshirt sway back and forth with the movement of her hips, then thought of Brad Daggett bending her over the carpentry table, lifting her skirt . . .

I went downstairs to the basement level, where our kitchen and dining room were located. I found a carton of red curry shrimp in the fridge and ate it cold, sitting at our butcher-block island.

My head was starting to ache, and I was thirsty. I realized that without having fallen asleep I was already hungover from all the gin I'd had in the airport lounge, and then on the flight.

The redhead from the bar had also been seated in business class, across from me, and one row behind. After boarding the plane, we'd kept talking across the aisle, even though we'd temporarily ceased our discussion of my wife's infidelities. The old woman next to me in the window seat saw us talking and said, 'Would you and your wife like to sit next to one another?'

'Thank you,' I said. 'We'd love to.'

Once she was settled in, and once I had ordered a gin and tonic from the flight attendant, I asked for her name again.

'It's Lily,' she said.

'Lily what?'

'I'll tell you, but first let's play a game.'

'Okay.'

'It's very easy. Since we're on a plane, and it's a long flight, and we're not going to see each other again, let's tell each other the absolute truth. About everything.'

'You won't even tell me your last name,' I said.

She laughed. 'True. But that's what lets us play by these rules. If we know one another, then the game doesn't work.'

'Give me an example.'

'Okay. I hate gin. I ordered a martini because you had one in front of you and it looked sophisticated.'

'Really?' I said.

'No judgment,' she said. 'Your turn.'

'Okay.' I thought for a moment, then said, 'I love gin so much I'm worried sometimes I'm an alcoholic. If I had my way I'd drink about six martinis a night.'

'It's a start,' she said. 'You might have a drinking problem. Your wife is cheating on you. How about you? Have you ever cheated on her?'

'No, I haven't. I have . . . what was it Jimmy Carter said? . . . I've had lust in my heart, of course. I've already imagined having sex with you, for instance.'

'You have?' Her eyebrows raised, and she looked a little shocked.

'Absolute truth, remember?' I said. 'Don't be surprised. Most men you meet are probably thinking disgusting things about you within five minutes.'

'Is that really true?'

'Yep.'

'How disgusting?'

'You really don't want to know.'

'Maybe I do,' she said, and shifted toward me in her seat. I drank a little of my gin and tonic, the ice knocking against my teeth. 'It's interesting,' she said. 'I just can't imagine what it would be like to meet someone and know right away that I want to have sex with them.'

'It's not that, exactly,' I said. 'It's more like an ingrained response where you just picture it. Like when we were standing in line at the boarding gate, I looked at you and pictured you naked. It just happens. That never happens to women?'

'Like suddenly imagining sex with a man? No, not really. With women it's different. What we wonder about is if the man we just met wants to have sex with us.'

I laughed. 'Well, he does. Just assume it. Trust me, though, you don't want to know more than that.'

'See, isn't this game fun? Now why don't you tell me more about how you want to kill your wife?'

'Ha,' I said. 'I don't know if I was really serious about that.'

'You sure? The way you told that story I couldn't tell.'

'I'll admit that after seeing them together in our house, I think if I had a gun on me that I could easily have shot them both through the window.'

'So you are thinking of killing her,' she said, the plane starting its pre-takeoff hum. We each buckled in, and I took a longish sip of my gin. I had always been a nervous flyer. 'Look,' she continued. 'I'm not trying to trap you into saying something you don't want to say. I'm interested is all. This is just part of the game. Absolute truth.'

'Then you go first. All you've told me is that you don't like gin.'

'Okay,' she said, and thought a moment. 'Truthfully, I don't think murder is necessarily as bad as people make it out to be. Everyone dies. What difference does it make if a few bad apples get pushed along a little sooner than God intended? And your wife, for example, seems like the kind worth killing.'

The plane's hum turned into a whine, and the captain told the flight attendants to take their seats. I was grateful for a moment when I didn't need to immediately respond to the woman next to me. Her words had echoed the persistent thoughts I had been plagued with for a week as I entertained fantasies of killing my wife. I'd been telling myself that killing Miranda would do the world a favor, and along came this passenger who was suddenly giving me the moral authority to act on my desires. And while I was shocked by what she had said, I was also in that state of drunkenness – gin buzzing through my body – that makes one wonder why anyone wants to ever be sober. I felt both clear-headed and uninhibited at the same time, and if we'd been anywhere semiprivate I think I would have taken Lily in my arms right then and tried to kiss her. Instead, after the plane took off, I kept talking.

'I'll admit that the thought of actually killing my wife is appealing to me. There was a prenup so Miranda doesn't get *half* of all I have but she gets a lot, enough to be comfortable for the rest of her life. And there's no clause about infidelity. I could hire a lawyer, get him to hire a detective, and make a case, but it would be expensive, and in the end I'd waste time and money, and I'd be humiliated.

'If she'd come to me and told me about the affair – even told me that she'd fallen in love with Daggett and wanted to leave me – I'd have allowed a divorce. I would have hated her, but I would have moved on. What I can't get over . . . what I can't get past . . . is the way that she and Brad acted that day I saw them fucking in my house. When I'd spoken to them earlier, they were both so calm and convincing. Miranda lied so easily. I don't know how she learned to be like that. But then I started to think about it, to add up everything I knew about her, the different ways she acts in front of different people, and I realized that this is who she is – a shallow, fake liar. Maybe even a socio-path. I don't know how I didn't see this before.'

'I imagine she acted the way she thought you wanted to see her. How did you meet her?'

I told her how we'd met, at a housewarming party of a mutual friend in New Essex on a summer night. I'd spotted her right away. Other guests were wearing summer dresses and button-up shirts but Miranda was in cutoff jeans so short that the white pockets hung below the tattered edges, and a tank top with a Jasper Johns target stenciled on the front. She was holding a can of Pabst Blue Ribbon, and she was talking with Chad Pavone, my college friend who'd bought the house we were there to celebrate. Miranda's head was thrown back in laughter. I thought two things right away: that she was the sexiest woman I'd ever personally seen, and that Chad Pavone had never uttered a funny line in his life and what was she laughing at? I quickly looked away from them, surveying the party for someone I might know. Truth was, seeing Miranda had felt like being punched in the chest, a sudden realization that women like her existed outside of dirty magazines and Hollywood movies, and that, in all likelihood, she was here with someone else.

I learned her name from Chad's wife. It was Miranda Hobart. She was house-sitting in New Essex for a year. She was some sort of artist, and she had found a job at the box office of a local summer theater.

'She single?' I asked.

'Believe it or not, she is. You should talk with her.'

'I doubt I'm her type.'

'You won't know if you don't ask.'

When we did end up talking, it was Miranda who approached me. The party had gone late, and I was sitting by myself on the sloping lawn at the back of Chad and Sherry's house. Through a cluster of roofs I could make out the purple sheen of the ocean, lit periodically by the rotating beam from a lighthouse. Miranda sat down next to me. 'I hear you're very rich,' she said, her voice deep and accentless, slightly slurred. 'It's what everyone's talking about.'

I had recently engineered a buyout between a small company that had developed a picture-uploading program and a major social media site for a sum that even I considered vaguely ridiculous. 'I am,' I said.

'Just so you know, I'm not going to sleep with you just because you're rich.' She was smiling, in a challenging way.

'Good to know,' I said, the words sounding clumsy in my own mouth, the line of roofs in the distance tilting slightly. 'But I bet you'd marry me.'

She threw her head back and laughed throatily. It was the way I'd first seen her, laughing at something Chad had said, but up close, the gesture did not seem as fake. I studied her jawline, imagined how it would feel to press my mouth against the softness of her neck. 'Sure, I'd marry you,' she said. 'Are you asking?'

'Why not,' I said.

'So when should we get married?'

'Next weekend, maybe. I don't think we should rush into something like this.'

'I agree. It's a serious commitment.'

'Just out of curiosity,' I said. 'I know what I'm bringing to this relationship, but what exactly do you bring? Can you cook?'

'Can't cook. Can't sew. I can dust. You sure you want to marry me?'

'I'd be honored.'

We talked some more, and then we kissed, right there on the lawn, awkwardly, our teeth clicking, our chins bumping. She laughed out loud again and I told her the wedding was off.

But it wasn't off. We did get married. Not a week later but a year.

'Do you think she was playing me from the beginning?' I asked Lily. The plane had taken off, and we were in that peculiar bubble known as air travel, between countries, speeding at a terrifying velocity at ice-cold heights, yet lulled by fake air and soft seats and the steady purr of engineering.

'Probably.'

'But the way she approached me . . . the way she brought up how rich I was right from the beginning. It seemed like a joke to her, like something she would never say if she were trying to land a husband.'

'Reverse psychology. Bring it up right away, and she looks innocent, somehow.'

I was silent, thinking about it.

'Hey,' she continued. 'Just because she used you

doesn't mean that she doesn't have feelings for you, that you don't have a good time together.'

'We did have a good time together. And now she's having a good time with someone else.'

'What does she get out of Brad, do you think?'

'What do you mean?' I asked.

'What's the angle? She's risking the marriage. Even if she gets half, she probably won't get her dream beach house that she's building. Being with Brad could wreck it for her.'

'I've thought a lot about this. At first I thought she was in love with him, but now I don't think she really loves anyone. I think she's bored. She's obviously done with me, except as a source of income. She's not going to change, and she's still young and beautiful enough to hurt countless people. Maybe I really should kill her, just to remove her from the world.'

I turned toward my neighbor but didn't look her in the eye. Her arms were folded on her lap, and I saw goose bumps spread along the exposed skin of her arms. Was the airplane making her cold, or was it me?

'You *would* be doing the world a favor,' she said, her voice quiet enough that I had to lean toward her a little as I raised my eyes. 'I honestly believe that. Like I said before, everyone is going to die eventually. If you killed your wife you would only be doing to her what would happen anyway. And you'd save other people from her. She's a negative. She makes the world worse. And what she's done

41

to you is worse than death. Everyone dies, but not everyone has to see someone they love with another person. She struck the first blow.'

In the circle of yellow from the reading light I could see flecks of many different colors in the pale green of her eyes. She blinked, her papery eyelids mottled with pink. The closeness of our faces felt more intimate than sex, and I was as surprised by our sudden eye contact as I would have been had I suddenly discovered her hand down my pants.

'How would I do it?' I asked, and felt goose bumps break out along my own limbs.

'In such a way that you don't get caught.'

I laughed, and the temporary spell was broken. 'That easy?'

'That easy.'

'Another drink, sir?' The flight attendant, a towering, slim-hipped brunette with bright pink rouge, was holding a hand toward my empty glass.

I wanted one, but turning my head toward the attendant had caused a sudden rush of dizziness, and I declined, asking for a water instead. When I turned back, my neighbor was yawning, her arms outstretched, finger pads touching the back of the soft seat in front of her.

'You're tired,' I said.

'A little. Let's keep talking, though. This is the most interesting conversation I've had on a plane.'

A prickle of doubt passed through me. Was I just an interesting conversation? I could hear her talking to a friend the next day: *You're not going to believe this guy I met at the airport . . . Freak told me all about how he planned on killing his wife.* As though reading my thoughts, she touched my arm with her hand. 'Sorry,' she said. 'That sounded flip. I'm taking this seriously, or as seriously as you'd like me to take it. We're playing a game of truth, remember, and truthfully I don't have a moral problem with you killing your wife. She misrepresented herself to you. She used you, married you. She took the money you earned, and now she's cheating on you with a man who is also taking your money. She deserves whatever she gets as far as I'm concerned.'

'Jesus. You're *not* kidding.'

'I'm not. But I'm just someone you don't know sitting next to you on a plane. You need to decide for yourself. There's a big difference between wanting to kill your wife, and actually doing it, and there's an even bigger difference between killing someone and getting away with it.'

'Are you speaking from experience?'

'I plead the Fifth on that one,' she said, yawning again. 'I think I'm actually going to take a little nap. If you don't mind. You keep thinking about your wife.'

She tilted her chair back and closed her eyes. I considered sleeping myself but my mind was racing. It was true that I had been considering the very real possibility of killing my wife, but now I had spoken it out loud. And to someone who seemed to think it was a good idea. Was this woman for real? I turned and looked at her. She was already breathing deeply through her nostrils. I studied her profile, her delicate nose, creased slightly at the tip, her pressed-together lips, the upper lip barely curving over her lower one. Her long, slightly wavy hair was tucked behind a small, unpierced ear. The darkest freckles on her face were across the bridge of her nose, but, looking closely, there were pinprick freckles across most of her face, a galaxy of barely noticeable marks. She took a sudden chest-swelling breath and twitched toward me. I turned away as her head settled against my shoulder.

We stayed that way for a while, at least an hour. My arm, which I refused to move, began to ache, then turned numb, as though it weren't there at all. I ordered another gin and tonic, thought about what she had said about murder. It made sense. Why was the taking of a life considered so terrible? In no time at all there would be all new people on this planet, and everyone who was on the planet now would have died, some terribly, and some like the flick of a switch. The real reason that murder was considered so transgressive was because of the people that were left behind. The loved ones. But what if someone was not really loved? Miranda had family and friends, but I had come to recognize, in the three years that I'd been married to her, that they all knew down deep what she was. She was a shallow user, content to get by on her looks, and have things handed to her. People would mourn, but it was hard to imagine anyone truly missing her.

The plane began to rise and dip a little, and the pilot's deeply American voice came over the speaker. 'Folks, we've hit just a little bit of turbulence. I'm going to ask you to return to your seats and fasten your seat belts till we've passed through this rough patch.' I finished my drink just as the plane dropped suddenly, like a car going too fast over a hill. A woman behind me let out a sharp gasp, and my new accomplice jerked awake, looking up at me with her green eyes. I don't know if she was more surprised by the plane's sudden lurch or by her position, snuggled up against my arm.

'It's just turbulence,' I said, although my stomach, which had lurched with the airplane's first dip, had tightened with fear.

'Oh.' She straightened up, rubbing at both eyes with the palms of her hands. 'I was dreaming.'

'What were you dreaming about?'

'I don't know anymore.'

The plane bucked a few more times, then began to straighten out. 'I've been thinking about what we were talking about,' I said.

'And?'

CHAPTER 4

LILY

A year before the arrival of Chet, back when my beautiful orange cat Bess was still alive, I found her one morning trapped against the vegetable garden fence by a huge, matted black stray. Bess was hissing, her fur ruffled, but she was clearly in retreat. I watched as the feral tomcat leaped onto her back, sinking his claws into Bess's haunches. I know that cats don't really scream, but that is the only way I can describe the sound that Bess made. An almost human scream of terror. I charged forward, clapping my hands, and the stray tore off. I took Bess back into the house, and searched her fur for blood. There wasn't any, but I knew that the horrible cat would be back.

'Just keep Bess inside,' my mother said.

I tried, but Bess cried at the door, and it was a semester during which my father was hosting his senior seminar at our house; students came and went Tuesday and Thursday nights, swinging through the front door to smoke cigarettes on our steps, and Bess could easily escape.

It was spring and starting to get warm and I slept with my window cracked. One morning, just past dawn, I heard Bess yowling outside, a ferocious, terrified sound. I pulled on sneakers and ran downstairs, exiting out toward the back garden. In the gray, early morning light I spotted them right away, Bess backed against the fence again, the horrible black stray crouched and ready to attack. They were each frozen in the terrible moment, like a diorama at the Museum of Natural History. I clapped my hands together, yelling, and the stray merely turned its ugly matted head my way, appraised me with indifference, and turned back to Bess. I knew right then that the feral tom would kill Bess if he got a chance, maybe not on that morning but some morning, and that I would do anything to stop that from happening.

There was a pile of paving stones on the edge of our unfinished patio. They had been there so long that moss had grown on some of them. I picked up the largest one I could carry; its edges were sharp and it was slippery with dew. I walked quietly and quickly to stand behind the stray. I didn't need to be quiet. He was unafraid of me, intent on terrorizing Bess. Without thinking about it, I lifted the paving stone above my head and hurled it down onto him as hard as I could. He turned his head at the last moment and made a squalling sound as the edge of the stone caught him on the skull, the whole stone coming to rest on his body. Bess bolted, racing across the backyard as fast as I'd ever seen her move. The stray's body shivered, then lay still. I turned to the house,

47

expecting to see a bedroom light turn on, the house woken by the sound of murder, but there had hardly been any sound.

It had been easy.

The bulkhead to the basement was unlocked. I crept down the dark, leaf-slicked steps and groped around the entryway, finding one of the snow shovels that lined the wall. I used the edge of the plastic shovel to slip the paving stone off the stray, then pushed the shovel under the inert body. I could see no damage on the matted head; I was terrified that the cat was not dead, just knocked unconscious, and would spring up any moment, come at me hissing and full of vengeance. But when I lifted the cat it flopped like a dead thing, and I was suddenly struck with a bad smell, a trail of defecation that had sprayed from the cat when it died. I had expected blood but hadn't expected shit. The smell sickened me, but I was happy I'd killed that disgusting cat.

He was not as heavy as I thought he would be, his stiffened fur giving the impression that he had been larger than he was, but he was heavy enough. I managed to carry the cat about ten feet away, to the edge of the woods, and dropped the body on top of some rotted leaves. I spent another five minutes digging up debris and tossing it on top of him till he was covered. It was good enough. My parents never went in the woods anyway.

Climbing back into bed, shivering from the cold,

I didn't think I would fall asleep again, but I did, easily.

I checked on the corpse of that stray for the next few days. It lay there, undisturbed, buzzing with flies, till one morning it was simply gone. I guessed it must have been dragged away by a coyote or a fox.

Bess resumed her cat's life, coming and going from the house, and sometimes, when she brushed against my ankles, or purred in my lap, I imagined she was thanking me for what I had done. She had her kingdom back, and all was right with the world.

After what happened with Chet the night of the party, I immediately thought about the incident with the stray cat. It gave me ideas about how I would kill him and get away with it. It seemed crucial that the body never be found. And if that was the case, then I needed to find some things out about Chet.

After the party Chet seemed to disappear for a little while, not coming out of the apartment, and not visiting the house. I did see him one night. He was on the lawn, looking up at my bedroom window. I'd just turned the light off to go to bed, and that's when I saw him there, swaying a little, like a tree in a breeze. He'd been watching me. I'd left the window cracked and the shade slightly up so that some air got into the room. I felt stupid and afraid, and tears pricked at my eyes, but I told myself that Chet would not make me cry again. I now knew for sure that he was simply biding his time, waiting for a good opportunity to rape and murder me. I did consider telling my mother about what had happened but I thought she'd be on Chet's side, that she'd wonder why I was making such a big deal about it. And my father was still away with Rose, the poet, and the way that my mother sometimes talked about it late at night, it sounded as though he wasn't coming back. I asked her once, while she was making a giant batch of hummus in the kitchen.

'Has Daddy called?'

'Your daddy has not called,' she said, spacing the words out for maximum effect. 'Your daddy, last I heard, has made a fool of himself in New York, so I expect we'll see him back here soon enough. You're not worried, darling, are you?'

'No. I was just wondering. What about Chet? Did he leave?'

'Chet? No, he's still here. Why'd you ask about him?'

'I just hadn't seen him. I thought that maybe he'd moved out of the apartment and I could go up there again.' I loved the small apartment above my mother's studio, with its whitewashed walls and huge windows. There was an old red beanbag chair that had once been in our house and been moved to the apartment. It had a small rip along its vinyl bottom and was slowly losing its little pellets of filling, but I missed it. When the apartment was empty I'd bring books over there to read.

'You can still go up there. Chet won't bite.'

'Does he have a car?'

'Does he have a car? God, I don't think so. I don't even think he has a place to live right now, besides with us.'

'How'd he get here if he doesn't have a car?'

She laughed, then licked hummus off a finger. 'My bourgeois daughter. Darling, not everyone has a car. He took a train from the city. Why are you asking so many questions about Chet? Don't you like him?'

'No, he's gross.'

'Ha, now you really do sound like your father. Well, whatever you two think, Chet is a real artist, and we are all doing the art world a huge favor by allowing him some space to focus this summer. Keep that in mind, Lily, that it's not all about you all the time.'

I had gotten what I wanted to get from my mother. Chet didn't have a car, and had arrived here by train, which meant that he could easily pack up his stuff and leave for good. That made my job a whole lot easier. I began to prepare, spending time in the meadow next to the old farmhouse, gathering the largest rocks that I could carry. I also made myself visible to Chet, dragging one of the old lounge chairs out to the sunny patch of yard between the main house and the studio. I didn't want him to keep avoiding me, since it was crucial that he trust me to a certain degree, crucial that we establish some sort of relationship. The

51

first few days when I lay in the sun, reading, my headphones on, Chet did not make an appearance. Once or twice I thought I saw his silhouetted frame in the slatted glass door of the apartment as he watched me. But one day he wandered out to smoke a cigarette, standing on the top landing in his paint-splattered overalls, no shirt on underneath. I peered over the top of the Agatha Christie I was reading and he nodded in my direction, raised a hand. My gut reaction was to ignore him, to not give him the pleasure of a response, but I forced myself to raise my hand and wave back.

The next day when I went to my reading spot, it was hot and muggy, the kind of day when you wake up sweaty and take a cold shower, and start sweating again as soon as you get out of the shower. I pulled on my green bikini. I'd had it for two years but my body hadn't developed much. It fit up top, although it was a little tight down below, where I now had hips. I pulled on a pair of shorts – ones I'd asked my mother to buy me earlier that summer. They were madras plaid and she said they made me look like a Kennedy, but she bought them for me anyway. I took my book and a bottle of sunscreen to the chair that faced Chet's apartment. I hated the sun, and I hated heat. I had red hair and freckly skin so all the sun did was make my freckles darker. I slathered myself with the sunscreen, trying to remember if the high number on the bottle was a good thing or a bad thing. I kept an eye on the apartment and pretty soon I saw Chet peering through the window. I could make out the orange tip of his cigarette winking on and off. Fifteen minutes passed, and I was listening to my tape of *Les Mis* and reading *Sleeping Murder* when Chet emerged with a mug of coffee, descended the studio steps, and casually wandered toward where I was lounging.

'Hi there, Lily,' he said, standing about five feet away, the already high sun lighting up the hair along his bare arms and shoulders so that he almost shimmered. He smelled like he hadn't showered in days.

I said hi back.

'What are you reading?'

I started to hold up the book cover toward him dismissively, then remembered that I needed to be a little bit nice so that he wouldn't suspect anything when I came to his apartment later. 'Agatha Christie,' I said. 'It's a Miss Marple.'

'Cool,' he said, and slurped at his coffee mug. Like everything else he owned, the mug was covered in paint. 'Things okay with you?' he asked.

I knew that what he wanted to ask was if things were okay with *us*, with what had happened the night he came into the room. He wanted to know if I remembered him being in there. 'Yeah,' I said.

He rocked his head back and forth. 'It's fucking hot out here, man.'

I shrugged and returned my eyes to the book. I'd done enough and I really didn't want to talk to Chet anymore. I pretended to read but I could feel him still studying me. Sweat had pooled where the two triangles of my bikini top met, and a single drop was inching its way down my rib cage. I willed myself to not wipe the sweat away with Chet watching, even though the unbearable progress of the drop felt as though Chet's eyes were slicing me with a razor. He took another loud sip from his mug and wandered off.

My father came back. There was a lot of yelling and some tears. The Russian left, and for some time, my parents were constantly in each other's company, drinking like they used to on the unfinished back patio, listening to jazz albums. I was glad that my father was back for a few reasons, one of them being that with my parents' attention turned toward one another, I could focus on getting rid of Chet. I had set up everything perfectly in the meadow, the pile of rocks growing every day, and the rope in place down the old well. It had just become a matter of picking the perfect day, a day when no one would see me cross the front yard to where Chet was living, or see the two of us walk together into the woods. That day came on a quiet Thursday three days after the return of my father. I spent the afternoon in my room rereading *Crooked House* and listening to the muffled sounds of my parents drinking. They'd started early, sharing a bottle of wine at lunch, then moving to the patio outside, drinking gin and listening to music. When the last record ended, a new one hadn't begun, and I heard their bedroom door thunk shut, then laughter. I looked out my own bedroom window; it had just become dusk, the shadows from the nearby woods lengthening across the weedy yard. I knew the timing was perfect. There were no other visitors at Monk's House right then, and my parents were unlikely to emerge from their bedroom until morning.

I pulled on a pair of jeans, socks and sneakers. The no-see-ums would be out and I didn't want them biting my ankles. I found a white tank top that I'd had for a few years. It was embroidered with a butterfly and was a little bit tight. I wanted to make sure that Chet would follow me to the meadow. I slid the little pocketknife that Grandpa Henderson had given me into my front pocket. I didn't plan on using it but it felt good to have it pressed against my thigh. Chet was unpredictable and I didn't want him to try and have sex with me before we got to the well. I also grabbed a small penlight from the top drawer of the bureau at the bottom of the stairs. The woods were always dark, especially at dusk.

I went out the front door and down the wooden steps to the asphalt driveway. I cut across the yard, worried suddenly that the light was fading too fast. Behind the studio the sky was streaked with flat pink clouds that looked like watery strokes of paint. Walking past my lounge chair I caught a whiff of cigarette smoke, and looked up to see Chet stepping out onto the landing. It was perfect.

I wouldn't have to knock on the door, or worry about being dragged into the apartment.

'Hey, little Lil,' he said, the words sounding slurry.

I stopped and looked up at him. 'Chet, can you do me a favor?' I don't think I'd ever used his name before, and the word sounded strange in my mouth, like a swearword I wasn't supposed to say.

'A favor? Anything, anything for you, my Juliet, my rose by any other name.' He put his hands over his chest. I knew he was doing that Shakespeare play but he had it wrong. Juliet was on the balcony and Romeo was down below.

'Thanks. Can you come down here?'

'I'll be with you anon, my Juliet,' he said and flicked his cigarette in a high arc. It landed on the driveway, showering sparks. He went back inside his apartment and I waited. I thought I would be nervous, but I wasn't.

CHAPTER 5

TED

After retrieving our luggage at Logan, I walked with Lily past the idling taxis at Terminal E and toward Central Parking. She stopped me as soon as we were alone in the dark lot. The pilot had told us that the current temperature in Boston was fifty-four degrees, but a whistling, litter-dispersing wind made it feel much colder.

'Let's meet in one week,' she said. 'We'll pick a place. If I change my mind, I won't show up. And if you change your mind, then don't show up either, and it will be like this conversation never happened.'

'Okay. Where should we meet?'

'Name a town where you don't know anyone,' she said.

I thought for a moment. 'Okay. How about Concord?'

'Concord, Mass., or Concord, New Hampshire?'

'Concord, Mass.'

We agreed to meet in the bar of the Concord River Inn the following Saturday at three o'clock in the afternoon. 'I won't be shocked if you're not there,' she said. 'Or upset.'

'Ditto,' I said, and we shook hands. It felt oddly formal to shake the hand of someone who had offered to help you murder your wife. Lily laughed a little, as though she felt the same way. Her hand was small in mine and felt as frail as expensive porcelain. I resisted the urge to pull her toward me.

Instead, I said, 'Are you for real?'

She released my hand. 'You'll find out in a week.'

I arrived early that Saturday at the Concord River Inn. When Lily had asked me to pick a town where no one knew who I was, I had picked Concord, and while it was true that I knew no one there, it was also true that it was a place that had played a large part in my childhood. I grew up in Middleham, about ten miles west of Concord, and about thirty miles from Boston. Middleham is an old farming community, a sprawl of open fields and new-growth forest. In the 1970s, two extensive developments had gone in – dead-end streets named after the trees that were no longer there, and single-acre lots with cookie-cutter deckhouses, all popping up to accommodate employees from nearby Lextronics, the company where my father worked.

My father, Barry, was an MIT graduate, and a computer programmer when most people didn't know what a computer programmer was. He met Elaine Harris, my mother, at Lextronics, where she was a receptionist, and undoubtedly the prettiest woman he'd ever seen. I don't know for a fact that my father had never dated anyone before meeting my mother in his thirtieth year, but it would shock me if he had. My mother, on the other hand, had spent her twenties in an on-again, off-again relationship with a fellow Boston University grad who played professional hockey for two years before a knee injury ended his career. She told me once that when their relationship ended – and she realized she had wasted eight years with a 'playboy type' – she swore on the spot that she would find a husband who was plain and dull and reliable. And that turned out to be Barry Severson. They dated for six weeks, were engaged for another six, then were married in a small ceremony in West Hartford, Connecticut, my mom's hometown.

The reason that Concord became an important place for me was that my mother dreamed of moving there. Early in the marriage, she had decided she hated the isolation of Middleham, and had become fixated on this particular wealthy suburb, with its gabled houses, its well-dressed housewives, its arty jewelry stores. My father got sick of hearing about it, so my mother would dress me up and take me, and sometimes my older sister as well, to lunch in Concord, often at the Concord River Inn, and afterward we would visit shops; she would buy new outfits, or jewelry, or Roquefort and pinot grigio at the Concord Cheese Shop. It was not a surprise to either my father or me when, during my senior year at Dartford-Middleham

High School, Elaine left my father and moved into a rental apartment along Main Street in Concord Center. She lived there for a year, before moving to California with a divorced accountant.

My father, retired now, still lives in Middleham, where he spends his time creating Revolutionary War dioramas. I visit him on Thursday nights. If the weather is above sixty degrees, he cooks me a steak on his grill. If it's below sixty, he makes a pot of chili. My sister visits every other year for Thanksgiving. It's the only time we see her, since she lives in Hawaii with her second husband and his four children. She sees my mother far more often, partly because my mother still lives in California, and partly because my mother and my sister are so much alike. I sometimes think that when the divorce happened the family split along gender and geographical lines, my father and I staying east, my mother and sister going west.

Clattering up the steps at the Concord River Inn, it was impossible to not think of my mother and me sitting in the wallpapered dining room with our seafood Newburg lunches, my mother sipping a Pink Lady and me with a Pepsi with a slice of lemon. Lily and I had agreed to meet at the bar, and not the dining room. What I had forgotten was that there were two bars in the rabbit's warren of the inn, a snug L-shaped one immediately opposite the dining room, and a larger one toward the back. I chose the smaller bar, since it was empty, and from my barstool I could watch the hallway that led toward the bar at the back. I ordered a Guinness, told myself to sip it slowly. I had no intention of getting drunk this afternoon.

I had spent a lot of time with my wife in the previous week since returning from my business trip to London. Miranda was filled with ideas for furnishing the house in Maine. We had a vintage card table in our library and she had covered it with clippings from catalogs and printouts from the Internet. I tried not to think of her and Brad Daggett as she showed me item after item of things the house absolutely needed to have. I agreed to everything: the heated tile floors in all the bathrooms; the twenty-thousand-dollar Viking range; the indoor lap pool. And while I was agreeing, what kept me going was the knowledge that she was going to die, and I was going to be the one who made that happen. I thought about it constantly, turning the idea around in my mind like looking at a diamond from every possible perspective, looking for flaws or cracks, looking for guilt or second thoughts, and I found none. All I found was the renewed conviction that Miranda was a monster that I needed to slay.

She returned to Maine on Thursday, making me promise that I would come join her on the weekend. Before leaving she brought me to the library to show me a few more items she wanted to order from her pile of catalogs. Then she brought up an image on her cell phone, a painting she thought would be perfect for the dining room.

'It's six feet by nine feet,' she said. 'It will be perfect for the south wall.'

I looked at the tiny image. It appeared to be a man's head, his ears on fire.

'It's a Matt Christie self-portrait,' she said. 'It's guaranteed to be a good investment. Look him up if you don't believe me.' Then she named a ridiculous figure in a sentence that also included the word *bargain*.

'I'll think about it,' I said.

She did a little jump without quite leaving her feet, then kissed me. 'Thank you, thank you.' She pressed a hand against my crotch, running a finger along the zipper of my jeans. Despite my feelings for her, I felt myself getting hard. 'When you come to Maine I'll give you a proper thank-you, okay?' she said in a lowered voice.

I had a sudden urge to spin her around and bend her over the card table, the way I'd seen Brad Daggett fuck her, but I didn't trust myself. I didn't trust that I wouldn't smash her face into the catalogs, or call her a cheating bitch. Instead, I told her that I probably wouldn't get to Maine till Saturday night at the earliest. She didn't seem too disappointed.

After she'd packed for the long weekend, I walked her to the garage where we kept our cars. After loading up the Mini Cooper, I said to her, 'I hope Brad doesn't give you any trouble up there. All that time you spend together.'

'What do you mean?'

'He's never hit on you, has he?'

She turned, a thoughtful expression on her face. 'Brad? No, he's a total professional. Why, you jealous?'

She delivered the line perfectly, a mixture of surprise, contemplation, and casualness. If I hadn't seen them together through the binoculars, I would never believe that there was anything going on between my wife and my contractor. The first few years I knew Miranda, I thought of her as someone whose every emotion was on the surface, someone incapable of deception. How had I been so wrong?

She folded herself into the driver's seat, and blew me a kiss through the window before whipping her car away through the tight channels of the garage. A sense of certitude washed over me. With those few simple words – denying her relationship with Brad – any doubt I had was erased.

Lily was late, and as I slowly sipped my Guinness, I became convinced she was not going to show up. I felt a strange combination of relief and disappointment. If I never saw Lily again my life would return to normal. Could I honestly say that I would still murder my wife without her help and her encouragement? Would I even be willing to try? If I did get away with it, what would stop Lily from coming forward, from telling the police that I'd drunkenly preconfessed my crime on a transatlantic flight? No, if Lily didn't show up, then I would confront my wife, tell her I knew about the affair, and ask for a divorce. What would follow would be an eternity of legal wrangling and ritual humiliations, but I would survive. Miranda would take a lot of my money – even with the prenup – but I could always make more. And Brad would get what he deserved. My wife.

But some of the disappointment I felt as I sat alone at the Concord River Inn, now convinced that I would never see Lily again, was that I was secretly hoping that part of her reason for this meeting was a romantic one. I had not been able to shake the image of her pale, beautiful face, or the feel of her slender hand in mine. Maybe an affair with Lily would be the real revenge that I could unleash upon Miranda and Brad. An eye for an eye. And it had not escaped my notice that the place we had chosen for an afternoon drink was also a hotel. I could feel the presence of all those empty beds just above the half-timbered ceiling of the bar.

As I'd been doing all week, I began obsessively reconstructing the night flight to Boston, the sudden appearance of a woman who wanted to help me murder my wife. I remembered the evening well, despite the gin. Perfectly, in fact, line for line, but it was like recalling a slightly unreal dream. I wasn't sure I trusted the clarity of all my memories, or whether I had begun to project my own ambitions and desires onto the event. Since being home, I had tried to find out information about Lily, of course. I visited Winslow College's Web site, found a bare-bones page that summarized the goals and accomplishments of the Winslow Archives. There were two names listed in the department. Otto Lemke, college archivist, and Lily Hayward, archivist. Each had a phone number, but their mutual e-mail address was the same: archives@winslow.edu. I searched the Web for anything else about a Lily Hayward, and found nothing that seemed to relate to her. No Facebook page. No LinkedIn page. No images. I wasn't surprised. She hadn't seemed the type who would have any kind of Web presence. And even if she had a Web presence, I doubted that it would have shone any light on what I really wanted to know. Why does a stranger agree to help someone murder his wife? What does she get out of it?

I had just finished my pint when I spotted her. She was slowly walking down the crooked hallway, peering into doorways, and I spun on my stool to wave her into the bar.

'You're here,' she said, sounding surprised.

'You're here, too,' I responded. 'Let's go sit at one of those tables. What can I get you?'

She asked for a glass of white wine. I ordered her a sauvignon blanc, got another Guinness for myself, and brought both glasses to the corner table she had selected. She looked as I'd remembered her, except that her long red hair was pulled back into a simple bun. As I placed her wine in front of her she was sliding out of a gray blazer.

65

Underneath, she was wearing a beige cardigan over a dark blue blouse. Her cheeks were flushed from the outdoors.

There was a moment of awkwardness as we each took sips of our drinks, and neither of us said anything right away.

'It's like a bad second date,' I said, to break the ice.

She laughed. 'I don't think either of us expected the other one to show up.'

'I don't know about that. I thought that you would.'

'I guess that I didn't expect *you* to show up. I figured you woke up the following morning with a terrible hangover, and a vague memory of plotting to murder your wife.'

'I did have a terrible hangover, but I remembered everything we talked about.'

'And you still want to kill her?' She said this as though she were asking me if I still wanted to order French fries. But there was amusement in her eyes, or maybe a challenge. She was testing me.

'More than ever,' I said.

'Then I can help you. If you still want my help.'

'That's why I came here.'

I watched as Lily leaned back fractionally in her chair, her eyes leaving me to look around the small bar. I followed her gaze, taking in the unvarnished wood floor and the ceiling that could not have been much higher than seven feet. There was one other customer in the bar, a man in a suit who had taken over my vacated stool and was drinking an Irish coffee with whipped cream on top. 'Is this place okay?' I asked.

'No one knows you here, right?'

'I've been here before, but no, I don't know anyone in Concord.'

I thought of my mother, of the year that she spent living in this town. I wondered if she had frequented this bar. Was this where she came to look for a second husband? Had she met Keith Donaldson here, the divorcé who talked her into moving to California? They hadn't married but she was still in California, with another man now. I saw her less than once a year.

'You seem nervous,' Lily said.

'I am. Don't you think it would be strange if I wasn't nervous?'

'Are you nervous about what we're planning to do, or are you nervous about me?'

'Both. Right now I'm wondering why you're here. Part of me thinks you're some sort of law enforcement and you're going to tape me saying how I want to murder my wife.'

Lily laughed. 'I'm not wearing a wire. If we weren't in such a public place I'd let you frisk me. But even if I were wearing a wire, could I even arrest you for planning to kill your wife? Wouldn't that be entrapment?'

'Probably. I suppose I could just say that I was trying to seduce you by talking about killing my wife.'

'That would be a first. Are you?'

'What? Trying to seduce you?'

'Yes.'

'Are we still playing the game from the plane? Absolute truth? Then I won't lie and say that I haven't thought about you in that way, but, no, everything I said about my wife, and how I feel about the situation, is true. I was honest with you on the plane.'

'And I was honest with you. I want to help.'

'I believe you,' I said. 'It's just that I don't entirely understand your motives. I understand what I get from what we're planning . . .'

'A quick divorce,' Lily said, and took a small sip of her wine.

'Yes, a very quick divorce . . .'

'But you wonder what I get out of it?'

'I do. That's what I'd like to know.'

'I thought you might be wondering about that,' she said. 'I'd have been worried a little if you hadn't.' She fixed her intense eyes on me. 'Remember when I was telling you how I felt about murder? How I believe that it's not as immoral as everyone thinks. I truly believe that. People make a big deal of the sanctity of life, but there's *so* much life in this world, and when someone abuses his power or, as Miranda did, abuses your love for her, that person deserves to die. It sounds like an extreme punishment, but I don't think of it that way. Everyone has a full life, even if it ends soon. All lives are complete experiences. Do you know the T. S. Eliot quote?'

'Which one?'

'"The moment of the rose and the moment of the yew-tree are of equal duration." I know it's not justification for murder, but I think it underscores how so many people think that all humans deserve a long life, when the truth is that any life at all is probably more than any of us deserves. I think most people fetishize life to the point of allowing others to take advantage of them. Sorry, I'm offtrack here. When I met you in the airport lounge, and then we talked on the plane, you chose to tell me that you fantasized about killing your wife, and that allowed me to tell you about my philosophies of murder. That's it, really. I like talking with you, and if you are serious about killing Miranda, then I will help you, in any way I can.'

I had watched Lily, in the course of her short speech, become briefly passionate, her face pushing toward me like a sun worshiper tilting toward the sun to get the most of its rays. Then I had watched her retreat again, as though she had revealed too much. She turned the stem of her wineglass between her fingers. I wondered briefly if she was insane, and as soon as I had that thought I decided to plunge forward anyway. I knew this feeling well. It was the way I had made enormous sums of money, by taking foolish risks.

'I want to do this,' I said. 'And I want you to help me.'

'I will.'

She took another sip of her wine, the light from a brass wall sconce above her making the glass glow, and reflecting onto her pale face. She looked more beautiful, I thought, with her hair pulled back, but also more severe. She reminded me of models in some of the catalogs my wife received. Catalogs full of tall, rich-looking girls in tweeds and jeans, posing next to horses, or in front of country houses made of stone. The models from those catalogs were never smiling.

'I have one question,' I said. 'Exactly, how many people have *you* killed?' I wanted to phrase it as a joke to give her a way out of the question, but I also wanted to know if she had practiced what she preached.

'I'm not going to answer that,' she said. 'But only because we don't know each other well enough yet. But I promise you that after your wife is dead I'll tell you everything you want to know. We won't have any secrets. It's something I look forward to.'

Her face softened as she said this, and I felt as though there were an implied promise of sex thrumming in the quiet room. My glass was empty.

'Have you been thinking about it, about how it should be done?' I asked.

'I have, a lot,' she said, and slid her wineglass away from her, so that it lined up with my pint glass. 'We have a huge advantage and that advantage is me. I can help you, and no one knows that we've ever met. I'm an invisible accomplice. I

70

could provide you with an alibi, and since no one knows we know each other, the police would trust me. We have zero connection, you and I. And there are other ways I could help you, as well.'

'I don't expect you to do the killing for me.'

'No, I know. It's just that, with me helping you, we can greatly reduce the chances of getting caught. That's the hardest part. Committing the crime is easy. People do that all the time. But most people don't get away with it.'

'So how do we get away with it?'

'The way to commit murder and not get caught is to hide the body so well that no one will ever find it. If there was never a murder, then there can't be a murderer. But there are many ways to hide a body. You can leave a body out in the open but make it look like the opposite of what happened actually happened. That's what needs to happen with Miranda, because if she goes missing the police will keep looking until they find her. When the police look at her body it needs to tell a story that has nothing to do with you. It needs to lead them down a road where you'll never be. I have a question for you. How do you feel about Brad Daggett?'

'What do you mean?'

'Do you have an opinion on whether he should live or die?'

'I do have an opinion. I want him to die.'

'Good,' she said. 'That's going to make this a whole lot easier.'

71

CHAPTER 6

LILY

When Chet came back out of the apartment and joined me in the yard, I was glad that he had put a shirt on underneath his overalls. He still smelled bad, like apple cider that had turned sour. I told him that I had found something in the meadow on the other side of the woods and needed his help. I told him that I would have asked my father but he was busy. Chet grunted in solidarity, as though he knew that my parents were reuniting in their bedroom.

We entered the narrow band of pine forest that separated my parents' property from the derelict property next door. 'Have you been over to the meadow?' I asked. He was behind me, stumbling slightly, holding up a forearm, as though branches might suddenly lash at his face.

'I took a walk down to the old railway tracks when I first got here,' he said. The tracks were in the opposite direction of where we were going.

'The meadow's cool,' I said. 'It's behind an old farm that no one lives in anymore. I go there all the time.'

'How far is it?'

'Just through the woods here.' We clambered over the toppled stone wall that lined the edge of the woods. A ghostly light from the low sun turned the meadow's scattered wildflowers into electric colors. The sky above was transforming from pink to dark purple.

'Beautiful,' Chet said, and I felt a brief, unreasonable annoyance that he was sharing my meadow.

'Over here.' I began to walk toward the well.

'You, too. You're beautiful, too.'

I forced myself to turn and look at him.

'Sorry,' he said. 'I told myself . . . But, God, just look at you. You don't even know how beautiful you are, do you, little Lil? You don't mind, do you? Just if I look.' He swayed a little, one hand rubbing at his unruly beard.

'It's okay, but I need you to help me first. There's an old well and there's something down there attached to a rope and I can't pull it up.'

'Cool. Let's go take a look. How'd you find a well out here?'

I ignored his question and led him across the meadow. I'd known about the well for years. It wasn't too deep. With a flashlight you could see the bottom, nothing down there but pieces of rock, and sometimes standing water if it had rained. I wasn't even sure it was initially a well, so much as a deep hole, maybe the beginning of a well that had failed. I had come across it when I was probably nine years old, running back and forth across the meadow. One of my footfalls had made a hollow, wooden sound and I pulled away dry, yellow weeds to discover the well cover, a rotted wooden square that looked like it had been put there just to keep someone like me from falling in. It barely covered the rectangular well hole and was easily pulled off. The sides of the well were lined with layered rock. I didn't have a flashlight with me then, so I dropped rocks down to judge its depth. They hit something solid after only a second or so, so I knew it wasn't that deep. At the time, I thought maybe it was a hiding place for treasure, or a clue to a larger mystery. I raced back to get a flashlight, but I ended up disappointed. The well hole was just that, a hole in the ground, collapsing in on itself.

When I showed Chet the well, he said, 'Hey, look at that. When did you find this?'

'About a week ago,' I lied. 'I spotted the rope first and then pulled off the well cover. It isn't deep, I think, but I can't pull the rope up myself. There's something heavy on the other end.'

Putting the rope down the well had been part of my preparation. I had found the rope, a weathered-looking length, in the cellar of our house, along with an old metal stake, and had brought both to the meadow days ago. I tied one end of the rope tightly around one of the larger rocks I'd unearthed from the meadow, and lowered that end down the well, then staked the other end deep into the earth. I didn't think it looked particularly genuine but it didn't matter. All I needed was for Chet to want to find out what was on the other end of that rope. That morning I'd gone into my parents' bathroom and found something in the cabinet, a small tub labeled pomade. I'd brought it with me earlier to the well and rubbed the hair goop all over the first few feet of the rope, making it hard to hold. I had been worried that the rope would be too easy to pull up and that Chet could manage it from a standing position. I needed him to kneel in front of the well hole. As it turned out, I didn't need to worry. Chet, acting like an excited little boy, dropped to his knees in front of the well and took hold of the rope.

'Ugh, what's on this?'

'I don't know,' I said. 'Some sort of muck.'

He put his fingers to his nose and smelled. 'It doesn't smell natural. Smells like shampoo.'

'Maybe someone doesn't want us to pull it up.' I had moved so that I was standing directly behind him. He craned his neck to look at me. I could see one of his wet, puffy eyes stare at my chest. My skin tightened, goose bumps breaking out along my arms.

'You like butterflies?' he asked, his eyes still on the embroidered front of my tank top.

'I guess,' I said, and involuntarily shifted backward. I felt a sudden revulsion, plus anger at myself, that I had brought this man with me to my secret meadow. Of course he wouldn't care what was down the well. Of course all he cared about was sex. He'd want to stick his penis in me before pulling up the rope. I'd been foolish. I tried to think of something to say, but my brain had emptied out and my mouth had gone dry.

But then Chet asked, 'You didn't tell your parents about this?'

'No,' I said. 'They'd just get mad at me, and if they found anything cool down there they probably wouldn't let me keep it.'

'Might as well take a look,' he said and turned his eyes back toward the well hole. 'Now, what's in it for me if we find a treasure chest down there?'

He was doing what I hoped he would do, working his way down the rope to get a better grip. He ducked his head partway into the hole and shifted forward on his knees. 'Don't fall in,' I said. It was something I had planned on saying, to make him feel more safe.

'How far down is it?'

'Not that far, I think.'

Chet made a couple of whooping sounds into the well that echoed back up.

'Let me hold on to you.' I had planned this as well, wanting to get him used to having my hands on his back. I didn't want to just try and push him in and have him rear back suddenly and fight me.

I grabbed the fabric of his overalls with both fists, just as he said, 'I got it. It's coming up.'

I conjured all the strength I had and shoved as hard as I could. He tried to lift his head but it was in the hole and he banged the back of it on one of the layered stones that lined the well. His whole body tilted forward, falling, and for a moment I thought I was going to go down the well with him, a possibility that hadn't even occurred to me. But somehow he managed to jack his legs out and stop his forward progress. I rolled to the side, listening to his surprised scream. One of his heavy boots was jammed between two of the flat rocks that lined the well entrance. 'Jesus,' he yelled. Then: 'Help me.' I heard a clattering sound as something struck the bottom of the well. His glasses, I thought.

I stood. One of my fingernails had snagged on his overalls and torn. I only noticed because I had reflexively shaken my hand and flecks of blood had spattered me in the face.

'Lily, God, help me.'

I crouched near where his foot was lodged between the rocks. It was pretty clear that it wasn't going to hold him, and that he would fall anyway, but I took hold of the edge of the worn sole and shoved it forward. Chet made a grunting sound, then I heard the sound of scraping followed by a loud crash as he hit the bottom of the well. I expected to hear him yell some more but he was quiet. There was only the sound of falling dirt and debris still pattering down the well, plus two crows cawing at each other on the other side of the meadow.

I pulled the penlight I had brought out of my back pocket and twisted it so it turned on. It didn't produce a very powerful beam but it would be strong enough for me to see into the darkness of the well. I thought my hands would be shaky but they weren't. I felt focused, and lost in my own brain, the way I felt when I was reading a good book and the afternoon disappeared. I peered over the edge and pointed the beam of the flashlight down toward the bottom. I was so sure that Chet would survive the fall and would be begging me to help him up. I had been prepared for it. Instead, he lay still at the bottom of the well, on his back, his legs against the side, and his neck at a funny angle. I stared at him for a while. My penlight beam was weak and the well was filled with shifting dust, but it didn't look like he was moving. Then I saw an almost unnoticeable shift and heard a low sigh that could have come from Chet or could have come from something settling in the disturbed well.

I stood and walked the few feet to my low pile of heavy rocks that I'd been collecting. I selected the largest, a jagged hunk of gray stone with a vein of quartz running through it. I had to carry it with both arms so I gripped the penlight in my teeth. Waddling like a penguin I came back to the well, straddled it, and bent at the waist. Pointing the penlight into the darkness, I lined up the rock as best I could and dropped it straight down toward Chet's head. I didn't watch the rock after I dropped it but I heard the noise it made when it struck Chet's head. It was a sound like a watermelon cracking open. If Chet had still been alive after the fall he wasn't anymore.

My arms ached from carrying the rock and I stayed crouched for a moment. A crow watched me from his perch on a dying maple tree on the outskirts of the meadow. I wondered if he could smell the death in the air, and thought that he probably could. He dipped his head, ruffled his black wings. I felt like he was welcoming me to a special world.

After turning the penlight off and returning it to my pocket, I pulled the stake out of the ground, dropping it and the greased-up rope into the well. Then I walked back and forth from my pile to the well and dropped about six more large rocks down toward Chet. I would cover him more later but figured that it wouldn't hurt to get a head start on the process. I would have kept going but the light in the sky was fading, the clouds now purple and dark, the meadow and the surrounding woods losing their color, fading into grainy variations of gray. My initial plan had been to return to the apartment above the studio, and start packing up Chet's things, bring them back through the woods to the well and dump them in. Then I would cover everything over with rocks and re-cover the well hole. But as I walked back through the blackness of the woods, my penlight's beam only carving out a small patch of forest floor in front of me, I decided that I could pack up Chet's things now, and move them to the well in the early morning. I knew that my parents would sleep late.

I was very familiar with the small apartment above the studio. It was one of my favorite places when it was empty, but I hadn't seen it since Chet had moved in at the beginning of the summer. I had been worried that he would have a lot of stuff that I would need to pack up, but he didn't. He was still living out of a large army-green duffel bag that was spread open by the single bed. I began to search the place using the penlight, then realized I could simply turn the lamp on. On the off chance that either of my parents looked out their bedroom window toward the studio they would hardly be surprised to see a light on in Chet's apartment. In fact, they'd be more surprised if there wasn't a light.

The lamp cast dim yellow light across the white-washed walls and the wide, bare planks of the floor. There was very little furniture in the studio apartment, just my beloved beanbag chair, looking deflated, and two upholstered chairs, each with rips in its fabric, foam coming out. The chair with the pastel sprigged print was another of my favorite reading spots. I was glad to see that Chet had used it to stack some books. It meant he hadn't been sitting in it.

There were some clothes scattered around the cot, a couple of T-shirts and a pair of white under-pants. I used one of the T-shirts to scoop the underwear off the floor and put both in the duffel.

A stale, itchy smell of body odor came out of the half-filled bag, but the apartment didn't smell as bad as I thought it might. Mainly turpentine and ash. In the center of the floor was a coffee can nearly filled to the brim with cigarette butts. I picked it up, and tried to think where to put it, then realized I could dump it in the duffel. Chet would not be wearing his clothes anymore.

From the bathroom I grabbed Chet's toothbrush, a nearly empty tube of toothpaste, a white crystal stone in some packaging that said it was a deodorant, a bright green bottle of Pert. I left behind the sliver of hairy soap in the dish. From the kitchen – really a corner with a sink, a few cabinets, and an electric hot plate – I grabbed two packages of ramen noodles and a large plastic bottle of Popov vodka. I dumped the vodka down the sink and left the bottle in one of the cabinets. I suddenly worried that I was leaving my fingerprints all over the apartment, that I should be wearing gloves. But I would have time tomorrow to wipe things down. Besides, if things went the way I thought they would, then no one would suspect that Chet had been killed. It would simply look as though he had taken off. It was hard to imagine that anyone would miss him.

After filling the duffel, I zipped it closed and lifted it, making sure I would be able to carry it in the morning. It was heavy but manageable. All that was left of Chet's in the apartment were his painting supplies. There were four canvases, three that were leaning against the wall, faced so that I couldn't see what they looked like. The fourth canvas was still on the easel. It was in the early stages, just a few blocks of color over some pencil marks, but I could tell that it was of the swimming pool at the back of the house, and that a figure had been sketched in the corner of the pool. There were no details but I knew it was me. It was a pretty small canvas, not a lot bigger than a normal TV screen. I took it off the easel and twisted it so that its fragile wood frame snapped, then I put it on the floor, and stacked the other canvases on top of it. I barely looked at them but they all seemed like finished paintings. Abstract splotches of color with, here and there, something that resembled a figure. I could have painted them.

The easel was Chet's, since I was pretty sure there had never been an easel in the apartment. It was small, with three telescoped legs supporting it. I collapsed it and folded it into itself till it was the size of a small briefcase, a block of stained wood with a handle to carry it. I added it to the pile of paintings.

I looked around the room, thinking that I had gotten everything. Even if something was left behind it would merely look as though Chet had left it himself.

My finger throbbed where I'd torn at the nail. I looked at it closely. The blood had clotted, turning brown and sticky, and I didn't think that I had splattered anything in the apartment. Suddenly, I wanted to get out of there, and be back in my bedroom. And I was hungry. Unless my parents had gotten to it, there was leftover shepherd's pie in the fridge.

I set my alarm for six the next morning. But when my owl-shaped clock whoo-whooed I was already awake, out of bed, and half-dressed. I'd slept some, but it was the kind of sleep where you are aware of every squeak and click and scrape that old houses make, where you think you haven't slept at all and then realize that the strange thoughts in your head were actual dreams, and that the pulled curtain is glowing slightly, that dawn has broken.

It took three trips to bring everything from the apartment to the well. I brought the duffel bag first and that was the hardest. I had to drag it for a while when it got too heavy to carry. The meadow was covered with a cool dew that dampened the bottoms of my jeans. I peered down into the well before dropping the duffel in. Chet was still there, buried under the rocks I'd dropped on him. A few clumsy blackflies batted around his body. On the next trip, I brought the three larger canvases. They weren't heavy but they were awkward, and I had to break one of them to get it down the well. On the last trip, I brought the small backpacker easel and the painting that Chet had started, the one of me in my pool. After dropping them down the well, I grabbed the rest of the rocks I'd been unearthing and dropped those in. It was satisfying, especially as I watched all evidence of Chet disappear under a pile of rocks. I had used an old rusty trowel to pry some of the rocks loose. It was still in the meadow and I used it to dig up clumps of dirt, dumping them down the well until it looked as though there was nothing down there except dirt and rocks. I knew it wasn't perfect but I was satisfied.

The last thing I did before leaving the meadow was to drop the rusty trowel down into the well, then replace the cover. Using my already filthy fingers I swept some of the long, dried-out grass across the cover to try and camouflage it. I circled the area before leaving it, an eye on the ground to make sure that nothing had been left behind, but there was nothing, not even a cigarette butt. Chet was gone from the world. The morning was quiet, just the rising hum of bugs, and the cawing crows that were the true owners of this meadow. I cawed back at them, like I sometimes did, and wondered what they thought of me.

Back at the house I showered for a long time, scrubbing at my fingers to get at the last of the dirt. The hot water humming over my body made me feel both powerful and safe at the same time. When my mother opened the bathroom door and said my name, I jumped and nearly fell, my foot squelching along the bottom of the shower.

'What's wrong?' I said.

'Nothing, darling. Daddy and I were wondering if you wanted to go get breakfast at Shady's?'

'Okay,' I said. 'When?'

'Soon as you're out of that shower.'

We used to go to Shady's Diner more often. It was my father's favorite and probably my favorite, too, especially for breakfast. I got the French toast with a side of extra crispy bacon. My parents sat across from me in the booth, their shoulders touching, even sharing a fruit bowl to go with my dad's corned beef hash and my mom's omelet. Thoughts about Chet crept into my mind all during breakfast, then they would disappear when one of my parents said something to make me laugh, or when I was thinking about how good my food was. My stomach felt like a hollow bowl that I could fill forever.

'You're hungry, Lily,' my mother said.

'She's a growing girl, almost a woman,' said my father.

Breakfast was a good time, even when my parents ruined it by asking me again if I wanted to skip another grade. Some of my teachers had recommended it at the end of the school year and I had already said no at the beginning of the summer. My mother had kept bringing it up, so I punished her by refusing to go to art camp in July. I knew that the two weeks when I was away was something she looked forward to. I was surprised that the subject came up again, but it didn't last long and it didn't entirely ruin breakfast.

I didn't hear anything about Chet for a week, and began to worry, wondering if it was unnatural that I hadn't said anything about it. So one day during lunch, my father nowhere to be found, and my mother in a silent mood, I asked what happened to Chet.

'Chet left. Didn't you know that?'

'Where'd he go?'

'God, Lily, I don't know. Someone else's couch, I guess. He never said good-bye, ungrateful prick.'

That afternoon I wandered out to the apartment. It looked as though my mother or father had been in and straightened it out a little. The cot had been stripped of sheets and the trash bucket in the kitchen area was emptied. I sat on my chair for a moment, even though I didn't have a book. The windows were open and a cool breeze, the first we'd had for a while, came through into the apartment. I'd been waiting for two things since killing Chet. Waiting to get caught and waiting to feel bad. Neither had happened yet, and I knew that neither would.

CHAPTER 7

TED

When I told Miranda that I was planning on coming up to Kennewick for a week at the beginning of October, there was a look of genuine pleasure on her face. We were sitting across from one another in the first-floor kitchen of our brownstone, eating linguini with clam sauce (the one dish I can make), and finishing a bottle of pinot gris. 'That'll be amazing,' she said. 'I'll get you all to myself for an entire week.'

I watched her face for any signs of deceit, but saw none. Her dark brown eyes had brightened with what looked to me like real excitement. And for a moment, I believed her and felt the warmth and reassurance one feels when someone else wants to spend time with you. A second later that feeling passed, and I was again amazed at my wife's acting skills, her duplicitous nature. Did she feel no guilt for what she was doing with Brad Daggett?

'Should we get that suite again?' she asked.

'Which one?'

'Boo. How soon you forget. The first place we stayed. With the whirlpool tub.'

'Right. Sure.'

After cleaning up, we went upstairs to watch television, settling on a remake of *Sleuth* that was being shown on one of the five hundred movie channels we had. Miranda had changed into the short nightshirt she'd taken to wearing in the evenings and was stretched out along our couch, her feet in my lap. I studied her toes, meticulously painted a deep shade of pink. I took one of her feet in my hands and pressed a thumb along its baby-soft sole. She said nothing but her body reacted by sliding almost imperceptibly closer to me, her feet arching. Her languid presence made me acutely aware of myself, my knotted shoulders, the uncomfortable shirt I was still wearing, the way I sat rigidly by the armrest, my elbow cocked unnaturally. I took my hand off my wife's foot, but she didn't seem to notice. I knew that she would be asleep soon, before the movie had finished.

Going to Maine for the week had been Lily's idea, suggested toward the end of our meeting at the Concord River Inn. She said it was important for me to know what went on up there, what Brad's work schedule was like, how Miranda spent her days.

'With me up there, everything will be different,' I had said. 'Miranda and Brad will act differently.'

'It doesn't matter. I'm more interested in the work habits of the crew on your house. How many people are there on a regular basis? How often is Brad there alone? Just observe. The more information you get, the better off we'll be.'

I'd agreed. The hardest part was clearing my schedule for a week. But I'd insisted, and Janine, my assistant, had managed to reschedule everything. The plan was that I'd go up to Kennewick late on a Friday and return to Boston nine days later on a Sunday afternoon. In a strange way I had begun to look forward to the extended time away, and I was secretly reveling in the idea that I would be putting Brad and Miranda's affair on hold. I wondered what Brad's reaction would be when Miranda told him. Even sitting there on my couch having broken the news to Miranda I felt the power shifting in my favor.

Miranda twitched and I turned to look at her in the flicker of the television's eighty-four-inch screen. Her eyes were closed, her lips slightly parted. She had fallen asleep. I stared at her for a while instead of at the movie. Deep shadows accentuated her curves, and her face, cast in the TV's light, seemed a black-and-white version of herself. Her mouth opened a little farther, a nerve fluttered in her temple. I was fascinated by her raw beauty while at the same time realizing that she would not age well. Her face, rounded and doll-like, would turn puffy, and her pinup body would sag. But she wouldn't grow old, would she? I was going to kill her, wasn't I? That was the plan, and the thought of doing it, and getting away with it, filled me with a sense of gratification and power, but also fear and sadness. I hated my wife, but I hated her because I had loved her once. Was

I making a mistake that I would regret for the rest of my life? When I thought this way, when I began to be frightened by what I was planning to do, I wanted to make contact with Lily, to hear her talk about murder in her casual way, as though she were talking about throwing away an old couch. But we had agreed to not talk for a while, to not meet until I had spent my week in Maine, and that was another reason I was looking forward to that week in Kennewick. Each day was getting me one day closer to being back with Lily.

John, the hotel concierge who often manned the check-in desk, told me that Miranda was in the Livery, then offered to have my bags taken to the suite. I thanked him and went to find Miranda, navigating the narrow, Colonial-era stairs that pitched steeply toward the inn's lower levels. The tavern, named for the livery stable it had once been, had stone floors, a stone fireplace, and a long oak bar that curved like the lines of a yacht. Miranda was alone at the bar but talking animatedly to the tattooed bartender, whose name was either Sid or Cindy. I could never remember.

I interrupted them, kissed my wife, noting the absence of the taste of cigarettes on her mouth, then ordered a Hendrick's martini. I shed my wool blazer, soaked from the walk from the car to the inn. It had been drizzling in Boston, but in Maine, the rain had become biblical, my wipers on full speed barely able to clear the windshield.

'You're soaked,' Miranda said.

'It's pouring.'

'I had no idea. I haven't been outside all day.'

Sid/Cindy was delivering my drink. 'She lives the life, your wife,' she said and laughed hoarsely as she said it.

'I know she does.' I turned to Miranda. 'What did you do all day?'

'It wasn't an entire waste. I made decisions on furniture for all the guestrooms, and I got a massage, and I waited, with bated breath, for my husband. Oh, I almost forgot.' She held up her nearly empty beer. 'To one whole week.' I clinked it with my glass of cold gin and took a long sip, the drink instantly making me feel warmer. 'Have you eaten?' Miranda asked.

I told her that I hadn't, and flipped open a menu to take a look.

We stayed till closing time, and I got drunk enough so that when Miranda and I stumbled to the suite at the back of the inn, then fell naked across the king-size bed, I barely thought of the reasons I was in Maine for an entire week, or of Brad Daggett, or even of Lily.

The following morning the rain was done, the clouds all swept out to sea, and it was one of those October days that sell calendars. The sky was a hard, metallic blue, and the trees had turned into bouquets of red and yellow. After lunch, Miranda and I walked to the house. I timed it; it took twenty-five minutes along Micmac Road, not

91

much longer than it took along the cliff walk. Route 1A was the busiest road in this part of the world, but this section of Micmac was scenic, with its periodic views from the bluff above the Atlantic, so a lot of cars went by during my walk. Micmac Road branched out from 1A at Kennewick Center, then passed Kennewick Harbor and Kennewick Beach, the three major sections that formed the town. Kennewick Beach was the less exclusive section of the Kennewick shoreline, a long sandy stretch bunched with rental cottages and, across the road, a campsite that became filled with Winnebagos in the summertime. I didn't know this for a fact but I thought I remembered Miranda telling me that Brad owned one of those semicircular clusters of rental cottages, and that, since his divorce, he was living in one of them year-round. I hadn't paid attention when she told me these facts because at the time I didn't know that he was sleeping with my wife. But now I was paying attention. To everything.

There was only one vehicle parked in our driveway, a Toyota pickup truck with a bumper sticker that read if god didn't want us to eat animals, he wouldn't have made 'em outta meat.

'That's Jim,' Miranda said. 'Brad's having him do the drywall in the basement.'

We walked around to the back of the house and entered through the patio doors. It was impossible to not think of the last time I'd been here, of first spying on Brad and Miranda sharing a cigarette in the kitchen, then later, crouching at the terminus of the cliff walk, watching them fuck in our future living room.

'Wait till you see the bar downstairs.' Miranda led me across the finished hardwood floors of the foyer, her steps echoing sharply in the empty space. Jim was downstairs, listening to classic rock on a dusty radio, and eating his lunch, perched on a plastic Quikrete barrel that had been turned upside down. He seemed flustered and embarrassed by our presence, as though he'd been caught asleep on the job instead of simply eating a sub.

He turned the music down. 'Brad'll be out a little bit later. You looking for him?'

'We're just looking. Ted hasn't even seen it down here since, since . . .'

She turned to me, and I shrugged. I didn't think I'd been to this part of the house since just after the house had been framed. I knew that Miranda was insisting on making an extensive man cave for me, even though it was something I had never asked for. She was picturing leather furniture, a pool table, a full bar, and dark red walls. When she had first mentioned this, I had viewed it as a sign of Miranda's generosity, that she wanted to make a special place in the house just for me. Now, thinking about it, it just pissed me off that she was spending my hard-earned money on something I wasn't sure I would ever use.

She gave me a tour, showed me the finished bar shelving, the space where the pool table would go, and let me see swatches of the possible color she had in mind for the walls. When we left, Jim had finished his lunch and resumed his work. A Steely Dan song played from the radio.

We didn't see Brad that day till we were all done with our tour and walking back down the driveway toward the road. He roared up in his truck, scattering gravel as he came to a sudden halt. He killed the engine and swung out of the driver's seat. He wore navy blue chinos and a tucked-in flannel shirt, and moved with an easy athleticism. He shook my hand, as he always did, and made solid eye contact when he asked me what I thought of the progress so far. As we talked, Miranda appeared disinterested, gazing back toward the house, and its view of the ocean, placid and still in the quiet afternoon.

'I hear you're here all week,' Brad said.

'Thought I'd take a little vacation. Keep an eye on Miranda.'

Brad laughed, and maybe I was overanalyzing, but he laughed a little too heartily. I could see the fillings in his teeth. In my peripheral vision I saw Miranda swing her head back to take a look at him.

'She's the *real* general contractor on this job. She missed her calling, this one,' Brad said.

'That's what she keeps telling me.'

'I'm right here, you know,' Miranda said. 'You can include me in this conversation.'

Before Miranda and I left to walk back to the inn, I told Brad that he should swing by the tavern that night, have a drink with us. He told us he'd try and make it.

'Aren't you chummy,' Miranda said when we were back on Micmac.

'He's your chum. I was just trying to be friendly so that he doesn't feel like he has to stay away now that I'm in town.'

'What do you mean?'

'I thought you two were friends. He's never met you at the inn for a drink?'

'God, no. He lives in this town. He's not going to pay five bucks for a Bud Light.'

'Where do people who live in this town go to drink?'

'There's someplace called Cooley's, along Kenne-wick Beach, where *I* have not personally been invited yet. We should go sometime this week. We can't eat at the inn every night.'

'I'd be up for that,' I said. The sidewalk narrowed for a stretch, and Miranda slid her arm through mine, pulled us closer together. Despite the brightness of the sun, it was cold where the sidewalk was shaded.

I asked, 'So you don't think Brad will show up tonight?'

'I have no idea. Maybe he'll feel he has to, since you're writing the checks and you asked. But I wouldn't be surprised if he doesn't.'

'You and him have really never had a drink together? I just figured you had, since you shared cigarettes and all that.'

'God, that really bothered you, didn't it? No,

95

Brad and I are not friends, but we are friendly. He's an employee and he's doing a great job, and I respect him, but I don't necessarily need to become his drinking partner. Besides, from what I hear, he has plenty of drinking partners already in this town.'

'What do you mean? What do you hear?'

'I've heard from some of the other guys on the crew that he drinks a lot, and screws around a lot. That's why his wife left him. Not that it's any of our business so long as he gets the job done. Why are you suddenly so interested?'

'I'm up here for a week. I thought I'd get to know some folks, some of the people you've been spending time with.'

'I've made one friend here, and it's Sid. She's the one who told me about Cooley's, and about Brad's reputation. Let's go back to our room, take a nap, then get a drink. Sound good?'

Brad didn't show up that night at the tavern. Miranda and I sat at the curving end of the bar, drinking wine and talking with Sid, even though she was busy with the Saturday night crowd. Sid had spiky blond hair, and intricate tattoos that covered one entire arm. When she spoke to us she never took her eyes off Miranda, something I was familiar with, and something that at other points in my life I had actually enjoyed. Maybe Miranda and Sid were having sex as well. Maybe Miranda was having sex with every Tom, Dick, and Sally in Kennewick.

Throughout the course of the evening, every time someone swung through the heavy tavern doors I would glance over to see if it was Brad. Miranda never looked. Either she knew he wasn't coming, or she didn't care, and since I doubted that she didn't care, I assumed that somehow she knew something I didn't, that they'd found a way to communicate, or that she already knew he had plans.

I didn't see Brad again until Monday afternoon, when a cold mist was coming off the ocean, and I decided to explore the cliff walk. Miranda was napping. That morning we had driven up the coast to look at a lighthouse that was apparently worth looking at. It was at the end of a hook of land where the fog was particularly thick. We took photographs in which the lighthouse was barely visible, then drove farther up the coast and ate lunch at a clam shack that was closing for the season that week. Returning to the inn, Miranda suggested a nap, as she did every afternoon, and I joined her. In a strange way, the sex we'd been having since I knew that Miranda was unfaithful was better than it had been before. Anger toward my wife had made me become selfish, less inter- ested in her needs, and only interested in mine, and she was responding to me in ways she never had before. That afternoon I had flipped Miranda onto her stomach and entered her from behind, holding her in that position even after she told me she wanted me facing her. I spread my body along hers, pushing my face into the tangled hair at her neck, gripping her wrists. I was surprised when she came shortly before I did, emitting a strange yelping sound. Afterward, she murmured, 'You were quite the animal today. I liked it.' She curled into the fetal position and I watched her fall asleep. I counted the knuckles of her spine, studied the dual dimples above her buttocks, wondered about a quarter-size bruise high up on her thigh. As she began to lightly snore, my thoughts turned paranoid again. Was she this relaxed after having sex with Brad? Did she consider this her due, a lifetime of men catering to all her needs? All the tension that the sex had temporarily extinguished came flooding back. I wondered what it would feel like to punch her as hard as I could in the back of the neck.

I dressed and slipped out of the room, not leaving a note. I felt better once I was on the cliff walk, enveloped in the cold mist, staring out toward the opaque ocean. I walked fast, concentrating on the slippery footing, trying not to think of the last time I had taken this route to the house. When I reached the end of the walk, I checked my watch, noting that it had taken a little over thirty minutes to reach my new home from the Kennewick Inn. I stood on the bluff, staring toward the rear of my house. I wasn't afraid of being spotted this time. I was a lord surveying my manor. I walked across the damp stretch of land, then looped around toward the front of the house through a stand of balsam firs. As I approached the driveway, I watched a truck pull away, and assumed I had just missed Brad. But as I came fully around the house, I saw his two-toned pickup truck, with him next to it, a cigarette jutting from his lips. He was punching a number into his cell phone, but stopped when he spotted me. He smiled and the cigarette bobbed up and down. I smiled back and walked toward him, hand outstretched.

It was time I got to know Brad Daggett.

CHAPTER 8

LILY

I hadn't planned on falling in love, but who does? Eric Washburn was a junior, and president of a 'literary' fraternity at Mather called St Dunstan's, although I didn't know that at the time I met him. We met in the library. It was closing time on a frigid February night, and we were the last to leave, passing through the swinging glass doors together into an eye-watering wind. Eric offered me a cigarette, which I didn't accept, then lit his own, and asked me what direction I was going in. He walked me to Barnard Hall, a gesture that at the time seemed born entirely from gallantry, and not from more sinister motives. At my entryway, he invited me to a Thursday night party at St Dunstan's. I told him I would come. He wasn't particularly handsome; he had a long face and a high forehead, a bony nose and too-big ears, but was tall and slender, and his voice was deep and almost melodic. That night he was wearing a long, charcoal gray coat and a burgundy scarf that he had wrapped several times around his neck. I had heard of St Dunstan's, knew that it was the most elite society at a college that already had its share of prep-school snobbery, and I was very familiar with its location, the Manor, a stone and slate piece of Gothic Revival architecture that broached the northern edge of campus, where Mather spilled out into the urban wasteland of New Chester's streets. It was a beautiful building, its stonework gilded with carvings and gargoyles, its front door tall and arched, and its windows all of stained glass. It was the type of architecture that had attracted me to the college in the first place. I'd looked at several places, but Mather, a two-hundred-year-old private college with just under a thousand students, had been the only place that felt right. With its gabled brick dorms, its archways, its elm-lined quad, it was like a campus stuck in some earlier time, the campus of a mystery novel set in the 1930s, where boys sang in barbershop quartets and girls in skirts walked briskly from class to class. To the deep dismay of my mother – who had been lobbying for Oberlin, her own alma mater, since I was five – and the unsurprising indifference of my father, I'd chosen Mather.

'Lily,' Eric said, after inviting me to Dunstan's, 'what's your family name?'

'Kintner.'

'Oh, right. You're Kintner. I heard you were here.' The way he'd said it sounded a little rehearsed, as though he'd already known who I was.

'You know my father?'

'Of course I do. He wrote *Left over Right.*'

I was surprised. Most of my father's fans mentioned *Slightest Folly,* his boarding school farce, and I had never heard anyone mention his comedy about the life of a London tailor.

'What time?' I asked. I was propping open Barnard's exterior door and was anxious to get inside.

'Ten-ish. Wait, hold on.' Eric dug into the pocket of his large coat and pulled out a small square card that he handed to me. It was white, printed with a letterpress image of a skull. 'Show this at the front door.'

I said good night and entered my dorm. Jessica, my roommate, was still up and I told her about the invite. She was deeply invested in the social life of Mather and I was curious what she would know about Eric Washburn and the Thursday night party.

'You got a skull card,' she said and snatched it from my fingers. Then said, even louder, 'You got a skull card from fucking Eric Washburn.'

'What do you know about him?'

'He's like royalty. I think his great-great-great-great-grandfather basically built Mather. You honestly hadn't heard of him?'

'I've heard of St Dunstan's.'

'Well, of course you've heard of St Dun's. Is the invite a plus one?'

'I don't think so. He didn't say it was.'

I went to the party, and I went alone. Eric was there, behind the bar when I first arrived, and he made me a vodka tonic without asking me what I wanted first. Then he took me by the arm and introduced me to several St Dunstan's members before returning to his bartending duties. He said it was a rotating Thursday night job and he'd drawn the short straw. I was slightly disappointed with the interior of the Manor, expecting something that more closely matched its Gothic exterior. I don't know what exactly. Persian rugs and leather chairs? Instead, it was a slightly nicer version of the other fraternities I'd been to my freshman year. Low-ceilinged rooms, tatty furniture, and the ubiquitous smell of Marlboro Lights and cheap beer. I wandered its first-floor rooms, talking to several members, many of whom asked me about my father. After drinking my third vodka I went to the bar to say good-bye to Eric and thank him for inviting me.

'Come next week,' he said, and dug out another skull invite for me from his pocket. 'I won't be bartending.'

When I got home, Jessica pressed me for every detail. I told the truth, that there was nothing particularly interesting about St Dunstan's, and that everyone there seemed nice while not being wildly fascinating. I told her there were no secret passageways, or initiation rituals. I told her that there wasn't a room lined with the skulls of freshman girls.

'Gross, Lily. You didn't meet Matthew Ford, did you?'

'I met a Matthew. He was short with long bangs.'
'God, he's hot.'

For better or for worse, St Dunstan's became my primary social life that winter and spring. I went to all their Thursday night parties, and an occasional dinner party as one of the members' date. I wasn't sure why I was invited as often as I was. Eric seemed to have a girlfriend, a fellow junior named Faith who tended to hang around him toward the end of most parties. One night, I walked into the billiard room at the Manor and saw them kissing. They were pressed up against a built-in bookshelf. Faith was on the tips of her toes, and even so, Eric had to stoop to kiss her. One of his hands was tangled in her hair and the other was pressed against the small of her back. Eric was facing me and we made brief eye contact as I backed out of the room.

Other members of the society (St. Dunstan's was technically not a fraternity, and they didn't refer to themselves as brothers) would occasionally make a pass at me, but never in the groping, sweaty way that I had experienced at fraternity houses the few times I had gone with Jessica my fall semester. No, the passes at Thursday night parties were usually slurred compliments about my looks, followed by clumsy offers of another drink, or some other recreational drug, in their dorm room. I always refused, not because the boys who made the offers were particularly repellent but because, despite the presence of beautiful, dark-haired

Faith, I was in love with Eric Washburn, and had been, since the first party at the Manor, when he had slipped from behind the bar to guide me around the rooms, introducing me to his friends. It was the way he had held my arm, just above the elbow, as though he were telling me, and others, that I belonged to him, if only slightly. Eric was the reason I kept going to St Dunstan's, although I enjoyed talking to other members, even when they were making drunken passes. The boys I met there could easily have been classified as preppy snobs, boys who had been born on third base and thought they hit a triple (as my mother often quoted), but they were also usually polite, and made conversation in which the main point was not how wasted they had been the night before, or how wasted they planned on getting tonight. They were boys pretending to be men, so they tried a little harder to impress me with thoughts on politics, and ideas about literature. And even if it was all a ruse, I appreciated the effort.

Because I had first been invited to St Dunstan's by Eric, I would usually seek him out to say good-bye when I left one of the Thursday night parties. He would press one of the skull cards into my hand and ask me to come the following week. If he wasn't around at the end of a party, he would manage to find me at some point during the week to give me an invite, and once, he left a card in my mailbox at the student center. I considered the invites evidence of a small romance. A very small one, but it was also my first. And it was enough for me.

My last exam of freshman year was on a Tuesday afternoon, and I had arranged to take the bus the following morning from New Chester to Shepaug, where my mother would pick me up and drive me to Monk's. After my exam I had planned on packing up my few belongings while enjoying the solitude of a final night in Barnard Hall. Jessica had finished her exams early and left the day before. Coming back from my American Lit Survey exam I found a skull card on the linoleum floor of my dorm room, a message from Eric scrawled on the back. 'Two full kegs. Come help us finish them tonight.' After finishing my packing, I walked across the muddy campus toward the Manor, and wasn't surprised to find only a few members and a few girlfriends circled around the bar. Most students had already left. Eric seemed wildly pleased to see me, and I drank more than I usually did, happy to note that Faith was nowhere around. I even asked Eric about her.

'Oh, she's gone, Kintner. Literally and figuratively.'

'What do you mean?' I had a sudden horrific feeling that she'd died and I hadn't heard about it.

'She's gone from here.' He gestured around him with an open palm. 'And she's gone from here.' He pointed at his heart, and several of his friends

106

guffawed. I realized that Eric was drunker than I'd seen him before.

'I'm sorry,' I said.

'Don't be sorry. She was not for me. Good riddance and good luck.' He made another theatrical gesture. I suddenly knew that Eric had invited me to St Dun's that night in order to seduce me, and that I was going to let him do it. It was what I had been waiting for. I had no illusions that it would be anything other than a one-night stand, but I was a virgin and I had decided that the time was right. I was not so foolish as to believe that I had to lose my virginity to someone who was in love with me, but it was important that I lose my virginity to someone that I loved.

St. Dunstan's Manor had three single bedrooms on its second floor. Since Eric was president, he had the largest room, a high-ceilinged single with a view toward the college chapel. Instead of a single utilitarian cot, he had a four-poster bed made of darkly stained wood. Eric seemed more nervous than I was at first as we lay, fully clothed, kissing on his bed. He excused himself to go to the bathroom, so I took off my clothes and got under the covers. When he returned he had splashed cold water on his face and his mouth tasted of toothpaste. He stripped to his boxers and slid under the covers with me.

'Should I wear a condom?' he asked.

I told him yes. I didn't tell him I was a virgin because I didn't want him to have second thoughts.

We had sex twice that night, the first time with him on top of me. Because of his height I found myself fixated on the few sparse hairs that covered the center of his thin chest in a triangle formation. He moved awkwardly and I wasn't sure he was enjoying himself but when I lifted my knees high up by his sides he said my name in a high, breathy voice, and it was over. Later that night, we had sex again with me on top. It was helpful to see his face below me, lit dimly by a streetlamp through his window. I had come to love his face, even for all its awkwardness. The saucer ears, the expanse of forehead, the thin lips. Eric had stunning eyes, dark brown and with beautiful thick eyelashes like a girl's. While on top of him, I changed the rhythm, slowing down, then speeding up again. After doing this several times, Eric suddenly pulled me down toward him, took one of my nipples into his mouth, and shuddered. Later he asked me if I'd had an orgasm. I told him that I hadn't but that it had felt good, which was the truth. I left before dawn. He was stirring as I dressed, but I managed to get out of the room before he woke. I didn't want to listen to false promises. Over the summer, I wanted my memories of Eric to only be good ones.

That summer was the first one after my parents' divorce was final. My mother was manic, obsessing over rumors that David was already engaged again, and frantically putting together a show for a New York gallery. I spoke with my father on the phone twice; he invited me to visit him in London, but

I declined, happy to spend a summer in Connecticut, reading. Monk's was blessedly empty of house-guests. My benign aunt was around for all of August but my mother had elected for a moocher-free summer, as she put it. I didn't hear from Eric, but even if he had wanted to, he had no way to contact me. As far as I knew, he didn't know where I lived, or my mother's unlisted phone number.

For my housing request my sophomore year at Mather, I had applied for a single, despite Jessica's protests that we made perfect roomies. In August I got a letter from the housing department that I had been given a quad with three roommates, a trio of girls I didn't know. Either I was stuck with three other students who were antisocial enough that they all requested a single for their second year of college, or they were three friends who had put in for a triple. The good news was that the room was in Robinson Hall, the oldest dorm on campus, a brick tower that fronted the quad. All of the four-bedroom dorm rooms had built-in window seats, and a few had working fireplaces.

I arrived late in the evening on move-in day. My three new roommates were clearly a trio of close-knit friends, and had decorated the common room in posters from David Lynch films and the Smiths. I recognized them from freshman year but didn't know them personally. They all had pitch-black hair and pale complexions: Goth versions of prep-school girls. To me, they looked like Winona Ryder from three different films. The most radical had spiked hair and wore only black, like Winona from *Beetlejuice*. The other two were preppier: Winona from *Reality Bites* (bobbed hair swept off the forehead) and Winona from *Mermaids* (cardigans, pearls, and bangs, maybe ironic, maybe not).

I don't know how the Three Winonas viewed me that September night, as I arrived in Capri pants and a collared linen shirt, but, despite their dark lipstick and double-pierced ears, they were friendly, offering to turn down Joy Division as I unpacked. I had just accepted a glass of wine from *Mermaids* Winona when there was a rap at the door. It was Eric Washburn. I was so surprised that for a brief moment I thought he must be there for one of my new roommates. But he was there for me. He was wearing cargo shorts and an oxford shirt and smelled of cigarettes and whiskey. I went with him back to the Manor and straight up to his room. He told me how he'd thought of me all summer, how he'd tried desperately to find out where I lived. He even told me that he was sure he loved me. And, like a fool, I believed him.

CHAPTER 9

TED

Brad and I had started off by drinking beers, then had switched at some point to Jameson and gingers. We were sitting at a high-backed booth at Cooley's, one of the few year-round bars in the Kennewick Beach area. The menus boasted that they'd been open since 1957. No one would doubt the truth of this claim. The back of the bar was cluttered with grimy knickknacks, delivered by a thousand liquor reps throughout the years. Schlitz wall sconces. A Genny Light mirror. A Spuds Mackenzie light-up dog. I was happy with the switch to Jameson and ginger – it made it easier for me to get myself a pure ginger ale when it was my turn to get the drinks.

After finding Brad at the house site getting ready to leave, I had been the one to suggest we get a beer. He happily accepted, offered me a ride, and took me the couple miles to Cooley's at Kennewick Beach. It was just after five when we arrived, and we were the first customers. The bartender, a college-age girl in tight black jeans and purple tank top, said, 'Hi, Braggett,' when we walked in.

'What did she call you?' I asked after we'd slid into a middle booth.

'Braggett. It's my nickname around here. Brad plus Daggett. High school thing. First round's on me, boss.' He slid back out of the booth and toward the bar. I didn't know exactly what it was I was hoping to get from Brad by drinking with him, but Lily had asked me to gather information, so that was what I was doing. The more I knew about him the better off I would be.

For the first hour of the evening, Brad and I talked about the progress on the house. He struck me as he'd always struck me – 80 percent consummate professional and 20 percent bullshitter, like the car salesman who honestly steers you away from the leather upholstery, but still manages to sell you the expensive navigation system. We drank Heinekens, and as we talked, I watched him closely. He was a serious drinker, consistently polishing off a bottle of beer in three long sips. And while he was still handsome, some wear and tear was starting to show. There were dark patches of sun damage on his tanned face, and the beginnings of a rosy drinker's hue on both cheeks. Despite his muscular frame, there was a softness beginning under his chin that was only partly disguised by his salt-and-pepper goatee. His best feature was his dark brown eyes, and a full head of black hair that was going gray at the temples.

After talking about the house through several

beers, I said, 'I hope Miranda hasn't been driving you too crazy. She's very particular about what she wants.'

'That's a good thing. The worst clients are the ones who keep changing their minds. No, Mrs Severson's been great.' Brad slid a Marlboro Red out of the pack that had been sitting on the table since we'd sat down. He tapped the filter a few times against the varnished wood, then asked if I'd mind if he stepped outside to smoke.

While he was gone, I took a look at my phone, which had been vibrating silently off and on in my pocket for the past twenty minutes. Miranda had sent me a succession of texts, culminating in: seriously, where the f are u? I texted her back that I was having a few drinks with Brad and would be back to the hotel shortly. I told her to feel free to get dinner without me. She texted back ok, then a few seconds later xoxoxo.

I spun around in my booth and looked out through Cooley's front windows toward where Brad was standing, blowing smoke into the now-dark evening. From the angle of his head, it looked as though he were staring at his phone as well, possibly typing into it. Maybe he was texting my wife as well. A moment of rage flared up in me, but I reminded myself that I was on a fact-finding mission. The war had begun with this slightest of skirmishes, and the more Brad drank, the more chance I had of discovering his weak points. I went to the bathroom, bringing my three-quarters-full beer, and dumped most of it down the sink, in an attempt to keep relatively sober.

When Brad returned, the subject of Miranda did not come up again. He started to ask me questions about my work, and my life in general, and when he learned that I'd gone to Harvard he began questioning me on what I knew about their hockey program, and how many Beanpot tournaments I'd been to. Despite not caring, I had actually been to a couple of hockey games with my sophomore-year roommate, a sports-obsessed English major who went on to become a successful magazine editor. From hockey, we moved on to the previous year's Red Sox season, a subject I knew a little more about. I told him how I shared a block of season tickets in one of the luxury boxes, and I promised to take him to a game the following year. After switching to Jamesons, and feeling that I had exhausted my limited repertoire of sports conversation, I asked him about his divorce.

'I have two great kids,' he said, after removing another cigarette from his hard pack and tapping it down on the table. 'And a fucking ballbuster of an ex-wife.'

'Does she have the kids?'

'Except for every other weekend. Look, I'll say this for her, and it's all I'll say, but she's a good mom, and the kids are better off with her. But if the marriage hadn't ended when it did, I was going to kill her, or she was going to kill me, and that's all there is to it. It was fucking nonstop. *Brad,* where the fuck are you? Come home early and fix the toilet, *Brad. Brad,* when are you going to take me and the kids to Florida again. *Brad,* doesn't it bother you to work on all these beautiful homes while your wife and kids live in a shithouse. Nonstop. It's a good thing I didn't own a goddamn gun.' He grinned. His teeth were slightly yellowed from the nicotine.

'You know what I'm talking about, brother,' he continued. 'Or maybe you don't. What's the dirt on Miranda?'

'No dirt. We're like newlyweds. All's well in paradise.'

'Oh, fuck,' he said in a loud voice. 'I'll bet it is,' he said. He had begun to slur. *I'll bet it ish.* Then he presented me his fist from across the table, and I bumped it, awkwardly, grinning back at him. How had he suddenly become so drunk? Even though we'd been drinking steadily for about two hours, Brad had seemed sober five minutes earlier.

'No, Miranda's great,' I said.

'No shit,' Brad said. 'I mean, don't get me wrong, you're not a bad-looking guy or anything, but how did you score a wife like that?'

'Just lucky, I guess.'

'Yeah, luck and a few million dollars.' As soon as he had said it, his face fell with regret. I didn't have a chance to respond because he instantly put a hand, palm up, toward me, and said, 'Aw, man. That was uncalled for. I didn't mean that the way it came out.'

'It's okay,' I said.

'No, it's not okay. Totally uncalled for. I'm an asshole, and I've had too much to drink. Sorry, man. She's lucky to have you. I'm sure it has nothing to do with the money.'

I smiled. 'No, I'm sure it has *something* to do with the money. I can live with that.'

'No, man. I don't know Miranda well at all, but she doesn't care about that stuff. I can tell.' Brad seemed to be ramping up for a long apologetic monologue, so I was pleased when a heavily made-up blonde slid into the booth next to him and bumped him on the hip.

'Hey, Braggett,' she said, then extended a hand toward me. I gripped her limp fingers in what was technically a handshake as she said, 'Hi, Braggett's friend. I'm Polly. I'm sure you've heard nothing at all about me.'

'Pol,' Brad said. 'Meet Ted Severson. He's the one building the new house out on Micmac.'

'No shit.' Polly smiled at me. Even with the clownlike makeup you could tell that she was pretty, and had probably once been beautiful. Natural blond hair, blue eyes, and large breasts that she was showing off in a V-neck shirt and cardigan sweater. The portion of her chest that was visible was deeply tanned and freckled. 'Brad told me all about that house. It's gonna be beautiful, I hear.'

'That's the plan,' I said.

'Well, boys, I was going to intrude on your manly

little bonding session, but now that I see you're talking business, I have lost interest.'

'Have a drink,' I said.

'Thanks, anyway. I'll let you two talk.'

She slid out of the booth, leaving behind a hefty waft of perfume.

'Girlfriend?' I asked Brad.

'In eighth grade maybe,' Brad said and laughed, showing a lot of his teeth. 'But now that she's here I wouldn't mind taking off. I live right around the corner. You got another drink in you, then I'll take you home?'

'Sure,' I said, although the last thing I wanted was another drink, and the next-to-last thing I wanted was to get in a vehicle with a drunken Brad behind the wheel. But this was a chance to see where Brad lived, and I couldn't pass that up.

The night had turned cold, but the mist had lifted and a multitude of stars wheeled in the sky. Even though Brad's rental cottages were about three hundred yards away, he drove me in his truck, parking erratically in front of the first of about a dozen boxy cottages that formed a semicircle across the road from the beach. A hand-painted sign said crescent cottages, then a phone number.

'Miranda told me you own these,' I said as he unlocked the dark cottage. All of them were dark, illuminated only by a streetlamp, and by the bright night sky.

'My parents own them but I run them. We're out of season now but they do good in the summertime.'

117

He flipped on a tall floor lamp as we walked through the front door. It was nicer inside than I expected but also bleaker, just a few pieces of utilitarian furniture, the walls painted white and mostly empty. The one item that marked it as Brad's home and not a rental was an enormous TV on a stand that looked out of place in the relatively small living room. I thought it would smell of cigarettes inside but it didn't.

Brad went straight to the fridge in the alcove kitchen, and I shut the flimsy front door behind me. I heard two caps popping off bottles, and he returned and handed me a cold Heineken. We sat on the beige couch. Brad slumped a little, his legs spread wide. The beer bottle looked small in his big tanned hands.

'How long have you lived here?' I said, just to say something.

''Bout a year. It's a temporary situation.'

'Yeah,' I said. 'I can see that. I mean, you wouldn't want to live here too long.'

As soon as I said it, I felt a little bad, and I watched a hateful flicker darken Brad's face that he quickly replaced with a thoughtful frown. 'Like I said, only temporary. Till the old ship comes in.'

I said nothing back and we lapsed into a silence. I looked around, noticing that the stack of fishing magazines on the coffee table were squarely lined up with the corner of the table. On top of the magazines was the remote control, also squarely lined up. On the side table closest to me was a framed picture of a boy and a girl, taken on a boat. Both kids, who looked to be about twelve and ten, wore orange life vests.

I picked up the picture. 'These your kids?'

'Jason and Bella. That's taken on my old boat, though. I sold it the beginning of this summer, and bought myself my Albemarle. You fish?'

I told him no, but he continued to talk about his boat. I was barely listening, but it didn't really matter. I was learning some things about Brad Daggett. Putting aside for now the matter that he was sleeping with my wife, I was discovering that I didn't like Brad Daggett at all. He was a selfish drunk, who was probably only going to get more selfish and alcoholic as he got older. He didn't care about his kids beyond placing a photograph of them in his home, and it wasn't clear if he really cared for anyone besides himself. He was a negative in this world. I thought of Lily, and I thought about Brad coming to a sudden end, and I didn't really mind. In fact, I wanted it to happen. Not just because it would punish Brad for what he was doing with my wife, but also because Brad disappearing off this earth would be a good thing. Whose life was he making better? Not his kids, or his ex-wife. Not Polly at the bar, who maybe thought she was his girlfriend. He was an asshole, and one less asshole around was good for everybody.

I interrupted Brad in his monologue about his boat, and told him I was going to the bathroom.

It was as clean as the rest of the apartment. I dumped my beer down the sink, and took a look in Brad Daggett's medicine cabinet. There wasn't much to look at. Razors and deodorant and hair product. A large bottle of generic ibuprofen. A box of hair dye that hadn't been opened. A prescription bottle for antibiotics that had expired over five years earlier. I opened it up and looked inside; the bottle was filled with blue, diamond-shaped pills that I recognized as Viagra. So Brad the stud wasn't such a stud, after all. I actually laughed out loud. When I returned to the living room, Brad hadn't shifted position from the couch, but his eyes were closed and his chest was lifting and falling steadily. I watched him for a while, trying to feel something besides disgust – trying to feel some pity, maybe, just as a way to test myself. I felt none.

Before leaving I quietly searched a few of the drawers in the kitchen alcove. One of them was a utility drawer, filled with tools, measuring tape, a spool of twine, a roll of duct tape. Toward the back of the drawer was a Smith & Wesson double-action revolver. I was surprised, only because he had made that earlier joke that he would have killed his wife if he'd owned a gun. For one rash moment, I considered stealing it, then realized he would most likely know who took it. I left it where it was, but I did take a newly minted key from a small box filled with similar keys. He would never miss it, and it was possible that it

120

opened the door to this cottage, or maybe all of the Crescent cottages.

I took one last look around before leaving. Brad hadn't moved from his position. I stepped out into the cold, brackish air, then quietly tried the key on Brad's front door. It slid in and turned. I left the door unlocked, and pocketed the key. I pulled out my phone and was about to call Miranda to have her come and pick me up, when I decided I might walk. The cold felt good against my skin. I breathed deeply through my nostrils, the salt in the air making me feel more alive than I'd felt in a while. I began to walk. It was only a few miles, and I felt like I had all the energy in the world.

CHAPTER 10

LILY

For all of my sophomore year, and Eric's senior year, I spent almost every Thursday, Friday, and Saturday night at St Dunstan's Manor in Eric's second-floor bedroom. At the time, I thought of this period as the happiest of my life. In retrospect, and not just because of what happened later, I realized that it was also a time of uncertainty and anxiety. I was in love with Eric Washburn, and he said he was in love with me. I believed him, but I also knew that we were young, and that Eric was graduating soon, with plans to move to New York City and get a job in the financial sector. And my plan was to spend the following school year in London at the Faunce Institute of Art, studying conservation. Even though Eric and I would talk about our future, I told myself I knew that everything was going to change when he graduated.

I led two separate but compatible lives that year. From Sunday to Thursday I did all my reading and schoolwork. My roommates, the Three Winonas, played loud music and smoked nonstop cigarettes, but were surprisingly quiet, and relatively good-natured. I found I had a lot in common with *Mermaids* Winona, a bookworm who, like me, grew up idolizing Nancy Drew. On Thursday evening I would go to St Dunstan's Manor for the weekly party. I would bring my largest purse, packed with a change of clothes and a few of my toiletries, since I would always spend the night, and sometimes the weekend. From Friday morning until Sunday evening Eric and I were rarely apart, with the exception of classes, and Eric's racquetball matches, or Ultimate Frisbee, or any of the numerous pickup games that it was important for him to win. We saw movies at the campus repertory theater, and would venture into New Chester to eat Italian food, and would sometimes go to parties not hosted by St Dunstan's or any of its members, but that was rare. We slid into a comfortable relationship filled with predictable routine, a day-to-day of inside jokes and what seemed to me to be some highly well-suited sex. We called one another Washburn and Kintner. We were blessedly free of the dramatics of disappointment or infidelity. I cherished what we had become but kept it to myself, telling Eric and no one else how strong my attachment was. He echoed my feelings, and sometimes talked of our future together after Mather.

Eric's ex-girlfriend Faith was also a senior, and still a regular at Thursday night parties. She was now dating Matthew Ford, and because Faith and I were the respective girlfriends of the two most prominent members of St Dun's, Faith attached herself to me that year, even occasionally asking me questions about my relationship with Eric, although I never took the bait. I didn't particularly like Faith, who was bubbly and devious and liked to be the center of attention, but I didn't mind spending time with her. If Faith hadn't been around at all, curiosity about the girl who had spent two years with Eric might have escalated into obsession. But she *was* around, and I got to know her, and, because of that, she had no place in my imagination.

I could see what had attracted Eric to Faith. She was round-faced and sexy, with short black hair. Her clothes were straight out of *The Official Preppy Handbook* but her sweaters were always a little too tight, and her skirts were always a little too short. When she talked, she came in close and made disarming eye contact, but she laughed often, and made funny jokes about herself. If we went anywhere together, Faith would push her arm through mine, and if she was standing behind me, she would run her fingers through my hair. Neither of my parents had been physically affectionate with me, so I found Faith's touchiness often disturbing and occasionally reassuring. Once, when Faith was drunk, she told me she wanted to study the color of my eyes. She came in close, her own brown eyes huge in my vision.

'It's like a tapestry in there,' Faith said, her breath warm against my cheek. 'There are flecks of gray and yellow and blue and brown and pink.'

Eric rarely spoke of Faith, but one night as we lay in his bed, he asked if it bothered me that Faith was around so much.

'Not really,' I said. 'She's decided we're best friends. Have you noticed that?'

'She's best friends with everyone. No, delete that. I think she genuinely likes you and wants to be your friend, it's just that . . .'

'Don't worry. I know what you mean. I have no intention of becoming her best friend. I'm not sure we have anything in common. Besides you.'

'No, you have nothing in common. I can vouch for that. She's not a bad person, and she and Matt make a good pair.'

'I guess so,' I said.

And that was the extent of our conversation on the subject of Faith.

That summer I returned to Monk's. My mother had a new boyfriend, Michael Bialik, a bearded linguistics professor from the university, who was surprisingly grounded. He had his own place about a half mile from ours, a converted barn where he lived with his son, a piano prodigy named Sandy. Michael loved to cook, and because of this, my mother spent a lot of her time at his house, leaving Monk's to me. My library job was only four hours a day Monday through Friday, and I spent the rest of my weekday time either reading or puttering around the property. I was in love, and I was at peace. I even returned to my favorite meadow, the final resting place of Chet. The well cover was still in place; it looked the way it had – years ago – when I had first discovered it, hidden by winter-yellowed grass. The nearby farmhouse was still unoccupied.

My plan had been to visit Eric in New York on the weekends, but when Eric came to visit Monk's he fell in love with it, or at least he claimed he had.

'I want to spend every weekend here, Kintner. This will be the perfect life. Weeks in the city, and then I can take the train out Friday evening and be here with you. Country weekends.'

'You won't get bored?'

'Not a chance. I love it here. What about you? I'd be asking you to spend all your time here.'

'You're describing every summer I've ever had. I don't mind. And I'll have you to look forward to on the weekends.'

And so our summer turned out to be a replication of our school year. Weeks alone. Weekends together. I didn't mind, because I had never minded spending time alone. And the days I spent alone were days that were getting me closer to the weekend, to seeing Eric step off the commuter train, overnight bag slung across his shoulders, huge grin on his face. And these weekends were that much more intense. Away from Mather, our relationship seemed more mature, more comfortable. We felt married. So, no, I didn't mind just seeing Eric two days each week.

And Eric didn't mind, for reasons of his own.

I might never have found out about those reasons, and might have left for London in the fall feeling as though Eric was still the love of my life, if it hadn't been for my father's visiting New York in the last week of August and asking to see me for lunch. He had a new book coming out, a collection of short stories, and was in New York to meet with his American agent and his American publisher, and to give a reading at Strand Books. He hadn't invited me to the reading, which wasn't a surprise. I'd asked him once – my junior year of high school, I think – if I could go to one, and he'd replied, 'God, Lily, you're my daughter. I wouldn't expose you to that. It's bad enough you'll eventually feel the need to *read* my books, let alone have to listen to me speak them out loud.'

So I took a day off from the library and caught the train to New York City. My father and I ate lunch in a swank restaurant attached to the lobby of his midtown hotel, and we talked about my upcoming year in London. He promised to e-mail me a list of friends and relatives I had to visit, along with a few of his favorite London landmarks, most of which were pubs. Then he drilled me for tidbits about my mother and the new boyfriend. He was very disappointed to hear that the linguistics professor was, on the whole, a decent man. After lunch, we parted ways in front of the hotel. 'You turned out all right, Lil, despite your mother and me,' he said, not for the first time. We hugged good-bye. It was a strangely nice day for late August in the city, so I headed downtown, toward Eric's office, a place I had never visited. The air that had been stifling for the entire month was suddenly free of humidity, and I was just happy to be walking along the quiet midday corridors of the city. I hadn't decided whether I would intrude on Eric's workday to surprise him or not, but was considering it, beginning to imagine the look on his face as I stepped into his office. I was taken out of this reverie by hearing someone shout my name. I turned to see Katie Stone, a junior at Mather, and someone I knew from St Dunstan's parties, crossing the street and waving at me.

'I thought that was you,' Katie said, stepping onto the curb as a yellow cab hurtled by. 'I didn't know you were in the city this summer.'

'I'm not. I'm at my mom's house in Connecticut, but my dad's here and I had lunch with him.'

'Do you want to get coffee? I got let out of work early. God, New York's depressing in August.'

We went to a chain coffee shop at the nearest corner and both ordered iced lattes. Katie prattled on about Mather students we both knew, and several I'd never heard of. She was a gatherer and purveyor of gossip, and I was surprised that she wasn't asking me about Eric, so I asked her, 'Do you see Eric much?'

Katie's eyes widened a little at the mention of his name. 'Oh. I wasn't going to bring him up.

No, not much, but a little. He works around here somewhere, you know.'

'Yeah, I know. Why weren't you going to bring him up?'

'I just didn't know how you felt, now that you're not seeing each other. I didn't know if you wanted to hear about him.'

A cold flush went over my skin. I very nearly told Katie that of course I was still seeing Eric but something stopped me. Instead, I asked, 'Why, what's going on with him?'

'Nothing that I know of. I've seen him a little, but he's never here on the weekends. His dad's sick. Maybe you knew that?'

'No,' I said. 'What's wrong with him?'

'Cancer, I think. Eric goes there every weekend. They must be close?' She phrased it like a question, and I managed to nod, despite the sudden need to get out of the coffee shop, and away from Katie. Fortunately, Katie's cell phone began to ring, and as she dug within her enormous purse, I excused myself. I borrowed the key from the barista, then locked myself into the closet-size restroom. My mind galloped, desperately trying to understand the information I had just received, and while there was a part of me that was questioning what Katie had said – that it must be some ridiculous misunderstanding – there was a more logical part of me that knew it was true, that I had been a fool. Eric was leading two lives, and no one knew that he was seeing me on the weekends. After returning the key I saw that Katie was still on her phone, and I took the opportunity to tap her briefly on the shoulder, point at my watch, and move quickly toward the door. Katie lowered the phone and stood, but I simply mouthed the word 'sorry' and kept moving.

Once outside, I went down a residential side street. One of the brownstones had stone front steps that were shaded by a leafy tree. I crouched high up on the steps, not caring if the owner spotted me and told me to leave. I don't know how long I sat on those steps, but it was probably about two hours. I felt miserable for some of that time, but pretty soon I began to feel calm. I analyzed the situation. Eric had compartmentalized his life with me so that it only happened on the weekends and never in the city. It was the way he operated; it was the way he had operated at college. But why was he lying about where he was on the weekends? There could be only one reason – that Eric was involved with someone here in New York.

A little before five o'clock I walked down toward Eric's office building. I knew the address but not what it looked like. I walked slowly, my eyes scanning the crowd. I knew that I would not be able to handle running into Eric, but I wasn't ready to leave the city yet. I wanted to see where he worked, maybe even see him without letting him see me.

His office was in a nondescript four-story stone building next to a Gray's Papaya. I sat on a bench across from its entrance, and pulled a *New York Post* from a nearby trash can, unfolding it in front of me but keeping my eyes on the building's front doors. At a little after five a few men in suits, plus one woman in a skirt and blouse emerged. No Eric, but he came out in the next group of three men. He wore a light gray suit, and as the three men hit the sidewalk, they all simultaneously lit cigarettes. I wasn't surprised to see Eric smoking, even though he'd told me he quit on the day of graduation. He'd never once smoked a cigarette while visiting me in Connecticut on the weekend, but that was because he was two people. His coworkers, their cigarettes lit, began walking downtown, but Eric stood for a moment, glancing at his phone. A yellow cab pulled up, and I thought that Eric was going to get into it, but instead, a redhead in a retro minidress got out and kissed Eric on the mouth as he flicked away his cigarette.

They spoke for a moment, Eric's hand on the curve of her hip.

My chest hurt, and the world shimmered in front of my eyes, and, for a brief moment, I thought I was having a heart attack. Then the worst of it passed. I straightened my back, and took a deep breath, studying the girl. She looked familiar, but I had yet to see her face. The fact that she was also a redhead was a twist of the knife, even though I could tell from this distance that this woman's hair came from a hairstylist and not from genetics.

Eric and the redhead turned and for one horrible moment I thought they were going to step off the curb and cross the street toward me, but they headed north, arms linked. I watched them from over my newspaper and finally caught a good look at the face of Eric's city girlfriend. It was Faith, a redheaded Faith. Looking back, I wasn't really surprised at all that it was Faith – *of course it was* – but I remember being shocked by the way she had changed her looks, her hair now red like mine. And I was angry. I was the angriest I'd been in years.

CHAPTER 11

TED

Before saying good-bye at the Concord River Inn, after we had decided that it made sense for me to spend some time in Maine with Brad and Miranda, Lily and I had planned our next meeting. It was to be two Saturdays from our first meeting, at the same time, but in the Old Hill Burying Ground, a hillside cemetery that rose above Monument Square in Concord Center. There were benches there and we could sit beside one another and talk, and we would be less visible than we had been at the inn's tavern.

I showed up early that Saturday afternoon. There were tourists in town, but none of them were on the hill. I sat alone on a cold, wrought-iron bench, looking out over the shingled roofs toward Main Street. The sky was low and the color of granite. A steady purposeful wind blew colored leaves through the air. I looked for Lily, studying the cars that circled Monument Square, even though I had no idea what kind of car Lily drove. I tried to guess. Something classic, I thought, but with just a little bit of flair. A vintage BMW maybe, or an original Austin Mini. But when I spotted Lily, she wasn't coming out of a car, but walking briskly down Main Street, wearing a knee-length green coat, her red hair bouncing with each step.

I watched her walk toward the cemetery, losing sight of her when she dipped below the rooflines. I felt a surge of excitement that I was going to see her again. Part of that was my burgeoning romantic fixation, but I was also excited to tell her about my trip, and to tell her about the key I had stolen from Brad that opened his front door. In a way, I felt like a child bringing home a good report card to my mother.

Lily came back into view along the cemetery's flagstone path. She smiled at me before sitting down on the opposite side of the bench. 'Quite the view,' she said, her voice slightly breathless from the steep hill.

'I saw you coming down Main Street. Could you tell you were being watched?'

'No, I wasn't even thinking about it. I was worried I was late and that you would have left.'

'Oh, I wouldn't have left. I have too much to tell you.'

She turned toward me. In the gray October light her face seemed bleached of color, while her hair was redder than I remembered, an alarmingly alive color among the monochrome graves. I wanted to reach out and touch her, to make sure she was real, but held back. 'You went to Maine?' she asked.

'I did,' I said, then told her the story of my week,

of the time spent with Brad, of being in his house, and taking his key.

'You don't think he'll miss it?' she asked.

'I don't. He had a whole pile of them in his drawer. It's a business he runs, so I assume he needs lots of keys. For all I know, those are masters that open all of the cottage doors.'

'Well, it can only be helpful. Just remember to make sure that after all of this happens, you get rid of that key, or leave it back in his house. You can never get caught with any kind of physical evidence. You know that.'

I nodded, and Lily asked, 'What else did you find out about your house? Is there a completion date?'

I told her that Brad had told me that he expected to be done with his work in early December, early January at the latest.

'That means we need to act relatively fast. It's important that it happens before the house is finished, I think.'

We created a plan, where I would need to be and when, and what we would both be doing. Lily discussed it as if we were a couple of seniors in high school discussing who would be doing what when we presented our final science project. I was a detail-oriented person – I had to be, for the work I did and the money I made – and my natural inclination was that I should be taking notes, but I knew that nothing could be written down. Ever. As Lily had said earlier, this would be the last time we saw each other before I became a widower, and then we could meet again, accidentally, as though we'd never met before. As we talked, and as I memorized what needed to be done, I felt the start of some tightness in my chest, a feeling of constriction in my throat and jaw. I tilted my head. My neck cracked.

'You okay?' Lily asked.

'Fine. It's just becoming real. It was one thing to plan my scouting trip to Maine, but this is a little different.'

Lily straightened up, pulled her lower lip under her upper. There was concern in her eyes. 'You don't have to go through with this, you know,' she said. 'This is for you, and not for me, and the last thing I want is for you to do something that will haunt you for the rest of your life.'

'I'm not scared of that. Maybe I'm worried about something going wrong.'

'If we do this the way we're planning, then nothing will go wrong. Let me ask you – if there were an earthquake today in Maine and Miranda and Brad were killed, how would you feel?'

'I would be happy,' I said, without having to think about it. 'It would solve all my problems, and they would deserve it.'

'That's all we're doing, then. We're creating an earthquake, one that will bury them both. And if we do it right, everyone, including the police detectives assigned to the case, will naturally assume that Miranda was murdered by Brad, and that

Brad skipped town. All their efforts will go toward finding him, and they never will. They might suspect you briefly. It would be strange if they didn't, but nothing they find will point them toward you, and your alibi is going to be rock solid.'

'Okay, I trust you.'

'Look, if at any point you decide you don't want to do this, then just let me know. But if you're worried about something going wrong, I don't think you need to worry. If we stay sharp and do everything the way we planned it, you're not even going to be a suspect. Miranda and Brad will get what they deserve, and not only that, but think of the sympathy you'll receive. Your beautiful young wife killed by her brutish lover. You'll be fighting them off with a stick.'

Lily was smiling. She pushed a strand of hair off her forehead.

'Just for the record,' I said. 'That's not my motive.'

'No?'

'No, not unless you . . . uh, you were volunteering for the position.'

Lily was still smiling. 'Ah, the plot thickens.'

'Or thins,' I said.

She laughed. 'Right. Or thins.'

We looked at each other for a moment, and Lily's smile faded. She hunched her shoulders, and buttoned her coat a little higher. 'Cold?' I asked.

'A little. Should we walk around? I've never been here before.'

I agreed, and we strolled among the tottering,

timeworn gravestones, Lily's arm through mine. We moved comfortably together, not having to talk, as though we were an old couple with years and years of memories between us. We read some inscriptions, most commemorating lives lived in the eighteenth century, many cut short at ages that nowadays would be deemed a tragedy. But they had had lives. And no matter how young they had been when they died, they would still all be long gone by now.

Some of the gravestones had lettering that had worn away to unreadable hieroglyphs, and many depicted winged skulls, and the words *Memento Mori. Remember that you will die.* I ran a finger over one of the carvings, a skull in the shape of a lightbulb with round owl's eyes and a full set of teeth. Between the skull and the inscription were two sets of crossed bones. 'I wonder when they stopped putting death imagery on gravestones,' I said. 'It's so appropriate.'

'Yeah, it is,' Lily said, pulling me in closer with her arm. The cemetery dipped a little on its far side, and we found ourselves below its highest ledge and underneath a tree, still festooned in yellow leaves. Almost simultaneously we turned, and I took Lily in my arms, and we kissed. I unbuttoned her coat and slid my arms inside of it, around her waist. Her sweater felt like cashmere. She shivered.

'Still cold?' I asked.

'No,' she said, and we kissed more, the kiss

getting wetter, each of us pulling the other closer into our bodies. I ran a hand up the front of her sweater, feeling the ridges of her ribs, then the small swell of a breast, a hard nipple. The sound of a branch snapping made us each turn our heads. On the cemetery's bluff a lone figure crouched, taking a photograph of one of the gravestones. We broke apart, but continued to look at each other.

'We should call it a day,' she said.

'Okay.' My voice was a little hoarse.

'Do you know the plan? Should we go over it again?'

'I've got it. All up here.' I tapped my forehead.

'Okay, then.'

Neither of us immediately moved. 'So afterward,' I said. 'Can we continue this?'

'I'd like that.'

'And you'll tell me all your secrets?'

'I will. I'll tell you everything. I'm looking forward to it.'

I remembered the half joke I had made at the Concord River Inn, asking her how many people she had killed. Again, I asked myself who I was becoming involved with. Again, I told myself I didn't care.

'We should leave here separately.'

'I know. Before we wind up in one of that man's photographs.'

I looked up at the bluff. The man was standing now, peering through his camera along a line of leaning gravestones. 'I'll go first,' Lily said.

'Okay. Until next time . . .'

'Right. Until then . . . and good luck.'

She walked away from me, up and over the cemetery's ridge, the man with the camera never even turning to watch her. I stayed where I was, the taste of her lips still on mine. I zipped up my coat, then shoved my hands deep into my pockets. The sky, still the color of granite, had brightened a little, so that I squinted as I watched her. For the first time since I had decided to kill my wife, I wanted it to happen right away. I felt like a kid the week before Christmas, the days stretching out, each one a miniature version of eternity. I wanted Miranda dead. She had taken our love and made a mockery of it. She had made a mockery of me. I kept thinking of the way that Miranda used to look at me, still looked at me sometimes, like I was the center of her universe. And then she had ripped out my heart. And how could I share the money I had made with a woman who had done that, who had ripped out my heart like it didn't mean a thing to her? This was my reason, and I told myself I believed in it.

But now I had a new reason. I had Lily. I was doing this because of Lily. I was going to kill my wife so that I could be with her. And this reason made more sense than any of the others.

CHAPTER 12

LILY

There was one full weekend before my flight to London for my year abroad and I told Eric that I had a terrible late-summer cold and maybe he shouldn't come. He agreed, on the condition that I let him drive me to the airport on the Tuesday that I flew from JFK. I thought it would be harder, those couple of hours with him in his car, but they were easy. I just told myself to act like nothing had happened.

Over the summer, Eric and I had discussed my year in London several times. I'd given him the chance to express any reservations, but he had insisted that we should stay together, continue to be mutually exclusive. His first visit was scheduled for October, six weeks after my arrival. Eric had already bought the ticket. So when we said good-bye at the loading zone at JFK, Eric said, 'Six weeks feels like a long time, but it isn't really. We'll see each other soon.'

'Hey,' I said. 'This is going to sound strange, but I want you to know that if you think this separation is too long I would understand. If you want to take a break, be with someone else, I won't like it but I won't hold it against you. Right now is the time to tell me. Not later.'

He looked concerned, his eyes locking into mine. 'Is that what you want?'

'No, not at all. But I want you to tell me the truth. I wouldn't respond well if you cheated on me.'

'You never have to worry about that. Ever.' I searched his face for any signs of deceit. It was something I had done for many years living with my parents, and I had come to regard myself as someone who could tell when I was being lied to. But I saw nothing in Eric's face except love and sincerity.

'I can't wait to see you in October,' I said, and held him tight for a moment while a trapped Range Rover behind us sounded its horn. In a way I wasn't lying. I was now looking forward to Eric's trip to visit me. That face he had made, that innocent, loving face, had sealed his fate. I didn't know how I was going to do it yet, but I did know that I would find a way to punish Eric when he came to visit me in London.

The Faunce Institute of Art accepted just a few foreign students per year, so for my orientation week, I was at a hotel in Russell Square mixed in with about forty American students all attending something called the Overseas Academy for Foreign Study, a college that catered exclusively to American college students on their year abroad. In that week – along with a meet and greet, and some orientation sessions – we were expected to form groups and look for housing. We were given a list of real estate agents that specialized in temporary flats, and told that our best chance of finding something was to form groups of either four or six. As it turned out, many of the American students had already come over from their respective colleges in groups. I was wondering if it would be possible to find a studio flat just for myself when I was approached by a pretty student gripping her list of agents. 'Have you found a group?' she asked.

'Not yet. You?'

'No, but my older sister did this program and she told me that they tell you that it's easiest to be in a big group but that's a lie – they just want you to be in big groups for some reason – and that it's much easier to find a flat for just two, and so I looked around and I saw you.' She said this all in one rush, and with a sharp Texas twang.

'I'd be willing to share if you want to,' I said, glad to have met someone who seemed to know a little bit about the process of renting a flat.

She bounced a little, her long brown hair jumping on her shoulders. 'Oh, goody. All these groups are boys and girls, and don't get me wrong, I like boys, but I'd just as soon not share a flat with one of them. My name's Addison Logan. My family all call me Addie but I thought I might try out my full name, Addison, while I was here in London, but you can call me what you want to call me.'

'I'm Lily Kintner,' I said, and we shook hands.

It took us two days of looking, but we finally found a one-bedroom basement flat along an Edwardian block of mansion flats in Maida Vale. It was a long Tube ride from the Faunce Institute and from Addison's classes, but it was in the nicest neighborhood we'd been shown. Addison told me it was the only place we'd seen that didn't make her want to take a shower right away, so I agreed. I called my father – who was a visiting writer that semester somewhere in California – to tell him I'd taken a flat in Maida Vale, and he said how posh I was, mentioned a pub called the Prince Alfred, and ended by telling me that 'the only bad thing about London's all the bloody American students.'

Addison and I turned out to be good roommates, mostly because our schedules meant we rarely saw each other. About three weeks after our arrival, I began to see even less of her, because she had started dating a fellow Texan in her program who had a flat in Camden Town. 'I know it's lame that I come all the way to London and end up dating some kid from Lubbock named Nolan, but he's a cute kid.'

'Don't apologize to me,' I said.

'When's your boyfriend – Eric, right? – when's he coming again?'

I told her and she promised to be out of my hair during his visit. I insisted that it didn't matter either way, even though I did want Addison to stay away while Eric was here. Along with immersing myself in my schoolwork at the institute, and exploring London's bookstores and museums, I had been spending my time trying to figure out a way to kill Eric and get away with it. And I was pretty sure that I had figured it out.

The first part of my plan hinged on Eric's competitive nature. I had spent enough time watching him play pool at St Dun's to know just how much he hated to lose. He tried to hide it, but when he lost, especially to someone he didn't like, his eyes would go blank, and he would find a way to play that person again, and to win. And just this past summer, when Eric visited me at Monk's, he'd asked me about the huge oak in the backyard. He'd spotted the two faded colored flags that had been nailed into its trunk, one at about the three-quarters mark, and one near the top. I explained that one summer my father's best friend from childhood had come for a month, and how they had taken turns climbing the oak, each trying to get his flag higher than the other's. It had gone on for weeks, only ending when my father, drunk, fell off the first branch one night and broke his wrist. After telling Eric this story I knew that he would have to try and climb the tree. And he did. It took him several tries but he made it higher than either my father or my father's friend had.

'How do you think your father would feel if I put my own flag up there?'

I laughed. 'I don't think he'd care at all. He'd be amused.'

'I don't need to, but if you thought he'd find it funny.'

'Have you always been this competitive?'

He frowned at me. 'I don't think I'm that competitive. You should see my brother.'

At the time, I chalked Eric's denial up to a lack of self-knowledge, but now I saw it as part of his fraudulent nature. He genuinely did not want people to know about his driving desire to win at all costs. It gave away too much of himself. And it gave away a part of himself that was unchangeable. So, when I heard about the beer challenge at the Bottle and Glass, a dowdy pub at the end of my avenue, I knew that I could get Eric to attempt it. I didn't need him to be drunk for what I had planned, but it would definitely help.

He arrived in London on a cold, wet Saturday. Addison, true to her word, packed a bag on Friday evening to spend a few days with Nolan. 'Honey, you must be so excited,' she said.

'I am,' I said.

'Well, try and look it.'

'I'm just nervous,' I said. 'I don't really know why, but I am.'

'That'll go away about five minutes after he gets here. You just both need to get laid.' She laughed, and covered her mouth with a hand.

Eric's flight had left New York the previous night and was scheduled to land around eight in the morning. I'd e-mailed him directions on how to get to my flat. I hadn't been lying to Addison when I said I was nervous, but I wasn't nervous about what I planned on doing to Eric, I was nervous about the time we needed to spend together before I put my plan into action. I knew that he'd probably want to have sex as soon as he arrived, and I was steeling myself to go through with it. I told myself it was a test, a way to see how I really felt about him. I knew that being with Eric would never change my feelings about the way in which he had betrayed me, but I did wonder if it might change my plans to end his life. I doubted it, but it was a way to find out. And, if all went according to plan, Eric would only be around for another twelve hours. I could manage.

The buzzer sounded at nine thirty, and I walked up the brief flight of stairs to the chipped marble landing to let him in. He looked tired and wrinkled from the flight, his hair sticking out in the back. We hugged and kissed, and I led him down to the basement flat, showed him around. 'You must be exhausted,' I said.

'I am, but I don't want to sleep all day. Maybe I'll take a nap, and then we can go somewhere.'

'There's a good pub down the street. The Bottle and Glass.'

'Okay. Just let me sleep. One hour tops, and only if you join me.'

I told him to get into the bed and I'd join him later, hoping he would fall asleep. But after he entered the bedroom, and after I'd killed fifteen

147

minutes by slowly making myself a cup of tea, I decided I actually did want to join him. It was not just a test – it was a way of saying good-bye. I entered the small dark bedroom; Eric shifted under the covers and I could hear his steady breathing. I took off all my clothes and slid in behind him. He stirred but didn't wake. He was naked, too, and the feel of his long warm body against mine didn't make me cringe the way I thought it would. I ran a hand along his hard chest, down his flat stomach, and touched his penis. He instantly became hard, mumbling something into the pillow that I didn't understand, then slowly turned toward me. I spread my legs and moved him between them. He began to say something but I pulled his head down so that it was beside mine. His hair smelled unwashed but good. I guided him into me, then pulled the sheet and blanket over our heads, and we made love in that smothering dark cave, neither of us talking, moving together in a slow, sleepy rhythm.

He fell asleep again after we finished, and I slid away from him, pushing the sheets down around my waist. The cool air felt good against my naked torso, my skin damp with sweat. I thought about what I planned to do to Eric later that night, and tried to feel bad about it. I compared him with Chet, who wanted to have sex with a child, but at least Chet didn't pretend to love anyone. Eric was bad through and through, someone who would go through life taking only what he wanted and hurting the ones who loved him. I had handed him my love – my life really – and he had treated each with disdain.

Eric woke, disoriented and starving, a little after noon. He showered and dressed and we went out to explore my neighborhood. I took him to a take-away spot and we bought sandwiches and drinks and brought them to a small park called Rembrandt Gardens that abutted a canal. It had stopped raining, but the skies were still low and dark, and water dripped from the trees and puddled every-where. I spread my jacket along a wooden bench and we sat and ate the sandwiches, finishing them just as a sparse rain began to patter at the leaves above us. 'Sorry for the weather,' I said.

'It's pub weather,' he said.

'Ready to get a drink? The Bottle's not too far from here. No attempting their beer challenge, though. That's all I ask.'

'What's that?'

It was all I had to do. When we arrived at the Bottle and Glass, a pub that was plain and boxy by London standards, with uncarpeted floors and wooden benches, Eric read about the beer chal-lenge, and studied the names of those who had succeeded. To be immortalized on the Bottle's walls all you had to do was drink one pint each of the pub's ten draft beers, in the order in which they were lined up behind the bar, in the space of five hours. They monitored your toilet visits to make sure you didn't throw up. Eric told me it didn't sound particularly hard. I had thought the same thing, and brought it up to Stuart, the bartender, the previous week. He said the combination of beers, from porters to bitters to pilsners and ciders, was a rough ride and was much harder than it looked. He'd seen many a beefy guy give up, or throw up, before the end.

'I'm doing it,' Eric said, to both me and that day's bartender, an older woman I hadn't seen before.

'Seriously? Eric?' I said as the bartender said, 'Right, luv,' and produced a sign-in sheet. 'Print your name here where it says "start," along with the time, and I'll initial it. When you've finished your tenth pint, all you've got to do is walk back up to this bar, sign your name at the end, then the rest is up to you. Most of them lose their last few pints in the toilet.'

I complained a little more, just for show, but I knew Eric wouldn't change his mind. The first beer was a Fuller's ESB, and I joined him. We took our pints to a corner table. 'I'm on vacation,' he said, then took a long swallow.

'I don't want you to be sick the whole time you're here.'

'I won't be. Ten pints in five hours. Not a problem.'

I stayed for about three and a half hours. It was clear that Eric was determined to finish the challenge, but he was on his seventh pint, a porter, and drinking it fairly slowly. 'I'm more full than anything,' he said, but his words, from jet lag and from beer, were thick-sounding in his mouth.

'Let's call it quits,' I said. 'I'm sick of sitting in this pub.'

'I'm not going to come this far, and then quit.' He looked around. Some of the locals who had showed up around quitting time had taken notice of Eric's attempt to make it onto the wall. I knew that Eric would keep going no matter what.

'Then I'm leaving. I'm starving, and I don't want to keep eating crisps. I'll get take-out Indian food and have it at the flat.'

'I'm sorry, Lily.'

'Don't be sorry. Have fun. Try not to puke at the bar, and I'll see you in a couple of hours. You know how to get back?'

'Just down the street, right?'

I left. It was dusk, the bloated sky a dark purple, and there was a fine mist in the air. I walked straight to the corner Indian restaurant that I'd been to many times. I ordered a rogan josh and a chicken korma, plus a Coke to drink while I waited for the food. 'No nuts in the rogan josh?' I asked as the owner rung up my order. I knew the answer but I wanted to be on record as asking.

'No nuts in the rogan josh but, yes, cashews in the chicken korma.'

'Right, I know. Thanks.'

I took the bags of food back to the flat. I left them on the small wooden table in the kitchen and went into the bedroom to look through Eric's suitcase. He'd brought several changes of clothes, *One Up on Wall Street* by Peter Lynch, and a running outfit. His two EpiPens were in a plastic sandwich bag in an interior zippered pocket. He should have had one of them with him – I'd told him that a hundred times – but I knew that he wouldn't. His nut allergy was fatal, but it was vanity that kept him from taking the pens around with him. 'What am I supposed to do, Kintner, wear them in a fanny pack?' He convinced himself that he would never eat anything in public that would remotely have the chance of having nuts in it. I took the EpiPens and shoved them under the mattress, then went back to the kitchen. I was hungry and ate some of the Indian food directly from the containers before dumping the chicken korma into a wide bowl. I spread the chicken and its yellow sauce out evenly and methodically picked out every cashew, placing them into the stone mortar I'd found in one of the cluttered cabinets of our kitchen. When I was sure that I had found every cashew, I got the pestle and ground half of them up into a fine paste, then mixed the cashew paste back into the korma, and put everything back in its container. I took the remaining cashews, placed them in a folded piece of paper towel, and hid them behind the condiments in the fridge. I washed the mortar and pestle, plus the bowl, and put them back where I'd found them. I put the containers of Indian food in the flat's quarter-size refrigerator. Chicken korma was one of Eric's favorite, and the restaurant we'd gotten it from in New Chester never put nuts into it. The stage was set. All I needed to do now was wait.

I tried to read *Gaudy Night* but had trouble concentrating. I wasn't nervous, exactly, but I wanted it to be over with. Eric had started his challenge at around one thirty, so he would be finished, one way or another, at six thirty. At about six fifteen the harsh din of the door buzzer sounded. I jerked upright. I wondered if he'd given up, but when I got to the front door and opened it, I found Addison. She was crying, her shoulders hitching up and down, and searching through her purse for the key.

CHAPTER 13

TED

My junior year at Dartford-Middleham High School I asked a sophomore girl named Rebecca Rast to the junior prom. She was a popular blond student I'd gotten to know while we both worked at the school newspaper. She seemed happy when I asked her, even though I knew she was more interested in the school's jocks. It was fine with me; I was just looking for a date.

But a week before the prom, I ran into Rebecca at a beer party at an abandoned military base the next town over. I'd heard about these parties but had never gone to one. About a hundred students were there, cars parked on the broken asphalt of the base's old parking lot, the kids milling around the sloping hill on the south side of the boarded-up buildings. Most of the kids had brought six-packs lifted from their parents' homes, or bought by older brothers and sisters. I had come with my best friend, Aaron, who was, like me, neither popular nor an outcast. Before getting out of our cars we had nearly turned back, intimidated by the scene, and embarrassed that we had brought no alcohol. But then I spotted Rebecca clambering out of a nearby convertible with a bunch of her girlfriends, and I convinced myself that I should, at least, say hello to the girl who would be going with me to the prom the following week.

To my surprise, she seemed thrilled to see me, and we spent most of the party together, drinking warm beers on the hill, then exploring the abandoned base. We wound up on a low flat roof that we reached by a rusted fire escape. We stared at the stars, the beer we'd drunk making them slide in and out of focus, then we started to kiss. It was a warm spring night, and Rebecca wore a midriff-baring halter top and a short denim skirt, and she let me touch her everywhere, at one point whispering to me that we should slow down unless I had a condom. I didn't, but, lying in bed later that night, I told myself that I needed to get one as soon as possible and definitely before prom night. It was an exhilarating thought, but more exhilarating was the fact that I had my first girlfriend.

On the evening of the prom I picked Rebecca up at her parents' modest house near Middleham pond. While Rebecca's mother took pictures, her father leaned against his Dodge Dart, smoking a cigar and giving me icy looks from under a Patriots cap. I was glad when we were safely in my car on the way to the Holiday Inn where the prom was being held. Rebecca wore a light blue dress with a low neckline. Her hair was French-braided, and she smelled like vanilla.

Despite some bad nerves on my part, the first

few hours of the prom went well. Rebecca was chatty and flirty. We ate the dried-out chicken cordon bleu, and danced several times. During one of the slow dances, I gently kissed Rebecca on the side of her head. She pulled me in closer to her, and I thought about that foil-wrapped condom hidden behind my driver's license in my wallet.

It wasn't until about twenty minutes before the end of the prom that everything fell apart. I'd gone to the bathroom, and when I returned, Rebecca was no longer at our table. I spotted her on the far side of the ballroom, leaning up against the wall and talking to a junior I recognized as Bill Johnson, a linebacker on the school football team. I stopped in my tracks, my limbs turning cold and my throat tightening. Instead of crossing the endless yardage of the room to confront them, I went back to my table, and it was from there that I watched Rebecca and Bill hug, then kiss, then leave the prom together.

I saw Rebecca in the hallway of the high school on Monday afternoon. I thought she might apologize, but I watched as her eyes skidded over me, and she turned away. I learned that week that she and Bill were definitely an item. I don't know if it was easier or harder that very few of my fellow students seemed aware that I had been humiliated on prom night. I do know that if Rebecca had at least attempted to apologize to me, things might have turned out differently.

I plotted my revenge for over a year. It made sense that if I was going to do something to

Rebecca, I should wait for some time to pass. Otherwise, I'd be a natural suspect. I devoted my senior year to getting the best grades I could, keeping my head down, and not allowing myself to get into any more potentially humiliating situations. I was accepted at Harvard, surprising even my guidance counselor, and while this acceptance felt like one kind of revenge, I still wanted to pay Rebecca back. Ideally, I would find a way to humiliate her in the way she had humiliated me, but I couldn't figure out a way to do that. I opted for my second choice – I would scare her very, very badly.

A week before graduation I parked my Ford Escort at the back parking lot of Arnie's Liquors on a sunless afternoon, then walked through a brief stretch of state forest that led to the back of the Rasts' house. If anyone saw me, they would have seen a kid wearing a denim jacket and a baseball cap pulled low, something I would normally have never worn. But no one saw me. I had brought a crowbar in my backpack to break through the back door, but it was already open. I knew that no one would be home, that Mr Rast had left months ago, and that Mrs Rast worked day shifts at the CVS. And I knew, I hoped, that Rebecca would be coming home alone after school let out at three o'clock. I hid in her bedroom closet and waited.

Thinking back on it now, I remember the terror and excitement I felt in the small, dark space,

Rebecca Rast's clothes rustling up against me, the ski mask on my face starting to make me sweat. I had the closet door cracked a little and was able to hear Rebecca's car pull into the driveway, to hear her enter the house and walk slowly up the stairs. She went to the bathroom first for what seemed a long time, then the toilet flushed, and she entered her bedroom, humming tunelessly to herself. My heart was thudding so loudly in my chest that I wondered how she hadn't heard it. I had planned on leaping out of the closet in my ski mask, but I didn't need to. She came straight to the closet door and slid it open along its tracks. I stepped toward her, scissors in one hand, duct tape in another. She opened her mouth to scream but nothing came out. I watched all the color drain from her face, and I was sure that she was about to faint, but instead she turned to run. I tackled her from behind, realizing as I did it that she had stripped to just her underwear. I held her down and managed to wrap duct tape first around her face and mouth, and then around her hands and ankles. It wasn't easy; I got kicked several times but refrained from making any noise, from letting her know who I was. After she was securely bound in duct tape, I dragged her into the closet, and before I shut the door, I ran the edge of the scissors along her neck. Her eyes were squeezed shut, tears coming out of them. I could smell the sharp tang of urine.

I dumped the coat, the ski mask, the scissors, the crowbar, and the backpack into the Dumpster

158

behind the liquor store. I drove home shaking, my emotions alternating between enormous satisfaction that I had paid Rebecca back for the pain she had caused me, and a sickening shame that I had gone too far. Those feelings lasted through the summer, the shame temporarily replaced by the horrible fear that I was going to get caught. I would be publicly shamed, and sent to prison, and I wouldn't get to go to Harvard. But the police never showed up, and, as the summer progressed, I began to believe I'd gotten away with it. I did hear about the incident once, from a gossipy friend of mine named Molly. She told me that Rebecca Rast – 'You know her, right? Oh my God, you went to the prom with her, didn't you?' – had been assaulted in her own home, tied up and left in the closet, and that everyone thought it was her own father, that creepy dude who used to work at a gas station. That was all I ever heard about it.

I still dream about Rebecca Rast. In these nightmares – and they are definitely nightmares – Rebecca dies the night I duct-taped her and left her in the closet. In these dreams I am plagued with guilt, and terrified of being caught, and I can never remember whether I meant to murder her or whether I meant to just scare her. But either way, I am a murderer, and that knowledge has taken over my life.

On the Friday morning that Miranda was flying down to Miami Beach for a bachelorette party, I woke, having had one of these dreams. I was alone

159

in the bed, and I lay there for a moment, the images from the nightmare flashing in my brain, then disappearing. At first I thought it was a Rebecca Rast dream, but then I realized that the person in the dream that I had killed had been Miranda. I'd trapped her in Rebecca Rast's closet and she had died there. Other images from the dream came back to me. A funeral where no one would look at me. The terrible fear that I forgot to hide the body. An image of my father, water coming from his nose. A field that I was frantically digging in. For one terrible moment, I thought that these weren't pictures from my dreams, but recent memories. I'd had this feeling before, always when I was in the half state between sleep and wakefulness – this dreadful feeling that what I was dreaming about was in fact real, that I was a murderer, and it was only a matter of time until the whole world knew it. I shook my head and told myself I'd been dreaming, then rose from the tangled sheets and picked up my phone from the dresser. It was past eight, much later than I usually slept. Miranda's car service was coming at eight thirty to take her to Logan. I pulled on a pair of jeans and a cotton sweater and went downstairs.

'Hey, sleepyhead,' she said when I'd found her in the formal dining room. She was sitting at the long Stickley table, her luggage by her side. She wore a short blue dress and a pair of red cowboy boots and was avidly studying her phone.

'Aren't you cold in that?'

She looked up. 'Yes, but not for long. I'll tell the driver to turn the heat up to Miami temperatures.' She turned her phone off, slid it into her purse, and stood. 'What are you going to get up to while I'm away?'

'First of all, you're always away, so this is nothing new. And second of all, work, obviously.'

'You should have dinner with Mac tonight. I'm sure he's around.'

'He's not, actually. He's at his aunt's funeral. Remember, I told you about that? No, I'm going to take that lamb out of the freezer. Special dinner, just for me.'

'Please. Eat it all. Casey said we're going to Joe's Stone Crab tonight.'

I brought her luggage to the foyer, resisting the urge to comment on how heavy it was for a three-day weekend. Miranda peered through the front door's leaded window. 'Limo's here,' she said, and pulled me in for an unusually tight hug. 'I'll miss you, Teddy,' she said.

'How long exactly are you going for?'

She slapped my chest. 'Don't make jokes. I really am going to miss you. You're a good husband, you know.'

'I'll miss you, too,' I said, trying to get some feeling into my voice. The way Miranda was acting I wondered briefly if the bachelorette party was made up. Was she meeting Brad down in Miami?

Miranda pulled the front door open, and the driver jumped out of his Town Car, bounding up our steps to collect the luggage. Miranda followed him down to the car, a sharp wind plucking at the hem of her dress. She turned to wave at me, and she looked frail and cold in her inadequate clothes. Before I shut the door she pulled her huge sunglasses out of her purse and put them on, then blew me a kiss.

The day loomed before me. I had phone calls to make and a prospectus to proofread, but that would only take about half a morning. I gathered a cup of coffee, then went to my computer. I Googled the name Lily Hayward for about the hundredth time but nothing came up that seemed like her, besides her job listing at Winslow College. I Googled the town of Winslow and mapped a route from my house to a promising-looking restaurant in the town's center. What harm would it do if I drove out there for lunch? It was going to be a beautiful October day; after a hot, extended summer the leaves were just now at their peak. I could take a walk, eat some lunch, see the town that Lily lived in. And if I saw her – and the chances of that were slim – then what would the harm be? We wouldn't need to say hello, and if we did, would it possibly make a difference?

I did my work, then showered and dressed. At my garage I decided, on the spur of the moment, to take out my vintage 1976 Porsche 911, the car I'd bought after I'd made my first big deal, instead of the Audi. I avoided the Pike and drove toward the river, getting onto Storrow Drive. The river was filled with college rowers, prepping for the upcoming Head of the Charles weekend. The day was perfection, the sky only creased by the vapor trails of airplanes. I looked up, wondering if I was seeing the remnants of the plane that was taking my wife to Florida.

From Storrow Drive I got onto Soldiers Field Road, then wound my way through Waltham and Newton till I found Boston Post Road, and headed west through the suburbs toward Winslow. Shifting gears, I wondered why I had ever gotten the automatic transmission on my Audi. The next car I bought would be a standard.

I drove down Main Street in Winslow center, looking for parking in the surprisingly busy downtown. Students were crossing the street in large groups. Mostly girls in jeans and boots, with hair pulled back in ponytails. Waiting for several to cross the walkway, I peered through the abutting metal gates toward the college campus. I could see three low brick buildings that bordered a carefully manicured lawn. A line of oaks marked a path across the campus. Was Lily in one of the buildings I could see? Was she the type who brought a sensible lunch and ate in her office or did she walk into the town center for lunch? It was a Friday, after all, a sunny October day. The car behind me honked and I put the Porsche in gear, then turned off Main onto a side street with metered parking. I found a spot, and walked back toward the group of restaurants I'd passed earlier.

The place I'd read about – the Carvery – was there, but I chose a restaurant called Alison's, that had an open outside table that faced both the high midday sun and Wins-low's campus. I ordered a Bloody Mary and a Cobb salad from the college student waitress, and watched the pedestrians pass by. The students had the scrub-faced look of earnest young feminists. They hauled backpacks that looked as though they'd put a football player into traction. The nonstudents were mostly middle-aged housewives out for shopping and lunch. They wore handmade scarfs and flouncy clothes that hid their hips. I saw a few professor types – men with bad haircuts and tweedy jackets, and women who looked like older versions of the solemn young students. But I didn't see Lily, even when, after lunch, and a second Bloody Mary, I took a walk through Winslow's campus.

It was a pretty college, its campus gently sloping away from Winslow center down toward a pond that was circled with a walking path. I sat for a while on a wooden bench in the botanic gardens, next to a conservatory with a high peaked roof. There was no one around, and I imagined that this might be the type of place where Lily would bring her lunch. To this very bench maybe. I stayed seated until clouds appeared in the sky and the sun disappeared and suddenly it was cold.

I'd forgotten to refeed the parking meter after lunch and I had a Town of Winslow parking violation under my wiper. Fifteen dollars. I slid it into my jacket pocket and lowered myself into the Porsche. I was tired all of a sudden, and took the Pike all the way back to Boston, arriving at home just as I received a text from Miranda that she had safely landed in Miami and the festivities had begun. I texted her back, then went to my computer to check my e-mails. It was a slow period for me, not that I needed the work. The stock market, after years of stagnation, was surging again. My portfolio was healthy, and work was just a matter of filling my time.

Another text from Miranda: don't forget take the lamb out of the freezer.

I wrote back, thanking her for the reminder.

I had actually forgotten and walked down to the basement kitchen, taking the loin chops out of the freezer and putting them under running water. The text from Miranda was strange, as was the overly sentimental good-bye. Was she up to something sinister? Or was it possible that she had broken it off with Brad and was suddenly contrite? Even so, that didn't take away from what she had already done to me.

I went into the adjoining wine cellar and picked an Old World Syrah that would go nicely with the lamb. I opened the bottle and decanted it. The chops were starting to soften so I left them in their plastic wrap in a bowl of cold water, and went upstairs to the living room. I hadn't seen the paper yet that day, so I sat in the leather recliner and read the day's news while sipping a gin and tonic.

After a while, I put the paper down and just thought about Miranda and Brad and Lily and everything that had happened, or that was about to happen, since meeting Lily on the plane from London. I kept involuntarily flashing back to the dream I had awoken from that morning. That awful feeling that once you've murdered someone you can never go back and unmurder them. You will never again awake from a dream and be able to lie there, telling yourself that your life may be a catalog of sin, but that you are not a murderer. And I suddenly realized that my plan to kill Miranda and Brad had become a means to an end, had become a way to get closer to Lily, and that I didn't necessarily need to commit murder to get there. I could simply tell Miranda I wanted a divorce, then e-mail Lily and ask her if she were free for dinner. No one but us would ever know about the plans we had made. Miranda could have Brad, and I'd have Lily, and the world would keep on spinning. I had always been good at compart-mentalizing, and I would put all my rage and shame over what had happened with Miranda into a box and close it. I would hand my marriage to the lawyers; half of all my money was more than enough. A feeling of relief swept through me. It was like waking from a bad dream and realizing that it was just a dream, that it hadn't actually happened.

The doorbell chimed, and I jumped a little in my chair.

Walking to the door I instinctively looked at my watch. It was just past six. Who would be stopping by? I told myself it was probably a deliveryman, and tried to remember if I was waiting for a package.

I put the chain across the door and swung it open five inches. It was Brad Daggett, a slightly embarrassed smile on his face. It took me a moment to register that Brad, from Maine, was on my doorstep in Boston. It felt incongruous, like seeing a man in a tuxedo at a country fair.

'Ted,' he said, and he sounded a little breathless, 'I'm glad you're here. Can we talk?'

'Of course,' I said, undoing the chain and opening the door. 'Come on in.'

As soon as the words were out of my mouth, I regretted them. There was no good reason for Brad to come all the way from Maine to see me. He was halfway into the house and I pushed slightly against the door, stopping his progress. 'Brad, what are you doing here?'

'Just let me in, Ted. I'll explain.' His voice quivered, and I could smell the booze on his breath. Our eyes met, and I was suddenly scared. I pushed a little harder against the door, but Brad wasn't moving. He fumbled in his jacket pocket and I looked down at the gun he had removed. 'Let me in, Ted,' he repeated, and I stepped back as Brad entered my house.

CHAPTER 14

LILY

'Addison, what's the matter?' I asked.

'Fucking Nolan,' she said, and came through the door, following me down the stairs. She was brushing rain from her coat, spatters of it striking the back of my head.

'You two have a fight?' I asked as we entered our flat.

She looked at me, wiping tears off her cheeks with the palms of her hand. 'He has a girlfriend back at TCU. A *serious* girlfriend.'

'Shit,' I said. 'How'd you find out?'

Addison told me how she'd gone onto his computer and read his e-mails, and how he confessed to everything, telling her that he'd been meaning to tell her about Linda, but at first he thought that they – Addison and him – were just having a fling, and now he didn't know. I half-listened, opening a bottle of wine and pouring Addison a glass, but my mind was frantically trying to figure out what to do when Eric returned. Should I abandon the whole plan, telling Eric that I was pretty sure the chicken korma had cashews in it, or should I allow it to play out, with Addison

168

as a witness? In some ways, having Addison here might be better. She would back up my story – that a drunk Eric mistakenly ate Indian food that had cashews in it, and that we couldn't immediately find his EpiPen. But there were also so many ways that it could go wrong with Addison here. She could call for an ambulance that might get here in time. She could notice that Eric's EpiPen was not where he thought it was. And if Eric asked about the chicken korma – whether or not it had nuts in it, then I couldn't lie in front of her. And, most important, it wasn't fair to Addison to let her watch Eric die from anaphylactic shock. I decided it was off.

'Wait. Where's Eric? Didn't his plane make it here?' Addison asked, her head swiveling around our small flat as though he were here and she had somehow missed him.

'You know that pub challenge at the Bottle and Glass?'

'The ten-pint thing?'

I told her about Eric insisting he could do it, and I told her how I got hungry and sick of waiting for him, and just took off.

'I guess neither of us is having a good night with our men.'

'Well, I'll live,' I said. 'You're the one who got screwed over. What are you going to do about it?'

Before Addison could answer, the door buzzed again. 'That's Eric,' I said. 'Prepare yourself. He's going to be smashed.'

'Lily, I'll just leave. I totally forgot he was coming in tonight.' Addison stood, snatching her purse from the kitchen table.

'Not a chance. You stay here.'

I climbed the stairs again, bracing myself for a drunk Eric, but when I opened the door it wasn't Eric standing there, but Nolan, his eyes red-rimmed from crying. 'Ah, the bigamist,' I said, and he gave me a confused look.

'Is she here?' Nolan was tall and skinny with bright red ears. His close-cropped hair was an almost-white blond and he wore a puka necklace tight around his neck.

'She's here,' I said, 'but that doesn't mean she wants to see you. You wait here and I'll go check.'

I left Nolan on the stoop and went back downstairs. Addison was refilling her wineglass. 'Guess who's here?'

'Who?' She looked genuinely puzzled.

'Nolan. I left him upstairs. You want me to send him away?'

She let out a long, dramatic breath. 'No, I'll see him.' She continued to sit there at the table, and I realized that she was expecting me to go get him. I climbed the stairs for what seemed like the twentieth time that night, and when I reached the door I could hear male voices talking loudly at one another. I recognized one as Eric; he was back from the pub.

'I see you two have met,' I said, opening the door to find them together, Eric with a hand on

Nolan's shoulder, telling him about the pub challenge. I knew that Eric had succeeded by the way he turned toward me, a handsome grin on his face. 'And it looks like you triumphed,' I added to Eric.

'Barely,' he said. 'It's much goddamned harder than it looks.'

'Come down, you two. Eric, let Nolan and my roommate be. They need to talk.'

We all trooped down the clattery stairs. Addison was now standing in our doorway, a look of determination on her face. Nolan said, 'Ad,' in a hoarse voice. Eric introduced himself, sounding relatively normal for someone with so much beer in him. It was one of his immutable traits, that he was always civil and friendly no matter what the circumstance. A politician, basically.

Eric and I went inside while Nolan and Addison stood just outside the door on our grim landing, lit only by a bare lightbulb hanging from its cord. I filled Eric in on what was going on, looking to gauge any reaction he might have to hearing that Nolan was, like himself, dating two women at the same time.

'You think they'll work it out?' he asked, then said, before I had a chance to answer, 'I need to eat something.'

I was about to tell him that there was Indian food in the fridge that I could heat up for him, and that he shouldn't risk the chicken korma because I thought it had nuts in it, when Addison pushed her way back into the flat. 'Don't worry, you two. We're going to give you some privacy. We're going to go get a drink.' Nolan was behind her, and I could tell by the redness around both their mouths that they had been kissing in the hallway. I don't know what he had said but it had worked. Addison grabbed her coat and purse and they went back out into the damp night. I realized suddenly that my plan was back on if I wanted it to be. My stomach roiled with anxiety, but if anything, what I had just witnessed between Nolan and Addison had given me added resolve. Guys like Nolan and Eric got away with breaking hearts far too often.

'Look, Eric,' I said. 'I'm exhausted. I drank too much myself, and Addison wiped me out. I'm getting into bed. There's Indian in the fridge if you want. I got you a chicken korma.'

'You goddamn saint,' he said, and kissed me sloppily on the side of my mouth. I went into the bedroom, swung the door so that it was partially open, and took off my jeans and sweater, slipping into the wool pajamas that kept me warm in our cold flat. I could hear Eric rummaging around the kitchen; there was the sound of clanking dishes, then the loud hum of the dingy microwave. I could smell the korma – the tang of spice and coconut milk – as it heated up. I was sitting on the edge of my bed. I felt calm but my mind was feverish, filled with images. I pictured Chet in the meadow at dusk, swaying above me, not knowing he was about to die. I saw Eric emerging from his office, lighting a cigarette, meeting Faith. I saw Eric the night we first made love, his dark brown eyes an inch from mine.

The microwave stopped humming and I heard Eric open and shut the door, then it was quiet for a moment. I assumed he was rapidly eating, maybe still standing.

A minute passed and the bedroom door swung open. Eric stood there, the food container in his hand, the skin of his face already reddish. And there was a puffiness around his eyes. 'There's nuts in here,' he said, pointing at the container. It sounded like he was speaking through a mouthful of cotton.

'You sure? Where's your EpiPen?' I said.

'Bag.' He jabbed frantically at the air with his hand, finger toward where his bag was.

I pulled his bag up from where it was resting on the floor and put it on the foot of the bed. Eric put the container down on my bedroom's bureau and went quickly to the bag, shoving me out of the way. He searched through the zippered pocket where he'd left the pens, then turned toward me, panic in his eyes, and the redness of his skin now rising. One hand was now scratching at his neck. 'You didn't bring them?' I asked in a raised, panicky-sounding voice.

'Yes,' he said, and I could barely make out the word. It sounded as though it was coming from a great distance, the shout of a man trapped far underground in a narrow damp cave.

Eric dumped the contents of his suitcase on the bed, then began rapidly searching through them. He sat down, his body held rigidly, his lips pursed as he tried to pull air into his lungs. I began to help him sort through his clothes and toiletries but he grabbed my arm, mimed the action of making a phone call. 'You want me to call for help?' I asked.

He nodded. The redness around his neck and throat had puffed out alarmingly, like landmasses on a topographical map. But his face stayed pale, now taking on a bluish tinge. I ran into the adjoining room, picked up the phone, and stood for a moment, just listening to what was happening in the bedroom. I heard another zipper being opened, then a soft thwumping sound. I put the receiver gently back onto its handset, slowly counted to ten, then walked to the doorway, peered toward the bed. Eric was laid out, one hand still at his neck, but he was no longer scratching at it. His hand was just lying there, still. I watched him for long enough to know that he wasn't breathing, then, just to make sure, I waited a minute, then crossed the room and placed two fingers along his throat and felt for a pulse. There was none. I went back to the phone and dialed 999, gave my name and address, told the woman with the chirpy voice on the other end that my boyfriend was in anaphylactic shock.

After making the phone call I moved quickly. I took the few whole cashews from the paper towel

174

in the refrigerator and put some in the chicken korma that was still in Eric's bowl (and still warm from the microwave) and some in the take-out container. Then I flushed the paper towel and washed my hands. In the bedroom, Eric hadn't moved. I slid my hand beneath the mattress and pulled out the plastic Baggie with the two unused EpiPens. Eric's belongings were spread around the room. I wiped my prints off the Baggie with a pair of socks, then pushed the entire thing into one of his running sneakers. It seemed like a place where someone might keep emergency medicine. Eric never would have, but he wouldn't tell anyone that. And he wouldn't tell anyone that I had said the chicken korma didn't have nuts in it. I would tell them that he was drunk, and that he must have just decided to eat the chicken anyway, and I was in the bedroom, and then we couldn't find the EpiPens. I tried to think if there was anything else I needed to do to set the scene. I thought it might look good if I pressed on Eric's chest a few times, just to make it look as though I had tried CPR. Would a coroner be able to tell that sort of thing? I was about to start when the buzzer sounded again.

I ran up the stairs to let the medics in.

Three days later, after Eric's family had been notified, and arrangements had been made to have the body shipped home, the constable who had arrived after the medics that Friday night came to my door to tell me that there would be no inquest.

I was pleased, of course, but surprised. I had read so many English mysteries that I just assumed that any slightly unusual death would result in an inquest, one in which all the evidence would point toward an accidental and tragic death. In a small way, I was disappointed.

'Okay,' I said, making my face look confused. 'What does that mean?'

'Just means the coroner deemed the death accidental and doesn't see the need for further review. It's the right decision, I'd say, although an official inquest might have called into question the Bottle and Glass and that pub challenge of theirs. I might pop over there myself and talk to them about it.' The constable had kind eyes and a mustache that obscured his upper lip. Twice now, I had told him all the relevant facts. How Eric was drunk, and how I had let him know about the nuts in the korma and how he ate it anyway, and then he didn't remember where he kept his medicine.

'Thank you so much,' I said.

'Yeah, I'm thinking I might go round that pub and talk to them some more,' he repeated. He lingered briefly in the doorway, then turned to go. He had told me his name, but I didn't remember it.

My adviser at the Faunce Institute asked me if I'd like to return to America, and I told her that I was fine staying in London. That if there was a memorial service I would probably go back for that, but that, despite the trauma, I was happy in London and happy in the program. It was the truth – I loved my basement flat in Maida Vale, and I loved that Addison, since the incident, was almost never there. I had never thought of myself as a city person, preferring the quiet of Connecticut to the oppressive humanity of New York City, but residential London was different. There was something calming about its long rows of flats, its leafiness, its anonymous, polite bustle. The streets near where I lived were so quiet that birdsong was more common than the sound of humans. I was happy when I heard via e-mail that the Washburns had decided on a private family funeral, and that there would be a larger memorial service planned for sometime in the future. I planned on attending. For one, it would look strange if I didn't, but I also wanted to see if Faith showed up, and if she did, what her reaction to me would be. I still wondered if she had willingly conspired with Eric to cheat on me during the summer, or if she was a fellow victim of his duplicity. It was something I intended to find out.

A month and a half after Eric's death, I took a different route from the Tube station back to my flat and walked past the Bottle and Glass. It was a cold, dark evening, and the windows of the pub brimmed with soft light and the outlines of after-work drinkers. I had not been in since the day Eric died. I pushed through the doors into the crowded space, filled up with the murmur of low English voices. I ordered a pint of Guinness at the bar and took my glass over to the wall that explained the rules and regulations of the beer challenge. Nothing had changed, and I wondered if the friendly constable had ever popped around to talk with the pub owners about changing the challenge. If he had, they hadn't listened to him. Next to the rules was a large wooden board, filled with embossed name plates, the mostly male names of those who had completed the challenge. I went to the end of the list. Eric Washburn was the second-to-last name. There was also a bulletin board, covered with tacked-on Polaroid photographs. All the snapshots looked the same – pale, bleary-eyed men holding aloft an empty pint glass. I found Eric's picture in the upper-right-hand corner. He held his head slightly back at an angle, and his eyes were bright with what I recognized as pride. He was still a little tan from the summer, and with his head cocked back, his girlish beautiful eyelashes were even more apparent. I thought of taking the photograph for myself but decided against it. It belonged here. A testament.

Finishing my Guinness, I thought that my career as a murderer was over. Not because I had lost the stomach for it, but because there would never be the need. I would never allow anyone to get that close to me again, to hurt me in the way that Eric had. I was a grown woman now. I had survived the vulnerability of childhood, and the danger of first love. There was comfort in knowing that I would never be in either of those positions again, that, from now on, I would be the only person responsible for my own happiness.

I walked back that night to my empty flat, made myself a simple dinner, then settled into my favorite chair to read.

A long, uncomplicated life stretched out before me.

CHAPTER 15

TED

I backed into the foyer, my eyes on the gun in Brad's hand.

'What the fuck?' I said, and glanced at his face. He didn't look well, his normally ruddy complexion gray, and his neck muscles taut. He was wearing a jean jacket with a sheepskin lining and there was a sheen of sweat across his forehead. He seemed drunk.

'Nice place you got here,' he said, and the words came out in a strange rhythm, as though he'd rehearsed them.

'Can I show you around, Brad? Can I get you a drink?'

His brow lowered, as though my words had confused him. 'Yeah, a lot nicer than my temporary little shithole, right? This is where a real man lives, right?'

A memory flashed through me. The night that Brad and I were drinking. Me saying something about where Brad lived. A hateful look on his face. And suddenly I knew that Brad was here to kill me, and instead of panicking, I became calm and rational, my mind in overdrive. I knew I could talk him out of this. I knew that I was smarter than he was.

'Seriously, Brad, what are you doing with that gun?'

'What do you think I'm doing?' he said, and raised it so that it was pointed at my head. Everything in the room disappeared except that gun.

'Jesus, Brad, think for a moment.' I stared at the gun, probably the same one I'd seen in Brad's drawer in Kennewick. A double-action revolver. I watched as Brad slid his thumb onto the hammer. Did he not know that he could just pull the trigger? I needed to make a move, either attack or run. I was less than two feet from him, and I found myself lunging forward. The last time I'd been in a fight I was a third grader and I'd lost to a kid named Bruce in the first grade. I simply shoved at Brad as hard as I could, spinning his body so that the gun pointed away from me. He flew backward, his head striking the front door with a loud crack. I thought he might have been knocked out, but he hissed out a word I didn't understand. I turned and ran toward the stairs. As I hit the first step, already thinking about the phone on the first landing, I heard the loud pop of Brad's gun, and felt a slap of air at my back, as though the bullet had missed me by less than an inch. I kept bounding up the stairs. By the time I reached the top I could hear Brad behind me, his work boots hitting the first few steps of the stairway. I reached toward the phone, sitting on an antique phone table, and stumbled, falling to the carpeted floor, knocking the phone and the table over. Something warm had spilled across my stomach and I put my hand there. When I pulled it back I was surprised to see blood, and for a second, wondered where it was coming from. Then Brad was standing over me, the gun pointed in my direction. He was breathing heavily, a strand of saliva hanging from his lower lip.

'Why?' I said, but as soon as I said it, I knew. Brad was no psychotic, deciding to kill me because I'd insulted where he lived. He was doing this because of my wife. And in a few moments, it all unfolded in front of me. Miranda was using Brad to get rid of me. She wanted all the money for herself. Why hadn't I seen this before? A sharp pang of pain went through my gut, and I grimaced, then almost laughed.

I looked up at Brad with his stupid face and shaking gun. 'Miranda would never be with you,' I said.

'You don't know a fucking thing.'

'Brad, she's using you. Who do you think they're going to suspect? She's in Florida. You two are having an affair. Everyone knows it.'

I saw an expression of doubt on his face, and felt a sliver of hope. I held my hand against the exit wound on my stomach. The blood pulsing through my fingers was warm and thick.

'You think you're such a big deal,' he said.

'Brad, you're an idiot.'

'We'll see,' he said, and pulled the trigger.

PART II

THE HALF-FINISHED HOUSE

CHAPTER 16

LILY

'Hello, there,' I said to Ted Severson. He was sitting at the bar in the business class lounge at Heathrow Airport. I had recognized him right away but doubted he recognized me. We'd only met once, a couple years ago, when I had run into Faith Hobart at an outdoor market in the South End.

'I go by Miranda now,' Faith had said to me, then.

'Oh.'

'It's my actual name. Faith's my middle name. Miranda Faith.'

'I don't think I knew that. So you've lost your faith.'

She laughed. 'I guess you could say that. This is my fiancé, Ted.'

A handsome, somewhat stiff man turned from looking at a vintage letterpress tray and shook my hand. He had the dry, firm grasp of the professional hand shaker, but after a cursory few words about how nice it was to meet me, he turned back to the stall. I told Faith/Miranda that I was meeting someone, and needed to go. Before leaving, she said, in a low voice, 'That was terrible about Eric.

I'm sorry I didn't get in touch with you afterward but you were in London, and . . .'

'Never mind, Faith, it's okay.'

I walked away. I had thought many times about what might happen if I ran into Faith again. (I suppose I should call her Miranda now.) How would she react to me? Had she been surprised when she found out Eric died in London while visiting me? Had she been two-timed as well? But after meeting her at the market, seeing her with her new ink black hair and her five-hundred-dollar boots and with an oblivious fiancé, and seeing the casual way she expressed concern for me, I knew. I knew that she had actively deceived me as well. When she was with Eric in New York, she knew he was still seeing me on the weekends in Shepaug. Was it payback for my dating Eric in the first place? Was she just one of those women who got off on taking men away from other women? For a brief moment, there in the South End of Boston, I re-experienced that stab of pain in my chest I had felt when I knew for sure that Eric had betrayed me with Miranda, and that my life would never be the same again.

I told myself not to worry about it, and I didn't particularly, but when I saw Ted Severson at the airport (Miranda and he were married now; I'd read the announcement in the *Globe*) I decided to talk with him. 'Hello, there,' I said, giving him a chance to recognize me, even though I doubted that he would. He looked up, no idea who I was. He was visibly drunk, his eyes red-rimmed and his lower lip slack. He was drinking martinis. I ordered one as well, even though I hated martinis.

We shared a flight back to Boston, and he told me all about his sad life, about how Miranda was cheating on him, about his feelings of rage and resignation. He told me these things because he thought he would never see me again. At another time, another place, he would never have told me what he did. He even told me how much hate he felt for his wife, and jokingly said that he wanted to kill her. I told myself not to get involved, but I knew the moment we began to talk that it was too late. Miranda had come into my orbit again, and for a reason. Maybe it was selfishness, or maybe it was justice, or maybe it was something else altogether, but over the next few weeks I convinced Ted Severson to murder Miranda, as well as Brad Daggett, her lover. It wasn't hard. And just when the plan was set to happen, I gathered the *Sunday Globe* from my stoop one morning, and over coffee at my kitchen table I saw a picture of Ted, a small pixelated square on the top of a column in the Metro section.

I read the accompanying story, my mug of coffee halfway to my lips.

SOUTH END RESIDENT SHOT IN OWN HOME

Boston – Police are investigating the homicide of a Boston resident that occurred in the Worcester Square section of the South End early Friday evening.

Police responded to a call for shots fired at 6:22 P.M. According to Boston Police Detective Henry Kimball, the victim, 38-year-old Ted Severson, was found on the second-floor landing of his residence and pronounced dead at the scene.

'We are also investigating a burglary that occurred on Friday night on the same block as the homicide,' Kimball said. 'We don't know yet if the two crimes are related, but we are asking anyone who might have information to step forward.'

Ted Severson, president of Severson Inc., a consulting firm, is survived by his wife, Miranda Severson, née Hobart, who was in Florida at the time of the shooting.

According to a neighbor, Joy Robinson, Ted and Miranda Severson 'were a beautiful young couple. They looked like people you would see on television. I can't believe this happened to them. And in this neighborhood.'

Anyone with information on either the homicide case or the burglary may call the Boston Police Crime Stoppers line.

I set my coffee down, then read the story again. I felt cold all over.

It had never occurred to me that, while Ted and

I were setting up Miranda to be killed, she might be doing the same thing with Ted. It *had* to be Miranda, with the help of Brad. There was no way this was a random burglary that had turned into a murder. It was too perfect that Miranda was out of town in Florida, with a solid alibi. Brad must have come down from Maine and shot Ted. Maybe he burglarized a nearby house to muddy the waters. Maybe not. Either way, Ted was out of Miranda's way, and all his money would go to her.

I thought of Ted. He had been found shot to death on the second-floor landing of his house. He must have let Brad into the house, then made a run for it. He must have known he was about to die, and he must have known that Miranda had engineered it. My throat closed up and I felt tears well up in my eyes, but they didn't fall. I had grown fond of Ted. When we talked on the plane, I had seen him only as a way to find out more about my college nemesis. Miranda Faith Hobart was a loose thread in my own narrative, and I had told myself that, even though she had wronged me by stealing away my boyfriend, I was never convinced that she was a truly poisonous person. But after talking with Ted on the plane, and hearing his story of her betrayal, I knew that this was not the case. She was rotten to the core.

And maybe I was excited to have a prey again. I will admit that. Killing was a little bit of an itch that I hadn't scratched in many years.

But Ted grew on me. More than grew on me,

really. When we kissed in the cemetery in Concord I was surprised by my reaction, by how much I felt from a kiss. I told myself – as I always told myself when getting involved with a man – that falling in love was never an option. I knew I could never go through that again. But I liked Ted a lot. He was handsome, and yet somehow awkward, as though he had never really grown accustomed to his good luck. One of those men who own the world but don't quite know it. I could see how Miranda would have appealed to him. Not only was she the sexiest woman in any room, but she was also incredibly comfortable with herself. He must have been attracted to that quality. But besides the intensity of our kiss – the yellow leaves around us, his hand on my sweater – what I really felt with Ted was the unusual sensation of being able to be myself with him, of being able to share secrets with another human being. He was telling me his deepest thoughts, his desire to murder his wife, and, one day, I told myself, I might be able to tell him about my past.

But now Ted was gone.

And all I could think about was how badly I wanted to see him again, and how that was never going to happen.

I went online to see if I could learn anything more about what had transpired on Friday night. There was nothing, just a few newspaper articles that repeated the information from the *Globe* piece. I thought more about the murder, and how

Miranda had engineered it. It had to have been Brad that pulled the trigger. There was a possibility that there was a third person involved, but I doubted it. So how did they work it? Miranda leaves town and makes sure that Ted will be home alone on that Friday night. Brad drives down from Maine. First, he breaks into a neighbor's house and burgles it. It would have been a neighbor about whom Miranda had information. She would have known the homeowner was away, and that he didn't have an alarm system. That would be fairly easy. After the burglary, Brad must have gone to Ted's house and knocked on the door. Ted would have let him in, then all Brad had to do was shoot him. It would look like a burglary gone wrong. Then Brad returns to Maine.

I wondered about Brad's alibi. He had to have one, but how could he if he drove from southern Maine to Boston and back and committed two crimes? It would take at least three hours, probably more, because he'd need to keep to the speed limits on the highway. Maybe Miranda was counting on the fact that absolutely no one knew about her and her building contractor. But was that a possibility? Ted had found out. Someone else in town must have known. Members of his crew? The bartender at the Kennewick Inn? It didn't seem likely that they'd managed to keep it a total secret.

I knew, of course. It put me in a unique position – possessed of all this information from Ted

Severson, and no one in the world was aware that we had even known each other. I could go to the police, of course, and tell them everything, without ever mentioning that Ted had also been planning on killing his wife. But I wasn't going to do that. There was a good chance that the police would botch the prosecution and Miranda would go free. And even if she was arrested and convicted, she would become a national celebrity. I could see it already – a woman with her looks who had convinced her lover to murder her husband. It would play out on television for years to come.

Miranda deserved punishment, now more than ever.

I sent a text message to my friend Kathy, telling her that I didn't feel well and canceling our plans to catch an afternoon movie. Then I sent an e-mail to my boss at Winslow College, letting him know that I felt a cold coming on, and planned on taking the following day off. My boss was deadly afraid of germs, and always happy to grant sick days.

I had work to do, and the first step was to visit Kennewick and meet Brad Daggett. I knew I had to move fast, because the police might already be closing in, and I needed to get there ahead of them.

CHAPTER 17

MIRANDA

It was just past ten in the morning and I could smell the alcohol on his breath. There were dots of sweat along his hairline, and the skin under his eyes was puffy and bruised-looking.

'You here alone?'

'Yeah,' Brad said.

We were standing on the gravel driveway of the half-finished house in Maine. It was Sunday. Brad had killed my husband on Friday night, and I knew, just looking at him, that I'd misjudged his capabilities. He looked feverish, his eyes too bright.

'It went okay,' I said. 'Police think it's a burglary that went wrong. Just like we planned.'

'Yeah,' he said again.

'How do you feel? You look sick.'

'I don't feel so good. It was harder than I thought it would be.'

'Baby, I'm sorry,' I said. 'You won't feel that way for long. I promise. We're going to get married. You're going to be rich. Trust me, this feeling won't last.'

'Yeah, I know that.'

'Then you've got to pull yourself together. If the police come and talk with you, you can't look like a zombie. Okay? It's done now. Ted is dead, and there's no going back.'

A car slid past on Micmac Road, and Brad turned his head to watch it. I watched Brad. It was a cold morning, and his breath condensed in the air. He turned back to me. 'I don't know if we should be meeting here like this,' he said, and pulled a Marlboro Red out of the hard pack in his jacket's front pocket. He lit it with a match, cupping with both hands even though there was no wind.

'You're my building contractor. My husband was just murdered, and I needed to tell you to suspend work for a few days, just while I figure out what needs to be done. It's no big deal. I'm on my way to see my mother. No one knows about us. No one. You've got to pull it together, Brad.'

'I know. I will. It's just that . . . You weren't there. He looked scared.'

'Of course, he looked scared, baby.'

'And there's something else, too.'

'What?'

'I think he knew about us.'

'What do you mean?'

'He said some things. He said you'd never be with me, and that you were using me.'

'He probably just put it together. As soon as he saw you coming through the door with the gun,

194

he figured that you and I were together. There's no way he knew about us before.'

'I think he did. It's not like he was surprised. He acted like he'd known all along.'

I thought for a moment, wondered if it were possible, but decided it wasn't. 'How would he have known?' I said to Brad.

'I don't fucking know, Miranda, but I'm telling you. He knew.' His voice was pitched high, and his hand with the cigarette bobbed up and down as he spoke.

'Shhh, it's okay. Maybe he knew about us, but now he's dead, so it doesn't matter, okay?'

'He could have told someone.'

'Who would he tell? I know him. He had no close friends. Maybe he just suspected us, but he wouldn't have told a soul. I promise.'

'Okay.' He took a long gulping drag at his cigarette.

'Baby, listen to me. You've got to be prepared with your story. You're a building contractor, and you were working for Ted and me. Ted was never around but I was. I seemed a little bit bored, had my nose in every detail, but other than that I was all right. I never hit on you. You never hit on me. Why would you mess up a sweet deal like the one you had? They were filthy rich. You have no idea who might have killed Ted. You have no idea if Ted and I were happy. We seemed happy when you saw us together, but, honestly, you weren't paying that much attention. That's it. That's all you know.'

'Okay.'

'Repeat it back to me.'

'Jesus, Miranda, I got it.'

'Okay. So tell me about your night with Polly. How'd that go?'

'Fine. We had lunch at Cooley's, kept drinking and left around three. We went back to my place. She was hammered, passed out before I left.'

'Did you fuck her?'

'Jesus, Miranda.'

'I'm not asking for me. I don't care. It's probably best that you fucked her, in case she gets asked about the story.'

'Why would she get asked? I thought you said—'

'She's not going to get asked, but I'm just making sure. She's your alibi. I want to know what she's going to say on the off chance that the police check your alibi.'

'She'll be good. She'll probably say I'm her boyfriend, and we did some drinking, then had sex back at my place. She'll say I was there all night. She's not going to say she passed out. I know her.'

'She was still there when you got back?'

'Yeah, she hadn't moved.'

'You woke her up?'

'Yeah, I did just what you said. I woke her up. It was about ten, and I took her back to her car.'

Another car wound by out on Micmac, and Brad watched it again. He'd tossed his cigarette, and with his free hand he tugged a little on one of his sideburns. 'Okay,' I said. 'I'm going to get going.

Tell the crew to take a couple days off, okay, just till I figure out what I'm going to do. I'll call you, but only for work reasons, okay?'

'Yeah, I know.'

'Nothing bad's going to happen, Brad. I promise. I don't think the police are ever even going to talk to you.'

'I know.'

I stepped forward, glancing toward the road to make sure it was empty, then took Brad's big knuckly hand and guided it down the front of the yoga pants I was wearing. I wasn't wearing any underpants, and on Friday, during the few hours that I was in Miami, I'd gone with my girlfriends to a spa and suffered through a complete Brazilian. I pushed Brad's fingers down far between my legs. 'And when this is all over,' I whispered, 'you and I are going to take a long vacation on some tropical island where no one knows us, and I am going to fuck you blind.'

'Okay, Jesus,' he said, pulling his hand away from me and taking a step back. 'Someone will see us.'

'You worry too much,' I said. 'That's your problem.'

'Okay,' he said again, and pulled another cigarette from his pack. He glanced back at his truck, probably thinking about the bottle he kept there in the glove compartment.

'Gotta go, baby,' I said, and got in my car. 'Stay cool, okay?'

He nodded, and I U-turned out of the driveway. Brad had been a big mistake. That was pretty clear, and all I could do was hope that the police kept their investigation to Boston, and never questioned him.

I got back onto I-95 and settled in for the long haul to Orono. After marrying Ted I'd tried to talk my mother into moving closer to Boston, but she'd insisted on staying up in Maine. I gave her some money and she ended up buying a 1,600-square-foot town house that she fell in love with because of a stainless steel fridge and some granite countertops. I told her that owning a nice house in Orono was like owning half a parking spot in Boston, but she still didn't want to move down. I think the reason she wanted to stay in Maine was to rub her newfound money in the faces of her friends. Along with the condo, she also got a new wardrobe and a Mercedes.

'Did you tell your father I'm driving a Mercedes now? We had one once, you know, for about five minutes,' she said to me after she'd bought the car.

'Dad doesn't care what car you drive, Mom.'

'You think because he's some kind of intellectual he doesn't care what car someone drives.'

'No, he just doesn't care what kind of car *you* drive, Mom.'

That had been a few weeks ago. We hadn't spoken again till yesterday, when I called her to let her know that Ted, her son-in-law, had been killed in an attempted burglary. I told her I was coming up for a couple of nights, that I didn't want to stay in Boston.

'Of course you don't, Faith.' My mother still called me Faith, my middle name and the name I'd gone by from the age of six to the end of college. I'd insisted on changing it when there was another girl with the name of Miranda in my first grade class. When I told my mother I was switching back to Miranda, she'd refused. 'I've only just gotten used to it, Faithy, and I'm not turning back.'

I could tell that Detective Kimball wasn't too pleased when I told him I was driving to Maine to be with my mother. 'We could get you a hotel room here in town,' he'd said. 'Your mother could come down here.'

'Is it important that I stay in Boston?'

'It would be helpful to have you here to answer any questions we might have.' Detective Henry Kimball talked in a low voice, and seemed far too nervous to have reached any kind of rank in the police department. He had brown hair that was a little too long, and brown eyes. He wore a tweedy coat over a pair of jeans. I thought he looked like one of the lost souls who used to work at the literary magazine at college. I wondered how quickly I could make him fall in love with me. Pretty fucking quickly, I thought.

'I'm only going to Maine. You have my cell phone number. I can't stay . . . I can't stay in my house, right now. You understand . . .'

'Of course, I understand, Mrs Severson. Completely. Well, then, we'll be in touch. I'll call you immediately if something comes up in the investigation.'

We'd had this conversation after I'd identified Ted's body. I took a cab from the police station back to our house, and packed a bag. Brad had thought that driving to Maine so soon would look suspicious, but I thought it would look completely natural.

After losing my husband it would make sense that I would want to spend time with my mother. That is, if you didn't happen to know my mother. But driving up to Maine gave me a chance to stop over in Kennewick and check on Brad and find out how much I needed to worry about his nerves. And, as it turned out, I definitely needed to worry.

Up past Portland I started losing decent radio stations and slid in one of the mix CDs that Ted had made for me. It began with a song that he claimed was playing at the party where we met. 'Mansard Roof' by Vampire Weekend. I couldn't remember the song from that party, but I liked it, and sang along. When I married Ted I hadn't planned on killing him. I didn't love him, but I liked him enough. And he was generous. He let me spend his money without complaining. Not that he really had anything to complain about; as far as I could tell, the money would never run out. Then one morning I woke up in Boston, sun coming through our bedroom window. I looked over at Ted, still deep in sleep, his face pillow-creased. I studied a little patch of dark stubble under his chin that he must have missed while shaving the previous day. He was snoring, lightly, but each ragged breath began with a little nasal hiccup, like his breath had caught on the edge of something. It was infuriating to listen to, and I realized that I was going to spend the rest of my life waking up and looking over at the same face, growing older, and older, and snoring more and more. That part was bad enough, but I also knew that, as soon as Ted woke up, he was going to look over at me, and his face was going to look so pleased, and he would say something like, 'Hey there, beautiful.' That was the worst. I'd have to smile when all I wanted to do was smash that stupid grin off his face. Ted stirred a little, and I knew he was going to wake up. As quietly as I could, I pulled the duvet off of me and slid my legs over the lip of the bed. I wasn't fast enough, though. Ted woke and ran a finger along my back, and said, in a sleepy, dopey voice, 'Where you going, sexy?' And right then, I knew I couldn't do it. I wanted the money but couldn't spend a lifetime with Ted. Not even close. We'd just begun breaking ground on the house in Kennewick. I thought of Brad Daggett, our contractor, and wondered if he might be good for something besides house construction.

By the time I reached the outskirts of Bangor, the CD had played through twice, but I kept listening to it. I got off of I-95, drove past the Thomas Hill Standpipe and got onto Kenduskeag

Avenue, which took me all the way into town. It was grim, the leaves on the trees having already turned and fallen. Most had been bagged or mulched, and the city had settled back into its familiar color palette of shingle and brick, low dwellings underneath a low gray sky.

I got onto State Street, skirting the Penobscot River, heading north toward Orono. A quarter mile from my mother's condo my phone trilled. I turned down the radio and answered it.

'Mrs Severson, this is Detective Kimball.'

'Hello,' I said, and even though he could be calling about anything, my heart skipped a little.

'Sorry to bother you, but we have a question. Do you happen to know what your husband did on the day . . . on Friday, during the day?'

'Um. Far as I know, he was home all day. I saw him in the morning before my flight to Florida. He told me he had work to do, and that night he was planning on eating alone at home. He was going to make lamb. I texted him to remind him to take it out of the freezer.' I made my voice tremble a little.

'Uh-huh. Did your husband know anyone in Winslow, Mass.?'

I slowed the car down, looking for my mother's town house.

'Winslow. I don't think so. Why?'

'We found a Town of Winslow parking violation in his car. It was from 2:33 p.m. on the Friday that your husband passed away. We were just curious if you knew why he might have driven out there.'

I spotted my mother's driveway, the Mercedes coupe in Diamond White, and pulled in next to it.

'I have no idea. Where's Winslow again? That's where the college is, right?'

'Yes. Did your husband have business contacts there?'

'He might have. I have no idea. Why? Do you think it has something to do with what happened?'

'No, no. We're just following any lead. So as far as you know, your husband didn't see anyone he knew during the day on Friday.'

'As far as I know, yes, but I wasn't there . . .'

'Of course. Thank you very much, Mrs Severson. If you think of anything else, or remember who your husband might have known in Winslow, please get in touch. You have my number?'

'You just called me. I have it.'

'Right, thank you.'

I sat in my car a while, even though I saw the dark figure of my mother peering out of her second-floor living room window. I was a little concerned that the police were finding it necessary to investigate where Ted had gone the day he was killed. I was banking on their simply assuming that Ted fought back against a burglar. I took a deep breath, wondered for a moment if my mother was still smoking, and if there were cigarettes in the house, then calmed myself down. Of course they wanted to know where Ted had gone that day. It

203

was routine. But why had he gone to Winslow, and why hadn't he told me about it? I hadn't lied when I told the detective that, as far as I knew, Ted knew no one in Winslow. But the name of the town was ringing a bell with me, and I couldn't remember exactly why. Someone I knew lived there now, or was I getting Winslow confused with Winchester. And why would Ted have gone to Winslow? Could he possibly have secrets, as well? Now I had another thing to worry about, along with worrying that Brad was going to come apart at the seams. Story of my life.

I stepped out into the cold Orono air. Dead leaves were scuttling across the driveway. I pulled my bag from the backseat of the Mini and made my way to the front door of my mother's town house.

CHAPTER 18

LILY

On the drive from Winslow to Kennewick I kept thinking about what Miranda had done to Ted. He was an innocent. Even though he had been planning Miranda's own demise, as well as Brad's, I knew, down deep, he was not a natural murderer, not a true predator. And now I was realizing that he had been the prey all along. I wondered if he subconsciously sensed that Miranda was coming after him. Was that why he was willing to kill Miranda – because he felt her at his back, the way a mouse feels the presence of a cat, perched and still in the tall grass?

The day was cold and gray but I had the window cracked, and as I exited from I-95 onto the rotary just north of Portsmouth, I could smell the briny sea air. I didn't know Maine well. Since living in Massachusetts I had visited Cape Cod several times, staying in Wellfleet at the house of a work colleague and friend, but had only gone north of my state line on a few occasions. I got onto Route 1 and passed through Kittery, land of the outlets, and spotted the Trading Post, where Ted had bought the binoculars he used to spy on Miranda.

I could imagine him on this very road, just a few weeks ago; I could imagine how he must have felt, that terrible hollow feeling in your gut when you've been let down by someone you love.

Once I was past the outlets, the views from the road opened up, and I caught glimpses of sea marsh and, in the distance, the Atlantic, almost the same gray color as the low, placid sky.

It took me a while to find the Kennewick Inn. I got off Route 1 at Kennewick Beach, then had to backtrack southward toward Kennewick Harbor. I passed several small clusters of salt-faded rental cabins, and wondered which one belonged to Brad and his family. I also passed Cooley's, its neon sign unlit on that early Sunday afternoon. A pickup truck idled in its parking lot and I wondered if Brad was already there. Past Kennewick Beach, Micmac Road wound through some expensive real estate. I kept my eye out for the house that Ted and Miranda had been building, spotting it almost immediately – a beige monstrosity perched far out on a bluff, the dark ocean laid out behind it. There were two large Dumpsters at the front of the house but no vehicles that I could see.

I kept driving till I reached the inn, pulling into its nearly empty gravel driveway. Below the wooden inn sign, carved in ornate script, hung a placard that said vacancies. I knew there would be. It was a Sunday in October, and at this time of the year the tourists head to the mountains to leaf-peep, leaving the shoreline to its year-round residents.

I studied the Kennewick Inn. It was a post-and-beam structure built right up against the road, with a large extension behind it, designed to look as old as the original building. All the exterior woodwork had been recently painted white, and even in the gray light of the day it seemed to shine with the promise of luxury and comfort. I wasn't sure if it was smart to take a room; there was a slim possibility that Miranda was also staying there. Still, it was unlikely – her husband had just been killed, and I assumed she was in Boston taking care of business. But I couldn't be sure. Running into her would not be the worst thing. There was no reason for her to suspect I had anything to do with her husband. There was zero connection between us. Still, it might put her on her guard, and for my plan to work, I needed her to be relaxed.

I decided to stay. The truth was, I wanted to get a look at where Miranda had been living for most of the past year. People would know her here. There might be gossip. All of which might give me an advantage.

Walking from the car to the reception area, the raw air smelled of woodsmoke. A workman in paint-splattered overalls was coming out of the inn's side door as I reached it, and he held the door for me as I passed through with my bag. I walked across the uneven, wide-planked floors to the unmanned reception desk. I waited for a minute, then rang the bell. A gray-haired man with a handlebar mustache appeared from a side office. His name tag identified him as John Corning, concierge.

'Checking out?'

'Checking in, actually. If there's a room. I don't have a reservation.'

It took about fifteen minutes, as John described several of the available rooms. I settled on one in the old section of the inn. I was warned that the ceilings were low, but that there was a good view of the ocean.

'Just visiting?' John asked.

'I had a couple days off and I've never been up here, so I thought I'd treat myself.'

'Well, yah picked the perfect place. There are spa services here, but they're not walk-in. You need to call ahead. Dining room's closed tonight, but the Livery's open down in the cellar, and the food's just as good, if you ask me. Try the lobster BLT. And I'd be happy to recommend nearby restaurants. Do you need someone to show you to your room?'

I told him I didn't, and climbed the narrow stairwell to the second floor. The view from my room was a narrow slice of ocean past a cluster of huddled trees on the bluff across the road, but the room was nice, with dark blue walls, Shaker-style furniture, and a four-poster bed with an actual red-white-and-blue quilt on it. I wondered, of course, if this were a room that Ted and Miranda had stayed in. Had they slept together in this bed?

I unpacked my bag. I had told John at the front desk that I would be staying for two nights, but I had packed clothes for more than that. I would play it by ear. The room was too warm, the radiator clicking and hissing, and I opened the window, standing there while the cold air spilled over me. The low clouds were thinning as the afternoon wore on, and I could make out the lengthening shadow of the inn as it stretched across the road. It would be dark in less than an hour. I had planned on walking the cliff walk but decided that I could do that the following day. I left the window cracked and lay down on the soft bed. The ceiling was crossed with dark beams, and I imagined Miranda in this room staring at the same view. I pictured her alone, naked under the sheets, thinking about the two men in her life – her husband and her lover – and plotting murder. I tried to think of Ted, but my mind kept slipping toward Miranda. Was it possible that I was wrong about her, and that Ted had really been killed by a surprised burglar? I didn't think so but knew it was a possibility. It was the first thing I needed to find out, and the reason why I needed to meet Brad as soon as possible.

Miranda flooded my thoughts. I remembered her from years ago, staring into my eyes that drunken night at St Dunstan's. She had wanted to study them, she said, and I'd let her. I could smell the sweet trace of vodka on her breath, and one of her hands was touching my wrist. She told me all the colors she could see in my eyes. I wondered at the time what she was up to. I thought that it had to do with Eric, that she was trying to spook me, since I was now going out with her ex-boyfriend, but now I wonder if it had something to do with me. What had she seen in my eyes? Had she seen Chet at the bottom of that well? A commonality that went beyond Eric Washburn?

Some guy whose name I've forgotten had yelled, 'Kiss, already,' from across the room and we broke eye contact, but I've never forgotten that moment. I wondered if she remembered it, too.

I stayed in the room until a little after five, then changed into my tightest jeans. I pulled my hair back into a ponytail, and put on more makeup than I normally used, including dark eyeliner. After dinner at the Livery, I was planning on checking out Cooley's on the beach, and I needed to look the part.

The Livery was quiet when I took a seat at the bar. The bartender, a dyspeptic-looking giant in suspenders and a tie, was cutting lemons and limes, and a waitress was wiping down tables. The bar area was long and narrow. At one end was an unlit fireplace, and at the other, a man with long gray hair was unpacking an acoustic guitar, and setting up an amplifier. I hung my purse from a hook beneath the oak bar and ordered a bottle of light beer. Football highlights were playing on the TV mounted above the bottles, and I pretended to be interested. I wondered if anyone would show up on a Sunday night, but by six o'clock, as I was nursing my second beer, at least fifteen customers had arrived, most of them taking seats at the bar, and the man with the acoustic guitar had already sung two Eagles songs. I hadn't eaten since breakfast and ordered a turkey burger with sweet potato fries. Just as it was arriving, John, the hotel concierge who had checked me in, sat down two stools over and ordered a Grey Goose martini.

'Hello, there,' I said, swiveling my barstool fractionally in his direction.

I watched his eyes hunt my face. I knew I looked quite a bit different from when I had checked in. After a long second, he said, 'Hello, guest with no reservation. How'd you like your room?'

'It's lovely. You were right.'

'Didn't bump your head going through the door?'

'Almost.'

His drink arrived, the vodka forming a trembling meniscus at the brim of the glass. 'Now, how do you expect me to drink this?' he said to the bartender, who, without a word, plucked up a small black bar straw and dropped it into his martini. John lowered the level of the vodka a quarter inch, then flicked the straw back toward the bartender, who let it bounce off his chest and fall to the floor.

'Nice to leave your job and be able to go less than a hundred yards to get a martini,' I said.

'I wasn't kidding when I said how good this place was. See what a great advertisement I am, drinking at my own place of work.' His laugh was almost like a giggle, his shoulders hitching up and down.

We chatted while I ate my burger, and he worked his way through the martini, adding ice as he drank it. I was about to give up any hope that I would stumble into gossip about Ted and Miranda, but when John's second martini arrived, he asked, 'You said you were from Boston?'

'No, but Massachusetts. Winslow, about twenty miles west.'

'Did you read about the murder in the South End? Ted Severson.'

'I did. It was a home invasion or something, right?'

'Right. He was building a house up here, just about a mile up the road.' He pointed north with one of his large, meaty hands. 'They stay here – stayed here – all the time.'

'Oh, my God. You knew him?'

'I knew him really well, and Miranda, his wife, she practically lived here the past year.'

'She did live here,' said the bartender, breaking his silence. 'She was down here for dinner more nights than she wasn't.'

'Has Sidney heard yet?' John asked the bartender, and I noticed that two young women down the bar had stopped talking to each other and were now paying attention to our conversation.

'I don't know, but I'm sure she has. It's gone all over town.'

'Is the house finished?' I asked, wanting to keep myself in the conversation.

'No, not yet,' John said. 'If you walk to the end of the cliff walk you can look at it. It was going to be huge. Little bit of an eyesore, I thought, but don't quote me on that.'

'What do you think will happen to it?'

'No idea, really. For all I know, Miranda will finish it and move up here.'

'Oh, she'll definitely move up here.' This was from one of the two women eavesdropping. They were both in their twenties, one in a sweatshirt from UNH, and one in a windbreaker and a Patriots cap. The woman who spoke, the one in the sweatshirt, already had a raspy voice, as if she'd been smoking for all her young life.

'You think so?' John asked.

'Yeah, I mean she practically lived up here anyways, and she was always talking about how much she loved it, and how awesome the house was going to be, and on and on. She's from Maine, you know. Orono. I mean, maybe she won't want to move into such a big house now that her husband's dead, but I just wouldn't be surprised if she came up here. She can live anywhere with her money.'

'Why was she up here all the time if the house wasn't finished yet?' I asked.

John answered. 'She was supervising. She said she practically designed the place. Her husband used to come up weekends. We all knew him really well.'

'What was he like?'

'What was he like? He was nice but a little

distant, I guess. Everyone felt like they got to know Miranda really well, and Ted not so much. Maybe just because she was here so much.'

'Also, Miranda always bought drinks for the bar and Ted never did.' This was from the woman with the Patriots cap, and as soon as she said it, her face went pale as she remembered that Ted had been murdered. She covered her mouth and said, 'Not that . . .' and trailed off.

'Were they rich?' I asked.

Everyone in our little knitting circle of gossip immediately reacted – the two women each saying 'Oh yeah' in unison, John exhaling loudly, and the bartender nodding his head in one slow, exaggerated motion.

'Filthy,' John said. 'You should walk down the cliff walk tomorrow and see the house. You won't be able to miss it. It's got something like ten bedrooms. I'm not exaggerating.'

The solo guitar player broke into 'Moonlight Mile' by the Stones, and my new friends talked about how rich Ted and Miranda Severson were. The woman in the hooded sweatshirt used the word 'gazillionaire,' while John said they were 'very well off.' I went to use the restroom, and when I came back the two women were putting coasters on the necks of their Bud Light Limes to go out and smoke cigarettes, and John had bought me a new beer.

'Since we're gossiping,' I said, sliding back onto my stool, 'it seems strange that she spent so much time here at a hotel without her husband. You don't think she was seeing anyone?'

John stroked one side of his handlebar mustache. 'I don't think so. She always seemed thrilled when Ted came up.' A slight chilliness had entered John's voice, as though I'd possibly asked one too many questions.

'Just wondering,' I said. 'It's so sad.'

I stayed for a few more beers. John left after his second martini and I slid over and joined the two women, introducing myself. Their names were Laurie and Nicole, and both were waitresses, one at a fish place in Portsmouth, and one at the dining room of another seaside hotel two miles away. Sunday night was their going-out night. All they wanted to talk about was Ted and Miranda, the tenor of the conversation alternating between respectful and salacious. By eight, the Livery was nearly full, and another couple, friends of Laurie and Nicole, had joined us. Mark and Callie were in their thirties, also in the restaurant business, and a lot of what had been said about Ted Severson's murder was repeated after they sat down. I stayed and mostly listened. I'd already decided that I wasn't going to Cooley's till the following night. Even though I had been drinking light beers, I'd had too many, most of them bought by my new friends, and I felt too drunk to trust myself in a conversation with Brad Daggett.

As it neared closing time, and as the group got

louder, I asked again about the possibility that Miranda was screwing around up here in Maine.

'I don't think so,' said Laurie, who had designated herself the closest-to-Miranda in the group. 'If she was, then I don't know when she was doing it, because she was only ever here at night, and she always went straight up to her room at the end of the night. No, I don't think she was doing anything up here. I mean, slim pickings around these parts.'

'Yeah, there is,' Nicole said.

'No offense, Mark. You're taken, but seriously, I doubt it.'

'She's fucking gorgeous, though. It makes you wonder,' Mark said, and his girlfriend, Callie, nodded heartily in agreement, as did Nicole and Laurie.

'Was she?' I asked.

'Oh, my God, yes. She was like model gorgeous. Totally hot.'

'She must have gotten hit on?'

'If she'd gone other places, sure. Like Cooley's. But not here, not really. This is not exactly a pickup bar.'

'Sidney would've picked her up,' Callie said.

Again, they all reacted, nodding their heads. 'Yeah, Sidney's obsessed,' Laurie said. 'Lily, Sidney's the bartender here most nights. She was totally in love with Miranda but, you know, that only went one way.'

I learned nothing else, and when the bar closed

at ten, I went back to my room, got into the boxer shorts and T-shirt that I slept in, and slid into bed after loosening the sheets. I couldn't sleep if my feet were tucked completely in. I turned the bedside lamp off, and the room became intensely dark, a blackness that I wasn't used to. Where I lived in Winslow was quiet, but my street had streetlamps, and my bedroom was never completely dark. I tried to think of Ted, but the blackness of the room made me remember where he was now, and as I wound down into sleep, it was Miranda that kept entering my consciousness, her eyes an inch away from mine, her touch on my wrist becoming a grip, her sharp nails growing like talons and digging into me.

CHAPTER 19

MIRANDA

That night in Orono – after eating bad take-out Chinese food and watching my mother struggle to ask me questions about my dead husband instead of telling me about her pathetic life – I lay in the undecorated guest room on a twin bed that was the only piece of furniture in the room. The walls were a horrible lemon chiffon white, and even in the dim light from the streetlamps outside, I felt oppressed by their tackiness.

I was wide awake, still worrying about Brad and his ability to keep his shit together, and still wondering why Ted had gone to Winslow on the day that Brad had killed him. I'd been saying the name – *Winslow, Winslow* – all day to myself. I was still sure that I knew someone who lived there. Clearly it was someone Ted knew as well, and I wracked my brain, going through all of our friends, to try and figure it out. So far, nothing.

I chewed at the skin around the nail of my thumb until I tasted blood, then made myself stop. I thought of getting up, going downstairs to look for the cigarettes my mother was pretending she didn't have, but knew that if she heard me, she'd come out of her bedroom and yak some more. Instead, I tried to masturbate, the only sure way I knew of getting myself to sleep. I pictured blank-faced men, as I always did, but their faces kept getting replaced by Ted's or Brad's and I eventually gave up, resigned myself to a sleepless night. I stared at the ceiling, and at the occasional fan of light that wheeled over it when a car passed outside on the road.

I must have fallen asleep because I woke with my mother standing over me in a pink robe, her hair still damp from the shower.

'Jesus, Mom,' I said.

'Sorry, Faithy. I just wanted to look at my peaceful sleeping daughter.'

'That's exactly the point. I was peaceful and sleeping.'

'Go back to sleep, then. I'll be downstairs in the kitchen. I'll keep your breakfast warm.'

After she left, I lay awake in bed, checking my phone. It had been turned off since the previous evening and I had about a thousand voice mails and text messages from friends, sending their sympathy, and asking if I needed anything. I went online to see if there was anything new about Ted's murder, and it didn't appear that there was – the reports still focused on a random home invasion, the neighborhood banding together in solidarity and fear. No news was good news, I told myself, and decided I would return to Boston that day, or maybe to Kennewick. Another day and night with my mother was out of the question.

At breakfast we talked about my plans, my mother only asking questions for which she already knew the answer. It had always been that way. *What outfit are you going to wear for your first day of school? Where were you thinking of applying to college? Why do you think your father would go and do something like that?* That morning she asked me where I was planning on living now that Ted was gone. 'Not in Boston, of course,' she answered before I could. 'I know that already.'

'Boston, probably,' I said in response.

'Faithy, don't say that. After what happened. Your neighborhood is obviously not safe. I never really thought it was and I was right. I saw that movie with Matt Damon about Southie—'

'Mom, I live in the South End, not South Boston. They are entirely different neighborhoods.'

'Clearly they are not. Or if they are, they are both violent and dangerous. You could move up here, show everyone in Orono what you made with your life. With your money you could buy the biggest house here.'

'Mom, I don't want to talk about it – not right now, okay?'

To her credit, she nodded solemnly and began to wash dishes at the sink while making little sighs for my benefit. I forgave her for her bad manners and her selfishness. I always did. People say that personalities are formed and set by the time we hit the age of five, but Sandra Roy's personality, at least for the second half of her life, was entirely formed by the day my father, head of the history department at the University of Maine, lost his tenured position for coming on to a freshman girl. Until that moment, my mother thought she was living a life of luxury. I guess she was in a way – she'd been raised in a tenement in Derry, and she'd made it all the way to the University of Maine, where she met Alex Hobart, a grad student from a middle-class town in Vermont. She dropped out of college her junior year to marry him, and a few months later she gave birth to my brother, Andrew, then a year later gave birth to me. When we were both young, my father secured a tenure-track position in the history department at the university. He excelled, becoming the youngest department head in the school's history; his yearly-increasing salary was practically a fortune in Orono, and my mother, happy with just the two children, turned our custom-built Colonial into her special project. When I was nine, the family traveled to Europe, and my mother came back with a new way of speaking, sounding like an American actress in the 1950s, all clipped words and vaguely English vowel sounds.

Then it all fell apart the year I started high school. A freshman girl taking my father's seminar on ancient Egypt taped him soliciting her for sex in exchange for grades. The situation went public, and my father was immediately fired. My mother threw him out of the house and filed for divorce. I remember that year as one long rage-fueled monologue from my mother, who seemed to blame my father more for losing his well-paying job than for his attempt at sexual blackmail. These monologues were directed at me. Andrew had discovered pot, then Phish, and spent all his free time in his bedroom, his head encased in large headphones. There were no savings; all of my parents' money had gone into house furnishings and vacations, and two years after the divorce, my mother sold the Colonial, and we moved into a three-bedroom attic apartment normally rented to students. Andrew, a senior at high school then, stayed in the apartment for less than a month, before moving into a friend's house. My mother protested, but I knew she didn't really mind. She'd turned against all men, and that included my shiftless brother. 'Just us girls, now,' she'd say, insisting that the apartment was temporary. But we stayed there all through my junior and senior years of high school. My brother graduated, then spent a year following a Phish tour around the country, ending up in San Diego, where he still lived. Last I'd heard, he was working at a brewpub and shacked up with a woman he'd met who already had four children. He'd called and left a message on my phone after Ted had died but I hadn't called him back, and probably wouldn't.

After the divorce, my father moved to Portland, where he got an adjunct position at a community college. My mother got work as a receptionist in a dentist's office, and between her salary, and my father's meager child support checks, we made ends meet. The constant refrain of our two-women house was that my mother's life was ruined, but that mine could be better. And by better, my mother meant more money.

In high school I was pretty average, but I did turn myself into a world-class shoplifter. Most of my thefts occurred outside of Orono, in either Bangor or Portland during one of my visits to my father. I mostly stole from department stores, the places that employed store detectives who prowled around trying to look like customers. Those detectives were trained to look for shoplifters by observing their body language, looking for someone who was acting nervous or suspiciously. I was never caught because I never acted like a thief. I perfected the casual nonchalance of a girl with her parent's credit card doing a little aimless shopping. I brought a big purse with me wherever I went, and I looked for small expensive items. Scarves. Perfume. I became very skilled.

The only time I was spotted stealing was by a classmate at the pharmacy in Orono. I rarely shoplifted there – it was too close to home, and a store that I went to a lot. I was a junior in high school then. I purchased several items from one of the hawk-eyed old lady cashiers, but walked out with three packs of replacement razors for my Gillette Venus in my purse.

After exiting through the automatic doors I heard a guy's voice say, 'I think you forgot to pay for something.'

I turned. It was a kid I knew from school. James something. I didn't realize he worked at the pharmacy. 'Excuse me?' I said, trying to sound like I had more important things to do than talk to a drugstore employee.

'In your purse. I saw you put the razors in there.'

'Oh, Jesus,' I said, making my face look shocked. 'I totally forgot about those.' I began to step toward the store. 'I'll just—'

The boy laughed, and grabbed my arm and steered me away across the sweltering parking lot. It was August, that annual two-week period when northern Maine turns hot and muggy and mosquito-infested. The asphalt had softened and filled the air with the smell of hot tar. 'I'm not busting you,' he said. 'I just saw you. I don't give a fuck if you steal. I do it all the time.'

'Oh.' I laughed. 'I know you, don't I?'

We introduced ourselves. His name was James Audet, and he was a junior as well, although he'd started at Orono High halfway through the previous year. He was handsome, with light blue eyes, high cheekbones, and thick blond hair. He was also short, and tightly muscled to make up for it, which caused him to walk like a gymnast, bouncing on the tips of his feet. I was a bit of a loner in high school, biding my time until college, and determined to make sure my grades were good enough to secure financial aid somewhere out of state. James and I became fast friends. He confessed to me that he believed the only thing that mattered in life was money, and that he planned on making a lot of it.

'Then marry a rich woman,' I said. We were at the Friendly's two towns over where we liked to hang out.

'I'm too short. Rich women want tall husbands.'

'Is that true?'

'Proven fact. You, however, could definitely marry a rich man. Look at those tits.'

'Ugh. I look like a freak.'

'Trust me. You're the slightly awkward girl in high school who comes back for the reunion and looks like a model. I've seen it a hundred times.'

'Seen it where?'

'Movies, of course.'

After graduation we both got jobs in what passed for a downtown in Orono, James at a pizza place, and me at that same pharmacy I used to sometimes steal from. I had gotten into Mather, a private college in Connecticut. It was a school that primarily catered to rich kids from New York and Boston, but I'd graduated third in my class, and my parents' financial situation ensured that more than half of my tuition would be paid for with aid. James was going to the University of Maine, where his father coached the wrestling team. We were both virgins, and by July of that summer, decided to have sex with each other so that we wouldn't enter college with no experience. We did it in the back of James's Caprice Classic. Afterward, he asked me how it felt. 'Incestuous,' I said, and we both laughed so hard that James fell off the backseat and bruised his hip. We kept at it, though, telling ourselves that we'd seen every good movie that was out that summer, and the hookups passed the time. On our last night together before my father was going to pick me up and drive me to Connecticut, James said, 'It was nice knowing you.'

'Um, we'll see each other at Thanksgiving.'

'No, I know. I just assume you'll have some rich boyfriend by then and won't even talk to me.'

'I'll *talk* to you,' I said.

But he was right, and we barely saw each other again after we each started college. I only ever thought of him when I came back to Maine. I wondered if he knew how rich I was.

'You ever hear anything about the Audets?' I asked my mother after we'd cleared the breakfast things, and moved to the living room with the high bay windows that looked out over the Methodist Church adjacent to the graveyard.

'Their son Jim got married. You knew that. He works at a bank in Bangor, and I heard his wife's pregnant.'

'He goes by Jim now?'

'That's what Peg calls him. I haven't seen him since he was in high school. He's still short, I hear.'

My cell phone rang. I recognized the number

as Detective Kimball's from the night before. A pulse of fear went through me. 'Mom, I need to take this.'

I answered the phone while walking toward the kitchen.

'Mrs Severson?'

'Yes.'

'It's Detective Kimball again. How are you doing?'

'All right,' I said in a raw voice.

'I'm sorry to bother you, but I'm going to need to request that you return to Boston.'

'Okay. Why?'

'A neighbor of yours thinks she saw the man who may have killed your husband. We have a sketch, and we need you to come down and take a look at it.'

'Why? Do you think it's someone I might know?' I said, immediately regretting my tone. I sounded defensive.

'Not necessarily. We're still treating this as a burglary gone wrong, but we need to rule out every other possibility. It's a possibility that whoever did this was someone who wanted your husband dead, and if that's the case, then you might be able to identify him.'

'I'll drive back down this afternoon.'

'That's great, Mrs Severson. I know it won't be easy for you, but any help—'

'It won't be a problem.'

The detective coughed about six times in a row.

'Sorry, cold. One more thing. Any luck on coming up with anyone your husband might have known in Winslow? Remember, I'd asked you about it last—'

'No. I thought about it, but nothing. I'm sorry.'

'Just wondering. Please call me when you're back in Boston. I can bring the sketch to you wherever you're . . .'

'I'll call you,' I said and hung up.

I could hear my mother talking on her own phone in the living room. All I could make out was the word *terrible* repeated several times. I stared out the window. The afternoon had turned dark, the fast-moving clouds swollen and inky, a rainstorm approaching. Because of the darkness outside, I could make out my reflection in the kitchen window. I stared at myself, thinking hard about Winslow. I knew I knew someone who lived there . . . was it someone from high school, or someone from Mather? And then it came to me, and I suddenly knew who it was I was thinking of. It was Lily Kintner, that spooky girl from Mather who was with Eric Washburn when he died in London. I remembered hearing that she'd been living in Winslow, working at the college as a librarian. But she didn't know Ted. At least I didn't think she did. Was it possible they had met once, years ago, when I ran into her in the South End? Was it her that Ted was visiting?

My mom was still on the phone, whispering loudly, as though I couldn't hear everything she was saying, and I went upstairs to pack for my return to Boston.

CHAPTER 20

LILY

Ted had told me that Cooley's was a dive, and he was right. It was a bar that had gotten its look and feel from years of accumulated kitsch, to the point where it looked fake. If this place were in New York City or Boston you'd almost think that some enterprising hipster had opened it the year before. But here, the World of Schlitz light fixtures were coated with a genuine film of grime, and the grumpy bartender was in an actual bad mood, and not just some actor trying to look the part. I sat at the far corner of the bar with a view of the front door. I wondered if I'd recognize Brad Daggett when he came in. I thought I would. Ted had described him as a big handsome cretin who was starting to show his age. That could describe about half the men who would come to a bar like Cooley's on a Monday night, but I was also counting on my knowledge that Brad had recently killed a man. I knew I could recognize a murderer.

I'd arrived at just past five, driving over from the Kennewick Inn under a rainstorm that had blackened the dusky sky. There were three cars in Cooley's lot, but I was the first customer. I settled onto my stool, shucked off my damp jacket, and ordered a Miller Lite. The bartender, the spitting image of Disney's Ichabod Crane, uncapped and delivered the bottle, then placed a laminated menu with frayed corners onto the bar. I scanned it – Cooley's Clam Pie was the specialty of the house.

It was a slow night. While I had been surprised by the relatively lively crowd at the Livery the night before, I was not surprised by the scarcity of souls that decided to brave Cooley's on a cold, wet Monday evening. By seven the only other customers in the place were a lone man, at least seventy, who had hoisted his considerable weight onto a stool and ordered a bourbon sour, two past-their-prime blondes securing the opposite end of the bar, plus a pair of middle-aged tourists who had hesitated in the doorway, decided they didn't have the courage to turn around and leave, and sat in one of the high-backed booths. In my two hours at Cooley's I had sipped two bottles of beer, and tried the famous clam pie, a slice of which had arrived on a chipped plate next to a little pile of parsley sprigs. It was pie dough filled with a chopped clam and bread crumb mixture the color of wet sand. It tasted like a fishy version of the terrible filling you scrape off baked stuffed shrimp. I ate two bites, then ordered a plate of fries. The bartender looked amused.

I had spent most of the day at the Kennewick

Inn, reading the newspaper in the lobby by the fireplace, then having lunch at the Livery, where I'd been served by Sidney, the slender, pretty bartender who supposedly had a crush on Miranda. While I ate my salad, she moved behind the bar with a purposeful intensity, making sure every glass was clean, and all the surfaces were wiped. She wore an oxford shirt, sleeves rolled all the way up to show off her biceps. One of her arms was entirely tattooed in flowers and pinup girls. She didn't seem talkative, so I decided not to ask her about Ted and Miranda. But right before I left, a hotel employee came down to the bar to fill a to-go cup with Diet Coke, and I overheard their conversation.

'Have you talked with Miranda?' the employee, a heavily made-up brunette in a black suit, asked Sidney.

'I left a message on her phone, just saying how sorry we all are. I don't expect to hear back.'

'Jesus.'

'I know, right. I keep thinking about her . . . about it . . . Ted.'

'What do you think she'll do?' The woman in the suit, who looked like an events manager, took a long pull of her Diet Coke through a straw.

'That's what everyone's asking me. Honestly, I don't fucking know. She's a friend, I guess, but it's not like I know her *that* well. For all I know, we'll never see her again.'

I left cash on the bar and slid off my stool. I

had heard what I wanted to hear. Unless people were being coy, it didn't sound as though hotel employees and regulars at the Livery were aware that Miranda was fooling around with Brad on the side. I wasn't surprised. She'd obviously worked incredibly hard to conceal it, and if it hadn't been for Ted's watching them share a cigarette and growing suspicious, then no one but Brad and Miranda would know that they meant anything to each other besides employer/employee. It made me realize that Miranda probably planned on using Brad to kill Ted from the very beginning. She'd never gone to Cooley's. Brad had never come to the Livery. My guess is that the only place they had ever been physical was in the house that was being built, and only when no other employees were on the premises.

After lunch I returned to my room to get my hiking shoes and a windbreaker in order to walk the cliff walk. I was looking forward to it. The weather was brisk and gusty, the ocean that I'd seen from my hotel room window gray and wind-chopped. I'd checked the weather on my phone, and it looked like there would be a major rainstorm, but not till later in the day. I exited the hotel and crossed Micmac, the wind buffeting my clothes against me. I worked my way down the rudimentary steps that led to the brief snippet of beach where the cliff walk began. The only other beachgoers were a stationary man and a chocolate Lab that raced in great loping strides after a tennis ball that the man threw from a plastic grabber. I proceeded immediately to the path; it was high tide, and the first hundred yards were slick with seawater that had crested over the flat rocks, but after that, the path went higher and cut inland so that a strip of stunted trees and bushes – mostly bittersweet, its yellow berries splitting open to reveal the red underneath, and winterberry – protected me from the wind. I walked slowly, not so much to be careful, but because I was savoring the beauty of the walk. I have never been a fan of the seashore – all those sedentary oiled bodies spread out along the beach like pieces of meat under a broiler. Maybe I'm biased, since my pale, freckled skin turns to a blistering red instead of a tan. I do like to swim but prefer the water of lakes and ponds to the salty brine of the ocean, and I have never been able to abide the feel of sand clinging to my feet and legs. But this particular stretch of Maine shoreline felt different to me. Maybe it was just the dramatic weather and the scudding clouds, but along this path I felt enveloped by beauty, by the primal force of nature. The large slabs of gray rocks were so much more appealing than the impermanent stretches of beach most people crave. I took deep breaths of the air as though I were thirsty for it.

There was no one else on the path that day. I wasn't surprised. By the time I reached the end, with its view of the back of Ted and Miranda's house, the wind had picked up, and pockets of rain had begun moving sideways, drumming at my raincoat.

I looked around for the spot where Ted might have propped himself with his binoculars. There were several, but a grassy hummock behind a low twisted tree seemed to provide the most cover. Ted's binoculars must have been good ones, since the house seemed an impenetrable distance away, across a stretch of ugly bulldozed land. I considered crossing the grounds and taking a closer look at the house, but I worried that Brad, or other workmen, might be there. Instead, I turned back. Waves were breaking on the rocks and sending up frenzied explosions of seawater and foam. I turned my face into the slanting rain, no longer worried about getting soaked, and walked carefully and purposefully back along the path.

At the inn I went to the small fireside bar on the lobby level and ordered a hot whiskey – my father's go-to winter drink – and took the drink back up to my room, where I sipped at it while soaking in the extra-deep tub. I felt good and had to remind myself that I was in Kennewick for a purpose, that I had a friend to avenge. After my bath I took a short nap, then got back into the tight jeans I'd worn the night before, overapplied my makeup, and drove myself to Cooley's.

I'd been there three hours, had nursed four light beers, when I decided that Brad was probably not going to show. The tourists had left, and so had the two ladies at the bar. Three lone men had entered since then, and each time they had come swinging through the outside door, shrugging rain off their coats, I had expected Brad. But one was in his early twenties, one was a pear-shaped man with a full beard, and the third came in wearing a blue blazer over a collared white shirt and a pair of pressed jeans. He was the right age, I thought, about forty, but clean-shaven. Still, I watched him carefully. It was possible Brad had shaved the goatee that Ted had mentioned, and it was possible that he was dressed up for a reason. Maybe meeting a new client. Maybe waiting on a date. He caught me looking at him, raised an eyebrow in my direction, and lifted his pint glass of beer. I stared at my phone to discourage him from coming over. I had decided it probably wasn't Brad. He was seated close enough for me to see the softness of his hands, and the frosted tips of his hair, and unless Brad was a criminal mastermind who had entirely changed his appearance, I doubted it was he. I paid my bill with cash and tottered out of Cooley's on the high heels I wasn't used to wearing.

'Don't leave on my account,' said blue blazer as I walked past him.

I turned and appraised him. 'What's your name?' I asked.

'Chris.'

'Chris, where do you work?'

He seemed a little confused by my line of

questioning, but answered me. 'I'm manager at the Banana Republic over in Kittery. Do I know you?'

'No,' I said. 'I was just curious. Have a nice night, Chris.' I continued on my way out of the bar.

Outside, the gusting rain from earlier had tapered to a steady drizzle. The wind direction had changed, and even though the ocean was just over the road the air smelled of pine trees and fresh dirt. Straddling two parking spots, a pickup truck idled, its driver-side window rolled down. Walking past it, I caught the smell of cigarette smoke in the damp air. I got to my car and fiddled for a while with my purse, hoping that the driver of the truck would finish his cigarette and get out so I could get a look at him. Just as I pulled the keys out of my purse, the truck's engine cut out, and I turned and watched the graceful arc of the cigarette butt as it traversed the parking lot, landing in a puddle with an audible fizz. A tall man got out of the truck. He was illuminated by an exterior mounted light on the edge of Cooley's. He had dark hair, and wide shoulders, and when he turned to shut the truck's door I could clearly see his dark goatee. It had to be Brad.

I had no intention of following him back into Cooley's. 'Brad,' I said, and he raised his head to look at me. Even in the dim parking lot lighting, I could see that his eyes were puffy from lack of sleep, and that he had the jittery, ghostly look of a man who had done something very bad.

'Me?' he said.

'You're Brad, right?'

'Uh-huh.'

'Brad Daggett?'

'Yeah.' He took a quick covert glance around the parking lot, maybe looking for the SWAT team poised to take him down if he made a sudden movement.

'Can we talk for a moment? Out here? It's important.'

'Okay, sure. Do I know you?'

'No,' I said. 'But we have friends in common. I know Ted and Miranda Severson very well. Look, it's wet and cold out here. Can we sit in my car and talk, or else we can sit in your truck, if you'd feel more comfortable.'

Again, he looked around the parking lot. I knew his mind must be working on overtime, wondering who I could possibly be and what I could possibly want. 'There's nothing to worry about,' I said, making my voice sound as soothing as possible. 'Why don't we sit in your truck?'

'Okay, sure,' he said, and opened his door. I took the three steps across the wet parking lot and opened the passenger-side door. Before getting in, I unzipped my purse. Resting near the top was a six-inch stun gun designed to look like a flashlight. I didn't think I would need to use it, but I wanted to be careful. I had no idea how Brad was reacting to the fact that he'd murdered a man in cold blood less than a week ago, but I had to assume he was jumpy and paranoid, and possibly dangerous.

'So you know the Seversons?' Brad said, after we were both in the truck, with what sounded like forced casualness. The truck's interior was spotlessly neat, smelling of cigarette smoke and Armor All.

'Yes,' I said. 'Well, I knew Ted Severson, and I know Miranda.'

'It was horrible what . . .'

'What happened to Ted, I know it was. That's actually why I'm here. Let me talk for a moment, okay, Brad? You're not going to like what I'm going to say, but I need you to listen. Do you think you can do that?'

I looked right at him. His eyes were rimmed in red, and his skin, despite a deep, leathery tan, had the distended look of a man who was unwell. His breath smelled like wet grain, and I wondered how much he'd already had to drink. He nodded. 'Sure, sure.'

'Brad, I need you to do me a favor. A big favor. And if you do me that favor, then I won't tell anyone that you drove down to Boston last Friday night and murdered Ted Severson.'

I braced myself, one hand resting on the stun gun in my open purse. I thought he might lunge at me, or at least violently tell me that he had no idea what I was talking about. Instead, his heavy lower lip drooped a little, and his jaw tightened, and for a moment I thought he was going to burst into tears. Instead, he said, in a voice that sounded dry and desperate, 'Who are you? What do you want from me?'

'Right now,' I responded, 'I'm your best friend in the world.'

CHAPTER 21

MIRANDA

I left Orono the way I had come, driving back through Bangor. Before getting onto I-95, I stopped for gas at a locally run station, where a teenage boy pumped it for me. I sat in the car and worried about Brad. Had the idiot actually been spotted in my neighborhood on the night of the murder? I was just praying that whatever sketch the detective had was of someone else altogether, or else didn't look remotely like Brad, because if it looked like him – even a little bit – I was going to have to say something about it. And if that happened, then Brad Daggett would be questioned by the police, and I just didn't think he was going to be able to handle that. I pictured his sweaty face, and darting eyes; the police would take one look at him and know they had their man. And he'd crack, that much was sure. One hour in an interrogation room was about what it would take. And then my only option would be to claim that Brad was delusional, that he'd clearly become obsessed with me, and killed Ted all on his own. I could even tell the police that Brad and I had had sex, a couple of times, in the house I was building, but that I never suggested he murder my husband. It would be his word against mine, and they could never prove that I had anything to do with it. But people would know. Of course, they would. I caught myself clenching my teeth and stopped doing it.

I breathed through my nose, savoring the smell of gasoline while I waited for the attendant to run my credit card. The rain began – fat, intermittent drops that made snapping sounds on the roof of the car as I drove away from the gas station toward I-95.

I kept worrying about Brad for most of the drive to Boston. Maybe he'd rise to the occasion when the police spoke with him. Maybe his alibi would hold up. And maybe – hopefully – the sketch that the detective had wouldn't look anything like Brad. That would be the best-case scenario, but, down deep, I knew somehow that the sketch was going to look just like Brad, that he had fucked up and let someone see him. After a while, I forced myself to think of something else, and began to think about Lily Kintner, the woman who lived in Winslow, and about whom I would never be thinking if Ted hadn't gone there last Friday and gotten a parking ticket. There had been a time when Lily had been a constant and annoying presence in my life. She was two years behind me at Mather. I'd met her my junior year when my boyfriend Eric Washburn gave her an invite to St Dun's.

'Who is she?' I'd asked. I hadn't been invited to a St Dun's Thursday night party until my sophomore year, and only after I'd been fucking Eric Washburn for three weeks.

'Do you know David Kintner, the novelist?' Eric said.

'No,' I said.

'She's his daughter.'

She came to that first Thursday night party, and I almost didn't see her. She was like some waif from a Victorian novel – thin and pale with long red hair. I watched her, and at first I thought she was nervous, blending into the wall she stood against with a drink in her hand, too frightened to talk with anyone. But I got closer to her, took another look, and decided that she actually didn't care that she was at St Dun's. She seemed almost disinterested, like a girl in the back row of a boring lecture. Did she even understand what it meant to get a skull card as a freshman? I thought she'd never return, but she kept coming back, every Thursday, and it was clear that Eric had become interested. I found one of her father's books in the library and read some of it in a basement carrel. It was supposed to be a comedy but it was mainly about boarding school boys in England being cruel to one another. It struck me as the kind of stupid book that Eric would idolize. I didn't care so much at that point, since I'd started sleeping with Matthew Ford, who made Eric look practically middle class.

Senior year, Eric and Lily became a couple. I was fine with it. Matthew and I were a much better fit than Eric and I had ever been. Unlike Eric, Matthew was insecure enough to make up for it by buying me anything I wanted. I told him elaborate stories, how I came from a rich French-Canadian clan but that my father had been disinherited for moving his family to Maine and teaching his daughter only English. Before Christmas break of that year I told Matthew that I needed a thousand dollars to sneak into Montreal and visit my paternal grandmother who was dying. He gave me the money in cash. It was a good relationship, but I didn't harbor any illusions that it would continue past our senior year of college. I assumed that the same would be true of Eric and Lily, especially since she was only a sophomore, but the more I saw them together, the more I realized that they were serious about each other. At least Lily was serious; I could tell that much. I wasn't sure if Eric was capable of love. He was like me in that way, someone who could turn it on and turn it off. He told me once when we were together that he felt he could easily be in equal relationships with two women at the same time. I always remembered that he had said this, and reminded him of it during senior week, when our exams were done and underclassmen were still busy studying.

'You suggesting something?' he asked. We were sitting on the stairwell at St Dun's, sharing a cigarette and listening to the remnants of a party down below. Radiohead was playing, and someone was shouting to change the music.

'I don't know,' I said. 'Everyone thinks you and Lily are serious.'

'What about you and Matthew?'

'Over with as of graduation day.'

'Oh, yeah.'

'Look,' I said, and touched his prickly jaw. 'It's senior week. What do you say?'

We hooked up that night, and continued to hook up the rest of that summer. Eric visited Lily at her parents' place on weekends, and spent the weeks with me. Lily never came to the city, and he told his group of friends that he was visiting his sick father on the weekend. As a joke, I dyed my hair red and told Eric to just pretend that he had only one girlfriend. I loved my weekends alone that summer in New York. I was subletting my own one-bedroom in the Village, so Saturday and Sunday were entirely my own. I imagined Eric and Lily in the country, in love, and it didn't bother me one bit. In fact, it made me laugh.

Eric died that fall in London. He was visiting Lily and forgot to bring his allergy medicine. Dropped dead from eating nuts. I used to wonder what it had been like for Lily. I'd heard he died in her apartment while she watched. I imagined her frantically searching for his EpiPen, trying to keep him alive. I always thought that Lily lucked out. She only knew Eric Washburn as a faithful boyfriend. She never learned the truth about him.

I ran into Lily a few years later. She wasn't on Facebook, but I'd heard rumors about her – that she was some sort of librarian at Winslow College – and something else about her father being involved in a car accident that killed his second wife. I recognized her right away. She hadn't changed at all, pale and waifish, Pippi-Longstocking-color hair in the exact same cut, blank face. I told her I was sorry about what had happened with Eric Washburn, and she stared at me for a moment with a flat, unwavering stare. That was the extent of our interaction. I tried to remember if I'd introduced her to Ted, and I think I probably did but couldn't be sure. I did remember her cold stare, her green, almost translucent eyes. Did she know about Eric and me that summer? And if she knew, then was it a possibility that Eric hadn't accidentally died? I didn't think so, but it unnerved me somehow that she was back in my mind. There were many reasons why Ted might have gone to Winslow on Friday; the chance that it had something to do with Lily was incredibly slim.

I got back to Boston at four in the afternoon. I parked on the street about three blocks from my house, and went to the bar of a boutique hotel, where I drank a vodka on the rocks and ordered a plate of lobster orecchiette. I was starving. When I'd finished the pasta, I returned to my car and called Detective Kimball. He picked up immediately.

'I'm in Boston,' I told him.

246

'Great,' he said. 'Where are you? I can pick you up if you like, take you to the station.'

I told him I was just down the street from our house, parked on the street, not knowing what to do, or where to go. I put a little hitch in my voice as I said it.

'Understandable. If you just wait there I can come get you. Then, if you want, you can make some calls from the station. Maybe there's a friend's house you'd like to stay at, or a hotel . . .'

The detective arrived ten minutes later in a white Mercury Grand Marquis, and drove me to the station. The interior of his car smelled of hand-rolled cigarettes and peppermint. He was wearing jeans and a corduroy jacket. His tie looked vintage, and was frayed a little along one side.

'Thank you so much for coming back to Boston,' he said as he weaved through traffic, one hand on the steering wheel, the other on his knee, index finger tapping to nonexistent music. 'We're feeling very good about this lead. We think we have a detailed description of the man who killed your husband.'

'How?' I asked.

'There was a woman visiting one of your neighbors who was sitting in her car texting. She watched a man exit from the house that was burglarized – the Bennetts at 317, you know them? – and then walk to your house. She said she kept watching him because he seemed shifty and nervous. He passed right under a streetlamp and she got a good look at his facial features. She worked with our sketch artist and we have a pretty good likeness, I think.' The detective glanced toward me. He was smiling a little shyly, as though he wasn't sure how he should act. I watched his eyes scan my face.

'Why do you want me to take a look at the sketch? Do you think I might know him?'

'We think it's a possibility. Our witness said that the suspect rang the doorbell at your house. Your husband came to the door, and talked to the man for a while. In fact, the witness says she stopped watching because it seemed like they might have known each other. Next time she looked up he wasn't there, and she assumed that he'd entered the house.'

'Oh, my God,' I said. 'It was someone Ted knew?'

'It's just a possibility, Mrs Severson. It's possible he was a random burglar who talked his way into your house. That's why we want you to look at the sketch.'

'Are you sure that this man who came to the door was the same man who shot . . . who shot my husband?'

The detective casually spun the wheel of the car and looped his way into a parking space in front of the precinct.

'We think so,' he said, killing the engine. 'The witness said she was sitting in the car some-time around six at night, and that's approximately the time of death that the coroner came up with.

She didn't hear a gunshot, but her car was running and your house has thick walls, or so they tell me.'

I lowered my head and took a deep breath through my nostrils.

'You okay?' the detective asked.

'I've been better. Sorry. I just need a moment . . . let's go in and look at the sketch.'

We were quiet as Detective Kimball escorted me into the station, and had us buzzed past the heavily fortified reception area into a hallway with scuffed linoleum floors and brick walls. I followed the detective to an open-space area that had been carved into cubicles. I moved slowly. It was clear from what I'd heard that Brad had definitely been spotted. I controlled my rage, and thought about what I needed to say to the detective. If the sketch looked remotely like him I would need to say so, otherwise I would look suspicious when they did finally catch up with Brad. What I was desperately hoping for was a sketch that didn't look like him at all, so that I could honestly say that I had no idea who I was looking at.

We reached the detective's desk, in a cubicle framed by temporary partitions. He offered me a molded plastic chair to sit in and he settled onto a swivel chair with a padded seat. His desk was cluttered, but the piles of folders and loose paper seemed organized into distinct towers, each topped by a Post-it note in a different color. He pulled a folder off the top of one of the smaller towers and unfolded it. 'Can you see okay here?' he asked.

We were under a bright fluorescent light built into the low ceiling of polystyrene tiles, and I told him I could see fine. He slid out a piece of paper from the manila folder and twisted it so that I could see the sketch. It was a pretty good likeness of Brad – the thick neck, the black goatee, the dark eyes a little too close together under thick brows. His most distinctive feature – the thick hair and low hairline – was covered up by the baseball cap he wore. I could feel Detective Kimball's eyes on me. I could sense his giddy anticipation.

'I don't know,' I said, and jutted out my lower lip, studying the sketch to give myself another few seconds. But it was too close a likeness for me not to mention it. 'You know who he looks like,' I said. 'He looks like our contractor up in Maine. Brad Daggett. But Brad barely knew Ted, and he doesn't even live in Boston, so . . .' I sat up and looked at the detective. 'I don't know if that's helpful.'

'Brad Daggett?' the detective said. 'Can you spell that for me.' He wrote it down. 'What can you tell me about him?'

'Not much, really. I work with him closely, but I don't know anything about him personally. I really can't imagine any reason that Brad would have for coming down to see Ted, or for actually killing him. It doesn't make any sense.'

'He was your contractor? Is it possible that your husband and he were having some dispute over money?'

'Not without my knowing about it. I was the only one who worked closely with Brad, and I was making most of the money decisions. No. Not a chance.'

'So, had *you* had any disputes with him? Any issues at all?'

'Small stuff here and there, like maybe he bought the wrong ceiling molding, but nothing important. He was totally professional, and he was being paid incredibly well. There's just absolutely no reason I can think of that he would have anything against Ted.'

'Is he married?'

'Who, Brad? I don't think so. He *was* married because I'm pretty sure he has kids, but he's never mentioned a wife.'

'And was he ever inappropriate with you? Did he ever give you the impression that he . . . uh, that he found you attractive.' He stammered a little as he said it, and seemed uncomfortable, and I wondered briefly if his nervous energy was for real, or if it was an act.

'No. He might have, but if he did he never let me know. As I said, he was totally professional.' I looked again at the sketch, impressed by how much it looked like Brad, and pissed that Brad had been stupid enough to get spotted, then added, 'The more I look at it, it still looks like him, but only superficially. It's a man with a goatee, that's all.'

'Okay.' Kimball put his finger on the sketch and

swung it back toward him. 'We'll check him out. Do you have his number?'

I pulled out my phone and gave the detective Brad's number. 'I really don't think . . .' I said.

'No, no, I know. But we'll need to follow up, just to eliminate him from the investigation. My guess is that your husband's murder is exactly what it seems to be. Someone breaking into houses, looking for jewelry and other small items to steal. Maybe the killer had some sort of cover story that enabled him to talk his way into your house. Would you say that Ted was the trusting type? Would he have let a stranger past his door if that stranger had a good story?'

I thought for a moment, telling myself that the real answer was a resounding *no*. 'I could see that,' I said. 'He lived a charmed life and nothing bad had ever happened to him. You'd think that, with all the money he made . . . but he was pretty trusting.'

Detective Kimball leaned back in his swivel chair and nodded at me. I could feel that we were winding down. It made me nervous. I knew that as soon as he was alone, the detective was going to call Brad, and I did not trust that Brad would handle that call well at all, even though we'd been over what he was going to say a hundred times. I thought about trying to call him first to warn him and calm him down, then realized that there would be phone records, that the police would know I called him immediately after identifying him in a sketch.

'You know,' I said, realizing that it was important that I didn't hide any information from the police. 'I actually saw Brad Daggett yesterday morning. I needed to tell him to suspend work on the house. I was on my way up to Maine.'

'Oh.' The detective let the chair tilt forward.

'He was totally normal. A little shocked, I thought, about what happened to Ted.'

'Like I said, we just need to eliminate him. I'm sure he has an alibi. From what you're saying, it doesn't sound like he had anything to do with this. Oh, one other thing, Mrs Severson, the scene-of-the-crime officers are done at your house, which means you're free to go back there. I didn't know if you'd . . .'

'I need to go back,' I said, 'just to pick up some clothes, and then I'll see how I feel about staying there.'

'Okay.' He stood, and so did I. 'I need to stay here at the station,' he said, 'but can I get an officer to give you a ride back to your car, or to your house?'

'No, thanks. I can take a taxi.'

'Well, then, I'll call you a taxi. I can't thank you enough for coming in and looking at our sketch. You've been very helpful, and in my experience, once we get a likeness, an arrest is not far behind. Someone will know this guy.'

I continued to stand for a moment, hesitant to leave, knowing that things might start to unravel fast. My mind reeled, knowing that Brad would be questioned, probably within hours, by the police. I'd coached him, but not enough. And then there were other things, like the fact that Ted, on that last visit to Kennewick, had met up with Brad and gotten drunk with him at that bar at the beach. It was such an odd thing for Ted to do. It made me wonder about what Brad had said the day before – how he was convinced that Ted knew about us. Maybe he did, but how was that possible? And if he did, would he have told anyone? But even if he hadn't known, the fact that Brad and Ted had drinks together would only make the police more suspicious of Brad.

'You okay?' Detective Kimball asked awkwardly, and I realized he'd caught me standing there, lost in thought, for about five seconds. I dropped my shoulders, pretended to suppress a sob, then looked up at him, and let tears run out of my eyes. He quickly glanced around the office, but I stepped into him and he was forced to take me in his arms. I began to sob, pulling him in close to me, burying my head under his chin. I pressed hard enough so that I could feel my breasts flattening out against his chest. 'It's okay, Mrs Severson,' he said, and put a hand around my shoulders, keeping his other one down by his side. I separated from him, apologizing madly, just as Detective James, his partner, a tall, black woman, floated over, and asked me if I needed anything.

'Just a taxi,' I said. 'I'm sorry. So sorry.'

'Don't worry about it. I totally understand.'

Detective James had smoothly taken over the distraught widow and was gently but firmly leading me away from Kimball's desk. I stopped and turned.

'Oh, Detective,' I said. 'Remember what you asked me yesterday, about whether I knew anyone from Winslow?'

He was still standing, his cell phone in one hand. 'Yeah, I remember.'

'I thought of someone. Her name's Lily Kintner. I went to Mather College with her. I'm sure she has nothing to do with why Ted went out there on Friday, but . . .'

'Did they know one another? Were you close with her?'

'No. We weren't. She stole my boyfriend in college, actually, so I'm not a huge fan . . . but Ted and she didn't know . . . well, they might've met a couple of times, if I think about it. I ran into Lily in Boston a couple of years ago.'

'How do you spell her name?'

I told him. There was obviously no connection between Ted and Lily, but I figured it couldn't hurt to give the police another lead to track down. It might delay what now seemed inevitable – that Brad was going to get caught, and that he'd most likely give me up as well.

I told Detective James that I was okay, that I'd just like to leave. 'You sure I can't get you a drink of water before you go?' she asked in her husky voice, looking down at me. I figured she was close to six feet tall. She must have been a little bit self-conscious about it, because every time I'd seen her she was wearing flats. Dark pantsuit, collared shirt, and flats. And she never wore jewelry. She made me nervous in a way that Detective Kimball didn't. It wasn't that I thought she suspected me; it was that I truly had no idea what she was thinking. She looked at me the way she might look at a tollbooth collector.

'Can I walk you out, Mrs Severson?'

'No. I'm fine. And it's Miranda.'

She nodded at me and turned away. I was pretty sure she didn't wear any makeup either.

Detective Kimball must have made a call because when I got to the front of the station a taxi was waiting. It was already dusk, rain beginning. It felt as though the bad weather had followed me all the way down from my mother's house.

CHAPTER 22

LILY

I checked out of the Kennewick Inn very early on Tuesday morning, figuring I could drive directly to Winslow College. It didn't make sense to miss another day of work and draw attention to myself. I'd drunk two cups of coffee at the inn, but stopped in Kittery at a Dunkin' Donuts for another coffee to go. I was exhausted. Brad and I had talked for several hours the night before, first in his truck, then in the rental cottage that he lived in. Despite what he'd done to Ted, I felt a little bad for Brad. He was a wreck, and once he realized that I wasn't going to turn him in, he latched onto me like a drowning man coming across a lifeboat. He told me he would set up the meeting with Miranda for that night at 10:00 p.m. If she agreed, he would call me at my house from the public phone at Cooley's. He would only let the phone ring twice, but the number would appear on the digital readout on my landline.

I made it into my office before anyone else arrived. After logging in to my work e-mail account, I wasn't surprised to learn that my boss, Otto, had left early on Monday, the previous afternoon, having felt a cough coming on himself, and that he thought he'd take Tuesday off as well. Otto Lemke was easily the most suggestible man alive, especially when it came to any kind of ailment. Just letting him know on Sunday that I wasn't feeling well had probably sent him into a spiral of psycho-somatic illness. I spent the morning writing short descriptions of our archived collections to go on our internal site for students and faculty. When I'd done enough to justify a morning's worth of work, I walked across campus to the student-run café where I got most of my lunches. The rainstorm from the previous day had left the world looking bright and washed, like a car emerging from a car wash. The cloudless sky was a deep metallic blue. The air was crisp and smelled of apples. At the café I got curried tuna salad on wheat, and took my sandwich out to one of the stone benches with a view of the line of oak trees, bright red and bristling in the high breeze, that split Winslow's main quad. My life was good, and I wondered briefly why I'd gotten involved in the sordid affairs of Miranda and Ted and Brad. What I was plan-ning on doing in Kennewick tomorrow night was a huge risk. It was dependent on Brad, who was so fragile you could almost see the cracks in him, and it was also dependent on Miranda's not becoming suspicious when Brad suggested the meeting. I felt exposed, and less than 100 percent confident, but knew that I had gone this far, and would go to the end. Ted deserved to be avenged, and Miranda deserved to be punished, now more than ever.

That afternoon I had scheduled an off-site visit to a former student, now in her eighties, who was offering to donate items from her school years to the archives. These visits were often the best part of my job, and sometimes the worst. It all depended on the lucidity and expectations of the former student or professor. Sometimes all they had were a few battered textbooks and some class notes; these were often lonely people looking for someone to talk with for a while, someone who would have to listen to long tales from their college days. Sometimes, however, these former students would turn out to have treasure troves of archival materials. These were the girls who kept every-thing. The printed menus from the Midwinter Formal of 1935. Photographs from the March blizzard of 1960, when the drifts of snow were seven feet high. A handwritten poem from when May Gylys was the visiting writer. I never knew what to expect with these visits, and I only sched-uled them when the person was within close driving distance. Otherwise, we would ask the donors to mail us their materials.

I nearly canceled that afternoon's visit. I was still tired from lack of sleep, and was not sure that I had it in me to accompany some stranger down her own personal memory lane. But I told myself that I should keep my schedule as normal as possible, so I went, driving several towns west to Greenfield, where Prudence Walker, class of 1958, lived. She was raking leaves when I arrived and had filled several bags, all of which had already been placed on her curb for pickup. Her house was a neat, orderly Cape Cod in a neighborhood of Colonials and deck houses. I pulled into her driveway behind a new-model Camry, and Prudence Walker put down her rake and came over to greet me.

'Hello, there. Thank you so much for coming out. You've done an old lady a huge favor.' She was wearing a faded denim skirt and a green windbreaker. Her gray hair was pulled back in a bun.

'It's not a problem,' I said, getting out of my car.

'It's all boxed up, and right there on the front step. I'd carry it over to you, but it took all I had to get it from the attic to where it's sitting. Apparently, back then, I decided I needed to keep *everything*. Most of it's my scrapbooks, but I included all my notes from class, and syllabi, and there's a bunch of exam papers, as well. You said you wanted those, didn't you?'

'I'll take it all. Thank you, again, for this.'

I walked over to the front step, and picked up the heavy box. Prudence Walker came with me, walking with an uneven gait that dipped her right shoulder down every time she took a step with her right leg.

'I hate to make you drive all the way out here,

then send you off just like that, but I'm trying to get all these leaves raked up before we lose the sun. Can I get you a glass of water, or anything?'

'No, thanks,' I said, loading the box into my trunk.

As I backed out of the driveway, I watched her walk unsteadily back to the rake she had left leaning against a maple tree. I felt a surge of love for this woman, so willing to discard her old life, to not look back, but really I was just grateful that I didn't need to sit for an entire afternoon going through scrapbooks.

I dropped the box back at Winslow, answered a few more e-mails, then drove to my house, a cottage-style two-bedroom built in 1915. It overlooked a picturesque pond, lousy for swimming (it bred mosquitoes all summer), but decent for ice-skating in the cold winter months. I checked my phone, and there was no call yet from Cooley's. My doctor's office had called to remind me of an appointment, and my mother had called but had not left a message. It wasn't yet five o'clock, and I thought I'd try to take a short nap before making dinner. I lay down on the couch in my living room, and just as I was falling into a light sleep, the doorbell chimed and I jerked upright, confused for a second about where I was. I ran my fingers through my hair, stood, and walked to the foyer. I peered through the leaded glass that ran along the side of the front door. A slightly shaggy-looking man in his thirties stood there, scratching at the back of his neck. I partially opened the door, keeping the chain on.

'Can I help you?' I said.

'Are you Lily Kintner?' said the man, pulling his wallet out of his herringbone tweed jacket. Before I had a chance to answer, he flipped the wallet open to show a Boston PD Detective badge. 'I'm Detective Kimball. Do you mind if I have a quick word?'

I unchained the door and swung it open. He scraped his feet on my welcome mat and stepped inside the house. 'I like this house,' he said, glancing around.

'Thank you. What can I help you with? You've got me curious.' I took a few slow steps into the living room and he followed me.

'Well, your name has come up in an investigation, and I have a few questions. Do you have a moment?'

I offered him the red leather club chair and he perched on its edge. I sat down on the couch. I was scared to hear what he was about to say, but also anxious to hear it.

'What can you tell me about Ted Severson?'

'That man who was killed in Boston over the weekend?'

'Uh-huh.'

'I can tell you what I read in the newspaper, but that's about all. I do have a vague connection with him, but I don't know him. He was married to someone I went to school with.'

262

'You went to school with Miranda Severson?' The detective pulled a notebook from his coat and flipped it open. He pulled a small nub of a pencil from its spiral binding.

'Yes, Mather College. She was Miranda Hobart then. Faith Hobart actually.'

'She went by a different name?'

'Faith is her middle name, I think. That's what she went by in college.'

'Have you kept up with her? How did you know that Ted Severson and she were married?' He sat up a little, pushing back fractionally into the chair. His hair was a little long, especially for a police detective. He had round brown eyes under thick eyebrows, an imposing nose, and a mouth that could belong to a girl, with a plump lower lip.

'We met in Boston a few years ago, just by accident.'

'Was she with her husband then?'

'You know, I was wondering that myself after I read the story. She was with a man, I think, and she introduced us but I don't remember much about him. I couldn't believe it when I read about what happened in Boston. Detective . . . is it Kimball? . . . I was going to make coffee. Should I make enough for two?' I stood, aware that I was potentially acting suspicious, but I needed time to think.

'Um, sure. If you're going to make it for yourself.'

'Unless you think we can wrap this up right away.

I'm actually pretty curious as to why you're here,' I said as I walked toward the kitchen.

'No. Make coffee, and I'd love some.'

Once in the kitchen, I took a deep breath, put the water on to boil, and put ground coffee at the bottom of my French coffee press. I needed to think clearly. Something had happened to connect me with Ted Severson and I had to be extremely careful to not get caught in a lie, not to contradict myself. They had found something out, but I didn't know how much. When the water had started to boil I poured it over the coffee, inserted the plunger. I put the coffee on a tray with two mugs, a carton of milk, and a bowl of sugar cubes, and brought it back into the living room. I was startled to see the detective standing, peering closely at the bindings in my living room's built-in bookshelf.

'Sorry,' he said, sitting back down on the lip of the chair. 'You have some interesting books. I hope you don't mind my asking . . . you're David Kintner's daughter, right?'

I placed the tray on the coffee table and sat down on the couch. 'Uh, yes. Do you know him? And please just help yourself to coffee.'

'I do know him. I've read several of his books, and I saw him read once. In Durham, New Hampshire.'

'Oh yeah?'

'He was quite the showman.'

'So I've heard. I've never seen him read before.'

'Really? I'm surprised.'

'Don't be. He's my father, and what he does for work is not exactly fascinating to me. At least it wasn't when I was younger.'

I watched the detective assemble his coffee, adding milk but no sugar. He had beautiful hands with long slender fingers. I was suddenly struck with how similar he looked to Eric Washburn. Thin and masculine, but with almost girlish facial features. Rosebud mouth. Thick eyelashes. He took a sip of his coffee, put the mug back on the coffee table, and said, 'You know, you weren't easy to find out here. Are you still a Kintner or did you officially change your name to Lily Hayward?'

'No, I'm still Kintner, legally. People here know me as Lily Hayward. Hayward was my father's mother's maiden name. Don't read too much into it. It's just that – working at a college – people are familiar with my father and all his baggage, and when I got the job here, I decided to go by another name.'

'Understandable.'

'So you know what's happening with my father?'

'The accident in England.'

'Right.'

'Yes, I heard about it. I'm sorry. I really am a big fan of your father's. I've read *all* his books, actually. I think I remember that he dedicated his last one to you.'

'He did. Too bad it wasn't a better book.'

The detective smiled. 'It wasn't so bad. I think the reviews were a little harsh.' He took another sip of his coffee, was quiet for a moment.

'So,' I said. 'Back to Ted Severson. I'm still confused why you're here.'

'Well, it could all be a coincidence, of course, but Ted Severson came here to Winslow on the day he was killed. We know that because he got a parking ticket. He wasn't coming to see you, by any chance?'

A flash of anger at Ted's stupidity went through me, followed by a touch of sadness. He had come looking for me. He had come to my town. I shook my head. 'Like I said, I don't know him, and he doesn't know me. We might have met once or twice . . .'

'You were in England in September, right?'

'I was. I went over to see my father after he got out of prison. In fact, he's going to be moving back to America, and I was there to help him with some of the logistics.'

'Do you remember the flight you took back?'

'I can look it up for you if you'd like.'

'That's okay. I know the flight. It was the same one that Ted Severson was on after a business trip he took to the U.K. Do you remember seeing him on that flight?'

I was prepared for this. So they knew that Ted and I were on a flight together. It was still highly doubtful they knew that Ted and I met later at the Concord River Inn. Did they know I traveled to

Kennewick the day before? Probably not, but it wouldn't be hard to find out.

'Do you have a picture of him?' I asked

'I don't with me, but if you have Internet . . .'

'Right. I'll double-check it, but I did talk with a man on that flight, and now that I think of it, it was probably Ted Severson. We met, actually, in the airport bar at Heathrow. I remember thinking when we met that he seemed to know me. The way he said hello. But then we introduced ourselves and talked for a while. He didn't really look familiar to me.'

'You didn't exchange names?'

'We did, but I didn't really catch his. Or if I did, I didn't remember it.'

'But you gave him your name?'

'I did. And I told him that I worked here in Winslow.'

'So if he wanted to he could have looked you up, come out here to try and find you?'

'In theory,' I said. 'Though if he'd really wanted to get in touch with me, I don't know why he wouldn't have tried to call me.'

'You gave him your number?'

'I didn't, actually.'

'So it's possible he tried to find your number and couldn't, then drove out here.'

'Sure, I guess it is. It just doesn't seem likely. We had a nice conversation but it wasn't flirtatious, and he's a married man, and . . .'

The detective smiled and shrugged. 'You might

have just missed it. We see it all the time. Some guy meets some woman, and the woman thinks nothing of it, and the next thing she knows, he's stalking her. And vice versa, as well, but that's not as common.'

'You think I was being stalked?'

'I have no idea. We were just curious as to why he drove out here on the day he was killed. It's a suspicious death, so we look at anything that happened recently that seems out of the ordinary. But if he drove out here in the hopes of running into you, then I can't imagine it had anything to do with his death.'

'No. I can't imagine.'

'Do you mind my asking if you're in a relation-ship, Miss Kintner?'

'No, I don't mind. And no, I'm not seeing anyone. And you can call me Lily.'

'Just checking, Lily. No jealous ex-boyfriends in your life?'

'Not that I know of.'

The detective looked at his spiral-bound note-book and was quiet for a moment. I had relaxed. As far as I could figure, I had covered myself as best as I could. I couldn't deny having met Ted on the plane. There were witnesses. But there was no reason for me to admit anything else. If the police figured out that I had stayed for two nights in Kennewick immediately after the murder, I would just have to claim it was coincidence. It might look strange, but what could happen to me?

It's not as though I had actually been involved in the Friday night murder.

'Sorry, Lily, but I need to ask this. Can you tell me where you were on Friday evening?'

'I was here. I was alone. I cooked dinner for myself, then watched a movie.'

'Anyone stop by? Anyone call?'

'Sorry, no. I don't think so.'

'That's okay.' He finished his coffee and stood. 'Is it possible to look at a picture of Ted Severson online so you can give a proper identification?' he asked.

'Of course,' I said, and got my laptop. Together, we found a picture that accompanied a news article on Ted's slaying, and I said, that, yes, I was pretty sure that it was the same man I'd talked with on the plane.

'It's so strange,' I said. 'I read the article and realized that I kind of knew this man, or at least I definitely knew his wife, and it turns out I'd met him recently, spoken with him.'

At the door, Detective Kimball reached into his jacket pocket, then said, 'Oh, one more thing. I nearly forgot.' He pulled out a single key, still shiny. 'Do you mind if I check and see if this key opens your door.'

I laughed. 'So dramatic. You think this man had a key to my house?'

'No, I don't, but we found it hidden among his things, and I need to check every possibility. I'm just eliminating your house is all.'

'No, please check. I understand.' It must have been the key that Ted had stolen from Brad's house, probably a master for all the rental cottages. If Brad became a suspect, it would only be a matter of time until they discovered that the key belonged to him.

I watched the detective insert the key into my front door lock. It slid in easily and for one confused and terrifying moment I thought the key might turn my lock, that maybe Ted really did have a key to my house for some reason. But it didn't. The detective jiggled it a couple of times, then pulled it out. 'Nope,' he said. 'I had to check, though. You've been very helpful. If you think of anything else . . .' He held out a card and I took it. Glancing down, I saw that his first name was Henry. I stood in the door and watched him drive away. It was almost dark, the sky crisscrossed with orange clouds. Behind me the phone rang twice and then stopped. I walked toward it, but I knew what the handset would tell me. I picked it up, the words missed call and the number on the digital readout. The area code was 207. I would double-check the number against the number of Cooley's pay phone that I'd jotted down on the back of the napkin, but I was pretty sure they would be the same. The phone call meant that Brad had set up the meeting with Miranda for later that night. It was all going as planned. The visit from the detective had made me a little nervous, but as he'd said, he was simply eliminating me from the investigation.

I opened the fridge and peered inside, deciding what to make for dinner.

CHAPTER 23

MIRANDA

Back when Brad and I had been planning Ted's murder, I had briefly considered getting a pair of untraceable temporary cell phones. Just in case. I had stupidly discarded that idea, not wanting any physical evidence that pointed to our guilt. Right now, I desperately wished we had them. I was pacing the house in the South End, going out of my fucking mind, wondering if I should just call Brad, warn him that he was going to be questioned. I didn't even know if it would help. Maybe he would panic more if he knew they were coming. And part of me wondered if I should tell Brad that he was recognized by a witness, and that he should pack his truck and leave town, go on the run.

Scenarios unfolded in my mind.

According to your cell phone records, Mrs Severson, after you identified Brad Daggett as the man who had been spotted entering your house, you called the same Mr Daggett that evening. And now we can't find him. What exactly did you talk about during that ten-minute conversation?

I'd tell them that I'd called Brad to let him know

that the police might question him, that I'd identi-fied a suspect as possibly looking like him. I told him not to worry, that no one really thought he was involved. I had no idea, Detective. I mean, why would I?

You'll be glad to hear, Mrs Severson, that we caught Brad Daggett this morning. He didn't get far, actually. They got him at the Canadian border. He's confessed to murdering your husband, and he has quite the story to go with it. Would you mind coming into the station for questioning?

No, Brad running was not an option. He needed to hold his nerve, long enough for the investiga-tion to become cold. I had plans for Brad eventually, but those plans needed to wait.

I stood in front of the wide window in the second-floor living room. It was dark outside, the rain steady, almost comforting. Across the street were the lighted rooms of my neighbors' brownstones. I saw a figure move across one of them, a curtain being pulled.

I stood at the window for a while. I had yet to turn on any lights in my home, and I felt invisible, looking out at my corner of the city. A car moved slowly down the street, hitting a pothole and sending a cresting spray of rain onto the sidewalk. Would the police be watching me yet? Was I a suspect? It was Monday. The murder had happened on Friday and no one had been arrested yet. They must be getting nervous, and I knew that, on one level, I would have to be a suspect. I was the wife of a rich man who had died a suspicious death. But was it more than that? I pulled the curtains across the window, making sure that they met in the middle, then snapped on a lamp. It sent a circle of pale light into the room. I blinked rapidly, then shut the lamp off. I lay down on the couch in the dark, wondering if it had been a mistake to return to my house. Maybe I'd have been better off in a hotel room, like that baby-faced detective had suggested.

I kept imagining Brad at the moment when a detective approached him with questions about where he had been on Friday night. I pictured him sweaty and stammering, the detective instantly suspicious. I knew that the wheels would come off fast. I'd misjudged Brad. When we'd first met, all I saw was a cocky, slightly stupid contractor. Seducing him had been way too easy. I'd waited until we were alone in the house. I bummed a cigarette, telling Brad not to tell my husband. 'Hey,' he'd said. 'I won't tell your husband anything you don't want me to tell him.' It was early August and I was wearing a short dress that buttoned up the front. I pulled it over the top of my head, shucked my underpants, and slid on top of the finished kitchen counter. The height had been all wrong, and Brad had to slide a box of tiles over and stand on them. It was awkward and unsatisfying, but afterward I lied and told Brad, tears in my eyes, that it was the first time I'd had sex since the week after my wedding, that my husband had no interest in me that way. We got dressed, and I cried for a while, and then we got undressed again, and had sex with Brad sitting on one of the folding chairs the crew had brought in for their lunch breaks. I straddled him, facing forward, my leg muscles shaking. The look on Brad's face, his eyes raking over me, told me all I needed to know. 'Never anywhere else,' I said that afternoon. 'Only here, and only when we absolutely know that no one will be showing up. Okay?'

'Okay,' he said.

'You tell anyone about this . . .'

'I won't.'

A week later I told him that sometimes I dreamed about killing my husband. Two weeks later Brad told me he'd do it for me if I wanted. It was that easy. I told him if we did it right, and made no mistakes, that no one would ever suspect either of us, and we'd be able to marry, buy a yacht, take a yearlong honeymoon. When I'd mentioned the yacht, Brad's eyes had lit up in a way I'd never seen, even when we were having sex. Sex had hooked him, but greed would keep him, and I had thought all along that he would hold his nerve, but now I wasn't so sure.

I got off the couch, shook my arms out, bounced up and down a couple of times on the balls of my feet. My skin was crawling, my mind racing. I poured myself some Ketel One on ice, and wandered through the dark house. There was a stain on the second-floor landing where Ted had bled out. The police had told me about it so I wouldn't be shocked. I touched it with my bare toe, a dark brown pool that almost matched the stain of the wooden floor. The cleaning service was coming tomorrow and I would make sure to tell them about it. I brought my drink into the media room and flipped through channels for a while, settling on *Pretty Woman,* my favorite film from when I was a young girl. It had been on television all the time then, as well, and I'd loved it, years before I even understood what a prostitute was. It seemed stupid now, but I watched anyway, saying the lines to myself before they said them on TV. I calmed down, and when the film was over, and my drink finished, I knew that I needed to drive back to Maine and talk with Brad. He needed to be prepared for what was coming, and I felt that if I had a little time with him it could make a difference.

My car was on the street instead of in the garage. I dressed in jeans and a dark green sweatshirt with a hood, and left the house. Walking to my car through the rain, I resisted the urge to look around, to see if somehow I was being watched. I didn't think I was. My car was parked at the corner of my street. I got in, pulled straight out of the spot, and drove toward I-93. The roads were quiet, and it didn't seem as though anyone was behind me, any lights suddenly appearing. I merged onto the highway, still feeling sure that I wasn't being followed. I settled into a middle lane, slid a CD into the player, and tried to relax. The rain-shiny highway unspooled in front of me. It was late by the time I reached Crescent Cottages, the steady rain now a drizzle. Brad's truck was not in front of his unit. I assumed he was at Cooley's but I'd wait him out. It meant he'd be hammered when I finally got a chance to talk with him, but I hoped he wouldn't be so far gone that nothing would sink in. My plan was to prep him for being questioned, make sure he knew what he was going to say, then drive back to Boston before daylight.

I parked my car across the road, under an oak tree, its branches lowered by the rain, and waited. I didn't have to wait long. Brad's truck slid into his spot in front of his unit about 11:00 p.m. I'd cracked my window, but even so, the inside of the Mini had steamed up while I waited, and Brad's truck was a blur. I rolled my window all the way down and watched as another car, a boxy Honda maybe, slid in next to Brad. Fuck, I thought, probably Polly. I watched as first Brad, then a tall, slender woman, got out of their respective cars. Brad held the door open, and the woman entered his cottage first. She wore some kind of slick, reflective jacket and tight jeans. Way too thin to be Polly, and way too steady on her feet. Brad followed. Something about the way they entered the house made me think this wasn't a typical pickup. They'd moved like businessmen entering a meeting room. I waited five minutes, then pulled my hood up over my head and got out of my car. I thought it was still raining but it was just the oak tree, rain dropping from its few remaining leaves.

I crossed the road and approached Brad's cottage – I'd never been inside, but I'd stood in the doorway once, months ago, delivering blueprints, back before Brad and I had become involved. I remembered noticing how neat it was, and how sterile. I crept toward a window that was to the left of the front door. There were slatted blinds, but the way the interior light was coming through made me think I could see through them. I wanted to see if I recognized the woman. I was almost at the window when a light mounted above the door turned on, harsh white light flooding the front of the house. I moved fast around toward the side, my sneakers crunching on the crushed-shell driveway. I pressed my back against the wooden siding where the shadows were the darkest, and waited for the exterior light to extinguish itself. It did, after a very long minute. I heard no one stirring inside the house, and the road remained quiet. There was one window on the side of the house, just low enough that I could look through it while standing on tiptoe. The blinds were closed but there was a little space between them, and I could see through into a kitchen – a white refrigerator, an empty countertop – and, beyond that, into the living area, where Brad and a woman with red hair sat talking on the couch. In front of them, on the coffee table, sat two bottles of beer. For one brief moment, I thought it was Lily Kintner from Mather, and a shiver went through me, but the woman moved her head a little and I decided it wasn't Lily. She wore cheap makeup: dark eyeliner and bright lipstick, and unless Lily had changed, she was not the type to wear makeup at all.

I watched for a while, Brad and this woman talking intently, and I couldn't for the life of me figure out what they must be talking about. Brad seemed beaten down, his shoulders slumped, his mouth hanging open. The woman, whoever she was, was doing most of the talking. Brad looked like a dumb student trying to follow what his teacher was saying. This was not what I had expected to see at all. I expected to see Brad and some slut from Cooley's writhing around his couch. I wouldn't have liked it much, but I would have preferred it to what I was seeing now. What could they possibly be talking about?

Brad nodded, several times in a row, like a puppet having a string pulled, then he fumbled around in his jacket pocket, pulling out his cigarettes. The woman stood, stretched, her shirt lifting to reveal a sliver of pale stomach, then walked toward the kitchen. It took all my will but I kept looking through the slats, praying she wouldn't glance in my direction. I wanted to get a better look at her. She swung open the door of the refrigerator, bent at the waist to peer inside, and I was able to stare at her profile. She really did look a lot like Lily

Kintner – the same gamine body, pale complexion, red hair. But the clothes were wrong.

The woman pulled a water bottle from the fridge, uncapped it. Before she went back to the living room, she swung her head, her eyes scanning the spotless countertops of the kitchen. I got a better look at her, the kitchen's overhead fluorescent reflecting off her eyes, an unworldly green that seemed to glow for a moment. I dropped down off the tips of my toes. It *was* Lily Kintner. I'd seen her eyes and now I was sure. Without hesitation, I quickly walked back to my car, swinging wide of the front of the house so I wouldn't activate the motion-sensor light again. I slid back into my Mini. It was Lily. I was sure of it. But how was that possible? How had she possibly become involved with Brad? And it wasn't just Brad, obviously. Ted's trip to Winslow had clearly been to see her. So she must have been involved with Ted. Were they having an affair? Had she initiated it, after some long gestating need for revenge? But, more importantly, at this moment, how had she found Brad, and what did she want from him?

I slid farther down in my seat to wait. My mind reeled. The rain had stopped but the sky was still blanketed by clouds, and I felt protected in the black shadow of the tree I was under. I watched Brad's cottage, wondering if Lily would spend the night there, but knowing I needed to wait it out in case she didn't. My mind was filled with a swarm of possibilities, but in all of them, I was being hunted. Somehow, Lily was hunting me.

It felt like two hours but it was probably only one when Brad's front door opened and Lily emerged. The outside light flicked on and I watched her get into her car. She backed out of the driveway and turned south on Micmac Road. Part of me wanted to follow her, to see where she went, but it was more important that I talk with Brad and find out what was possibly going on. I forced myself to wait for five minutes, just in case Lily realized she'd forgotten something and turned around, then I bolted across the road and rapped on Brad's door. He cracked the door and looked out at me, his puffy eyes confused for a moment. I pulled the hood off my head. 'It's me, Brad. Let me in.'

'Shit,' he said and opened the door for me. I took a step inside and pushed the door closed behind me. I could smell cheap perfume.

'What the fuck was Lily Kintner doing at your house?' I said.

'Is that her name?'

'Jesus, Brad, what did she want?'

'I just met her tonight. She was at Cooley's. She came up to me in the parking lot.' His eyes were shifting, as though he were trying to figure out exactly what to say to me. I resisted the urge to punch him as hard as I could in the throat.

'Brad, what the fuck did she want from you?'

He slumped a little, looking like a dog that had

just been swatted in the nose, and said, 'She wants to kill you, Miranda. She wants me to set it up. She told me it's the only way I won't end up in prison. I was going to tell you, I promise.'

CHAPTER 24

LILY

I arrived in Kennewick at 8:00 p.m. on Tuesday, twenty-four hours after making the plan with Brad. Without traffic, the drive from Massachusetts was just over an hour. I parked my car at the Admiral's Inn, a brand-new resort hotel shoehorned onto a bluff on the other side of the beach in Kennewick Harbor. The parking lot wasn't full, but it wasn't empty either. I had circled and parked so that I was facing the short sliver of beach, and beyond it, the soft lights of the Kennewick Inn. I sat in my car for a moment. It was a cloudless night, the black sky pocked with yellow stars. A three-quarters moon reflected on the ocean. I had brought a small penlight so I could navigate along the cliff walk to Ted and Miranda's house, but I didn't think I'd need it.

Earlier, after making myself a simple cheese omelet for dinner, I'd called my boss at his home, and told him that I still had a sore throat, and that it might be getting worse.

'Don't come in tomorrow. Stay home. Get better,' he said, rising panic in his voice.

'Well, I'll definitely stay home tomorrow.'

'Yes, you should. Take the week if you need it.'

After the call, I went over the details of my plan. It was risky. It all hinged on whether Brad was able to set it up the way I'd asked him to, and I hated relying on someone else. I'd never done that before, and I wouldn't have done it this time except that I needed to act fast. The detective I'd met the day before – Henry Kimball – was probably closing in on Brad and Miranda, or maybe just Brad, fast, and I wanted to get there first.

I sat for a moment in the car. I was in my darkest clothes – black jeans and a black turtleneck sweater that I wore over several layers, since the temperature was supposed to dip into the 30s. I wore my hiking shoes with the good soles, and a dark green winter hat in wool, pompom cut off, my braided hair tucked under it. I had a small gray backpack designed for day hikes, and I filled it with a pair of gloves, my stun gun, the penlight, a thermos with hot coffee, a flask filled with apricot brandy, the fish fillet knife with the leather sheaf, a Leatherman multi-tool, and a handful of plastic bags.

When I stepped out of the car, it was colder than I thought it would be, a steady brisk breeze coming off the ocean, and I wished that I had brought a windbreaker. I put the penlight in my back jeans pocket, pulled the backpack over both shoulders, locked the car behind me, and walked down off the bluff toward the start of the cliff walk. I walked as casually as possible in case I was being watched, imagining myself as the type of person who always strolled along the shore on moonlit nights. As far as I could tell, there was no one to see me, however, and I reached the cliff walk unobserved.

I had plenty of time, and walked slowly, only turning on the penlight once, when the footpath passed below an alcove of twisted trees. As stunning as the walk had been two days earlier on that blustery afternoon, it was more beautiful now – the vistas of the ocean were silver beneath the high white moon. I felt as though I'd stepped into a black-and-white movie from the 1930s, the ocean and the sky some fantasy projection of a perfect glittering evening, romantic and moody at the same time. I kept moving, all my senses prickling, as though I were a small animal that had emerged from its burrow into a giant world. Something rustled in a bayberry bush, and I paused, waiting to see if it was another animal like me, or just the pulsing wind from the ocean. I heard nothing else and kept moving. When I reached the end of the path, I crouched and looked at the looming house. In moonlight, it looked finished, its three-gabled roof outlined against the sky. The stretch of land between the ocean and the back of the house, which in daylight looked like chewed-up dirt, was transformed by moonlight, resembling the sloping magisterial lawn it was destined to become. I looked behind me at the sky; a scrap of cloud was moving quickly, about to pass in front of the moon. I watched it progress, and when it blanked out the moon, and the world turned temporarily darker, I took a deep breath and crossed the property toward the house, making sure to skirt the half-dug hole where the swimming pool was supposed to go. I took the two wide steps up to the finished patio, crouched again, and removed the backpack from my back and unzipped it. I took out the stun gun and the knife, my pair of leather gloves, and two plastic bags, then rezipped the backpack and stood back up, putting the knife in one front jeans pocket and the stun gun in the other. I pulled the plastic bags on over my hiking shoes, tucking the ends down into my wool socks, then put on my gloves and tested the sliding glass doors that Brad said would be unlocked. They were, and I entered the pitch-black house.

I pulled the doors closed behind me and just stood for a moment, listening intently, and letting my eyes adjust to the blackness. It took a while, but they eventually did, the interior of the house becoming gray and fuzzy. I could make out the finished floors, piled here and there with stacked tiles, or large unopened boxes of Sheetrock. I moved forward into the foyer toward the front of the house, the plastic bags whispering along the floor. Something batted at my head and I jerked involuntarily, looking up at a pair of dangling wires where a light fixture would go.

I walked toward the south-facing kitchen, its

wide windows helping me to navigate, hoping that one of the windows would look out onto the front driveway. There wasn't one, so I turned back, moving in what felt like slow motion through the grainy light. The air in the house was as cold as it was outside, and smelled of sawdust and glue. I found the front door, twice the height of any normal human, and peered through one of its side windows. All I could see was the large Dumpster, something fluttering from its edge in the breeze, but no car yet. The window stretched from the floor to the ceiling, so I sat cross-legged and waited. I was an hour early.

I told myself several times during that hour that I could simply get up and leave, retrace my steps along the cliff walk, get back into my car and drive back home to Winslow. I had done nothing illegal yet, done nothing that would implicate me in any crime. I was untouchable. But I also told myself that if I did that, if I got up and walked away, I would be living in a world in which Miranda Hobart was allowed to get away with murder. Ted was dead. Eric Washburn was dead. And both might still be alive if it hadn't been for Miranda.

I heard Brad's truck before I saw it. He'd turned his headlights off, but the large pickup was crunching along the gravel driveway. He parked between the Dumpster and the house. It was still bright outside under the cloudless sky, and I could see Brad in the driver's seat and Miranda on the passenger side. They were a little early by my watch, and Miranda stayed in the truck for about a minute. I wondered what they were talking about. When she opened the door the truck's interior light popped on, and I watched Brad, an unlit cigarette in his lips, quickly put his hand over the light while Miranda swung down out of the truck onto the driveway. She walked toward the house, in that hip-swinging way I remembered, her hair tucked under what looked like a newsboy cap. As she neared the door, I stood and took a step backward into the deeper darkness of the house. My heart thudded a little faster in my chest, but I also felt an electric charge running over my skin.

I listened to a key being inserted, the lock snapping open. The door swung inward, Miranda taking a half step into the house, then pausing. The wind outside had picked up. I knew that she was letting her eyes adjust to the darkness as I had and that, for the moment, she couldn't see me. Her face was gray in the light, her eyes opened wide in an attempt to see, and her lips slightly parted. I looked at her hand on the doorknob. She also wore gloves.

'In here,' I said.

She turned, and I turned on the penlight, pointing its beam at the floor so she could see where I was standing. As soon as she located me I flicked it off.

'Lily?' she said.

'Come in. Your eyes will adjust.'

She shut the door behind her. 'Isn't this dramatic?' she said, and Faith the college girl came flooding back to me. Sarcastic, slightly loaded, talking to me in the dim lights of some St Dun's party, a drink in one hand and a cigarette in the other.

'Did Brad tell you what I wanted?' I asked.

She took a step forward. She wore a three-quarter-length coat, and her right hand was in its large pocket. I instinctively touched the stun gun, which was in my front pocket, its end protruding.

'He did,' Miranda said, stopping about a yard in front of me. I wanted to move backward a little bit, but I didn't want her to hear the rustle of the plastic bags on my feet. 'I was surprised.'

'Surprised by what?'

'Well, surprised by everything. Surprised you're here. Surprised you knew Ted. But mostly surprised that you want money from me. It just doesn't seem like you. Does it have something to do with your father?'

'What do you mean?' I said.

'He killed someone, right? In England. He must have legal fees.'

'No, the money is for me.'

'Fine. It doesn't matter to me,' she said. 'You know that I can't get you money right away. The estate has to be settled. These things take a lot of time.'

'I know. I just wanted to meet here tonight so I could hear from you directly. After this, things can go through Brad.'

'Can I ask you? Were you sleeping with Ted? How did that happen? How did you two even meet?'

'We were on a flight together. He knew everything about you, you know? He knew you were cheating on him with Brad. You didn't fool him.' In the fuzzy light I watched Miranda shrug. She was close enough so that I could smell her. Tobacco. Expensive lotion.

'So why didn't you just turn me in,' Miranda said, 'if you're so sure I'm this awful person?'

'I will turn you in, Faith, if you don't do everything I say.'

'Is this really about Eric?' she asked. I heard a door rattle somewhere in the house, the wind outside picking up.

'No,' I said. 'It isn't. This is all about you.'

Miranda turned first. Brad had emerged from the darkness to stand between us, a long heavy-looking wrench in his right hand. He must have come in through the patio doors, and had moved so quietly in the house that I wondered briefly if he'd taken his shoes off. His face in the half light was twisted, his jaw working back and forth, as though something was stuck in his throat. He was looking at me. I watched him lift the heavy wrench above his head and start to bring it down.

CHAPTER 25

MIRANDA

It took two hours, and a pot of coffee laced with whiskey, but Brad had told me everything. He told me how he'd spotted the sheriff's car in front of his place early in the evening. He'd panicked, driving straight by his cottages, then heading out to his dad's fishing cabin in Lebanon. He'd nearly decided to stay the night there, but then began to think that it would look strange, like something a guilty man would do. He'd driven back to Kennewick, going straight to Cooley's instead of going home, and that's where he'd found Lily Kintner waiting for him in Cooley's parking lot. They'd talked in his truck; she'd told him that she knew all about the murder. She knew that Brad and I were having an affair and that we'd planned on killing Ted together. She knew that Brad had driven down to Boston, had broken into a neighbor's house first to make the murder look like a burglary gone wrong, then knocked on Brad's door, asked to be let in, and shot him.

'How'd she know all this?' I asked.

'I didn't ask, Miranda. She just knew. She knew everything.' Brad's voice had risen an octave, and his hand was shaky as he drank from his coffee cup.

'Shh. It's gonna be okay. I'm here now.'

'I know. I was going to call you first thing in the morning, let you know all about it.'

'Baby, I know you were. But it's good I drove over tonight. It will give us more time to figure out what to do about her. What does she want?'

Brad hesitated. 'I'm supposed to tell you she wants money.'

'What the fuck does that mean, you're *supposed* to tell me?'

'Just listen. I'm telling you everything. I'm *supposed* to tell you she wants money from you, a million a year to keep quiet, and that she wants to meet with you tomorrow night at the house on Micmac. She wants to hear from you that you agree.'

'Tomorrow night?'

'Yeah. At ten. I drive you over, and you two meet in the house, one-on-one.'

'Jesus.'

'No, Miranda, you're not listening to me. This is only what I'm supposed to tell you. She wants to kill you. She's planning on killing you. That's what she told me.'

'How?' I asked. It was the first question that popped into my mind.

'She has a stun gun, and then she said she was going to strangle you.' Brad swiped at his nose with the back of his hand.

'I don't understand why she told all this to you.'

'She hates you. She said she's known you since college and you're an evil person.'

'Wow. Jesus,' I said.

'You look happy about this.'

'Do I? No, I'm freaked out.' I was freaked out, but I had another feeling I couldn't quite define. It was like being in high school and finding out that the cutest boy in class had been talking about you to his friends. I'd gotten under Lily's skin and I hadn't even known it.

'How did she think she was going to get away with it? How did she think *you* were going to get away with it? They already suspect you. There was a fucking witness down in Boston. Someone saw you, Brad, going into my house. That's why the sheriff was at your house tonight. You're going to be questioned.'

'What are you talking about?' Spittle flew from his lips, some of it striking me in the face.

'Relax, it's no big deal,' I lied. 'You have an alibi, remember? But that's why I drove up here in the first place. You're going to be interviewed by the police. I don't know when, but it's going to happen. You just need to remember everything we talked about. Stick to the story and everything's going to be fine.'

'But now this other person knows.'

'I know. Give me a moment to think.' I took two deep breaths, still trying to wrap my head around the fact that Lily knew everything, that Lily wanted to kill me. 'Did Lily say how she knew Ted?'

'No. I thought you'd know. But she knew everything about what had happened.'

'How does she think she'll get away with it, get away with killing me?'

'She said she's going to hide your body and your car, and that it will look like you skipped town. She said that it's the only way I won't get caught by the police. I'm supposed to drive you to the meeting tomorrow night, and then I'm supposed to help her get your body back to your car. She's got it all figured out.'

'And what? You told her you'd be happy to do this for her?'

'I was having a goddamn heart attack, Miranda. She knows everything. I told her I'd think about it. I'm supposed to call her phone from Cooley's tomorrow if it gets set up. Just let it ring a couple of times so it shows up on her caller ID. Obviously, I was going to tell you all about it, but I went along with her. What else could I do?'

'No, you were right. You did the right thing. I'm proud of you. Let me think for a moment.'

Brad tugged at a sideburn. 'I know what we need to do,' he said. 'I know what I need to do.'

'What?'

'I'll kill her, Miranda. It will be easy. She's sneaking up here to see you. No one knows she's involved in this. She told me. I'll take you to the house. You go in the front door and I'll go around and come in the back. Keep talking to her and

294

I'll sneak up and hit her with something. I can bury her in the yard.'

'You'd do that for me,' I said.

'I killed your husband for you, Miranda. I love you. Of course I'd kill this bitch.'

It made perfect sense. I knew that it was the only way out. If Lily knew everything, then she needed to die. But it worried me. 'Won't she expect that?' I said, speaking my thoughts aloud. 'It's so risky for her to come up here to meet with me—'

'She's not coming up to meet with you. She's coming up here to kill you. She told me that.'

'That's what I mean. How could she be so sure that she could convince you to do this for her. She just met you. She did *just* meet you, right?'

'Look. She was convincing. She told me it was my only way out – that you were going to throw me under the bus, that when the police came it was going to be my word against yours and there wasn't going to be any proof that you conspired to murder your husband. You could say that I was deranged, that I became obsessed with you. No one, besides me, could say otherwise.'

This was, of course, my plan if Brad was arrested for killing my husband. I would say that we'd gotten physical once, in a moment of weakness for me, but that there had never been any talk about killing Ted. *Now that I think of it, I did mention to Brad Daggett that I was going down to Florida for a long weekend. He must have thought . . . He must*

have thought I was telling him because I wanted . . .
Oh my God. They might suspect me, but there was
no way they could convict me. 'And you believed
all this shit she told you?' I said to Brad, a look
of disgust on my face.

'No, I don't. I believe you, but I told her that
I'd help her out. I pretended to believe her. We're
in trouble, Miranda. She knows everything.'

'Okay, okay. I'll meet her at the house, and
you'll kill her. It will all work out. It needs to
be done.'

We talked some more that night, but Brad was
drunk, and starting to not make sense, and he
needed to sleep. I was paying the price for enlisting
a gutless alcoholic to help me kill my husband.
Before I left, about an hour before dawn, I told
him that he should disappear the following day.
Take a drive up the coast and not answer his
phone. 'You're not in any condition yet to be
questioned by the police,' I said.

'I know,' he said.

'This is going to turn out fine. They might
suspect us, but they won't catch us. We knew this
all along.'

'I know.'

'If you wanted to, baby, you could leave after
tomorrow night. Skip town. Skip the country. Go
down to the islands, and I'll come and find you
when this is all over.'

'They'd know it was me.'

'They would, but they wouldn't be able to find

you. I could give you money to run with, and I'd meet you later, bring more money. You'd be free.'

'What about my kids?' he said, his voice cracking. He raised his big fat head toward me, and I saw that his eyes were genuinely wet. We'd never talked about his kids. Not even once.

'Shh,' I said. 'Let's not talk about it now. You need to get somewhere and sleep, and we can talk about this tomorrow night. Remember: stay away from your house and off your phone. Drive somewhere in your truck and sleep there, okay? Just in case the cops come early in the morning. I'll meet you in Portsmouth outside that restaurant that Ted and you and I went to way back when. Okay? At nine at night.'

I arrived back in Boston just as the rising sun was beginning to edge the city roofs in a thin cold light. I entered my house, taking Tuesday's newspaper in with me, and made a pot of coffee. While it brewed I showered and changed. I would try and nap later in the day but knew that I wouldn't be able to sleep right now. I was in a shit storm. The police hadn't bought the burglary angle, and they were closing in on Brad. And now, this craziness with Lily. I couldn't even wrap my head around it. There had always been something freakish about Lily Kintner. She was watchful. I remembered that. I'd met her when she was probably eighteen, but she seemed much older at the time. Composed, and sure of herself, and definitely not like other freshman girls.

Had she known that I'd stolen Eric from her that one summer before he died? I hadn't stolen him, not really, but we were sharing him without Lily's consent. Had she found out and been stalking me ever since, waiting for an opportunity to kill me? If Eric were still here, I thought . . . and suddenly I went back to that half-formed thought. *Had she killed Eric in London?* He'd died of an allergy attack, but she could have been the one to give him the nuts, knowing he couldn't get to his medicine. It was crazy, but it was also possible. I tried to remember back to what I'd heard around that time. All my friends in New York had been talking about it. He was drunk and went out for Indian food and the chicken dish he got had nuts in it, and he died. Something like that. One thing I remembered for sure was that Lily had been right there with him, probably watching him die. Had she kept his medicine away from him? It now seemed entirely possible that she had.

The day passed, in slow chunks of time. I kept changing my mind about what to do that night. I wanted Lily dead, but what worried me was being present at the scene of a crime. I'd been so careful to make sure that I would never be convicted for Ted's murder, that there would be no evidence connecting me to any crime. Picturing the night ahead, I felt like I was walking into a trap. I *was* walking into a trap – Brad had told me that much – but even knowing what Lily had in mind, I felt unsettled, unsure of myself for the first time in a long time. But I also knew, without a doubt, that if Lily somehow knew everything she said she knew, she needed to be eliminated. With Lily gone, I'd be able to breathe a little easier. And then I could focus on dealing with Brad.

My phone was charging on my bedside table. I went and lay down, scrolling through the missed calls and listening to the voice mails. One of the messages was from Detective Kimball, letting me know that the coroner was done with Ted's body, and I could alert the funeral home that they could pick him up at their convenience. He also asked if I knew of a good way to get in touch with Brad Daggett. Hearing that was a relief; Brad was doing what I'd told him to do, and disappearing for a while. I thought of calling the funeral home but decided against it. Instead, I sent text messages to a couple of friends letting them know that I was okay, just lying low. I called my mother, and we spoke briefly. I told her I was overwhelmed by all the little chores associated with a husband's death. 'Tell me about it, sweetheart,' she said. 'Divorce is no picnic either. All that paperwork.' I tried to sleep, falling into a doze as thin as tissue paper, but thoughts of Lily kept rippling up at me. I tried to remember what she looked like, and all I could see was her slender, hipless frame, her shiny red hair, her unsettling stillness. When I tried to picture her face, I could get a general sense of it, but I couldn't picture any specific features. What did her nose look like? Her mouth? Every time I thought I had it, it flew away from me, like a butterfly I couldn't quite net. I realized I was chewing at the edge of my thumb, and made myself stop before I drew blood. I was wearing yoga pants, and I touched myself through them, thinking of a featureless man, someone rich, in Italy, a married neighbor who came over to my lakeside villa to fuck me. It started to work, and I shucked the yoga pants halfway down my thighs, but before I could come, I started to think of Ted, how on the first night in this house, on this bed, he had sprinkled rose petals, and laid out an expensive negligee for me, and how much it had turned me off.

I parked my car in the back alley behind the restaurant in Portsmouth where Brad and I had agreed to meet. It had turned cold, and I wore a long coat and a cap with my hair tucked up under it. One of the streetlamps in front of the restaurant was busted, and I stood under it, watching for Brad's truck. It was a bright night, though, and I still felt exposed. Brad showed up, exactly at the time we had planned, and I hoisted myself up into the passenger seat, hoping that he was relatively sober.

'We still doing this?' I asked as he pulled away from the curb.

'Fuck, yeah,' he said, and I recognized from his overly loud intonation that he was at least partly loaded, but not wrecked.

'Tell me again what we're going to do.'

'On Micmac Road I'll turn off my lights and drive up to the house. You get out and go in the front door using the key. I'll go around to the back of the house and come in through the patio doors. Then I'll walk up to both of you and hit her on the head with a wrench.'

'Why don't you just shoot her?'

'I don't have that gun anymore. You knew that.'

'Right. I forgot. Then what?'

'I left plastic wrap in the house. You help me roll her up. She goes in the truck and I take you back to your car. I can get rid of her body.'

'Tell me again why I need to be there.'

Brad turned his head slowly toward me. We were heading north on Route 1, and the lights of an oncoming car lit up his features. For one moment, I saw real hatred in his eyes and I involuntarily flinched. 'Because she's coming there to see you. If I show up alone, who knows what will happen? And because you need to be part of this. I did the first one on my own, but I need you for this. I'm not doing this alone again.'

'Okay, okay,' I said. I knew that what he really wanted was for me to see someone die. I hadn't forgotten the haunted look in his eyes the first time I'd seen him after he shot Ted. He probably thought I couldn't handle it, but I was prepared. I was nervous about things going right, but I wasn't nervous about seeing Lily Kintner get her head bashed in.

We were a little early, so Brad drifted through the empty streets of Kennewick. Along the beach I looked out toward the ocean, a swath of it sparkling with silver moonlight. I really did like Kennewick, not to live all the time, but as a place to get away from the city. But after the estate was settled, and all of Ted's money was solely in my name, I'd sell the house along the bluff. There were better places to live. I pictured islands in the Mediterranean. I pictured palm trees and beach bars that didn't look like Cooley's. I'd wasted my life in New England for far too long.

It was close to 10:00 p.m. when Brad doused the lights on his truck and turned off Micmac onto the gravel driveway of my property. He drove slowly, the truck seesawing, the driveway more rutted than ever after the recent rains. The house loomed up, looking simultaneously massive, its dark outline dwarfing the landscape, and small and fragile against the expanse of the ocean. Brad parked next to the Dumpster and killed the engine. A steady wind buffeted the truck. 'She's probably already inside,' Brad said. 'Watching us.'

'Don't waste time, okay,' I said. 'Once I enter the house, then you should start to move. I don't want to be fending off a psycho bitch in there.'

'I'll be fast. I want this over with.'

'Okay,' I said. Even in the dim light of the truck's interior I could see that Brad was trembling slightly. I pressed a hand against his prickly cheek, and he jumped as though a snake had bit him.

'Jesus,' I said. 'Jumpy?'

'You scared me. I can't see a thing in this truck. You should go.'

I opened the door and Brad put his hand over the cab's light. 'See you in there,' I said, and shut the door. The engine ticked, cooling down. I pulled the keys from my pocket and walked toward the stone front steps. The moon was behind the house, and as I got closer, the house was like a black wall with nothing beyond it. I breathed deeply, shocked by how cold the air had become. I fumbled with the keys, finding the right one, and unlocking the door, swinging it inward and stepping inside. For a moment, I had the surreal sense that I had merely passed through the facade of a house, and I was still outside. I looked up to see stars, but there was nothing there.

'In here,' a voice said, and Lily materialized briefly in a pool of light, then disappeared again. 'Come in,' she said. 'Your eyes will adjust.'

I let the door shut behind me. The lofty ceilings of the foyer began to take shape in the gray light.

I tested my voice. 'Isn't this dramatic?' I said, and it echoed sharply in the house.

'Did Brad tell you what I wanted?' Lily said.

I moved toward the voice, one of my hands going instinctively to my pocket. I'd brought the small canister of pepper spray that I sometimes carried with me in the city. I told Lily I'd been surprised to hear that she wanted money. I asked her if it was to help her father, hoping that was a sensitive subject and that it would piss her off.

'What do you mean?' she asked, her voice sounding calm, almost casual.

'He killed someone, right? In England. He must have legal fees.'

'No,' she said, 'the money is for me.'

I told her I couldn't get her money right away, and she told me she just wanted to meet me face-to-face, to hear that it wouldn't be a problem. We were about a yard away, and I wasn't planning on getting any closer. My eyes had adjusted, but Lily was still just a featureless blob. She hadn't moved since I'd come in, as though she were rooted in place. If she moved toward me, I was planning on bolting. I knew every square foot of this house, and it was an advantage I planned on using.

'Were you sleeping with Ted?' I asked her. Brad would be arriving any moment, and I genuinely wanted to know. 'How did you two even meet?'

'We were on a flight together. He knew everything about you, you know? He knew you were cheating on him with Brad. You didn't fool him.'

'So why didn't you just turn me in?' I said. 'If you're so sure I'm this awful person.'

'I will turn you in, Faith, if you don't do everything I say.'

It was strange to hear my old name, and it brought me back to college, to the smoky rooms and boozy parties. Suddenly I could picture Lily's face, her cold green eyes.

'Is this about Eric?' I asked as I saw a dark figure moving toward us. Brad, coming to kill Lily. I almost wanted to make him wait a moment. I wanted to know if Lily had killed Eric in London all those years ago. I needed that.

'No,' Lily said, amusement in her voice. 'It isn't. This is all about you.'

And then Brad was there, his face ghostly, lifting his large wrench. I watched, fascinated, then realized that both faces, Brad's and Lily's, had turned toward me. The wrench came down, a sharp pain exploding in my head. My knees buckled, and I was suddenly on the cold sawdusty floor, a hand on my head. Brad was over me. He grasped my hand and moved it away from my head. My hat had fallen off. I'm about to die, I thought. I heard the whistle of the wrench as Brad swung it again.

CHAPTER 26

LILY

Brad brought the wrench down on Miranda's head. She dropped first to her knees and then to the floor, her hat coming off. She brought a hand up, touched herself where she had been hit. For a second I thought that Brad wasn't going to be able to finish, but he crouched and hit her several more times. Without the hat to block the blows, the wrench made sharp thunking sounds against her skull. The last time he swung it I heard a raspy crunch, the sound of someone punching his hand through a wall. I gently pulled him away when it was clear that she was dead, when, even in the fuzzy light of the house's interior, I could see that the side of her head was caved in, and that a black pool of blood had spread out across the floor.

'Leave the wrench here with her. Let's step outside for a moment,' I said.

Brad did as I said, laying the wrench almost gently beside Miranda's inert body. I gripped him above the elbow and led him to the front door and through it. The air outside was the same temperature as it was inside the house, but it felt cleaner, filled with the salty smell of the ocean. I let the door shut behind us. 'It's done,' I said to Brad.

'You think she's dead?' he said.

'Yes, she's dead. It's over. You did a good job. Did she suspect anything?'

'No, I told her everything just like you told me to. She saw you, though.'

'What do you mean she saw me?' I asked.

'Last night. After you left my house, she was there. She'd come up to see me and saw you there. She recognized you.' Brad had pulled his cigarettes out of his jacket pocket and was unsuccessfully trying to extricate one from the packet.

'Let's sit in the truck for a moment and have a cigarette,' I said. 'Then we can deal with the body.'

We got inside Brad's truck. I'd pulled my backpack off and held it in my lap. 'You cold?' Brad asked. 'I can turn the heater on.'

'No, I'm fine. But I'm going to have a drink.' I unzipped my backpack and pulled out the flask of apricot brandy. 'Do you mind? I'm freaking out a little.'

'No shit, right,' Brad said, and barked out a short unnatural-sounding laugh.

I tipped the flask at my lips but didn't drink any of its contents. 'You want some?' I said. 'It's apricot brandy. It's good.'

He took the flask from me and took a long pull, handed it back. 'Have another,' I said. 'I've had plenty tonight.'

'If we can't drink tonight, then I don't know . . .'

307

he said, and tipped the flask again. I listened to him swallow twice. He'd drunk enough. I'd hoped the apricot flavor would mask what was in the brandy, and it had. I didn't know how long it would take for it to kick in, but I wanted to hear more about Miranda's visit to Brad the night before.

'Tell me about last night,' I said. 'Then we'll deal with the body.'

Brad flicked his lighter and lit his cigarette, blowing a blue plume against the windshield. 'She scared the shit out of me is what she did. You left the house, and about five minutes later she showed up. I thought it was you returning at first.'

'Why was she there?'

'She came because she didn't want to call me on the phone. She said the police have some kind of witness and that they are going to question me, and I needed to keep my shit together. We didn't talk about that much because she was so freaked out about seeing you.'

'And you told her what we talked about?'

'Yeah. I told her exactly what we planned. I said you tried to convince me to help you kill her, and that I told you I'd think about it, but that I thought we should double-cross you. I told her I'd be willing to kill you for her. She bought it.'

The night before, when I'd approached Brad in the parking lot of Cooley's, my plan had been simply to get Brad to bring Miranda to the house on Micmac Road. That was step one. Once I was alone with Miranda, I knew that I could kill her, using my stun gun first, then either smother her with a plastic bag, or use my knife. But when I began to talk with Brad outside Cooley's, I recognized that he was a man on the verge of breaking. In the dim light of his truck's cab, I could see that his eyes were haunted and scared. I was reminded of an animal with his leg in a trap, half-starved and desperate. I changed plans immediately, telling him that I'd known Miranda since college, and I knew what she had done, and that he'd been set up all along.

'She's going to turn you in, Brad. You know that, don't you?' I said to him.

'I don't know,' he said.

'Brad, I'm not asking you. I'm telling you. Miranda is an evil person. Is there any proof whatsoever that Miranda had anything to do with killing Ted? Besides your word, that is. All she has to do is say that you did it on your own accord. You won't be able to prove otherwise. You're going to go to jail for the rest of your life, and Miranda is going to get off scot-free. You've been used.'

'Oh, God,' he said, and wiped at an eye with one of his large hands.

It had been that easy to get him on my side. It was clear that he had not been completely fooled by Miranda. Far from it. I told him we should go back to his house and discuss options. I followed him in my car to the rental unit where he lived. Ted had described it to me, telling me how sterile and bleak it was, and he was right. The furniture was solid but uninteresting. Magazines had been fanned across the coffee table, and the whole place smelled of cleaning products. I wondered if it was even cleaner than when Ted had seen it – wondered if Brad, in his distress, had been compulsively straightening his apartment. We sat on the couch. I had turned down the offer of a beer but Brad had got himself a Heineken from the tiny alcove kitchen attached to the living room. He emptied half the bottle with his first sip.

'Are you in love with her?' I asked him.

'I thought so,' he said. 'I mean, I don't know. You've seen her. You saw her. She's going to be fucking rich.'

'Yeah, she's going to be rich, but she's not going to share that with you. Trust me. This is how she operates. She gets men to do what she wants them to do and then she eliminates them. She got you to kill her husband for her, and she got you to do it when she was a thousand miles away.'

He nodded at me, his face slack. 'That's the worst part,' I continued. 'She turned you into a murderer, and that's something that you can never reverse. But it wasn't you, Brad. It was Miranda. She manipulated you. You never stood a chance.'

I watched as tears spilled in two steady streams from Brad's eyes, falling down his leathery face. I had told him what he wanted to hear: I had told him that he wasn't responsible for the murder of Ted Severson, and that Miranda was. I had absolved him. When he stopped crying, I asked

310

him to get me a beer. I wasn't planning on drinking it, but I wanted to give him something to do, and I wanted him to feel like I was now on his side. He came back with two bottles, sat down, and uncapped the bottles with an opener that was attached to his key ring.

'What should I do?' he asked. 'Should I just go to the police and confess. Tell them everything that happened?'

'That's not going to help. You're still the one who killed Ted. She was nowhere near when it happened, and she's going to say she had nothing to do with it.'

'So what should I do?' He drank his beer, dribbled a little down his chin.

The way he was looking at me I could have told him to break his own fingers and he would have done it. So I took a chance, and said to him: 'I need you to help me get rid of Miranda. It's what she deserves, and it's the only thing that's going to get you off the hook. Can you help me do that?'

'What do you mean, get rid of her?'

'I'm going to kill her, Brad.'

'Okay.'

So I presented the plan. I told him to tell Miranda that I wanted to meet with her, that I knew all about the murder, and that I wanted money. We would meet in the house the Seversons had been building, sometime the next night, after dark. 'She'll be suspicious,' Brad said.

'Okay,' I said. 'You're right. So instead of telling

her that I'm going to blackmail her, tell her that it's a setup, that I told you to tell her it was blackmail, but that I'm planning on killing her, that I've been waiting for my moment since college. She'll come. I know she will. Then I'll get rid of her, and you can help me bury her body. If she gets discovered I'll make sure that you have a solid alibi. I'll say that you and I met up here in Kennewick, and we hooked up, and you came back down to my house in Massachusetts. You'll be fine, I promise.'

'What about the money?'

'You're never going to see that money, Brad. Never. You're going to go to prison, and I'm offering you a way out. If Miranda's gone, then you are safe.'

He nodded rapidly, like he'd just been scolded. 'How are you going to kill her?'

'I'll take care of that,' I said.

'I could do it,' Brad said, and there was something new in his eyes. Not fear, anymore, but hatred, plus maybe a little bit of craziness. I wondered if he'd slept at all since killing Ted.

'What do you mean?' I asked.

'I could send her into the house, and then I could come in through the back patio entrance and sneak up on her. I have this big wrench. I could hit her over the head with it. That way you wouldn't have to do it. You don't want to know what it's like.'

It was perfect. It solved my biggest problem, that if I was the one to kill Miranda, there would inevitably be some sort of forensic test that would prove a five-foot-eight-inch female had dealt the deadly blow and not a six-foot-two-inch man.

'You won't need to sneak up on her,' I said.

'What do you mean?'

'Tell her that you're planning on killing me because I know everything. Tell Miranda that you're going to sneak up on me and hit me with the wrench. Then, even if she hears you coming into the house, she'll think you're after me. She won't even know it's coming.'

'Okay.' He nodded.

'Are you sure about this?'

He told me he was, and I believed him. We talked more, going over every detail of the plan. I reassured him several times that everything was going to be okay. When I left his house, I was convinced that he would do everything he had told me he would do.

And he had.

I had wondered, as I was standing in the dark with Miranda, whether I had been stupid, and Brad was going to kill me instead of Miranda. But at the last moment, when Brad lifted that massive wrench, I knew. I knew that I had won, and Miranda, like others before her, was going to die, and that I was going to live.

With the windows of the truck rolled up, and Brad smoking, the cab filled with pungent smoke. 'So she was willing to kill me?' I asked Brad, needing to know.

'Yeah. Like you said she'd be. She was surprised, though . . . she said you guys weren't that close in college.' He rubbed at his lips with his spatulate fingers. 'How'd you know about everything? How'd you know so much about what happened with Ted? I never asked you last night.'

'I met Ted Severson on a flight back from London. He told me that his wife was cheating on him with his house contractor. He watched you through binoculars from the path out along the bluff. We continued to meet. He decided he wanted to kill Miranda. And you, as well. I told him I'd help.'

Brad took another long drag on his cigarette, but it was down to the filter. He cranked the window down and flicked the cigarette away. I heard it sputter out as it hit a puddle. 'You're shitting me,' Brad said, swinging his head in my direction. The chloral hydrate was kicking in. Brad's speech was starting to slur, and his eyes were drooping.

'No. I wish I was. Ted was planning on killing Miranda and she was planning on killing Ted, but she got there first. Well, you got there first. It's all over now, though.'

'It is,' he said. 'It is.' His words were heavily slurred – *is* sounded like *ish* – and I could just barely understand what he was saying. His head was angled down, and he reminded me of a boxer trying to stay awake in the ring, not realizing that he's already been knocked out. He started to lean a little toward me, and I moved back in my seat, the bags on my feet rustling against the floor of the truck.

'Why do you . . . why do you have bags on your feet?' His words were almost complete mush and I would never have known what he was saying but I could see where he was looking. He fell forward, slumping sideways so that his right shoulder landed hard on my thigh. I grabbed two handfuls of his thick denim jacket and managed to move him upright in his seat. His head tipped backward, his mouth open. I unlatched my door and got out of the truck, shutting it quickly so that the light didn't stay on too long in the cab. I looked up. The night sky was filled with clustered stars, brighter now than when I had parked the car. The ocean shushed unseen. I allowed myself ten seconds of just standing there, and then I got to work.

I had brought extra bags, and I had my knife, but before resorting to either of those, I hoisted myself onto the bed of the truck to check out the toolbox that was secured with a bungee cord against the rear of the cab. The corrugated metal lid was unlocked and I used my penlight to look inside. There were all the tools I'd expected – hammers, handsaws, a tire iron, a plastic box that contained a drill – but what caught my eye was a length of coat hanger wire that had been repurposed into a long hook, for jimmying the lock when the keys were left inside. I picked it up and straightened it out. It would be perfect; I didn't want any blood in the truck.

I slid back onto the passenger seat, and shut the door behind me. I rolled down my window; the smell of Brad's last cigarette still lingered in the cab, plus there was something else . . . the chemical odor of distilled alcohol coming from Brad's breath. Maybe also his body. He had begun to snore – high nasal rasps on each outtake of breath. I grabbed him by the shoulder and shook him as hard as I could, and he showed no signs of coming out of his deep sleep. I wondered if the combination of alcohol – how much had he drunk today? – and the chloral hydrate would eventually kill him, but I couldn't take the risk that it wouldn't.

I got onto my knees on the passenger seat. I pushed Brad's head away from me so that it fell facing the driver's-side window. It was still tipped back and there was space between his thick neck and the truck's headrest. I circled the coat hanger wire around his neck, and twisted the ends together so that the wire was tight against his neck. I took out the Leatherman from my backpack, and clipped the excess wire from the coat hanger so that the twisted-together part was only about an inch long.

I gripped the ends with the tip of the Leatherman pliers and I twisted, tightening the wire until I knew that Brad was dead.

PART III

HIDE THE BODIES WELL

CHAPTER 27

KIMBALL

I couldn't sleep.

This was nothing new to me, especially when I was working on a case. I checked the clock on my bedside table. It was a little after three in the morning. Pyewacket the cat was sleeping on my discarded clothes on the floor. He looked cold, curled into a ball like a woolly bear caterpillar that's pretending it's dead. He probably wondered why those metal strips along his apartment's floor hadn't started making burbling sounds and getting warm. Late October had turned cold, but I liked to hold out till November, at least, before turning the heat on.

I thought of getting out of bed and going to see what was playing on Turner Classic Movies but knew that if I did, I would never get back to sleep again. I needed to be at least a little sharp for the following day. Ted Severson had been murdered on Friday night, and it had now just tipped over into the following Wednesday. Almost a whole week. We had a prime suspect – this Brad Daggett character – but he'd pulled a runner, and no one could find him. I'd spent the day up in Maine, in the company of the mostly helpful Kennewick police force, keeping an eye on Daggett's house, checking any and all leads as to his whereabouts. He was our man, for sure. After Miranda Severson identified our sketch as possibly being Brad Daggett, I'd checked the system, and Daggett was there. He'd been arrested twice. Five years earlier on suspicion of domestic assault, and two years ago on a DUI. I'd called him with the number that Miranda had given me, but he didn't pick up. Then I called the local police, and asked them to swing by and check to see if Brad Daggett was home, maybe do some initial questioning, ask him if he had any information on the death of Ted Severson. They did as I asked, but he wasn't at his house. I told them it could wait till the next day, that I'd be questioning the primary witness in the morning and we'd know more then. I printed Daggett's most recent mug shot, and took it to Rachel Price's apartment in Somerville the following morning. When she looked at the picture, she hopped a little on her toes, and said, 'Oh, that's him. That's definitely him.'

'That's the man you saw entering the house at six o'clock on Friday night?'

'Yes, that's him. I'm sure of it.'

That had been Tuesday morning. I'd called the sheriff, then driven up myself. Daggett was still nowhere to be found. Not at either of the construction sites that he was supervising, and not at his home, one of a string of rental cottages that he owned along Kennewick Beach. White paint and green trim. Made me think of my own childhood vacations at Wells Beach, just a little farther north. When it was clear he wasn't home, and wasn't coming back anytime soon, I tried out the key I'd found hidden in Ted Severson's bedroom drawer. It fit Brad's cottage door. Why did Ted have a key to his general contractor's house? Had *they* been having an affair? I peered into the tiny, immaculate cottage but didn't enter yet. A local judge granted a warrant just after his lunch break and we searched the place, finding nothing.

I'd been kicking myself all day that I hadn't acted faster after Miranda gave me Brad Daggett's name. I should have brought his mug shot immediately to Rachel Price, but Miranda's halfhearted identification hadn't left me with much hope. Of course, now it seemed abundantly clear that Miranda only identified Brad because she felt she had to, and she was covering herself. And she must have been the one who had warned Brad to stay away from his house and turn off his phone. It was the oldest story in the book. The wife had had her boyfriend kill her husband. The curveball was that hidden key in Ted's drawer, the key to Brad's cottage in Maine. Was it Miranda's key and she had hidden it in her husband's drawer? Possible, I supposed.

By early afternoon, we'd put an all-points bulletin out for Brad and his vehicle. His ex-wife had been interviewed, plus several employees and work colleagues. No one had seen him since the previous day at lunch, when he'd bought a large meatball sub at a pizza place in York that he frequented. He'd disappeared.

I left Maine late in the afternoon, taking I-95 back down toward Boston. On the way, I received an excited call from Billy Elkins, the officer I'd tasked with looking into Lily Kintner, the woman that Miranda Severson said she knew in Winslow, Massachusetts. He'd found out a lot. Lily Kintner worked at Winslow College in the library department, apparently under the name of Lily Hayward. But she owned a house on Poplar Road in Winslow under her real name. Most importantly, Ted and Lily had shared a flight back from London on the twentieth of September. I pumped my fist in the car, then took down her address.

Asking Billy to check passenger manifests had been a total hunch, but an educated one, and I couldn't believe that it had paid off. As soon as Miranda had identified Lily Kintner as the one person she knew who lived in Winslow, I had wondered if Lily Kintner was the same Lily Kintner who was the daughter of David Kintner, easily my favorite living novelist. I didn't know much about Kintner's daughter, just that her name was Lily, and that she was born in America while David had been living in Connecticut, married to an American artist named Sharon Henderson. Mather College was in Connecticut, and if Lily was Miranda's age, then she'd be just about the right age to be Kintner's daughter.

The thing about David Kintner was that he wasn't just famous for being a novelist; he had become infamous for accidentally killing his second wife in a drunk driving accident in England. It had been huge news in England, less so in America. I followed it because I was a fan of his books. He'd done time and just been released, less than a month ago. It would make sense that his American daughter had flown over to London to see him. I had also learned from Miranda Severson that Ted had flown to London recently for work, so it occurred to me that Ted and this Lily Kintner had possibly met on an airplane. I had Billy take a shot and check the manifests, and got a hit. After a fruitless day trying to find Brad Daggett, it felt good that some detective work had actually paid off. She *must* have been the reason he traveled to Winslow that day, even though she probably had nothing to do with his death.

When I reached the I-95/I-93 split, instead of getting onto I-93 to head into Boston, I stayed on I-95, looping west toward Winslow. I didn't expect much to come from questioning Lily Kintner, but I needed to check it out.

She'd been home, and she did turn out to be David Kintner's daughter, just as I suspected. She lived in a book-filled house on a pond with only a few other houses on its leaf-plastered shore. She greeted me at the door, looking a little disheveled, her eyes taking a moment to focus on my face. I wondered if I'd woken her from a nap. She invited me in. I asked her about Ted Severson and she told me she knew him, but only from the newspaper reports of his death, and from knowing that he had married someone she knew from college. She offered coffee and I accepted. While she made it, I looked over her bookshelves, finding a row of all of David Kintner's novels. I ran a finger across their spines, remembering pictures I'd seen of him. Tall and angular with a thatch of white hair. A drinker's face – sallow and hollow-cheeked. Lily returned with the coffee, her hair pushed back behind her ears, her sleepy eyes now sharp and watchful. I told her I knew her father's books, was a fan actually, and she seemed unimpressed, as though she'd heard way too much about her father's genius. I told her I knew about the situation in England, and that allowed me to bring up the flight she'd shared with Ted Severson. Something clicked in her luminous green eyes, and she told me that she *had* met a man on the plane, and that he'd seemed familiar, and it was probably him. They'd spoken at length, and it was possible she'd told him who she was and where she lived. We found a picture on the Internet and she confirmed that it was Ted Severson she had spoken to, but she claimed to have no idea why he would have come to Winslow.

I believed some of what she told me. I believed that she hadn't known Ted Severson had come to her town to look for her, and I believed that she was surprised that I'd shown up at her house, but I didn't believe that she hadn't figured out that the man on the plane was the husband of a friend of hers. It made no sense. But why would she lie to me about such a thing?

At her door I put my hand in my pocket, my fingers touching the key we now knew belonged to Brad Daggett's cottage in Maine. Even so, I asked Lily if she'd mind if I tried her door with it. I just wanted to gauge her reaction. She seemed perplexed, but not worried. I left, not really knowing what to think. But I did know why Ted Severson had gone to Winslow that day. He'd met Lily Kintner on a plane, and he'd fallen in love with her. That much was sure. I empathized. In fact, I'd been thinking about Lily Kintner almost nonstop since meeting her the day before. She was beautiful, that much I remembered, but I was having trouble reconstructing her facial features in my mind. I could picture her long red hair, and her green eyes, so much like a cat's, but her face kept slipping in and out of my mind's grasp. But more than her physical presence, I had been taken in by her almost otherworldly self-possession, and by the way she inhabited her book-lined cottage in the woods of Winslow. Was she lonely out there all alone? Or was she one of those rarities, a human who didn't need other humans in her life? It was something that I intended to find out.

My younger sister, Emily, who knows me better than anyone in the world, told me recently that my problem with relationships is that I fall in love with every woman I'm attracted to.

'Don't most guys?' I said.

'No,' she said. 'Most guys just want to sleep with all the women they're attracted to. The last thing they want to do is fall in love. You call yourself a detective, and you don't know that?'

'Trust me. I also want to sleep with these women.'

'Yeah, but then you fall in love with them, and either they break your heart, or—'

'Can we talk about your love life now?' I interrupted. It was how I got Emily to change the subject when she was analyzing my failed romances.

Pyewacket stirred, which meant it was 5:00 a.m. He leaped onto my bed, prepared to breathe on my eyelids to wake me up, but I swung my legs out from under the covers before he had a chance. I let him out of my apartment's side door, which led to the fire escape. He darted out, nimbly walking on the metal slats, heading down to the small backyard, where it was his job to protect our kingdom from falling leaves and rogue squirrels.

I got back into bed, now certain that there was no chance I'd get any more sleep. I kept a spiral-bound notebook and a pen on top of the pile of books by my bed. It was supposed to be an idea book, a place to record late-night thoughts about cases I was working on, but also lines of poetry. I still considered myself a poet (something no one in the force knew about), even though I'd lost the ability to write anything but limericks these days. I told myself I was at least writing something, and that maybe it would help me think about cases. Earlier the day before I'd written these two:

> There once was a husband named Ted,
> Who met his end in a volley of lead.
> It was clear he was rich—
> And his wife was a bitch—
> So it's not a surprise that he's dead.

> There once was a girl named Miranda,
> It was clear that no one could stand her.
> But beneath all that crass
> Was an excellent ass,
> So the rich men all lined up to land her.

To the same page, I added the following:

> There once was a novelist's daughter
> Whose eyes were the green of seawater.
> I hoped to remove
> Her clothing to prove
> That naked she'd look even hotter.

I wondered, not for the first time, why my limericks always turned out dirty. I tried to come up with one about Brad Daggett but failed. Instead I got up, made a full pot of coffee, and began to get ready to go to work.

I reached my desk at just past seven, calling up

and checking in with the Kennewick chief of police, and finding out that Brad Daggett never returned to his house.

'I'm not surprised,' I said, half to myself. 'Keep a patrol car there, though, just in case. Even though he's obviously made a run for it.'

'We talked with a girlfriend of his last night,' said Chief Ireland, his voice raspy, like he was fighting a cold. 'Polly Greenier. She's kind of a fixture at Cooley's, the bar where Brad Daggett liked to hang out. They were an on-and-off thing. Years and years, actually. They went to high school together.'

'She know anything?'

'She didn't know anything 'bout where he might be. I asked her when she last saw him, though, and she told me she was with him Friday night.'

'Last Friday night?'

'That's what she said. They were drinking at Cooley's and wound up back at his place. She says she spent the night there.'

'You sure she had the day right?'

'No, not sure, but we can check it. If they were at Cooley's and left together folks in the bar will remember. It's a small town, and people notice stuff like that.'

'You'll check it out for me?'

'Sure will.'

'And one more thing,' I said. 'Have one of your patrols swing back to the Severson house that Daggett was building. And any other houses that Daggett might have the keys for. If he's still in the area, it makes sense he might be hiding out in one of them. Check all the cottages, too, that he owns on the beach.'

'We checked them.'

'Okay. Thanks, Chief Ireland.'

'Call me Jim, okay?'

'Will do,' I said.

I sat at my desk for a while after the phone call, worrying about Daggett's alibi, and how solid it might be. It couldn't be real, that much I knew. He must have gotten this girlfriend of his to agree that they were together on Friday night. If that was the case, then the alibi would crack faster than a window in a hurricane. I wrote her name down on the notebook in front of me, circling it several times. Then my partner, Roberta James, swung by, depositing an Egg McMuffin on my desk ('Two-for-one menu item, so I thought of you'), and I caught her up on what I'd heard that morning. After she left, I wrote a few more lines under Polly Greenier's name in the notebook. *Why would she lie for Brad? Why did Ted have a key for Brad's house? Why did Lily Kintner lie to me?*

I was about to call Police Chief Jim Ireland back, tell him I wanted to come up and talk with this Polly Greenier, when he called me instead. 'You better come up here,' he said. 'There's a body. At the house Daggett was building.'

'Is it him?' I asked, already standing, pulling on my jacket, checking my pocket for my car keys.

'No, it's not a *him* at all. It's a woman. I haven't

329

seen her yet, but they're pretty sure it's Miranda Severson. Her head's bashed in.'

'I'll be right there,' I said and hung up the phone. I grabbed James, who had just settled at her desk, and told her we were heading back up to Maine.

CHAPTER 28

LILY

After making sure that Brad was dead I removed the coat hanger wire from around his neck. I grasped him by his denim coat and managed to drag him across the truck's front seat onto the passenger's side, where I strapped him in with the seat belt. I tilted the seat a little bit back so that he tilted with it, then zipped his coat all the way up, turning up the sheepskin-lined collar so that it covered the ligature marks on his neck. If someone saw us in the car, he'd look like a dozing passenger. At least that's what I hoped he'd look like.

I started the truck, and drove out of the driveway and back onto the road, keeping the headlights off till I turned on Micmac. I checked the fuel gauge, the needle hovering somewhere between three-quarters and full, and I thought it would be enough gas to get us down to Connecticut. I had been prepared to get gas at a self-service station, paying with cash inside, but was glad that I didn't have to. So far, no one had seen me in Maine, and I was planning on keeping it that way.

I drove north, toward the entrance ramp for I-95.

I got off Micmac before hitting Kennewick Beach, knowing that if the police were onto Brad already, they were probably staked out in front of his cottage. I would have loved to go back there, get a few of his things to make it look like he'd truly made a run for it, but it wasn't worth the risk. Before hitting the interstate, I pulled into a closed auto shop called Mike's, one of those backwoods garages surrounded by junked vehicles. With my lights off I pulled into a row of junkers and got out of the truck. I found a car that looked as though it hadn't been moved through at least two winters and, using my Leatherman, I removed its Maine license plate, then swapped it with the license plate from Brad's truck. It took about five minutes, no sound except for that steady wind that rustled the remaining leaves in the trees. Licenses swapped, I got back in the truck, the cab light briefly illuminating Brad, his head now lolling unnaturally to the side. I turned away from him, and my eye caught the plastic E-ZPass transmitter glued to the inside of the windshield. There were tolls on the interstate, two in Maine, then another when the highway briefly passed through New Hampshire. I debated whether it was better to zip through tolls with the E-ZPass, and possibly be tracked, or whether I should remove it and go through cash tolls. I decided that paying cash was better and pried the transmitter off the windshield, throwing it into the woods next to the garage. Brad really did just look like someone's husband sleeping off a drunk, and I would take my chances on anyone recognizing me. My hair was my most distinctive feature and it was hidden under my hat.

I didn't need to worry. The tollbooth operators barely looked at either Brad or me on the entire four-hour drive to my old neighborhood in Connecticut. There was no one on the roads, and I could probably have made the trip in three and a half, but I kept strictly to the speed limits, staying in the right-hand lane while cargo trucks rumbled past me in the passing lanes. I kept the radio off, but somewhere around Worcester Brad's body shifted and made a gas-expelling moan. I'd been prepared for this, telling myself that dead bodies make sounds, but I still jumped about two inches in my seat when it happened. After that, I turned on the radio, flipping between crappy stations until somewhere in Connecticut I found a late-night jazz show on a commercial-free station way left on the dial. I didn't particularly like jazz, since it reminded me of my parents, but I could recognize a number of standards. 'On Green Dolphin Street' by Miles Davis segued into Nat King Cole's 'Autumn Leaves.' I listened to the words, trying to keep my mind away from the fact that I was driving through the night with a dead man as my passenger. Even with the radio turned up loud, I heard two more expulsions, and the cab of the truck filled with the smell of both urine and excrement. I thought about that black stray cat I killed years ago when I was a girl, and the way I'd been shocked by the presence of shit. I remembered how the disgust over that dead cat had made me feel even happier that I'd killed it. It was the same with Brad Daggett next to me in the truck. He'd gotten what he deserved, maybe even better than he'd deserved. He was dead now, and couldn't hurt anyone, but I still had to deal with his disgusting body. And I had to survive the remainder of this trip. I put a little more weight on the gas pedal, thought it couldn't hurt to go a little bit over the speed limit. The miles ticked by, through 'There's a Small Hotel' and Chet Baker's 'Almost Blue' and Dinah Washington singing 'This Bitter Earth.' The songs began to fuzz in and out of range as I got closer to home, but I didn't flip away, preferring snatches of old music to furniture warehouse ads and bad talk radio.

I turned the radio off when I reached Shepaug, listened to silence as I wound along the familiar tree-lined streets. I passed the driveway for Monk's House, instinctively turning my head and seeing a single second-floor light still burning. I guessed that my mother had fallen asleep reading, the way she did every night, book splayed open across her chest, lamp still on. I took the next right, down the weed-choked driveway that led to the empty farmhouse. I killed the truck's headlights and slowed to a crawl. Just as it had been in Maine, it was a cloudless night in Connecticut, the black sky crowded with bright stars. The farmhouse, unadorned and colorless, rose up out of a yard that had become a pasture. A single tree, planted too close to the house, seemed to be enveloping the structure, one of its branches having punctured the roof. I stepped out of the truck, and was flooded with the familiar piney smell of the surrounding woods. I took my penlight and waded out into the adjacent meadow, its dried-out grasses crackling under my feet. I had been back to this meadow a few times since childhood, but this was the first time I'd been here at night since that summer evening when I'd killed Chet. I walked toward where I thought the well was, only turning the penlight on when I thought I was close, pointing the beam down at the ground. It took five minutes, but I found the well cover, covered by the grass I'd flattened over its top so many years ago. I propped the penlight on the cover's wooden edge, angling it slightly up so that I'd be able to see its weak beam, then walked back to the truck.

Except for the rainfall of the day before, it had been a dry September and October in New England and the ground of the meadow was soft but not muddy. Keeping my eye on the penlight's beam I drove the truck from the driveway onto the meadow, bumping up and over a few rocks that were all that remained of an ancient stone wall. Brad Daggett jolted back and forth on his seat, emitting another expulsion of gas. My window was rolled down, my head halfway out. I pulled the truck up to the left of the well and kept it running while I got out and circled around to the well cover. With my gloves still on, I ripped away at the meadow grass and loosened the cover. I pulled it away gently, trying not to break the rotten wood, and laid it next to the well opening. I picked up the penlight; in its beam I could see worms writhing in the bare earth where the well cover had laid. I pointed the beam down the well, seeing only the rocks and dirt that covered Chet. I imagined what was left of him down there – a withered corpse, some paint-splattered clothes, a few rotted picture frames, a pair of dark-rimmed glasses. The world turned suddenly dark, and a slight jolt of fear went through me. I looked up, and it was a single scrap of cloud that was blanking the moon. I watched it pass by, and the world was flooded again with moonlight.

I opened the passenger door of the truck, unbuckled Brad, and he tumbled out on his own accord, landing face-first onto the ground, one of his feet, in his large work boots, snagging on the edge of the door. I loosened his boot and his leg followed his body down onto the ground. He was about three feet from the well hole, but even so, it was not easy to move his bulk. I wound up rolling him over several times till his head and torso were flopped into the well, then I lifted his heavy feet till he slid over the edge. He hit the bottom of the well with a splintery thump, sending up a rush of acrid air.

Brad, meet Chet. Chet, meet Brad.

I pulled the cover back onto the well, tapped down its sides, and replaced the meadow grass, sweeping it over like hair across a bald spot. I checked my watch. It was nearly 3:00 a.m. It was all going just as I had planned. Before I got back into the truck to drive to New York City, I took a moment just for myself, standing under the starry night, surrounded by nothing but darkness and nature. 'Rare breed of animal,' my father had once called me, and that's what I felt like. Totally alive, and totally alone. My only companion at that moment was my younger self, the one who tipped Chet down that well. I imagined she was there with me. We locked eyes, not needing to speak to each other. We understood that survival was everything. It was the meaning of life. And to take another life was, in many ways, the greatest expression of what it meant to be alive. I blinked, and my younger self disappeared. She came back into me, and together we drove to New York City.

I was back in Shepaug by ten in the morning. I had driven the truck into the city, cruising around the Lower East Side till I found a place to park not too far from a subway station. It was a litter-choked block filled with shuttered shops. It was nearly dawn but loud music blasted from a parked car half a block away. I parked under a flickering streetlamp. I had worn gloves the entire night so there were no prints to wipe off, but I did it anyway, using a small towel that I found in the

truck's glove compartment. After wiping everything down, I spread the towel out and draped
it over the soiled passenger seat, then I gathered
any paperwork that had Brad's name on it in the
truck and took it with me. There was a nearby
trash bin and I pushed the papers down into the
stew of pizza crusts and coffee cups. Then I
dropped the keys to the truck on the pavement
next to the driver's side, where they would
catch the light. I hoped that the person who first
spotted the dropped keys would not be some
do-gooder who would alert the authorities. I was
counting on the likelihood that the truck would
be in several pieces in a chop shop by the time
the sun came up.

I took the subway to Grand Central, bought a
ticket on the Metro-North Commuter Rail to
Shepaug. It was an hour wait and I drank coffee
and ate a greasy doughnut, and watched as the
station slowly filled with early-morning commuters.
I managed to doze a little on the train ride to my
hometown, and woke up shivering from the cold
that had gotten into my bones from the long
sleepless night. From Shepaug station I walked
the three miles to Monk's House, staying on a
trail that skirted an unused portion of rail line. I
hadn't lived in Shepaug for close to ten years,
but I didn't want to risk getting spotted by someone
I knew.

When my mother opened the door to me, a large
mug of coffee in her hand, she said, 'Darling, there

you are,' and for a brief moment I wondered if I'd told her I'd be there, before realizing that she was covering for herself in case she'd forgotten about a visit from me.

'Were you expecting me?' I asked, walking into the house.

'No. Was I? He's not coming *today*, is he?'

The *he* she was referring to was my father, who was moving back to America and back into Monk's House. I'd arranged it over my last trip to London. Long story short: my father needed to live with someone who would look after him in his fragile mental state, and my mother needed money to pay her bills. I'd brokered a deal, and had no idea if it would work or not, but it was at least worth a try, or that was what I was telling myself.

'This weekend, Mum,' I said, making my way to the coffeepot in the kitchen.

'What are you doing here, and what are you wearing? You look like a cat burglar.'

Over coffee I told my mother that I had been traveling for work, picking up college archival material, first in Maine, then in New York City. I told her that I'd left my car in Maine and flown from Portland down to New York City but that I missed my flight back. I told her I'd decided to come out to Shepaug, see my mother, maybe get a ride up to Maine to get my car. It was a ludicrous story, I know, but my mother, for all her supposed instinct, was incredibly gullible, for the simple reason that she wasn't interested enough in other people's stories to properly process them.

'I don't know, Lily, I have my pottery group today . . .'

'It's only about a three-hour drive to Maine,' I lied. 'Afterward, I thought maybe you could follow me back down to Winslow. We could have a mother-daughter dinner. You could spend the night.'

She thought about it, but I knew she'd agree. For some inexplicable reason my mother was always trying to get invited to my house up in Winslow. She liked the university setting, and my 'tiny cottage' (her words), and she liked that I cooked for her. I knew that she'd drive me to Maine if it meant she could come to Winslow.

'Okay, darling,' she said. 'How exciting. A spontaneous trip to Maine, just you and me.'

It took a few hours to get her ready but we were on the road by noon, me driving her old Volvo. I hadn't properly slept in about thirty hours, and the thought of spending another four hours behind the wheel of a car was not a pleasant one, but everything had gone perfectly. And it was nearly over.

We spent most of the trip talking about my father. 'I hope he doesn't expect conjugal relations,' she said, not for the first time.

'You're not even married, so it would hardly be conjugal,' I said.

'You know what I mean.'

'I wouldn't worry about it. You're not even going to recognize him. He's not the same as he was before going to prison.'

'I should hope not.'

'He can't be alone in the house. Not at night anyway. He has panic attacks. You don't need to be near him at all times, but he needs to know where you are.'

'Yes, you've told me.'

I had told her, several times. Still, I knew she wasn't prepared for what had become of her ex-husband. He had always had quirks and phobias. He was scared of the dark, scared of crossing city streets, scared of sitting in the backseats of cars. It was hard to understand, because he was also a man who had zero fear of speaking in front of large audiences, a man who would sneak out of his wife's bedroom after she had fallen asleep, and let his mistress into the house, and have sex with her on the living room couch, a man who had climbed halfway up the outside of the Pilgrim Monument in Provincetown on a bet. But that side of my father, the reckless side, had disappeared after what had happened with Gemma, his second wife. He'd met her after the divorce with my mother had been finalized; he'd been living at a hotel on the Old Brompton Road in London. Gemma Daniels was an aspiring novelist, one year younger than me, who had probably come to my father's favorite pub for the sole reason of meeting him. They became inseparable, marrying only six

341

months after they'd met. One of the drawbacks to living in London for my father was that the English tabloids cared about the bad behavior of writers almost as much as they cared about the bad behavior of footballers and pop stars. My father and Gemma were photographed having screaming matches on the street; they were chided in headlines such as 'Dirty Davie and His Child Bride.' This was all before the accident, before my father plowed his 1986 Jaguar into a tree after drunkenly leaving a weekend house party late on a Saturday night. Gemma was in the passenger seat and broke her neck when she went through the windshield. My father, who always wore a seat belt, was uninjured. He managed to call for an emergency vehicle, but he didn't manage to exit the Jaguar to check on Gemma. It wouldn't have made a difference. She had died instantly. Still, word got out that he had been found cowering in his vehicle, his wife sprawled across the roadside hedge. It was deemed manslaughter by gross negligence, and my father was sent to prison for two years. The sentence was cut to one year on appeal, and he'd been released in early September. I visited him where he'd been staying at a friend's house in the Cotswolds and asked him to come back to America, to live with my mother. David still had substantial money, and my mother, after leaving her teaching because of a disagreement with her department head, had been struggling to pay the bills. Monk's House was in a reverse mortgage. My father, tears in his eyes, had agreed to move back to Connecticut. 'And you're not far away, Lil. You'll come and visit all the time, won't you?' My father, who was sixty-eight years old, had sounded like a small boy speaking to his mother before being sent to boarding school.

'This is pretty,' my mother said as I wound her Volvo toward Kennewick Cove. It was still light out, but the sun was low in the west, casting long shadows across the road. The sky was a deep electric blue.

I pulled into the parking lot of the Admiral's Inn, where I'd left my car less than twenty-four hours earlier. It was still there. Before driving back to Winslow, my mother and I stretched our legs, walking down to the edge of the beach, looking out at the slate-colored ocean. 'I always loved the ocean, but your father hated it.'

'Yes, he does,' I said, and laughed. 'He said it was like looking at death.'

'"It's like looking at death and everyone saying how lovely it is,"' my mother said in an English accent, mimicking my father.

'Right. That's what he always said. What was the other one? "I love the beach, everything except the fucking sand, the fucking sun, and the fucking water."'

'Yes, I remember that. What he meant was that the only thing he liked about the beach was the girls in bathing suits.'

We laughed together, then my mother shivered

343

from the cold, and we got back into our respective cars to drive to Winslow. I was tempted to drive north along Micmac Road a little ways to see if there was any activity at Ted and Miranda's house but decided not to risk it. I would find out soon enough how long it took the police to discover Miranda's body. I turned south instead, taking the fastest route to I-95. At a little before six, I pulled into the driveway in Winslow, my mother still behind me. There were no police officers waiting for me, no SWAT team emerging from the woods. I was home, and I had gotten away with it. A surge of elation went through me, a feeling similar to what I'd felt in the meadow fifteen hours earlier. I had changed the world, and no one would ever know it. And even if they found Brad's truck in New York City, they would assume that he had simply left it there. They would never find him, and they would never connect me to any of this. Miranda would be found dead, all evidence pointing to Brad Daggett as the killer. And Brad would disappear forever. The police would assume he went on the run, but they would never find him. Case closed.

I remembered telling Ted that there were two ways to hide a body. One was literal, but the other way to hide a body was to hide the truth of it, to make it appear as though something else had happened to it. *We did it,* I whispered as I got out of the car, allowing myself a moment to believe that there was someone out there to share this with me. My mother followed me into my house. I flipped on the foyer light, and took her overnight bag from her.

'Oh, so quaint,' she said, as she always did when she came to my house.

CHAPTER 29

KIMBALL

By the time Detective James and I reached the Severson house in Kennewick, there was barely room to park our car along the driveway. It was already a jurisdictional mess, as we knew it would be. The entire Kennewick Police Department had turned out, but because of the limited resources of their detective department, the state police detectives had been called in as well. The chief medical examiner was there, and I heard that the U.S. Marshals Service had been advised that a possible murder suspect had most likely crossed state lines. We did manage to work our way into the house, getting past the miles of yellow police tape and about seven uniformed officers, all determined to protect the scene.

I'd seen the gigantic house from the outside the day before, when we'd been looking for Brad Daggett, but hadn't been inside yet. The foyer was the size of my apartment. Miranda Severson was facedown on the unfinished floor. She wore an expensive-looking dark green coat over jeans and boots. One of her gloved hands was up near her destroyed head. Her hat – gray tweed with a short brim – had come off. Her black hair was loose, spilling around her head. It was hard to tell where the hair stopped, and where the blood, dark and congealed, began. Together, the hair and the blood formed a black halo around her head.

'Weapon?' I asked Chief Ireland, who had come up to stand next to me. He hadn't said anything yet – he was giving me a chance to look at the body.

'It just got bagged. Twenty-four-inch adjustable wrench. Laid out right next to her.' He gestured vaguely toward one of the many portions of the dusty floor that had been marked with tape.

'What else they find?'

'Plenty, from the looks of it. Footprints, fibers, hairs. You missed the bagging party.'

'Anything unusual?' I asked.

'You mean more unusual than a girl with her head beat in?'

'I mean anything that doesn't make it look like what it probably is. I mean, anything that doesn't make it look like Brad Daggett panicked, brought her here, and beat her to death.'

'Well, no. We didn't find the dropped wallet of the mayor of Kennewick, if that's what you mean. There were some pretty fresh tire tracks out front that didn't get run over by the dog and pony show. They looked like truck tracks to me, and they probably belong to Daggett's F-150. So nothing really strange. I mean, if you ask me, it's all strange. She put her hand up to block the blow' – Chief

Ireland raised his own wide hand to the side of his head to demonstrate – 'but that was all the fight she put up. So, yeah, that's a little strange. He marches her in here holding a giant wrench and she just stands there and lets him beat on her head.'

'That is strange,' I agreed. 'No sign of there being anyone else in here besides the two of them?'

'Well, they photographed everything, so we'll wait and see, but just eyeballing it, I'd say no. What was odd was that it looked like she probably came in through the front door, and Daggett came in through the sliding glass doors – these ones right here. See those big prints? Those are his.'

There was tape marking everything, but I picked out the small muddy ridges on the otherwise dusty floor that must have come from Brad's boots.

'Why would he do that?'

'I can think of some reasons. Not necessarily good ones. Maybe the front door was locked, so while she looked for the key he went around the back to see if those doors were open. Maybe he sent her into the house first, then went back, got his wrench, and came in the back door in order to sneak up on her and surprise her.'

'That makes sense, I guess,' I said.

'Maybe he wanted to look at the moonlight on the ocean.'

'You never know,' I said.

One of Ireland's officers was waving him down from across the room. He excused himself and went over to him. I stood for a while longer, looking at the body, wondering about the footprints. James came over to me. She wore a gray London Fog trench coat over her black pantsuit. Stylish as always, except she wore a winter hat in Celtics green with the awful logo of the little Irish leprechaun spinning a basketball on his finger.

'What'd you find out?' I asked her.

'All signs point to Daggett. Time of death was probably twelve hours ago, which means he could be pretty far away.'

'He'll get caught,' I said.

'Oh, yeah,' she said.

I told her about the footprints that came in from the front and from the back as well. She thought about it for a moment. 'Makes sense. He brings her here to kill her but he can't walk in with a big wrench in his hand. So he makes an excuse to return to the truck, gets the wrench, then runs around to the back of the house. Sliding doors were probably already unlocked. What makes less sense is how he talked her into coming to the house at all. I mean, if he told her he wanted to talk, they could've talked in the truck. It's not like this place is warm and comfortable.'

'Yeah, I know. That bothers me, too.'

We stood for a moment quietly. Then I said, 'Have you seen the view? Out the back.'

'No,' she said. Together, we walked toward the sliding glass doors that led to a stone patio, and through them out into the beautiful fall day. The view was stunning. The house was on a bluff directly over the Atlantic. You could see miles in all directions.

'Was that going to be a pool, you think?' James asked about the wide hole dug in the sloping back lawn.

'That'd be my guess,' I said.

'It's all a little bit obscene. Not the location, but the size of the house. It looks more like a hotel than a place for a couple with no kids.'

I stepped out farther and turned back and looked up at the beige facade of the house. The second floor was lined with little balconies. One for every bedroom, I guessed. There was a built-in fireplace on the stone patio, and a place for a grill and a minifridge. I wondered what would happen to this place. If someone would swoop in and pay to have it finished, or if it would just languish and rot, become a luxury home for a colony of bats or raccoons.

'Another thing,' James said. She was still looking out at the ocean. 'If our assumption is correct, if Miranda Severson talked Brad Daggett into killing her husband, he must have done it thinking he would come into all of this wealth eventually.'

'Maybe he was in love with her, James. Don't be cynical.'

'Whatever. It doesn't change my point, which is why does he kill Miranda less than a week after killing her husband? I mean, she's the reason he's doing all this. Killing her means it all goes away. No more money, no more sex.'

'Yeah, it's strange. There could be lots of reasons, though. He panics, thinks Miranda is going to turn him in.'

'If that's the case, then why not just run instead of killing her first and then running?'

'I don't know,' I said. 'Maybe he acted alone. Maybe he'd fallen in love with Miranda, thought that killing the husband would make her fall into his arms. When that didn't immediately work, he killed Miranda so no one else could have her.'

'I thought of that,' James said, 'but if that was the case, then how'd he get Miranda to agree to come here with him?'

'Well, we'll find out. They'll get him soon. Twenty-four hours, tops. In the meantime, we've got a case to build. I'm going to go talk with this Polly Greenier, Brad's alibi for Friday night.'

'You need me?'

'I always *need* you,' I said. 'But I can manage Polly. Something makes me think that as soon as I tell her we have a positive ID on Brad down in Boston her alibi will break.'

'Okay. Call if you need me. The state detectives want us to pass over all we have on the Ted Severson murder case, and I said I'd oblige.'

After getting the address from Chief Ireland, I drove north to Kennewick Beach, passing Cooley's, the bar that Brad had supposedly been in with this Polly last Friday afternoon. From the beach road I turned inland onto Sea Mist Road, going about a mile, the houses getting smaller, the woods getting thicker. Polly Greenier lived down a dead-end street called York Court in a small single-story gray house situated on a yard that hadn't been mowed all summer. I double-checked the number on the mailbox. The house, blinds pulled down in all the windows, looked unlived in.

I waded across the foot-high grass to the front door. The doorbell produced an echoey bong from within the house, and almost immediately, a blond woman with a phone tucked between her shoulder and her chin swung open the door. I had my badge out.

'Jan, I gotta go,' she said into the phone. She kicked the screen door open a half inch and gestured me in. 'Yeah, yeah, I'll call you back. I gotta go, the police are here.'

'What's going on?' she said to me after I'd scraped my feet on the welcome mat and entered the messy living area.

'I'm here to ask you some questions about the last time you saw Brad Daggett. Would that be okay?'

'Oh God, yeah, of course,' she said. She still held the phone in her hand. In her other was an unlit cigarette. She wore a long pink nubby robe, hanging loose in the front, the side of one of her heavy breasts visible. I kept my eyes on her face. She invited me in, bunching up her robe in the hand that held the cigarette, then pointed me toward a living area that contained a matching couch and recliner. A cocker spaniel in a dog bed turned his wet eyes toward me. Polly excused herself for a moment and I sat down on the corduroy recliner. The house smelled of cigarettes and Febreze.

When Polly came back into the living room, she was still wearing the robe, but had knotted it tightly around herself. Her blond hair was pulled back, and it looked like she might have put a little bit of makeup on but I couldn't be sure.

'Can I get you anything? Coffee?'

'If you're having some, sure. If not, I'm fine.'

She went and got us both a cup of coffee, adding milk and sugar to mine without asking. While I waited I bent down and scratched the dog on the back of his head. He was old, I realized, his big eyes filmed with cataracts. 'That's Jack,' she said, when she handed me my coffee. I took a sip as Polly settled herself across from me on the couch. She crossed her legs and the robe fell away from her legs. She was heavy in the middle, her stomach bulging against the robe, but Polly Greenier had lovely legs, lightly tanned and beautifully shaped. Her toenails were painted an iridescent blue.

I had wondered before coming here if Polly would have heard yet about the body in the Severson house, but I now knew that she had. I could tell as soon as she'd opened the door, the phone against her ear. She'd probably been talking about it all morning.

'You've heard?' I said. 'About the body that was found this morning?'

'Oh, yeah. It's all over town. Is it really Miranda Severson?'

'She hasn't been ID'd, but, yes, we believe it's Miranda. But I'm here because of Brad Daggett.'

'I don't know where he is. I swear to God. I told the police chief everything last night.'

'No, I know,' I said. 'I didn't come here because I thought you might know where he is. I came here because I wanted to hear more about the last time you saw him. I heard from Chief Ireland that it was last Friday night.'

'That's right.'

'Can you tell me about it? I know you've been through it already, but I'd like to hear it as well.'

She told me how she and Brad had had an on-again, off-again romance since practically forever, all the way back to Kennewick High, and that they both still hung out at Cooley's, and occasionally hooked up, and that the last time this happened was Friday. 'I'm not proud of it, but we go way back, you know. Sometimes I thought we were destined to wind up together.'

'You sure it was Friday?'

'Oh, yeah,' she said, leaning forward and plucking her pack of Marlboro Menthols off the table. 'You don't mind if I smoke, do you?' she asked.

'No, of course not.'

'You want one?'

'Sure,' I said and leaned across to pull one of

the cigarettes from the hard pack. I usually only smoked hand-rolled cigarettes, but I figured it couldn't hurt to bond a little with Polly Greenier. She lit her cigarette first, then passed the Bic lighter over to me. I hadn't had a menthol in years, and the first minty drag punched me in the throat. 'How are you positive it was Friday?' I asked.

'It's the only day of the week I get off work early. I do the five-to-one shift at Manor House Nursing Home on Friday. Afterward I went to Cooley's for lunch and that's where I saw Braggett . . . I mean, Brad . . . we had a few drinks, then went back to his place.'

'Did you plan on meeting him there, or was it just chance?'

'Half and half, really. I'd seen him earlier in the week, and he'd mentioned it to me. Asked me if I still got off early on Friday and told me that he was planning on being at Cooley's, and maybe we could have a few drinks, celebrate the weekend.'

'Was that usual for the two of you. Making plans to meet?'

She blew a plume of blue smoke from her nostrils and rounded the ash of her cigarette against the edge of a glass ashtray on the coffee table. 'No, not really. We didn't usually make plans. We'd just run into each other. It's a small town, you know.'

'Anything else unusual about that day, about Brad?'

'He was a little strange, I'll admit it. Like, he insisted on paying for my lunch and buying me

355

beers. He was kind of all over me. I mean, that's happened a lot in the past, but not usually in the middle of the day. I thought it was weird, but I also kind of liked it. I thought maybe he'd gotten lonely since his marriage broke up and decided he wanted a girlfriend.'

I finished my cigarette, put it out in the ashtray. 'Polly, Brad Daggett was positively ID'd as being in Boston on Friday night around six at night. Are you sure you want to stick to your story?'

'I don't understand. I was with him at his place.'

I paused, took a sip of coffee to try to get the taste of menthol out of my mouth. 'I want to make this very clear, Polly. Brad is in big trouble. He's the prime suspect in two murders. If you're lying about Brad being with you that means you are willfully obstructing justice, and you will do prison time. No doubt about it.'

She clamped a hand around her mouth. Her eyes looked shocked but also confused. 'Did Brad kill someone?'

'Were you with him on Friday night?'

'I was. I was with him, but I don't know. I can't remember much. I think I might have passed out.' Her voice had turned high-pitched. Jack the cocker spaniel lifted his head in concern but stayed in his bed.

'Just tell me exactly what you remember. If you tell me the truth you're not going to get into trouble, okay?'

'We were pretty drunk when we left the bar, doing shots and stuff like that. Back at his place, we kept drinking—'

'What time was this?'

'I don't know exactly. Three maybe? I got to Cooley's around one, and we were there a couple hours. I don't know the exact—'

'That's okay. Around three is good enough. So you were both drinking? What were you drinking?'

'Jaeger shots, mostly, then we started to fool around. We were pretty wrecked. Brad, he couldn't get it up. I remember that much. He said something like, let's sleep it off and try again, and then we went to sleep.'

'What time did you wake up?'

'It was late. I don't know. Around ten or something. I remember because I looked at the clock and didn't know if it was ten in the morning or ten at night.'

'And Brad was there in bed with you?'

'No, but he was there. Out in the living room watching TV. He drove me back to my car at Cooley's, and I went home. I felt like shit.'

'Polly, thank you. That is all very helpful. And you haven't heard from him or seen him since then?'

'God, no. Did he really do it? Did he kill them both?' Her hand was up around her face again, and her robe had gaped open. She had put her cigarette down on the ashtray without putting it out, and it smoldered away.

'That's what we're trying to find out. Did he ever talk with you about either of the Seversons?'

'No, never, but him and the man were friends. They used to drink at Cooley's together. I met him once.'

'They drank together?'

'At least once. I remember, he introduced me. He was the guy building that big house out on the cliff, right? They kind of seemed like friends.'

'And Miranda Severson? The wife? Did you ever see her at Cooley's?'

'No, never. I'd heard of her, but . . . Jesus Christ, I can't believe all of this is happening.' She reached for her cigarette in the ashtray, saw that it was down to the filter, and crushed it out.

I left her my card, told her to call me right away if she remembered anything else, then got back into my car. It was close to noon. My original plan had been to swing by Cooley's, talk to a bartender, see if I could corroborate Polly's story, but now I didn't feel the need. She was telling the truth. Brad had gotten her drunk, made sure she passed out at his house, then driven to Boston to kill Ted. I called James and told her what I'd found out, that Brad's alibi was never going to hold up. She didn't sound surprised. She was still at the state police headquarters in Portland, Maine. I told her I'd pick her up there in an hour or two. That gave me enough time to grab some lunch. I drove south, back past the Seversons' house, still surrounded with official vehicles. I pulled into the driveway of the Kennewick Inn; I'd heard it was where Ted and Miranda stayed when they were in Maine. A wooden sign that advertised vacancies swung in the breeze off the ocean. I thought to myself that when the national press got hold of this story their vacancy issue was going to be solved.

There was a smaller hanging sign at the front of the inn's main building that advertised the livery pub. I walked toward it along the narrow sidewalk, crunching through desiccated leaves, and went down an exterior stone stairwell to the basement entrance. Inside, the Livery was a long narrow space that smelled of woodsmoke and French fries. I took a seat at the bar. There were only a few people in the pub, but all of them were talking feverishly, no doubt spreading rumors about what had happened a mile up the road. I ordered a cup of coffee and a cheeseburger from the rotund bartender. While I waited, I pulled out my notebook and looked at what I had written earlier that morning.

Polly Greenier – why would she lie for Brad? I now knew that she hadn't lied, that she'd merely been used by Brad as an unwitting alibi.

Why did Ted have a key for Brad's house? I still didn't know, but I had learned from Polly that Brad and Ted had spent some social time together at Cooley's. Whose idea had that been? Could Brad have given Ted the key for some reason?

The final note I'd written was, *Why did Lily*

359

Kintner lie to me? I still wondered about that, even though I didn't think she had anything to do with what had happened between Brad and the Seversons. Still, I pulled out my phone, checked to see that I had service, and pulled up the one image of Lily Kintner that I knew was online. A low-res photograph of her and her father from about ten years earlier, but Lily hadn't changed much since then. Same red hair in the same style. Same pale skin and intense eyes. When the bartender delivered my cheeseburger I turned the phone around on a whim and asked if he recognized the girl in the picture. He bent close, studied the phone's screen for about five seconds. I was so prepared for him to say no that I barely registered it when he said, 'Sure. She was here earlier this week. Stayed a couple of nights. Pretty lady.'

'Why was she here?' I asked, trying to keep the surprise, and the excitement, out of my voice.

'Couldn't tell you. Drank Sam light, I think. Always remember a drink order.'

He moved away to greet a pair of customers that had just taken seats at the other end of the bar. I looked at Lily's picture on my phone – a few grainy dots that formed her face. Was it possible she had more to do with all this than I thought? I knew I would need to see her again, find out why she was lying to me, find out why she'd come to Maine after Ted had been killed. I didn't expect to find out much, but it meant that

I'd get to see her again. Sooner rather than later. I took a bite of my cheeseburger, which was far better than a cheeseburger had any right to be. Life was looking up.

CHAPTER 30

LILY

y father fidgeted and sighed on the entire drive from JFK out to Shepaug. 'It's just Mom,' I said. 'She's as full of shit as she ever was.' He smiled at me, but there was still watery fear in his eyes. 'Give it a shot,' I continued. 'If it doesn't work, then we'll figure something else out.'

'I could always come and live with you, Lil,' he said.

That was the inevitability I was hoping to avoid, of course, but I simply placed my hand on his knee and squeezed.

As we rolled over the low hills of Connecticut into familiar terrain, my father got quiet, looking out the window. The leaves on the trees were past their initial burst of radiant color. The reds had turned to rust, the yellows faded. Pulling into the driveway of Monk's my father said, 'I can feel my balls going into hiding – now I know I'm coming home.'

As we removed my father's two unwieldy suitcases from the trunk of the car, my mother came to the door, aproned and paint-splattered. She had applied two slashes of bright red lipstick to her mouth. 'The patriarch returns,' she said, and it sounded rehearsed. It made me realize she was a little nervous herself.

'Sharon,' my father said, pushing his glasses up onto his forehead so he could see her at a distance. 'You look the same.' It was probably the nicest thing he could have said to her under the circumstances. She nodded and went back into the house.

After helping my father unpack his things and get set up in the first-floor guest room toward the rear of the house, we took a quick walk around the property before the sun disappeared completely. 'It gets dark early, here,' my father said. 'I remember that.'

'Only in the fall and winter,' I said. 'Not all year round.'

'I suppose I could do some raking tomorrow.'

'Mom would like that. She hates to rake.'

'I remember that. She always had me do all the raking.'

'Well, you or that boy across the street.'

'Right.' My father tightened the scarf around his neck, even though it was warm for a late October evening. 'Remember when you were little you used to crawl into the pile of leaves?'

'I don't know,' I said.

'Other kids always wanted to jump on leaves, apparently, but you used to burrow into them. Stay inside them for hours. You don't remember that?'

'Kind of.'

'You were such a strange little girl. Before you got your nose into books we used to think we'd given birth to a wild animal. You barely smiled. You'd creep around outside for hours. You made animal sounds. We used to call you our fox girl, and say that you were being raised by humans. Hope we didn't cock you up too bad.'

'You did okay,' I said as a little bit of rain began to fall out of the sky. 'You're letting me get my parents back together. The dream of every child of divorce.'

'That wasn't your dream, was it?' my father said as we turned and headed back to the house, dark except for the light coming from the kitchen.

'God, no. I was only joking. Besides, you're not getting back together, I hope. Just living together. Mutual parasitism. Isn't that the plan?'

'Yes, that's the plan. Peace and quiet. Maybe write one more book. Maybe not. I just want to live out the rest of my life and not hurt anybody. That's all I'm really hoping for.'

Dinner went well. My mother roasted a chicken and my father didn't say anything bad about it, even though it was overcooked. We drank a single bottle of wine among the three of us, and, afterward, my father offered to clean up, saying he'd clean up after every meal. 'I can't cook, Sharon, you know that, but I'm happy to clean.'

She rolled her eyes, but just at me. My father was already clearing the table, making careful stacks by the sink. We went to the living room; there was a television in there now, something we'd never had when I was a child. I mentioned it. 'For PBS,' my mother said as we sat on opposite sides of the worn-out couch. I thought we'd talk about my father, but my mother told me in exhaustive detail about a glowing review of some artist she used to know. 'I never thought much of him, but I guess I was wrong all along, at least according to the *New York Times*.' I listened to her, and I thought that this crazy arrangement between my mother and father just might work, at least for a little while. Over their years of separation they had come to mean less and less to each other, and that might allow them to live together. They didn't love each other enough to hurt each other.

I left the following day after breakfast. I was in no rush and turned north at Hartford to drive up through the Pioneer Valley, eventually connecting with Route 2 and driving back to Winslow along more scenic routes. It really was my favorite time of year, the blustery air filled with dead leaves, the houses decorated for Halloween. One week ago I had learned of Ted Severson's death, and now that whole sordid chapter of my life was closed. Miranda and Brad were gone as well, and I had gotten away with it. Any anxiety I had had about being caught was gone. Now, I just felt relaxed, and full of power. I had even enjoyed spending time in my parents' company.

The murders had become a big story; from what

I gathered, Kennewick had been flooded with reporters, all trying to untangle the story of the glamorous young couple murdered within one week of each other. Brad Daggett had not been found, and he never would be. If they'd located the truck, that hadn't made the news. He had killed both Ted and Miranda, and forensic evidence would prove it. And he would never be found to tell his story.

I thought about what my father had said to me the day before – how he wanted to get through the rest of his life without hurting anybody else. Maybe I could turn that into my goal, as well. It was how I had felt after killing Chet, and how I had felt after killing Eric, in London. It was how I felt now. I didn't regret what I'd done in the past. Miranda and Eric had both hurt me. Chet had wanted to, and Brad – while he hadn't hurt me directly – had murdered an innocent man. It had probably been a mistake to invite Ted Severson into my life. I'd taken enormous risks in the past few weeks, and I was lucky to have gotten away with them. But now I was done. It was over. I would live a quiet life and make sure that no one could hurt me again. I would continue to survive, knowing, as I'd known that night in the meadow, the stars pouring their light down on me, that I was special, that I was born with a different kind of morality. The morality of an animal – of a crow or a fox or an owl – and not of a normal human being.

I got off Route 2 and drove through Winslow center toward my house. There was an Oktoberfest happening on the town green, a polka band playing and a beer tent set up. I rolled down my window. The air smelled of apple cider. I considered stopping but decided I'd rather get home. I drove the two miles toward my house. As I approached my house, I could see a long white car in my driveway, easy to spot through the now-leafless trees. A jolt of fear went through me, and I almost drove past, but I turned into the driveway, telling myself that all would be fine.

Leaning up against the car was the detective who had come to ask me questions earlier in the week. Henry Kimball from the Boston Police Department. When he saw me, he dropped the cigarette he was smoking and put it out under his shoe. I parked and got out of the car. He came toward me, an unreadable smile on his face.

CHAPTER 31

KIMBALL

After lunch on Sunday I drove out to Winslow again to talk with Lily Kintner. She wasn't home but it was a crisp fall day, not too cold, and I decided to wait. I figured she was probably out to brunch and would be back soon. I leaned up against my car so that I had a view of the pond beyond her cottage, and I carefully rolled a cigarette, one of my allotted two of the day.

Brad Daggett had not been found. The only solid lead was that a garage in Kennewick had reported that one of the cars it was working on had had its license plate swapped. Mike Comeau, the mechanic, noticed only because the new plate was so much cleaner than the rest of the vehicle. It turned out to be the plate from Daggett's truck. So Brad Daggett had been smart enough to switch plates before taking off from Maine. An APB was issued for the new plate number, but there hadn't been any hits yet. I was starting to doubt that there would be.

I lit my cigarette, tilted my head back, and let the sun hit my face. Overhead, a flock of geese toiled by. Just as I was finishing my cigarette, Lily turned her Honda Accord into the driveway. I tried to read her face through the windshield, but she seemed to be looking at me with nothing more than mild curiosity. After she parked and got out of the car I walked up to her, reintroduced myself.

'I remember you,' she said. 'It was only a few days ago.'

She had an overnight bag with her, dark blue with gray polka dots, and I asked her if she'd been away.

'Down with my parents, in Connecticut. My father just came back from London.'

'Oh, to live here?'

'That's the plan right now. What can I do for you, Detective? I heard about Miranda. It's shocking.'

'I have a few more questions. I was hoping we could . . . we could sit and talk, again.'

'That's fine. Just give me a moment to get settled. We could sit on the back deck, if you like? It's not that cold.'

I followed her into her cottage, through the living room, and out through a door in her kitchen to a small back deck that was plastered with leaves. 'Let me get you a rag, and you can wipe off the chairs,' she said.

I did as I was told, clearing two of the wooden deck chairs of the bright yellow fan-shaped leaves from a ginkgo tree. I took a seat and after about five minutes Lily returned. She was still wearing jeans, but she'd taken her coat off and was now wearing a white V-neck sweater that looked like cashmere. Her hair was down, and her face looked freshly washed and free of makeup. 'What can I do for you?'

I'd decided earlier that I would come straight to the point, so I said, 'I want to know why you lied to me.'

She didn't look surprised, but she slowly blinked her pale eyelids. 'About what exactly?'

'Your relationship to Ted Severson, and the fact that you went up to Kennewick on Sunday and Monday night of this week. You didn't think you should have mentioned that to me last time I was here?'

'I can explain,' she said. 'And I apologize for lying. I've been stressed-out by this situation with my father. When you showed up the first time I was terrified of getting mixed up in a murder investigation. It would've been too much for him. That's the reason I pretended not to know Ted. I hope you know I wouldn't have lied if I thought our relationship had anything to do with the murder.'

'What exactly was your relationship?'

'We met in London at the airport. I didn't even recognize him at first, but we got to talking, and we eventually figured out that we had met before, through Miranda. We were both in business class, and we wound up sitting next to each other, and he told me that he thought his wife was cheating on him with his house builder.'

'That's kind of important information,' I said. 'We would have appreciated knowing that a week ago.'

'I know, I know. I'm sorry. It's not like he knew for sure. He just thought it was probably the case. I knew Miranda in college, and I thought he was probably right. Anyway, we hit it off. He opened up to me, the way it sometimes happens on airplanes.'

'So you became involved.'

'No, not really. Not romantically. We met again once, at a bar in Concord for a drink, but we didn't pursue anything. He was married.'

'But you liked him?'

She slowly blinked again. 'I did. He was a nice man.'

'When did you hear that he'd been killed?'

'I read about it in the *Globe* on Sunday. The article made it sound as though he'd been killed by a burglar, but I wondered . . .'

'Wondered whether he'd been killed by Brad Daggett?'

'That's the name of the contractor, right? And you think he killed both Ted and then Miranda.'

'Just tell me why you decided to go up to Maine.'

'I don't know exactly. Lots of reasons. Ted had told me how much he loved it up there, so I decided to drive up. I guess to mourn him. We'd only met twice but both meetings were pretty intense. And I suppose I also went up there to see if I could find anything out. I guess I was pretending I was Nancy Drew. It's stupid, I know.'

'What did you do while you were up there?'

'Took walks. Ate dinner at the bar at the hotel. Everyone was talking about the murder and I listened in, but I didn't hear anything about Miranda having an affair. I thought I would; I thought everyone would talk about it. According to Ted, Miranda practically lived at the Kennewick Inn. If she was sleeping with someone local, you'd figure that everyone would know about it. That's what I thought, anyway. But no one said a thing. I even went to Cooley's – it's the bar down the street, the more local one – and had a drink there, thinking I might hear something, or even see Brad. But I didn't.'

'What exactly were you going to do if you found out Brad and Miranda were having an affair?'

'Trap him, obviously,' she said. 'Get a confession out of him. Make a citizen's arrest.' Her face hadn't changed, and it took me a moment to realize she was joking. I smirked, and she smiled back. There was a crease between her upper lip and her nose when she smiled. 'Honestly,' she continued, 'I don't know what I was going to do. I didn't have a plan. And just because Brad and Miranda were having an affair doesn't mean that had anything to do with his death.'

'We're pretty sure that Brad Daggett killed both of the Seversons.'

'And he's missing?'

'Yes.'

We were quiet a moment. I watched Lily touch

the fingers of her left hand in succession against the armrest of the chair. It was the first outward sign of nervousness I'd seen from her. Finally, she said, 'I screwed up. I should have told you everything the first time you came here. I should have told you that Ted thought his wife was having an affair with Brad. I'm sorry. Honestly, when you came, I assumed that Ted had been killed by a burglar. I was almost embarrassed that I went up to Maine to try and do my own investigation. It sounded stupid.'

'Like Nancy Drew,' I said.

'Um, are you calling my childhood hero stupid?'

'No, of course not. I loved Nancy Drew, too. Why do you think I became a detective?'

A ragged-looking cat came up onto the deck, mewling at Lily. 'You have a cat,' I said.

'Not really,' she answered, standing up. 'His name is Mog, but he mostly lives outside. He comes here when he's hungry. I'm going to get him some food. Can I get you anything from inside?'

'No, thanks,' I said. While she was gone I clucked at Mog, but he stayed where he was. His eyes were different colors, or else one of his eyes was damaged somehow. Lily returned with cat food in a bowl, and set it down on the edge of the deck. Mog squatted and began to eat.

I wanted to stay, but I had nothing left to ask. I still didn't believe that Lily was telling me the whole truth, but her answers were reasonable enough. 'Your father,' I said. 'How's he doing?'

'Oh, he's . . . he's about the same. I think getting him out of England is the best thing for him. He took a beating from the press.'

'Is he still writing?'

'He told me he thinks he might have one more book in him, but I don't know about that. We'll see. Maybe he'll get inspired now that he's back living with my mother.'

'I thought your parents were divorced.'

'They are. Thank God. This is just an arrangement. Strange, I know. But my mother needs money, and my father is going to help out now that he's staying in her house. Plus, my father can't be alone. It's a shot in the dark, but if it works, it will solve both their problems. If it doesn't, my father could come here and live with me.'

I wanted to ask her more about her father, partly because I was interested in him, but mostly because I wanted to stay out here on Lily Kintner's back deck. I wanted to keep looking at her. The sun was behind her, turning her hair into a fiery red. She had crossed her arms across her middle, tightening her sweater against her body, and I could see the high swell of her breasts, and the faint outline of a pink bra, beneath the thin white cashmere. I thought of ways to prolong my stay. I could ask more questions about her father, about her love of Nancy Drew, about her job at Winslow, but I knew that I shouldn't. This hadn't been a social call. I stood up, and Lily also stood. Mog finished eating and came and rubbed his side against Lily's ankle, then bounded off the way he had come.

'Oh, one more thing,' I said, remembering a last question that I'd meant to ask. 'You said the first time we met that Miranda and you knew each other in college.'

'Uh-huh. At Mather College in New Chester, Connecticut.'

'Miranda told me you stole her boyfriend.'

'She did, did she? Well, we dated the same guy. Miranda dated him first, then I did, then he went back to her. It was a mess at the time, but it was years ago.'

'So, when you met Ted and realized he was married to Miranda, and that he was unhappy, you didn't think it was your opportunity for revenge?'

'Sure. It crossed my mind. I liked Ted, and I didn't like Miranda, but no, that's not what was between Ted and me. We weren't romantic. I was just someone for him to talk to.'

Lily walked me back through her house and out to my car. She held out her hand and I shook it, her palm dry and warm. When we let go, Lily's fingertips gently ran along my hand, and I wondered if it was intentional, or if I was imagining something between us that wasn't there. Her face told me nothing.

Before getting into my car, I turned and asked her, 'What was the name of the boyfriend?'

'Excuse me?' she said.

'The boyfriend in college that both you and Miranda went out with?'

'Oh, him,' she said, and a slight flush of color crossed her cheeks. She hesitated, then said, 'It was Eric Washburn, but he's, uh, dead now.'

'Oh,' I said. 'How did that happen?'

'It was right after college. He died from anaphylactic shock. He had a nut allergy.'

'Oh,' I said again, not knowing what else to say. 'I'm sorry.'

'Don't be,' she said. 'It was a long time ago.'

I drove away. As I headed back to Boston, a ledge of low clouds began to blank the sun. It was early afternoon but felt like dusk. I was going over the conversation with Lily. I believed a lot of what she had said to me but still felt lied to. I knew that she had left some things out, just as she had the first time we talked. But why? And why had Lily hesitated at the end when I asked her the name of her college boyfriend? It felt as though she didn't want to tell me. She'd told me that it had been a long time ago, but it wasn't really. She was only in her late twenties. *Eric Washburn.* I said the name out loud to myself to make sure I remembered it.

CHAPTER 32

LILY

One week after I'd been interviewed for a second time by Detective Kimball, I drove back to Concord Center. I'd been following the progress on the Severson murder case every night on the local news, even though there were never any developments. I knew there wouldn't be. Brad Daggett was not going to be found. It felt good knowing that I was the only human being in the world who knew where Brad was – who knew that he was never going to be found drinking a daiquiri on some beach in the Caribbean. He was slowly rotting in a forgotten meadow. I knew it, and so did the birds and animals that passed his way. They'd smell him, and think that some large animal had died, and then they'd go about their day.

It was the first Sunday since daylight savings time had ended. The morning had started cold, snow squalls moving through at dawn, but the snow had cleared by noon, the sky now a low, threatening shelf of chalky clouds. I took back roads from Winslow to Concord, driving slowly, listening to classical music on one of the public radio stations. It was midafternoon by the time I arrived in Concord, and I parked my car along Main Street. The sidewalks were busy: a throng of families waited outside a popular lunch place; middle-aged women in sporty gear came in and out of the jewelry shops. I walked slowly toward Monument Square, crossing the wide intersection toward the entrance to the Old Hill Burying Ground. I squeezed through the stone markers and trudged up the steeply inclined path to the top of the hill. There was no one else in the cemetery.

I went to the very peak of the hill, passing the bench where I'd sat with Ted Severson the last time I'd met with him, just over a month ago, and looked out over the roofs of Concord. Since I'd last been here, the trees on the hill had shed all their leaves and I could see all the way to where I'd parked my car. I stood for a while, in my bright green jacket, enjoying the solitude, and the bite of the cold New England air, and the godlike view of the scurrying pedestrians, going about their errands on a Sunday that came with an extra hour. I looked at the spot where Ted and I had kissed, tried to remember what it had felt like. His surprisingly soft lips, his large strong hand sliding up against my sweater. After five minutes, I turned my attention back along the spine of the hill with its sparse stone graves. Dead leaves had been blown by the wind and piled up against the backs of several stones. I walked slowly back down the flagstone path, randomly picked a grave that was partially obscured by a twisted, leafless tree, and knelt in front of it. It marked a woman named Elizabeth Minot, who had died in 1790 at the age of forty-five. She 'met lingering death with calmness and joy.' At the top of the stone was a winged skull, a banner around it that said be mindful of death. I stayed crouched, studying the headstone, wondering what Elizabeth Minot's short, hard life had been like. Truth was, it didn't matter anymore. She was dead, and so was everyone who ever knew her. Maybe her husband had smothered her with a pillow to end her misery. Or to end his own. But he was long gone now, as well. Their children were dead, and their children's children dead. My father used to say: every hundred years, all new people. I don't know exactly why he said it, or what it meant to him – a variation on being mindful of death, I suppose – but I knew what it meant to me.

I thought of the people I'd killed. Chet the painter, whose last name I still didn't know. Eric Washburn, dead before his life really got started. And poor Brad Daggett, who probably never stood a chance from the moment he first laid his eyes on Miranda Severson. I felt an ache in my chest; not a familiar feeling, but one I recognized. It wasn't that I felt bad about what I had done, or guilty. I didn't. I had reasons – good ones – for everyone I'd killed. No, the ache in my chest was that I felt alone. That there were no other humans in the world who knew what I knew.

I came down off the hill and walked back into town. I felt my cell phone vibrating in my purse. It was my mother. 'Darling, have you read the *Times* yet?'

'I don't get the *Times*,' I said.

'Oh. There's a whole piece about Martha Chang. You remember Martha, don't you? The choreographer?' She described the feature in detail, reading parts out loud to me. I sat down on a cold bench with a view of Main Street.

'How's Dad?' I asked, when she was done.

'Woke up screaming in the middle of the night last night. I went in, thinking he was just trying to get me into the bedroom, but he was a wreck. Shivering and crying. I went to get him some hot milk and whiskey and when I came back he was asleep again. Honestly, darling, it's like having a child in the house.'

I told her I had to go, and she told me a few more stories about friends of hers I didn't remember. When we hung up I noticed that the crowds around the lunch place had thinned, and I went in, got a large coffee to go. Then I walked some more, back past the Concord River Inn, where I'd had drinks with Ted and plotted the murder of his wife. Our plan would have worked. It was very close to what had eventually happened. Framing Brad for the murder of Miranda, then making sure Brad disappeared forever, that his body was never found. The details were different. His body was going to be dumped in the ocean while I drove his truck into Boston, leaving it where it would get stolen and stripped, but the outcome would have been the same.

I strolled along quiet back roads, lined with stately Colonials. I was working my way toward the back side of the cemetery I'd just been in. A crew of gardeners was clearing leaves from one of the larger yards. A preteen boy was throwing a football straight up in the air, then catching it himself. I saw no one else. I got onto a dead-end street that abutted the back side of the cemetery. I hopped a short fence, leaned against a tree, and waited. I could see the top of the hill, the headstones spread along it like the knuckles of a spine. The sun, a glimmer of whiteness behind the pall of clouds, was low in the sky. I pulled my coffee close into my chest to keep me warm. My hair was up under the same dark hat I'd worn the night that Brad and Miranda had died. I wondered, not for the first time, what would have happened between Ted and me if things had gone according to plan. We would have become involved, I knew that, but how long would we have stayed together? Would I have told him everything? Shared my life with him? And would that knowledge – the knowledge both of us would have had about each other – have made us stronger? Or would it have killed us in the end? Probably killed us, I thought, although it might have been nice for a while, nice to have someone with whom I could have shared it all.

I finished my coffee, slid the empty cup into my open purse. And I waited.

CHAPTER 33

KIMBALL

I had discovered that if I parked my car at the Dunkin' Donuts at the five-way intersection just off of Winslow center I could spot Lily Kintner driving down Leighton Road away from her house. Very few cars came down Leighton, and she was easy to spot in her dark red Honda. I'd waited here every day since our second interview, following Lily a total of seven times. I'd followed her to and from her offices at Winslow College. I'd followed her to a grocery store, and to a farmers' market one town over. Once, she'd gotten onto the interstate heading south; I guessed she was probably going to Connecticut to see her parents, and I turned back. The few times she'd driven into Winslow center to do errands I'd followed her a little bit on foot, keeping a big distance. I had seen nothing of interest.

I was doing all of this on my own, using my own nondescript silver Sonata. I didn't know what I hoped to accomplish. I just knew, in my heart, that Lily Kintner was somehow involved, and if I kept watching, then maybe she might screw up somehow.

I was parked at Dunkin' Donuts on Sunday afternoon and just about to give up when I spotted Lily's Accord. She turned left on Brooks, heading east, away from the town center. I pulled out of the parking lot, slotting in about three cars behind her. Her Honda was an older model, boxier than the usual Hondas on the road now, and easy to follow. I trailed her through Stow, then Maynard, then into West Concord. I tried to keep at least a couple cars between us at all times. I only lost her once, going through Maynard Center, where I got stuck behind a UPS truck, but I guessed correctly that she was staying on Route 62, and I caught up with her again. She drove into Concord Center, parked on Main Street, and got out of her car. She was wearing her bright green coat, buttoned up to her neck. I watched her walk toward what looked like a large rotary that looped around a smallish park.

The only person who knew I was trailing Lily Kintner was Roberta James, my partner, although she didn't know how often I was doing it. She certainly didn't know that on two occasions I had parked after dark on Leighton Road and worked my way through the woods to spy on Lily's house from the edge of her property. I'd watched her for an hour one night, as she sat in her red leather chair, her legs tucked up under her, reading a hardcover book. While she read she absentmindedly twirled a long strand of hair in a finger. A cup of tea next to her sent up a ribbon of steam.

I had kept telling myself to leave, but I felt glued to the spot, and if she had suddenly come outside, and spotted me, I don't think I could have left even then. I would never tell James any of that – she was already suspicious of my motives. 'What does she look like, Hen?' she'd asked me the night before. I'd had her over for spaghetti carbonara and scotch.

'She's beautiful,' I said, deciding not to lie.

'Uh-huh,' James said, not needing to add anything more.

'Listen,' I said. 'Eric Washburn was her college boyfriend. He was also the boyfriend of Miranda Severson, or Faith Hobart, as she was known then. Miranda told me that Lily had stolen Eric from her, then Lily told me that Miranda had stolen him back. Eric died from a nut allergy the year he graduated from college. He was with Lily in London.'

'You think she killed him with nuts?'

'If she did, then it was pretty brilliant. You can't really prove that something like that wasn't an accident.'

'Okay.' James nodded, took a sip of her Macallan.

'Now, years later, she becomes friends with Miranda's husband. Maybe more than friends. And then he gets killed—'

'He was killed by Brad Daggett. We know this. Do you think Lily also knew him?'

'No, I don't. I just know that she lied to me, and that it's a pretty huge coincidence that she was somehow involved with both the death of this Eric Washburn and now with Miranda.'

'We can bring her in, question her some more. Did you ask her if she had an alibi for the night that Miranda got killed?'

'No, I didn't ask her. I mean, we know that Brad did that as well. Is it possible that she knew Brad all along, that she got him to do these two murders, and now she knows where he is?'

'Sure, it's possible, but why would she do it? People don't go around murdering the girl who stole their boyfriend in college.'

'Yeah, well,' I said.

'That's all you've got – "yeah, well"?'

'Yeah, that's all I've got.' James smiled. She didn't do it often, but when she did, it changed her face from something a little severe to one that radiated beauty. We'd been partnered up in the department for just over a year. The scotch and pasta nights had started about three months ago. So far, our partnership had been the greatest nonsexual partnership in my life. From day one, we'd slipped into an easy back-and-forth conversational pattern that made me feel like we'd been friends for years. It was only recently that I realized how little I knew about Roberta James, besides where she'd grown up (coast of Maryland), where she'd gone to school (the University of Delaware), and where she lived (third floor of a triple-decker in Watertown). I assumed she was gay, but we'd never talked about it. When I had finally broached the subject, at the first of our pasta nights, she'd said, 'I like men, but only in theory.'

'Meaning in reality you like women?'

'No. I mean I'm voluntarily celibate, but if I ever decided I didn't want to be celibate, I would be with a man.'

'Got it, James,' I said, and didn't ask for any more clarification. Her usually unwavering stare had wavered a little during the brief exchange.

Most of our scotch and pasta nights were at my place, probably since I always overdid the scotch, and when James hosted, she always made me sleep on her couch. On one of those nights, I'd gotten up from the couch to get a glass of water, and when I walked back down the hallway past James's bedroom, I noticed her door was cracked open, yellow light slanting through. I pushed the door open a little farther, saying, 'Knock, knock.' James was on the bed, reading a paperback. It was a warm night, and she had kicked one of her long legs out from under the single sheet that covered her. She wore reading glasses, and looked quizzically at me over the frames. 'Can't sleep,' I said. 'I thought you might like some company.'

I'm not sure how I expected James to react to my proposition, but I hadn't expected the explosion of deep laughter that I was greeted with. I held up both my hands and backed out of the doorway, saying, 'Okay, okay.'

She tried to stop me from going, but I quickly retreated to the couch. In the morning, James was up at dawn and brought me a cup of coffee. 'Sorry for the laughter last night,' she said as she handed it to me.

'No,' I said. 'Sorry for the late-night bedroom visit. Totally inappropriate.' My voice was gravelly, and my head felt like it was gripped in a vise.

'I think you caught me totally by surprise. The last three times I've been hit on was by a woman. Anyway, I feel bad about it.'

'You shouldn't. I was the one who was trying to cross the line. Besides, we make good partners at work. Why fuck that up?'

'Right. Why fuck that up?'

That had been the extent of our conversation on the subject. We'd been a little awkward for a while at work, but it went away. And now we were back to regular get-togethers, and discussions of my love life.

'So, are you planning on following her again tomorrow?' James said, pouring us each a little more scotch.

'I don't know,' I said. 'Maybe I should take a day off.'

'Maybe you should. I'm sure you're very good at it, but it's only a matter of time before she spots you, and makes a complaint.'

'You're right,' I said, knowing I wasn't going to listen to her.

When Lily was toward the end of Main Street, down near the rotary, I got out of my car and started to follow her on foot. I watched her cross the wide intersection, make her way toward a white, boxy church, its steeple wreathed in scaffolding, then turn right and enter a hillside cemetery. I sat on a low stone wall, and began to roll a cigarette. She was about two hundred yards away but easy to see in her green jacket. I watched her slowly walk up the cemetery path. She wandered for a while, briefly disappearing behind the slate roof of an old stone house with a pergola. I lit my cigarette, and a middle-aged woman in a spandex biking outfit clattering by on her biking shoes shot a look in my direction as though I'd just murdered her children. I kept my eye on the cemetery. Eventually, I could see Lily again, walking along the top of the hill. She must have found the grave she was looking for, a stone marker under a twisted tree. She crouched and read its inscription, staying in that position for a while before standing and coming back down the hill. I wondered whose gravestone that was, and if it meant anything.

When Lily reached the sidewalk in front of the cemetery, and began to cross Monument Square in my direction, I retreated, crossing Main Street, and going into an upscale women's clothing store that was fronted with glass. I pretended to study a rack of scarves – all priced at about the cost of a decent used car – and kept my eye on Lily, who had made her way to a stone bench, where she was now talking on her cell phone. I was close enough to see that one strand of her red hair had fallen out from under her dark hat.

'They're all cashmere,' said the shopkeeper, who was suddenly about two inches behind me.

I jumped a little. 'They're beautiful. So soft.'

'Aren't they?'

I moved away from the scarves, and looked around the little store some more. Lily looked like she would be at the bench for a while. After a few minutes I thanked the woman who worked there and headed back out onto the sidewalk. Lily was gone. I was worried that maybe she'd crossed the street toward me to shop and that I would accidentally bump into her, so I walked away from the shops, back toward the low wall I'd sat on earlier. What I really wanted to do was walk up the hillside cemetery myself and take a look at the gravestone that Lily had read with such interest. The grave was immediately under a gnarled tree that jutted out from the crest of the hill, and I was sure that I could find it. But it would be better to visit the cemetery when I knew that Lily wouldn't spot me there. I decided to wait.

I took a long look around from my perch. Lily had disappeared, and I began to get nervous that she would suddenly appear and spot me. I decided that I didn't need to find her again. Instead, I stood and walked away from Concord Center. I passed an old gray-shingled hotel called the Concord River Inn. Smoke was issuing from its chimney and it looked like the type of place that probably had a bar. I went in. There was a dining room in front with white tablecloths and ornately papered walls, but I could hear voices coming from the rear of the inn. I walked down a low-ceilinged hallway and found a small bar, wedged into a space not a whole lot bigger than a parking space. I quickly scanned the room to make sure Lily wasn't there – there were two couples finishing up their late lunches, and one lone man reading the newspaper and drinking a bottle of Grolsch. I pulled myself onto an uncomfortable wooden stool at the short bar, and ordered a Boddingtons on draft. My plan was to slowly drink my beer, then go and check out the gravestone that Lily had been looking at. I didn't expect to learn anything from it. In that old cemetery, it was probably a marker for someone who had died over two hundred years ago – but I felt a compulsion to look at it. Lily had stared so intently at its words and I wanted to know why. I thought of my dinner with James the night before, and her unspoken warning that I was becoming obsessed with Lily Kintner in an unprofessional manner. Probably I was.

I took a sip of my beer, ate a tiny pretzel stick from the bowl on the bar, and took out a pen from my jacket pocket. On one of the bar napkins I scrawled a limerick.

There once was a copper named Kimball
Whose brain was as big as a thimble.
He followed a girl
All over the world
In hope that at sex she'd be nimble.

I crumpled the napkin up and shoved it in my jacket pocket. I peeled a new napkin away from the pile on the bar and tried again.

> *There once was a girl with red hair*
> *Whose bottom I hoped to see bare.*
> *The chance this would happen*
> *Was one in a million,*
> *But I'd settle for lace underwear.*

I crumpled that as well, shoved it into my pocket with the other napkin, then continued to drink my beer. I suddenly felt ridiculous – not so much for the terrible limericks – but for the fact that I had been obsessively following a woman tangentially involved in a case without my department's knowledge. James was right. If I thought Lily Kintner was hiding something, I should simply pull her in and question her. The chances were that her only involvement in this case was that Ted Severson had fallen in love with her shortly before getting himself murdered. She had lied to me because of a stressful situation with her father, a public figure who was involved in his own murder case. She had nothing to do with Brad Daggett, who had killed both Ted and Miranda on his own, and disappeared off the face of the earth. The latest theory was that after killing Ted, Brad had most likely blackmailed Miranda, somehow insisting that the handoff of the money take place at the unfinished house. It would explain why they had

392

met there late at night, and it might explain why Brad was able to vanish so completely – a substantial amount of cash would make it that much easier. I finished my beer and paid for it. I would leave the inn, go back to my car, and return to Boston. Tomorrow I would talk with my superintendent, ask him if he thought pulling Lily Kintner in for questioning was a good idea. If he agreed that it was worth a shot, I'd have James accompany me. If he thought I was barking up the wrong tree, then maybe I'd wait a week, give Lily a call, see if she wanted to get a drink sometime.

I stepped back through the low door of the inn. The day had darkened considerably in the half hour or so that I'd been inside. I reminded myself that daylight savings time was over, and dusk would come earlier. As I was walking back toward my car, I took a long look at the hillside cemetery. It was empty. In the fading light I could make out the tree and the gravestone; it wouldn't hurt to take a look. I crossed the large intersection, found the small entranceway to the cemetery. A newish stone in dark polished granite told me that this was called the Old Hill Burying Ground. I walked up the steep path toward the tree, its leafless branches blackly etched against the stone-colored sky. I found the marker that Lily had studied so intently, crouched as she had done, and read its inscription. Mrs Elizabeth Minot, dead in 1790. I suddenly wondered what I had possibly hoped to find from coming up here. I ran a finger along the worn inscription. It was a beautiful gravestone, with a soul effigy carved at the top, along with a warning: be mindful of death. I shivered a little, and stood up, both of my knees making popping sounds. My head swam a little in the colorless light of dusk. A steady wind began to swirl the fallen leaves on top of the hill. It was time to return home.

I heard the snap of a branch coming from the other side of the hill. I turned; Lily Kintner was a few steps away, her hands in the large pockets of her coat, coming purposefully toward me. Her presence felt unreal, as though she were an apparition, and I smiled, not knowing what else to do. Should I admit to following her? Should I pretend this was a total coincidence?

She kept coming, till she was just inches away. I thought for a moment she was going to kiss me, but instead she said, in a low whisper, 'I'm sorry.'

I felt a stinging pressure against my ribs, and when I looked down I saw her gloved hand pushing the knife up and into me, up and toward my heart.

CHAPTER 34

LILY

From my spot under the horse chestnut tree on the outskirts of the cemetery, I spotted the solitary figure along the ridge. The light was fading fast, but I could see that it was Detective Kimball. I watched him crouch, and take a look at the gravestone, the same one that I'd looked at earlier. Mrs Minot.

I took a moment – shaking my arms to get the blood moving – to congratulate myself on how easily I'd lured Kimball to an isolated spot, just as dusk was coming on. As I began to walk toward him, I looked around, on the off chance that there were other visitors to this cemetery. But we were alone.

When I was less than five yards from Kimball, I stepped on a fallen branch, and he turned.

In one pocket was my stun gun, and in the other was my filleting knife. I had planned on stunning Detective Kimball first, then stabbing him, but he seemed so surprised, so dazed, to see me that I simply stepped in close and slid the knife between his ribs, angling it so that the knife would reach his heart.

It was all so easy.

His face went white, and I felt his warm blood as it spilled onto my hand.

With our eyes locked, and my own heartbeat loud in my ears, I only barely registered the thudding footsteps climbing the hill to my left. 'Step away from him and put your hands up,' barked a female voice over the rustling wind.

I turned and watched as a tall, black woman in a trench coat scaled the path, holding a gun in both hands. Her unbuttoned coat whipped out behind her, snapping in the wind. I let go of the knife, and Kimball fell to both knees, one of them cracking loudly on a flagstone. I raised both hands and took a step backward. I watched the woman's eyes scour Kimball as she kept moving forward. She registered the knife protruding from his ribs and began moving faster, reaching Kimball and swinging the gun one-handed in my direction. 'Get the fuck on the ground. Right now. Face the fuck down.' I could practically hear the adrenaline coursing through her as she spoke, and I did as she said, stretching out along the cold hard ground of the cemetery. I had no intention of fighting, or running away. I had been caught.

'Just lie there, and don't move, Hen. Leave the knife where it is, okay?' The woman's voice, talking to Kimball, was low and purring. I turned my head so I could just make out the scene, the woman rapidly punching numbers into her cell phone, the gun still pointed in my direction. She called

911, requesting an ambulance to 'some fucking cemetery in Concord Center. It's on a hill.' She identified herself as Detective Roberta James of the Boston Police Department and told the dispatcher that there was an officer down. She ended the call, checked briefly on Detective Kimball – 'This doesn't look so bad, Hen, just lie still' – then turned to face me. I heard a whiskering sound as she whipped her cloth belt out of the loops on her coat. She planted a knee in the center of my back and leaned all her weight on it. I felt the cold tip of her gun pressed against my neck. 'Don't give me a fucking reason,' she said. 'Hands behind your back.'

I did as she said, and, with one hand, she tightly and expertly knotted her cloth belt around the wrists of my hands. 'You move at all, and I'll shoot you in the head,' she said. I relaxed my body. The wind blew a crumpled leaf against my cheek. I closed my eyes, and thought, with disbelief and horror, how my life was over. I could hear the female detective's low voice humming to Kimball. He said something back, but I couldn't make out the words. Now that I'd been caught there was no reason for me to want him to die. In fact, I hoped he'd live, and thought he probably would. I hadn't pushed the knife all the way in. In the distance I heard the approaching siren of an ambulance. I listened as the woman detective told Kimball that he was going to be all right, that he was going to live. I opened my eyes. A strand of my hair was obscuring my vision, but I could partially see the tableau before me: Detective Kimball laid out in front of Elizabeth Minot's grave, the woman over him, her hand pressed against his side to slow the bleeding. The sky darkened to the color of slate, and the faint, flashing lights of the ambulance were just beginning to illuminate the scene.

Twenty-four hours later my bail was denied at the Middlesex County Courthouse.

'We'll try again,' my state-appointed lawyer said. Her name was Stephanie Flynn, and she was about twenty-five years old. She was small-featured and pretty but her fingernails were bitten down to the quick, and she looked like she hadn't had a good night's sleep in years.

She came back with me to my holding cell. 'They'll grant a bail review, and they won't be able to hold you. Not with these circumstances.'

'It's okay,' I said. 'You did your best. I do realize I stabbed a police officer.'

'A police officer who was harassing and following you,' Stephanie said, staring intently at me through her stylish glasses. 'He's in the clear, now, by the way,' she continued. 'Just got moved out of ICU.'

'That's good,' I said.

My lawyer checked her watch, promised me she'd be back at the same time tomorrow. I could have paid for my own lawyer, or had my parents send one, but I chose to have one appointed for me, and right now, I felt good about that decision.

After she left I laid back on my cot in my dark green jumpsuit. My lunch – a hamburger with a side of mixed vegetables – was delivered by a grim-faced policewoman in uniform. I wasn't particularly hungry but ate a little of the burger, and drank the plastic cup of apple juice that had come with the meal. I refilled the cup with tepid water from the tap in my cell and drank several glasses, then lay back down on my cot. My parents, whom I'd finally called this morning, collect, from a wall-installed pay phone down the hall, were coming soon, and I was savoring the little bit of quiet before they arrived. The previous day, as I remained still and quiet at the Old Hill Burying Ground, while first one ambulance, then several, then a flotilla of cop cars arrived, I thought about what I'd say when I was questioned later. I considered telling the truth, the whole truth, about the two bodies in the well, and what happened with Eric Washburn in London, and my involvement with Ted and Miranda Severson and Brad Daggett. I imagined what that would feel like – to confess it all – and pictured the cold, fascinated eyes on me as I told the stories, and then I imagined that this fascination would hover around me for the rest of my life. All those years in prison. David Kintner's infamous daughter. I would become a specimen, a curiosity. People would clamor to write books. I would lose all of my anonymity forever.

So I thought of a different story, a much simpler one. I would tell everyone that I had become terrified of Detective Henry Kimball, who had been following me for over a week. I would tell them I had spotted him several times – that part was true – and that I had begun to fear for my life. If they asked me why I didn't call the police, I would tell them that he *was* the police. I'd tell them that I'd taken to traveling with my stun gun and my small knife, and that on the day in question, I'd driven out to my favorite cemetery in Concord. When I'd spotted him there, I'd panicked, attacked him with the knife. I knew it was the wrong thing to do, but I wasn't thinking straight. It was a moment of insanity, brought on by stress.

And that was the story I'd told, first to the arresting officer who questioned me at the Concord Police Station where I was booked for attempted murder, then later that same evening to Detective Roberta James, the woman who had saved Detective Kimball's life. I tried to glean from the interview whether Kimball and Detective James had both been following me in concert, or whether the female detective had just stumbled upon the scene. I had been so positive that Kimball was following me on his own, and not in a professional capacity. It was clear that he'd become obsessed with me, and it was only a matter of time before he started looking into every facet of my life. I'd already given him Eric Washburn's name, and no doubt he'd checked records and discovered that we were together when he died. I had started to panic a little, and the thought occurred to me that if he really was following me on his own, then I could simply lure him to an isolated spot, and take care of the problem. I thought of the cemetery I'd been to with Ted Severson. I'd never seen anyone else there, and yet it was fairly open. If Detective Kimball followed me to Concord he could see me in the cemetery from the town below. I'd stare for a long time at one grave, and hope that he would visit it himself. Then I'd simply wait for him.

It worked perfectly, until Detective James showed up.

I felt confident in my story. I would probably wind up temporarily in jail, or in a psychiatric institution, but I doubted very much that I would be put away for any considerable length of time. My biggest concern was just how much digging they would do into Miranda's death and Brad's disappearance. I had no alibi for that night, but why would I? It was late on a Tuesday night, and I lived alone. Even if they questioned my mother, I thought it was a very slim chance that she would mention my needing a ride to southern Maine. I thought it was a very slim chance that she'd even remember it.

While thinking of my mother, I heard the unoiled hinge of the door at the end of the hall creak open, and recognized my mother's hectoring voice. I heard the word *bail* and the word *ridiculous*. Both my parents were brought to my barred door by the same officer who had brought me my lunch.

My mother looked outraged, my father looked old and frightened. 'Oh, darling,' my mother said.

Three days later, the day before my bail review, I was brought to an interrogation room after my breakfast of microwaved eggs and potatoes. I'd been to the room before, a windowless box, its walls painted a harsh industrial white.

Detective James entered, announcing her presence and the current time to the camera mounted in the room's high corner.

'How are you, Ms Kintner?' she asked, after taking a seat.

'I've been better,' I said. 'How's Detective Kimball?'

She paused, pursing her lips, and I caught her eyes flickering toward the rectangle of one-way glass that stretched across one of the room's walls. I wondered if he was watching this interrogation.

'He's recovering,' she said. 'He's very lucky to be alive.'

I nodded but chose to say nothing.

'I have some follow-up questions for you, Ms Kintner. First off, you said in our previous interview that you'd spotted Detective Kimball following you on a number of occasions prior to the Sunday when you traveled to Concord to visit the cemetery. Can you tell me what those occasions were?'

I told her about the times I'd spotted Detective Kimball following me. Once in Winslow town center, and once I'd seen him in his car driving slowly past my driveway. She asked me about my relationship with Ted Severson, and my reasons for going up to Kennewick after his death. I told her the same things I'd told Kimball.

'So what you're telling me,' she said, 'is that when you had crucial information on a murder that had taken place, you chose to withhold that information from the police and go investigate the crime yourself? Then later, when you believed that a police detective who was just doing his job was following and harassing you, you decided to murder him? You have some very interesting solutions to your problems.'

'I didn't decide to murder Detective Kimball.'

'Well, you did decide to put a knife in him.'

I didn't say anything. Detective James stared across the table at me. I wondered if there was something going on between her and Kimball, something romantic, but I doubted it. She was almost beautiful – with the bone structure and the tall, lanky body of a model – but there was something fierce and predatory about Detective James. Maybe it was just the way she was staring at me right now, as though she could see straight through me and out the other side.

The silence hung there, and I thought that Detective James had run out of questions. Then she said: 'Detective Kimball told me that you spoke to him right before you stabbed him. Do you remember what it was you said?'

I did remember, but I shook my head. 'Honestly,'

I said, 'I barely remember anything from that afternoon. I think I've blacked it out.'

'How convenient for you,' she said, and stood and walked out of the room.

I was left alone for what felt like thirty minutes. I wasn't wearing a watch, and there were no clocks in the room, so I wasn't sure. I remained in my seat, tried to keep my face expressionless. I knew I was being watched through the glass, analyzed, talked about. It was like I was tied down naked, being pawed at by a bunch of dirty hands. But I knew that if I stuck to my story, and if Brad's body was never found, they wouldn't be able to keep me here forever. I would get my life back, or *a* life back, at least. And I would never make the same mistakes again. I wouldn't let people in. It only led to trouble.

The door opened, and Detective Kimball came in. He wore his usual outfit, a tweedy blazer and a pair of jeans, but he had a week's worth of beard, and his skin was pale. He moved gingerly toward the chair, but didn't sit on it, placing one of his hands on its back instead, and fixing me with a stare that seemed more curious than angry.

'Detective,' I said.

'I know you remember what you said to me,' he said. 'Right before you stabbed me.'

'I don't remember. What did I say?'

'You said "I'm sorry."'

'Okay. If you say so.'

'Why would you say that, if you were scared of me, if you thought I was stalking you?'

I shook my head at him.

'I will find out what you don't want me to find out,' he said. 'I don't know where it is, or what it is, but I'll find it.'

'I hope you do,' I said, and stared into his eyes. I thought he'd break contact, but he didn't. 'I'm glad you're okay,' I said, and I actually meant it.

'Well, at this point, it's probably best for you that I am.'

I didn't say anything else, and he kept looking at me. I searched for the hatred in his eyes, but didn't see it.

The door punched open with a loud bang, and a man in a suit I hadn't seen before slammed into the room. He was middle-aged, and hefty, with a gray mustache. 'Out, Detective, right now.' Henry Kimball turned slowly away from me, then walked briskly out of the room, the man holding the door for him. Before the door latched behind them, I heard the man's loud voice again: 'Jesus Christ, what the fuck were—' I was left again in silence.

That evening, after I'd been returned to my cell, my lawyer visited me, pulling up a chair outside the bars on my door. 'You had an unexpected visitor today,' she said. She was doing something strange with her face, and I realized that she was trying not to smile.

'You mean Detective Kimball.'

405

'Yes. I hear he barged into an interrogation room. You shouldn't have been there alone, in the first place. You can always request to have me present for questioning.'

'I know.'

'What did he say?'

'He wanted to know if I remembered what I'd said before I stabbed him, and I told him that I didn't remember anything about it, which is true. And he said he was going to find out what I was trying to hide.'

Now my lawyer really was smiling, and I noticed, for the first time, that she had those almost invisible plastic braces along the bottom row of her teeth. 'Sorry,' she said. 'I know it must have been upsetting for you, and it never should have happened. Henry Kimball has been officially suspended from the police department. It was going to happen anyway, believe me.'

'So, he was definitely acting alone in following me?'

'Oh, yeah. We knew that already. His partner was keeping an eye on him because she was worried about his mental health – he'd admitted to her the night before that he was following you in his spare time. She thought he was getting obsessed. So the next day she drove over to see him, and wound up following him herself. That led her to Concord.

'Not only that, but apparently they found some things he'd written about you when he was taken to the hospital. Poetry.'

'Really? Like what?'

'It's pretty incriminating. I don't think Detective Kimball will ever work for a police department again.'

'So what does all this mean?' I asked.

Her cell phone must have vibrated because she pulled it out of her blazer pocket, punched a button, and put it away again. 'I don't want to get your hopes up, Lily, but I think we can make some sort of deal here. I need to ask you how you'd feel about a psychiatric evaluation, and maybe spending some time in a hospital working on anger management issues.'

I told her that I'd be happy to agree to that.

'Good,' she said. 'We're moving forward here.' She looked up at me, smiled again. 'One way or another, I don't think you'll be spending much more time in here.' She stood, then dug into her bulging briefcase. 'I almost forgot, you got another letter. They gave it to me upstairs.'

She slid the envelope through the slot where my meals were delivered to my cell. It was another letter from my father. In the three days since I'd last seen him, he'd sent me three letters. 'Thanks,' I said.

My lawyer left and I sat back down on my cot, not opening the letter immediately. I took a moment. The news was so much better than I thought. I was going to get my life back. Maybe not right away, but eventually. I opened the letter, looking forward to reading it. My father had been writing me letters since I was a little girl, and they always cheered me up.

My dearest Lil,

Your mother is off teaching her adult ed class (her only bloody income!) this evening so I'm here at home microwaving a frozen lasagna. Apparently this takes fifteen minutes so I'll jot down another letter. I spoke with your lawyer this morning and she said all sorts of hopeful things that made it sound as though you might be free to return to your life sooner rather than later. We can hope.

It feels as though it's about ten at night but it's only five! The nights get dark early here. I'm enjoying a lovely cocktail I've just invented. One tall glass of water topped up with about two fingers of scotch. In essence, a whiskey-flavored water. Very tasty, and I can drink it morning to night without ever getting in any way impaired. On the plus side, I am also never completely sober at any point during the day, yet I wake up the next day feeling bright-eyed and bushy-tailed. I wish I'd discovered this drinking method years ago. I would have patented it and made a fortune.

The microwave has dinged at me, and my drink needs refreshing. Your mother mentioned something about her driving us up this weekend

to see you. Until then – 'HANG IN THERE,'
said the kitten dangling from the branch.
   Cheers darling,
   Daddy

   Oh, PS. I forgot to tell you in my last letter,
but I have some bad news. The old Bardwell
farm next door has been sold to a teenaged
hedge fund manager from the city. He's leveling
the place and building a sort of weekend flop-
house with about fifty-seven rooms. The bull-
dozers have begun to arrive. I'm only telling
you because I know you loved that little meadow
next to the farm and I'm afraid they're going
to tear the whole thing up tomorrow. Your
mother has suddenly become an outraged envir-
onmentalist. Sorry for the bad news. For all I
know you're wondering what the hell I'm even
talking about. See you soon, Lil. Daddy loves
you, and always will, no matter what.